THE ARYAVARTA CHRONICLES
BOOK 2

KAURAVA

Krishna Udayasankar is a graduate of the National Law School of India University (NLSIU), Bangalore, and holds a PhD in Strategic Management from Nanyang Business School, Singapore, where she presently works as a lecturer.

Govinda, Krishna's bestselling debut novel and the first in the Aryavarta Chronicles series of mytho-historical novels, has received critical acclaim. She is also the author of *Objects of Affection*, a full-length collection of poetry (Math Paper Press, 2013), and is an editor of *Body Boundaries: The Etiquette Anthology of Women's Writing* (forthcoming, The Literary Centre, 2013).

When she is not watching Rajinikanth movies first-day, first-show, complete with applause and whistles, or hanging out with her fictional characters, Krishna can be found with her family, which includes two book-loving Siberian Huskies, Boozo and Zana.

Praise for
The Aryavarta Chronicles Book 1
GOVINDA

'Pick up the book for a leisurely read and see how elegantly Udayasankar weaves tales in your head.' – *Mail Today*

'Strikes an intriguing balance between novelty and existing ideas ... Surprises with retellings that are startlingly different.' – *DNA*

'Thoroughly engaging ... The drama, diplomacy and dispute in this reimagined version makes the book unputdownable.' – *Straits Times*, Singapore

'A fast-paced book, full of intrigue and guile.' – *Sunday Tribune*

'Udayasankar takes the Indian fascination for incarnation, renunciation, friendship, and of course, romance, to the next level.' – *Democratic World*

THE ARYAVARTA CHRONICLES
BOOK 2
KAURAVA

Krishna Udayasankar

hachette
INDIA

First published in 2013 by Hachette India
(Registered name: Hachette Book Publishing India Pvt. Ltd)
An Hachette UK company
www.hachetteindia.com

This edition published in 2014

3

Map on p. ix illustrated by Priya Kuriyan
Author photo on cover by Alvin Pang

ISBN 978-93-5009-935-3

Hachette Book Publishing India Pvt. Ltd,
4th & 5th Floors, Corporate Centre,
Plot No. 94, Sector 44, Gurgaon 122003, India

Originally typeset in Arno Pro 11/13.1
by Eleven Arts, New Delhi

Printed and bound in India by
Manipal Technologies Ltd., Manipal

Author's Note

Aryavarta, circa second millenium BCE

In a large glen somewhere in the verdant forests of Naimisha, a sattra, or conclave of scholars, has been convened by the sage Saunuka Kulapati. Here, in what is described as a sacrifice lasting twelve years, the finest scholar–seers of the land, the keepers of knowledge, have gathered to discuss the knowledge of their times and give final form to its codification as the Vedas, Books of Knowledge. At the centre of this conclave stands Ugrashravas Sauti, the bard, traditional keeper of the ancient narratives known as the Puranas. The story he tells them, however, is their own, the tale of who they are and how they have come to be there.

He calls it *Jaya*. Victory.

To the gathered scholars at Naimisha, that story was neither ancient nor mythological. It was itihasa, or history. *Jaya* was undeniably a tale of its time, and just as posterity elevated the great men of that time and saw them as gods, so too was the story's context adapted and its reality turned into metaphor. In order to go behind the metaphor, and to tell the tale as mytho-history rather than mythology, the essential question that came to my mind was: If Govinda and all the other characters of this grand narrative had walked the world as we know it today, bound by our language and constructions, our common perceptions of physics, psychology and politics, what might their story really have been? Surprisingly, at its core it may not have been very different from the one that took form millennia ago during the conclave of Naimisha.

Like societies, stories are made up of two elements that I call (admittedly, with neither theological nor philosophical expertise) moral *imperative* and moral *principle*. Moral principles are the relatively immutable values that guide human life, perhaps even underlie philosophical evolution, whereas moral imperatives are the derivative rules that are part of social structure, the behavioural norms embedded in everyday interaction. These norms are often context-specific, and change as the structure of society changes. At the same time, for any social institution to survive, it must either adapt to these changing imperatives, or else justify defying them.

Through a process of re-interpretation and interpolation, even some aggrandization, the many unnamed narrators who have passed down such epic tales through the centuries have recast some events and explained others differently to make them not just palatable but also plausible and relevant to their audience. What remains constant, however, are the broad sweep of the story and the moral principles that underlie it.

There began the quest for the story that lay hidden beneath the larger epic tales of ancient India. The story that emerged as a result is the product of research and analysis based on both mainstream and alternative (e.g. Bhil and Indonesian Kakawain) narratives, the details of which are given at the back of this book.

Based on these works, ranging from Bankimchandra Chattopadhyay's and K.M. Munshi's interpretations in their books *Krishnacharitra* and *Krishnavatara* respectively, to Van Buiten's critical translations of the epic's texts and Alf Hiltebeitel's scholarly research papers and books on their symbolism-rich language, and to alternative Bhil and Indonesian Kakawain versions, to name a few sources, it becomes possible to construct a story of why things may have happened as they did, a plausible narrative with reasonable internal logical consistency. Something that could well have been history, something that stands firm not just on faith but also on logic and science. In short, the story of why something might have happened.

And so, Aryavarta comes to life not as a land of demigods and demons in strife, but as an empire of nobles, commoners and forest-dwellers in socio-economic conflict. Kalas, Yugas and the Wheel of Time make sense as theories of revolution and renewal, and the terrible Rakshasas of legend can be seen as Rikshasas – Vriksha or tree-people – their horned heads and fanged teeth morphed back into animal-horn helmets and tiger-tooth necklaces. The mythical epic of old, a story of gods and all-encompassing divine will in action, then falls into place as the tale of a feudal, agrarian hierarchy based on natural law and religion, caught in the throes of technological and economic change. In fact, the moment we do away with assumptions of both preternatural and supernatural forces, of omnipotence and divinity, we find ourselves necessarily seeking out political, social and even psychological explanations – including theories of conspiracy and political intrigue.

We are the stories we tell. *The Aryavarta Chronicles* are neither reinterpretation nor retelling. These stories are a construction of reality based on a completely different set of assumptions – a distinction that is important because constructing shared reality is what links individual to society, however widely we may define the latter. To that extent, it no longer matters whether these events happened or not, or whether they happened in a completely different way, because the idea that such things have come to pass has affected the lives of many for a very long time now. There is a sanctity which has developed as a result of what people have come to think and do as they have interacted with the spirit of these epic tales and their characters, with the world of Aryavarta. At the end of the day, that spirit is much, much larger than any story, or a book.

I am simply one of those innumerable bards who passes the story on, contexualized and rationalized but not lacking in sincerity or integrity. It is you, the reader, who shall infuse it with meaning and bring it to life as you will.

narayanaya vid mahe
vaasudevaya dhi mahi
thanno vishnu prachodayaat

We shall know the divine spirit within
We shall meditate on the essence of all beings
Thus, the all-pervading shall blaze forth

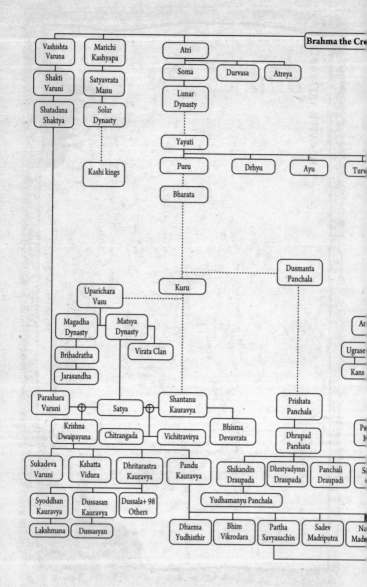

The Dynasties of Aryavarta

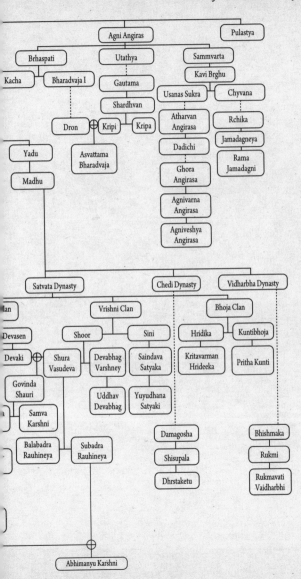

Cast of Characters

The Firewrights

The Secret Keeper: Head of the Firewright Order.

Ghora Angirasa: Former Secret Keeper of the Firewrights. Known for his revolutionary ideas and beliefs, many contrary to the traditions of the Firewright order.

Asita Devala: A Firewright faithful to the old traditions and beliefs of the Order. Known for his skill with hallucinogens and poisons, he is considered one of the most dangerous men in all Aryavarta.

The Firstborn

Krishna Dwaipayana: The greatest Vyasa – head – of the Firstborn Order that Aryavarta has ever seen, now retired. Also biological father to princes Pandu and Dhritarashtra of the Kurus.

Sukadeva Vashishta Varuni: Legitimate son of Krishna Dwaipayana and heir to his spiritual legacy.

Markand: Current Vyasa of the Firstborn.

At Dwaraka

Govinda Shauri: Commander of the Armed Forces of Dwaraka. Formerly a prince of Surasena, along with his brother Balabadra he brought together the warring Yadu tribes to form a Federation of Yadu Nations at Dwaraka. Also rumoured to have been responsible for the fall of Firewrights, despite having been Ghora Angirasa's student. For this reason, he is considered a traitor by many.

Balabadra Rauhineya: Govinda's older half-brother. Known for his fair and straightforward nature as well as his skill at wrestling and mace-fighting.

Yuyudhana Satyaki: Cousin to Govinda and Balabadra and former prince of the Vrishni clan.

Pradymna Karshni: The first of Govinda Shauri's adopted sons. Married to Rukmavati, princess of the Vidharbha kingdom.

Samva Karshni: The second of Govinda Shauri's adopted sons.

Daruka: One of the captains of Dwaraka's navy, and close associate of Govinda Shauri.

At Indr-prastha

Dharma Yudhisthir: Emperor of Aryavarta and king of Western Kuru. Son of Prince Pandu of the Kurus, has been elevated to the role of Emperor by Govinda Shauri.

Bhim Vikrodara: Second son of Prince Pandu. Known for his strength and skill with arms.

Partha Savyasachin: Third son of Prince Pandu. Known as one of the best archers in all of Aryavarta. Married to Subadra Rauhineya of Dwaraka.

Nakul Madriputra: First of the twin sons of Prince Pandu by his second wife, Madri.

Sadev Madriputra: Second of the twin sons of Prince Pandu by his second wife, Madri.

Panchali Draupadi: Empress of Aryavarta and Princess of Panchala. Married to Dharma Yudhisthir as a result of a wedding contest that was won by his brother, Partha. Close friend to Govinda Shauri, but banishes him from Aryavarta on her accession to the imperial throne.

Ayodha Dhaumya: Royal Priest and Counsellor to Dharma Yudhisthir and his family.

Subadra Rauhineya: Sister to Govinda Shauri and Balabadra Rauhineya. Married to Partha Savyasachin.

Abhimanyu Karshni: Son of Partha and Subadra, and adopted heir to Dharma Yudhisthir.

At Hastina

Dhritarastra: King of Eastern Kuru. Biological son of Krishna Dwaipayana, he is blind since birth and so was forced to yield the throne to his younger brother, Pandu. Becomes king subsequent to Pandu's abdication.

Bhisma Devavrata: Patriarch of the Kuru family and once Regent of the kingdom. Respectfully referred to as the Grandsire and remains, despite his age, an undefeated warrior.

Syoddhan Kauravya: Eldest son of Dhritarastra and Crown Prince of Kuru.

Dussasan Kauravya: Third son of Dhritarastra and second-in-line to the Kuru throne.

Shakuni: Former prince of the Gandhara kingdom and Dhritarastra's brother-in-law. Came to live at Hastina after Bhisma Devavrata annexed his nation and brought his sister to Hastina as Dhritarastra's bride. Is especially fond of his nephew, Syoddhan.

Vidura: Half-brother to Dhritarastra and biological son of Krishna Dwaipayana by a slave-woman.

Sanjaya Gavalgani: Prime Minister of Kuru and counsellor to Syoddhan Kauravya. Was formerly a student of Krishna Dwaipayana and one of his closest confidantes.

Acharya Dron: Teacher and martial instructor to the Kaurava princes, and one of the senior advisors at King Dhritarastra's court.

Acharya Kripa: Dron's brother-in-law and fellow advisor at King Dhritarastra's court.

At Kampilya

Dhrupad Parshata: King of Southern Panchala.

Shikandin Draupada: Son of King Dhrupad and once Crown Prince of Panchala. Known for his skills in the wilderness and for his distinctive braided hair.

Dhrstyadymn Draupada: Adopted son of King Dhrupad. He and his sister Panchali were foundlings who have no recollection of their lives before their escape from a burning structure in the middle of Panchala's forests. Since his adoption, King Dhrupad has declared him the heir to the Panchala throne, superseding Shikandin.

At Upaplavya

Chief Virat: Chief of the desert nation of Matsya.

Uttara Vairati: Virat's daughter.

General Keechak: Virat's brother-in-law, and General of Matsya's armies.

Others

Vasusena: King of Anga and faithful friend to Syoddhan Kauravya.

Jayadrath: King of Sindhu and Syoddhan's brother-in-law.

Asvattama Bharadvaja: Son of Acharya Dron and King of Northern Panchala. Brought up by his father as an incomparable warrior.

Part 1

1

'DO YOU KNOW WHO I AM?' THE WOMAN PRESENTED A SMALL BUT
imperious figure against the stately Elephant Throne of Hastina.

Krishna Dwaipayana, in his memory once again twenty-eight
and the youngest to have ever been chosen Vyasa of the Firstborn
Order, nodded in reply, and mumbled, 'Yes, Mother.'

The woman continued, 'You know then how I, Satya, came to
be here, queen of this lauded line of Kuru. Terrible wrongs were
done to my...to our people, Dwaipayana. All that I have lived for,
all that I have ever wanted, is a chance to take back what was
stolen from us. My father was the emperor of Aryavarta, the
great Uparichara Vasu of Matsya, and my soul will not know peace
until my children and their children sit on the Imperial Throne
once again.'

Dwaipayana willed the image of his younger self not to speak –
and, if he did, to say anything but the words that had defined his life.
But there was nothing he could do. The Wheel of Time had long since
turned, and Dwaipayana, now old, frail and almost forgotten, could
not undo what had already been done. The words that escaped his
lips bound him inextricably to the cause of his step-brothers, of each
and every Kaurava: 'Mother, I promise you now, so it shall be. Your
line shall rule all of Aryavarta. I shall see this done.'

Her eyes remained on him as he felt himself sliding into an
endless pit of darkness. When finally he stopped falling, he was in
another time, another place.

Dwaipayana entered a room where his mother, old and spent, lay dying. He knelt by her bedside and took her frail hand in his. She opened her eyes at his touch. They were as clear and keen as the day he had first seen her on the throne. Again, she wasted no time on affection. 'Do you know who I am?' she asked him.

Dwaipayana lived again the capricious emotions – the surprise, the sympathy, as he wondered whether her age-addled mind was merely re-enacting their first meeting. 'Mother?' he ventured.

Satya laughed, soundless, her shrivelled body shaking with the effort. 'You don't. Neither did your father.'

Dwaipayana longed to shut out the words he knew came next, but they echoed loud and unearthly in his mind. 'No!' he cried, and fell to his knees. 'No, it cannot be!'

As his mind swirled with disbelief, he heard Satya speaking again, her voice the feeble and hoarse rasp of an old, dying woman. '…and that is the truth, the truth that you have been blind to. But now you have no choice. Don't forget your promise to me, my son. Your blood – my blood – must sit on the imperial throne once again. You must not go back on your word, Vyasa of the Firstborn.'

'I won't,' Dwaipayana spat out.

Satya laughed again, her eyes fiery even as her spirit dimmed. 'This is my revenge,' she declared. 'And it won't end quite as soon as you think.' The old queen closed her eyes and sighed, a smile curving the corners of her mouth. Dwaipayana watched as life seeped out of her and she died, as though settling into a content sleep at the end of a long, tiring day.

Lightning cracked across the sky, the searing white flash lighting up the darkness outside the warm, oil-lamp lit hut. Dwaipayana sat up in his bed as the rumble of thunder shook the very core of the earth.

A dream.

A dream that was a cruel memory, a reminder of his near-failure as Vyasa of the Firstborn. The acknowledgement of it left his mouth as a quiet gasp.

He heard a gentle voice from the corner of the room ask, 'Are you all right, Father?'

Dwaipayana turned to look at the speaker, the one being he had allowed himself to truly love and cherish, the one familial bond that he had neither resented nor ignored. His son and the heir to his spiritual title as Vyasa: Sukadeva Vashishta Varuni. Dwaipayana felt nothing but pride when he heard the best of scholars praise Suka as the living embodiment of Vashishta, the first of the Firstborn. Though he did not admit it, even to himself, his son was also the very image of his father, Parashara of the line of Varuni – tall, handsome and strong. Unlike Dwaipayana himself.

Dwaipayana had no regrets. The power he had as the Vyasa was more than enough to compensate for his unseemly appearance. Yet, power alone meant little to him. He had a purpose; the reason why he had been conceived. He was Varuni, Firstborn, filled with the essence of life-giving water. His duty was to nourish and nurture, to protect and care for Aryavarta, and to keep its people safe – from themselves if need be. As he had kept them safe from the Firewrights …

Dwaipayana ran a hand over his sweat-stained forehead. He did not like to dwell on the complex journey that had brought him here, preferring to enjoy his well-earned rest in seclusion and silence. He rarely spoke, even with his own students and fellow scholars, and received no visitors from the outside, not even those who had once been his means to achieving his desired end, an empire ruled by Dharma Yudhisthir Kauravya. He hoped to spend the last of his days in such peaceful silence, engaged in nothing but meditation and penance. But the occasional dream, like the one tonight, returned to remind him that much could still go wrong. These days, the dreams came often, during the day as well as at night.

'Father, are you all right?'

Dwaipayana became aware that his son's gaze was still on him. He nodded.

Suka's reed stylus was poised over the scroll on which he had been working. Despite his father's response, he did not continue with his writing. With a soft grunt of effort, the elder got up from the thin reed mat that served as his bed, and made his way over to where Suka sat cross-legged on the ground, a sheaf of parchments set out before him. The younger man moved his shaded oil lamp to the other side, making room for his father to take a seat. Dwaipayana sat down, again with a little effort and, picking up a scroll at random, perused its contents with pride. 'You're better at this than I ever was, or your grandfather, even.'

Suka dismissed the praise with a chuckle, though his face beamed to rival a bolt of lightning. 'A few more years, and it will be done, Father,' he said. 'Soon, you will not just be Krishna Dwaipayana, but the *Veda* Vyasa, the great leader of the Firstborn who brought together the entire knowledge of Aryavarta in the Vedas, the books of knowledge.'

'Just an honorary title now, my son. For we must give serious thought to your investiture in my stead.'

'Father, I have been meaning to tell you… You should consider declaring Markand as your successor. He is, after you, the most senior among us.'

'He's a quiet old fellow, Suka. Seers are of three kinds – the good ones, at least. There is, first, the politician – that's what I am. Then there is the scholar…'

'That's me, I suppose?'

'Exactly. And then there is the holy man, the man of prayer and ritual, the one people turn to for blessings and consecrations and a word of faith in troubled times.'

'Ah. That might also be me, now that I think about it. But I suppose the description suits Markand more.'

'That is precisely what Markand is.'

'And that makes it the seventh time you've said so in the last two days.'

'It does? When did I last…?' Dwaipayana frowned, trying to recall the instance.

'Just before you also said that he would make the perfect successor in times such as these. The politican's work is done, for you now have an infallible empire. As for the scholar's work – that's another good reason to leave me alone, though you didn't mention that. And you did also say that Aryavarta now needed spiritual and ritual guidance. "This is the time for piety to lead prosperity" were your exact words.'

6

Dwaipayana laughed. 'Well did I name you "Suka". You do have the memory of a parrot! But if I appoint Markand as my successor will you reconsider your decision to … Well, you know what I want you to reconsider.'

Suka set down his quill with just a touch of exasperation. Dwaipayana smiled indulgently at his son, knowing him to be too mild a man to be so easily vexed. 'Really, Father,' Suka said, more amused than annoyed. 'I'm far too old for you to go on about my marriage. The time for that is well past. My life's work is to see your life's work done.' He gestured to the scrolls in front of them, and added, 'Truly, no wife could serve as a better companion than these tomes, nor could any child sing our praises better in times to come. I am content.'

A gust of wind whipped past the heavy hemp and cloth curtain that served as the only covering over the doorway to the modest hut. It brought with it a spray of rain, and the gentle flame of the oil lamp guttered as the wind howled through the confined space. Suka rose to his feet and secured the curtain in place, tying the threads that ran around its sides to the wooden slits set into the doorway for just this purpose. That done, he gathered the parchments that lay scattered on the floor of the hut and placed them in front of Dwaipayana. 'The world will speak of us, Father, of you and I, in millennia to come. I ask for nothing more. Announce Markand as your successor. And if you still wish, I am not so old yet that I may not ever have the honour of the title. And for whatever political threads that remain to be tied up, there is always your old student, Sanjaya.'

As yet another peal of thunder echoed through the sky, Dwaipayana felt a lump form in his throat. Suka, simple, innocent and pious, he thought, the epitome of all that he had worked to build and protect. He placed his hand on his son's head in blessing, feeling strangely grateful for the decision he had taken fifty years ago to never speak of his mother's last words, to never share with anybody the terrible secret she had laid on his conscience with her dying breath. In all these years, it seemed that no else had come to know of it either. No one could. Matsya, his mother's home, was nothing more than a barren wasteland, ostracized and looked down upon by all of Aryavarta. There was no way anyone could resurrect the past. But what if he was wrong? What if Suka ever found out?

Dwaipayana forced back the bile that rose in his throat, as he contemplated the terrible possibilities. *Suka will not survive such knowledge, the ultimate dishonour for the best of the Firstborn. Suka will not be able to weather the self-loathing and anger against his own kin that I have struggled with.* There were few things worse than looking upon your own parents with fear and distrust, as Dwaipayana knew well, and he could not bear even the suggestion that Suka might ever see him that way.

With effort, the old scholar dismissed the grey thoughts, reminding himself that they were of no consequence anymore. He had won. The danger was gone. Aryavarta's greatest days lay ahead. He wished for just one more thing – that someday his beloved Suka would be Vyasa in a land completely free of the worst kind of scourge its history had ever seen. The Firewrights.

2

THE SECRET KEEPER OF THE FIREWRIGHTS WAS A MAN OF FEW words and fewer emotions still. Nevertheless, it was with genuine warmth that he considered the figure sitting in a corner of the rustic inn on a rough wooden bench set against a table of the same unpolished wood.

The room was well lit, with torches burning on all the stone pillars around the room, but the man he had come to meet sat so that his face remained in the shadows. His eyes were closed, his long legs were stretched out insolently before him and he nursed a rough iron goblet in his dirt-stained hand. The rest of the fellow was equally unkempt. His grey-black wavy hair was in need of a wash; his antariya – the length of cloth covering the lower part of his body – had acquired the same veneer of dirt that streaked his nearly bare chest and had crept under his chipped fingernails. A rough stubble covered what could be seen of his jaw. Drink and travel both lay heavy on him, the Secret Keeper noted. A bundle that was little more than a heap of cloth lay nearby, on top of what looked like the outline of a thick staff or walking stick. These, apparently, were the vagabond's only possessions.

The Secret Keeper smiled to himself, amused at the thought that he, a scholar in ochre robes, was far more out of place in this surrounding than the man he had come to meet. Indeed, it was the best setting to discuss things discreetly – out in the open and private by obviousness. He stepped aside as two men, one more drunk than the other, stumbled their way out of the room. As a matter of habit, the intoxicated duo paused to pick a fight with him for partly blocking their way. Yet, at the last instant, their inebriation caused them to forget why they had stopped, and the two continued to sway on out of the drinking-house.

Despite his occupation, strict discipline had left the Secret Keeper with a body that many a warrior would envy. It served to deflect altercation in its own way. Yet, it took only a moment's study to see that even beyond his robes – partly hidden under a thick shawl – he was not a man up for a fight. He had never wielded a weapon except while training in his youth and he preferred that it remained so. The man he now approached, on the other hand, reeked of violence. He did not open his eyes as the Secret Keeper advanced towards him, but his hand slid slightly towards the ragged bundle that seemed, from closer quarters, even more tattered and dirty than its custodian. It was only when the Secret Keeper came sufficiently close for the man to hear the unique sound of his hard wooden footwear that he moved his hand away and looked up in greeting.

Taking the gesture as an invitation, the Secret Keeper slid into the seat facing the nearly recumbent traveller. A serving woman dressed in clothes that suggested she would not be averse to providing other forms of entertainment appeared at his side. She eyed him with open appreciation despite his robes of renunciation; whatever his occupation, a man who had made his way in here could well be tempted to do more, or perhaps the scholar's guise was just that – a guise. When he waved away the flagon of wine she held out to him, she set a cup of water flavoured lightly with basil leaves in front of him and turned her attention to his companion. Leaning in closer than was required, she refilled his empty goblet and was rewarded for it with a dazzling smile, which left her visibly breathless. Trying hard not to show it, she moved away.

'How do you do that?' the Secret Keeper asked, amazed at the effect his friend had on the girl.

'What do you care?' the man said from behind his cup. 'It's not like you're going to be warming her bed.'

'I'm curious. Humour me. As you said, it's not like I plan to give you competition.'

The man swallowed his wine in a single gulp and regarded the empty receptacle, pensive. He looked up at the scholar and said, 'What do you think?'

'I think you're capable of more love than the rest of us put together, Govinda. You don't just love humanity; you're in love with it, with every living being. I think *that* is what shows.'

Govinda waved off the analysis, unimpressed. 'Fine, now you know my secret. But then, you are the Secret Keeper...' A soft, satisfied smile spread on his face. It could have been a drunken gesture, but the Secret Keeper knew better. It was the smile of a man contented, replete with well-deserved peace. He wished he could bring himself to feel the same way.

'It is not a title that sits well on me,' he declared, a touch roughly. 'And it is you I have to blame for my position today.'

'Me? What did I ever do to you... *Acharya*?'

'*You*, you itinerant gwala, are the reason behind the empire we now live in. *You* had Princess Panchali married to Dharma of Kuru, *you* saw Dharma and his four brothers to their rightful inheritance of half a kingdom, *you* built the kingdom into one of the mightiest powers in Aryavarta. That was just another step in your scheme, was it not? You were determined to see Dharma rule as Emperor of Aryavarta – a great, united realm that would embrace the knowledge of the Firewrights while leaving behind the bitter legacy of their politics. Lest I forget, this plan of yours also served to rid you of your most deadly enemy, Jarasandha of Magadha. I'm sure I've left out many salient details of your manipulations, but surely this suffices to prove my point?'

Placing his wine goblet to one side with a hard thud, Govinda leaned forward, his arms on the table between them. 'I did what had to be done. *We* did what had to be done. If we are going to argue about the past, I suggest you consider the circumstances in which we acted. Ever since the Firewrights failed to turn the waters of the Saraswati, their days were numbered. They promised a new era in cultivation and farming, but brought only hunger and death upon the realm. Who could trust them, *us*, after that? Aryavarta was splintered and powerless. We, the rebel Wrights, were fighting the other Wrights, and all of us were battling the Firstborn. It would have only been a question of time before invaders took advantage of the chaos here and overran us. You know how close it once came to that! We had no choice; we *had* to destroy the Firewright order. And that is precisely why Dwaipayana has let me build this grand, united realm, as you so dramatically describe it.'

'But this empire is not an end in itself, is it? Rather, it is a means to an end.'

'Yes. But that end cannot be achieved without the empire. So it is as much an end in itself as it is a means ... Not unlike the primordial act of creation,' Govinda said, smiling at his own irreverent jest.

The Secret Keeper did not share in the mirth. He sat forward, his stance mirroring Govinda's, and fixed him with a steady gaze. 'And you? You left Indr-prastha nearly three months ago, barely days after Dharma was crowned Emperor. By now you should have left Aryavarta, set sail for a foreign land. But you're still here, roaming the empire though you shouldn't be! It speaks either of idiocy or of excessive inebriation, and neither is a compliment to the Commander of the armies of Dwaraka. Leave. Aryavarta no longer needs you.'

'Aryavarta never needed me, and I don't want to make the mistake of thinking it ever did. We are all products of time, of social inevitability, that's all. We are bound to fade into oblivion. Surely, that is a happy thought?'

'It is,' the scholar said. 'Soon, Aryavarta will remember neither Firstborn nor Firewright. The new empire that you have built stands on the trade of knowledge and resources, which shall fuel our rise and light the way – not just within Aryavarta, but across the world.

But there are elements of our plan beyond Dharma's ascent to the throne. Those aspects will take years, decades even, to mature. What of the interim, Govinda? If anything should go wrong, the empire is too young to stand on its own.'

Govinda bristled. 'You had agreed with me that this, too, was necessary. We destroyed the Firewrights to make sure their knowledge – and not their conflict-ridden order – would survive. Your words, not mine, mind you. By the same token, unless the Firstborn let go of their hold over Aryavarta, it would not be possible for the knowledge of the Wrights to spread, to be accepted and used. We had to weaken Firstborn and Firewright both, if the fundamental structure of our society was to change. Now, the iron-work of the Nagas, the medical science of Kashi's healers and the miners of the east – all these skills have been set loose across Aryavarta through the forces of commerce. They will drive the empire to new heights.' Waving his empty cup for emphasis, Govinda declared, 'You've spent too much time amidst politicians, Acharya. Your paranoia is compelling, but unfounded.'

'As is your optimism.'

'My optimism, as you call it, is nothing but faith in people and in the power of reason. The unified empire is the key to prosperity. Which ruler in his right mind will want to destroy that?'

'Don't be so complacent, Govinda. This is real! Dwaipayana's influence wanes. He has announced Markand as the next Vyasa, and that man is as ineffective as he is pious and gentle. I, on the other hand, cannot reveal my identity till the ultimate task that has been left to me is done. If I fail, or if I am prematurely discovered, it will destroy all that we have worked so hard to build. We must be careful!'

'Which is why you're the right man for this position, my friend. It takes great courage to make oneself useful at first and then redundant. Ghora chose you well.'

'Your faith in me is worrying. Even back when it happened, not many Wrights were happy that Ghora chose to teach me. And now, to be chosen the Secret Keeper – it feels like a borrowed mantle.'

'Ghora trusted you. That is why he taught you, and that is why he left the most important element of our plan to you. He declared you his successor. There is no room for argument.'

'Really? I doubt the man who sent the three mercenaries at the door would feel that way,' the Secret Keeper said, without looking back in the mentioned direction.

Govinda laughed softly as he glanced up at the well-built ruffians who stood in the doorway to the inn. 'I see Devala Asita has fallen on hard times. He did much to stop Dharma's imperial campaign at every point he could, and he was one of the most formidable enemies I've ever faced, but now… He could have done better than these three, for sure. Pity!'

The Secret Keeper clucked his tongue, disapproving of Govinda's blatant confidence. 'Those men didn't come cheap… Nor are they to be easily dismissed, I think.'

'Scared?' Govinda teased in return.

'Why should I be? It's you they're after.'

'What makes you so sure?'

'I am of no consequence to Devala. Besides, how do you think these men found you here? I brought them to you – in return for a ride here on their horse-cart, a few copper pieces, and some casual conversation, the details of which have since found their way to those who will use the information well. If you must know, Devala Asita is hiding on the outskirts of the Eastern Forests.'

'And you found my life worth bartering for this information?' Govinda continued in mock protest.

The scholar calmly took a sip of his water. 'You know what they say, Govinda. An individual for a family, a family for a village. And so, a Firewright for an empire. It is not a new exchange for us. Besides, didn't you just present persuasive arguments as to why you were now redundant?'

Govinda groaned under his breath, but his eyes held a discernible gleam. 'Don't tell me that for their kindness you've blessed them with good health, Acharya… You know I don't like getting into theosophical disputes with you about divine wish and human will. I'd hate to see your blessings fail.'

'I've wished them the best in their afterlife. It's up to you how soon they'll get there.'

Govinda rose from his seat but stumbled and knocked himself against the wooden table, toppling the glass of basil water and spilling its contents all over the surface. With a resigned sigh, the Secret Keeper swung his legs out of the way and sat back against the wall.

'My apologies,' Govinda offered, as he made a clumsy grab at his innocuous bundle, pushing the cloth off to reveal an engraved hilt that shone even in the dim lamplight of the room. He yelped as his inebriated grip slipped and the blade spun around on the bench to rap him on the knuckles. Looking very much like a truant who deserved that and more, he straightened up, weaponless, just as the three men rushed towards him with ready blades of their own.

3

THE INN CAME ALIVE WITH EXCITEMENT AND FEAR. FIGHTS HAD become rare in the past months but were not completely unheard of, and while the meek-hearted scrambled as far as they could from the fray, those who were bolder, or simply more bored, stayed where they were and looked on in anticipation as the three assassins sprang forward.

The men were trained killers and knew that their quarry was not to be taken lightly. They hemmed Govinda in from three sides, trying to put the crowded confines to good use by backing him further into his corner. The Secret Keeper sat as he was, with his back to the wall, making no attempt to hide from his recent acquaintances, but the assassins simply ignored him. The man in the middle advanced, swinging his axe hard in what he hoped would be a killing strike. His blade missed Govinda's ear by a hair's breadth, meeting the rock surface of the wall with a dull thud. The impact travelled up his arm, making him drop his weapon. Dully, the mercenary looked around for his quarry, only to realize that Govinda had shifted his position by a foot. Using the instant of surprise, Govinda rammed his elbow into the man's face, the impact breaking his adversary's nose even as he caught the man's left eye socket. Blood splattered on the walls and on a few of the inn's patrons as the assassin fell to the ground, writhing in pain.

Govinda did not wait to admire his bloody handiwork, but met the second of his attackers head on, grabbing the man's stabbing arm with his left hand even as he side-stepped the attack. His grip on the man's wrist still firm, Govinda pulled him close, caught his neck in the crook of his arm, and twisted. The man's neck snapped with a chilling crack that was lost in the fracas as the crowd cheered and shouted.

That left one assassin.

The Secret Keeper saw a veteran across the room, a fighting man by his scars, sit back and raise his drink to his lips with an appreciative gesture. For his own part, he had kept his seat but shifted in it to get a better view of the encounters in progress. The first man's blood had stained his ochre robes, but beyond making a mental note to burn the garment before he made his way home the scholar had not reacted to it.

'Your friend fights well.' The Secret Keeper turned to notice the serving woman standing next to him, one hand on her shapely hip. 'Who is he?' she asked.

'Didn't he tell you ... last night ... ? Or pehaps there was no breath to spare for conversation?'

'You're no holy one, you!' the woman lightly rebuked him before turning her attention back to the fight.

The last assassin had now joined the skirmish, having bodily thrown aside the table that had been barring his way and its occupant along with it. He charged at Govinda with a long, serrated sword. At a disadvantage in the cramped space, Govinda found himself being pushed back slowly against a table. His satisfied attacker paused, savouring the moment, and then whipped his blade down in a determined blow. Govinda reached up and grabbed the wooden rafters that ran the width of the room at even intervals. He hoisted himself up just as the serrated blade swished past his thigh. In the same motion, he swung himself forward, using the thrust to kick his attacker in the chest. Landing smoothly as his opponent staggered back, Govinda threw a hard punch at the man's face. As the man reeled back on his heels, he used both his hands to break his opponent's sword-arm. The serrated blade fell to the ground with a clatter. As the burly fellow doubled over in pain, Govinda brought his knee up hard into the man's chest, crushing his ribs.

The room fell silent, save for the whimpering of the first man, who lay on the blood-stained floor, his ample guts threatening to spill out through his bile-stained mouth. Govinda cursed at the sight before striding over to finally draw his silver-white blade from its scabbard, his every move betraying the least trace of what had earlier appeared to be inebriation. Raising his sword high he brought it down in one clean stroke, beheading the fallen man and putting him out of his torment, as the room erupted in a unanimous roar of approval.

Next to the Secret Keeper, the serving-woman reluctantly stirred. 'You two had best get out of here before the imperial soldiers arrive. Brawling is hardly tolerated these days, even in a place such as this. Go! We'll tell the soldiers you escaped.' She pushed at him gently, uncaring of his ostensible vows to avoid feminine touch. The scholar nodded his thanks and began making his way out, avoiding the dead bodies on the floor.

'Later then, dear,' Govinda winked at the serving woman before picking up his cloak and following his friend out.

'This way,' the Secret Keeper led Govinda away from the road outside and headed into the woods nearby. The wayside inn was one of the many that dotted the Great Road that ran the length and breadth of Aryavarta, girding its wide expanse into one united region. The road was the empire's pride, its life veins, and imperial soldiers patrolled its every stretch with diligence. It was imperative that the two men quickly put as much distance as possible between them and the road.

Govinda followed the Secret Keeper without protest, sheathing his sword as they walked into the darkness. With the knowledge that came of a common training, he knew the scholar was leading him to where his horse Balahak was tethered. As the two men emerged into a glade, the silver-white Qamboja stallion greeted his rider with a hushed whinny. Govinda lovingly stroked the horse's neck before turning back to the man beside him.

'Wash your sword and yourself as soon as you can. Unless, of course, you want to be brought before *your* Emperor on accusations of murder?' the scholar needlessly instructed.

Govinda nodded. 'What about you?' he asked.

'I'll be fine. Once I get rid of these blood-stained robes, they won't even think of looking for me. What is one harmless scholar, after all, in a land like Aryavarta?'

The statement carried an air of finality that Govinda did not like. He stepped forward to place his hands on the other man's shoulders. 'Why did you come here, my friend? Why did you really come looking for me? If anyone had seen us together, everything we've worked so hard for would be ruined!'

The scholar nodded his agreement, but added by way of counter, 'I had to see you, Govinda.'

'In Rudra's name, Acharya, *why*? You're not a man of sentiment.'

The scholar frowned. 'I can be on occasion, though this is not one such. I'm here because you're still here.'

'You think I'm keeping a secret from the Secret Keeper?'

'I think you have too sly a tongue to admit it and too much of a brain to ignore what I'm telling you.'

'And what are you telling me?'

'Leave! Your task here was done three months ago, yet you've tarried far too long and that unwise act worries me.'

'What doesn't worry you, Acharya?'

'Don't quibble, Govinda. I never worried in the least when you were busy being a decadent flirt, but you are an outcast now... Accept it, my friend.'

'You're right, Acharya. I *am* an outcast. My Empress...' Govinda chuckled as he corrected himself and let his voice betray a trace of affection, 'Panchali...my brave, petulant Panchali, has sworn me into leaving, to never return. I shall make one last journey to say farewell, and then...'

'Rudra help you, Govinda. You leave those you love behind forever.'

'We left them behind many years ago, Acharya. We left them all behind the day we became who we are.'

The Secret Keeper felt his heart grow heavy with the ties that had been broken and forged by that one truth alone. Reverentially, he whispered the word that bound them both: 'Firewrights.'

4

DEVALA ASITA MOVED THROUGH THE MISTY FOREST DAWN WITH the stealth of familiarity and the certainty of confidence. He felt no fear. He could hardly say the same of the men who were pursuing him, or at least those who remained alive and able after setting foot into these woods. In these times of plenty and prosperity, the dark depths of the Eastern Forests had become a haven for the last of the lawless, the ultimate refuge for those who were evil enough and desperate enough to continue with their outlaw ways. The unified dung pile of Emperor Dharma Yudhisthir's unified Aryavarta, as Devala liked to think of it.

It had been a hundred days since Dharma Yudhisthir had been crowned Emperor, and every one of those wretched days had lacked nothing in peace and bounty. It was, the people warmly said, as though Indra of the celestials himself sat on the imperial throne, for every dawn, if not every muhurtta, brought news of trade treaties with foreign nations, alliances with would-be invaders, and plans that promised development. The latter was a task to which the huge and well-trained imperial army had been assigned, effectively keeping the soldiers well-occupied and content in these times of no conflict. It was a brilliant plan, one that Devala knew the Emperor was completely incapable of devising on his own. The thought spurred a surge of hatred from the core of his heart for the man whose invisible hand had brought it all about. A man named Govinda Shauri.

A loud snarl slipped from Devala as the name came to mind, startling a colourfully plumed bird that had been watching his progress without demur. Before the bird could cry out, his hand went to the sash at his waist, drew out a slim dagger and sent it flying. The blade beheaded the bird just as it unfurled its wings. Its dismembered body dropped to the ground without a flutter, even as Devala moved under the branch to retrieve his dagger from mid-air before the sound of it falling into the thicket below could give his position away. He considered the carcass before him with a touch of satisfaction, but the mild violence he had indulged in could nowhere near enough assuage his anger. Far too much Firewright blood had been spilt and for far too long.

Once, his scholarly order had been the mightiest of powers in all Aryavarta, the mind, heart and sacred soul of this great empire. Till that miserable traitor of a cowherd, that rebel, Govinda Shauri, had destroyed them all for his own ambition. Govinda had ingratiated himself with the Firstborn, shed Firewright blood, and raised himself to power, building a new, mighty nation in Dwaraka. And then, when it had seemed that the death of the rebel leader Ghora Angirasa, the last Secret Keeper of the Firewrights, would change the face of Aryavarta and bring the true Wrights back to power, Govinda Shauri had again systematically destroyed them, this time under the pretext of building an empire in the name of Dharma Yudhisthir, the king of Western Kuru.

Devala was on the verge of tears as he thought of all that he had faced, all that he had been through to stop that treacherous bastard Govinda from annihilating what remained of the few secret clusters of Wrights that had survived. He wished yet again that he had gone after Govinda himself, instead of sending those hired assassins. But revealing himself was not a risk he could take, without being completely sure that his quarry truly was Govinda. He was, after all, the most wanted man in the entire empire. Devala would gladly offer his own life as sacrifice to the gods if they blessed him with one chance to kill the man who had brought them to this. In return, he would anoint their altars with Govinda's blood. *Yes!*

Rage coursed through the Firewright, bringing him to a halt. Shaking as he tried to bring his emotions under control, he looked around him. This was, he decided, as good a spot as any to lay his trap. He glanced around the small patch of less dense foliage that was not quite a clearing and made his way to one of the large banyan trees that marked its edge. Assuring himself of the cover it provided, he stepped out into the clearing. He drew a thick, copper cylinder from a hide bag and poured out its viscous contents to form a circular border around the periphery of the clearing, taking care to not, at any point, touch the colourless, odourless ooze with his bare hands. He watched as the liquid hardened, drying immediately to form a brittle border. Satisfied, he stepped back into the shadow of the banyan tree.

Soon, the forest around him came alive with an unnatural bustle as men attempted to close in on him from different sides. He had chosen his spot well, for no sound came from the direction of the banyan tree. He could easily escape that way once he had seen to his adversaries. Pulling out an arrow from the quiver on his back, he set it to his bow and waited. Moments later, a tall, light-skinned man emerged through the shrubbery.

'Stay where you are!' the man barked. The frantic rustling ceased, and confused exclamations and further orders filled the air.

'What happened, Asvattama?' a regal voice asked, irritated.

'We've found the bastard,' the tall man replied, taking a careful step forward. Asvattama's voice held a politeness as he addressed their quarry, though his eyes did not mirror it, 'Don't be scared, Devala. We won't hurt you … too much.'

'Scared, Asvattama? Of a traitor like you? Or of your pack of rats?' Devala meaningfully aimed his arrow at the dried dregs of the liquid he had poured out earlier. 'You know what that is. It will take the smallest impact to set it off. Quite a powerful explosion. You wouldn't survive, nor would your friends.'

'What in Rudra's name … ?' the irritated speaker now cut his way through the undergrowth. He cut a handsome figure and held his good looks with all the arrogance that came of his nobility.

'Careful now, Dhrstyadymn,' Asvattama said as he took in Devala and his arrow. He turned to the troops clustered behind him in the undergrowth and repeated the warning, adding instructions to stay close to the line of shrubbery.

Devala turned to the new arrivals with a mock bow. 'My, my! Two sworn enemies side by side. This is a fortunate sight indeed!

Crown prince Dhrstyadymn of Southern Panchala fights alongside Asvattama, king of Northern Panchala. And that's not all...you've brought friends along, I see. Sanjaya! The Vyasa does think highly of me if he sends so many men.'

Sanjaya Gavalagani, minister and advisor in the service of King Dhritarastra of the Kurus and faithful disciple of Krishna Dwaipayana Vyasa, squeezed the hilt of his sword, a gesture that suggested lack of experience rather than familiarity with the weapon. He gingerly kept his distance from the potentially explosive periphery as he made his way towards Asvattama. 'Well? What are you waiting for? Get him!'

'Muhira! Don't be an idiot, Sanjaya!' Asvattama snapped. 'Do you even know what that is? It's called a Ring of Fire – one of the most painful ways to die the Firewrights ever devised. It will take the slightest disturbance to set it off. Keep your thick feet well away from it.'

'That's right, Asvattama. See what happens when a pack of hyenas try to hunt down a lion? You never did stand a chance against me. You were dead the instant you set foot into these woods,' Devala gloated, malicious. With a leer, he added, 'And now that you realize what a terrible mistake you and your men have made, I have no further need to keep you alive.' He pulled back the string of his bow, drawing a yelp of panic from Sanjaya. An impetuous Dhrstyadymn made to throw himself at Devala but held back, grimly aware of the Ring of Fire in front of him. Around them, sharp sounds of weaponry being readied filled the air as the soldiers drew their swords and raised their bows.

It came without warning, even for those who expected it to happen sooner or later. One moment, Devala stood with the power of life and death in his hands; the next, he was bent over, screaming, his arrow-arm excruciatingly bent back, for it had been snapped at the elbow. But the Firewright turned out to be a hardier warrior than he had let on, for under the cover of his pain he turned around to confront his assailant. Using his other arm, he pulled out a menacing sword from its scabbard and swung it hard.

'Watch out!' Dhrstyadymn cautioned as he noticed the dark stain on the edge of the blade that hinted at a deadly poison. He need not have worried, for Devala's opponent reacted with the swiftness and precision of a hunting animal, bringing up his own sword to counter Devala's stroke even as he used the edge of his hand to land a hard blow on the Firewright's face. Then he struck Devala in the abdomen, using the force of the Firewright's fall to snap the sword-hand at the wrist and let the blade clatter to the ground. He used his grip on Devala's arm to lift the man and fling him over his shoulder and on to the hard ground. It was over as quickly as it had begun. Devala lay squirming on the mossy ground of the forest, the tip of a sharp sword aimed unerringly at his throat. His opponent stood towering over him, green-brown eyes blazing with undisguised wrath.

'Shikandin!' Devala managed to exclaim through gritted teeth. His eyes came to rest on the silver-white beads around Shikandin's neck. 'You…'

Ignoring the stream of expletives that followed, Shikandin gestured to the soldiers to come forward. The prone Firewright made a last attempt to grab at the explosive-coated rope with his good arm, his rage overcoming his need for self-preservation. The action only served to invite Shikandin's hide-soled foot to come down hard on the knuckles of his outstretched hand.

Devala cried out again, as Shikandin rasped, 'The only reason you're still breathing is because the Vyasa insists it be so. For my part, I would have liked to gut you alive and then slit your throat.'

'Calm down, Shikandin. This scum deserves to die many times over for what he has done. But that pleasure shall be denied us… for the time being,' Asvattama said. He added, 'We better get out of here before one of us steps on this infernal thing by accident. I'll set it off once we're a safe distance away. Sanjaya, he's all yours now. Take him, and don't lose him!'

Sanjaya made to retort but seemed to reconsider. He pulled his sword out of its scrabbard and pointed it, quite unnecessarily, in Devala's general direction. He signalled to four gigantic men who had been waiting quietly behind the soldiers. The men – guards of Hastina's prison as was evident from their metal and hide uniforms – gleefully stepped forward to take the Firewright into their custody. Once, their vocation had demanded gruesome excellence in various methods of torture, skills that had been perfected during the Great

Scourge when Firewrights, or those accused of being of the order, had filled Aryavarta's prisons in plenty. There was little demand for their art now, and the four guards regarded Devala with childlike joy.

Shikandin helped the men secure Devala's hands and legs so that he could walk with assistance, but do little else. Asvattama confiscated the Firewright's possessions and checked his person for concealed weapons. Together, the two pulled the prisoner to his feet. Devala looked from one to the other, making no effort to hide his contempt. Finally, Asvattama pulled out a scroll from a band on his upper arm. He did not bother to unfurl it, merely flashing the seal emblazoned onto the scroll for emphasis. In a strong voice, he declared, 'In the name of Dharma Yudhisthir, Emperor of Aryavarta, you are under arrest. You will be taken to Hastina for further interrogation, following which you will be tried and sentenced for your crimes.'

'And what crime might that be?' Devala spat out, his rage now heightened by his predicament.

Shikandin replied, 'The crime of being a Firewright.'

Devala laughed, cold and cruel. The sound filled the air with an unnatural sense of foreboding, and around them birds and small animals added disturbed cries of their own. He waited till all was silent again before saying, so that only the two men next to him could hear, 'Firewright, huh? In that case, tell your executioners to sharpen another blade. You both know that I'm not the only one.' With a last, defiant glance at the two, who refused to be provoked to show any reaction, he let the prison guards lead him away to the edge of the woods, where they had tethered their horses. Sanjaya followed right behind.

The sun had risen and the mist dispersed by the time the prison guards brought Devala out of the forest. He did not protest as the guards chained his wrists to his ankles and unceremoniously heaped him into a dark carriage that was little more than an airless wooden box mounted onto four wheels. Shikandin emerged from the woods, throwing a delighted glance in Devala's direction as he rode past the still-stationary carriage. By the time the prison guards were ready to leave on what Devala knew would be a slow, silent journey, Shikandin and his companions had long faded away.

Closing his eyes, Devala let out a deep sigh, a sign of weakness that he knew he ought not to show but nevertheless failed to hold back. He expected to be left alone with the pain of his defeat and capture but, to his disgust, Sanjaya clambered on to the carriage and perched himself on the rough wooden plank set into one of the sides.

'Go on,' Sanjaya ordered the prison keepers.

The guards exchanged glances, making it obvious that they neither approved of nor appreciated Sanjaya's presence in the carriage with their prisoner. Sliding open the small shutter that would admit a solitary beam of light into the otherwise sealed carriage, the guards lifted into place the heavy door and barred it shut with an iron rod. In the near-darkness, Devala and Sanjaya listened as the guards ran thick chains through rings set on the outside of the carriage. Shouts of instruction and coordination filled the air and, with a jerk, the carriage began to move. Soon, all conversation on the outside ceased, and the trundle of wheels and the rise and fall of the horses' hooves filled the air in a deceptively soothing rhythm.

In a soft voice, Devala ventured, 'I'm surprised, Sanjaya. You show more courage than I had expected, sitting here in the dark with me.'

'As am I,' Sanjaya replied. 'It is your sheer foolishness that I find surprising, in the dark or otherwise.'

'Foolishness? For all you know I have a dagger but a hair's breadth away from your throat.'

'If you do, that merely reaffirms my point. Only a fool lets his fear overcome his curiosity.'

'Oh? What should I be curious about?'

'For one, why the Vyasa insists that you remain alive when our dear friends Shikandin and Asvattama would both have loved to rip you in two and hack away at their half of your carcass? For another, why should I be here, suffering your presence, unless I thought it worth my while?'

A shadow flickered across Devala's face, the beginnings of uncertainty. 'What do you mean?' he asked, terse.

Sanjaya sat back in his seat. A beam of light fell directly into his eyes through a small crack in the wooden sides. Still, he did not blink. The carriage passed over a rut in the rough road and the beam shifted. He closed his eyes, welcoming the cool purple that swirled before them. 'You're not alone,' he suddenly announced. Softly, he added, 'You were never alone.'

Devala's breath was a hiss. 'You? A Firewright?' he asked with undisguised disbelief.

'Not just any Firewright, Devala. A true Firewright. One born of the blood of those destined to rule these lands and, by Hara and Agni, I will claim that destiny!'

Many questions needed to be asked, but Devala knew there would be time, later, to swap stories. What mattered now was the hope that had risen in him against all odds. It was therefore with reluctance that he asked, as though he would be remiss if he did not, 'How do I know you're telling me the truth? I've neither seen you, nor heard of you, though I've spent much of my life among the Wrights. How do I know you are who you say you are?'

Sanjaya gave an approving nod. 'My life is my proof. I have always shown loyalty to the Kuru kings and to the Firstborn, but I have done so to achieve certain things, and they will speak for themselves. Unless you would rather set your faith in whatever sychophant Secret Keeper that rebel Govinda Shauri will install to lord over us all... Perhaps you can worship a puppet that makes the right noises, but I would rather die than have a traitor command me in the name of my order, my kin! We will rise again, Devala, and not under some self-serving cowherd.'

The sheer improbability of Sanjaya's assertions gave his claim more credence than any reasoned argument could. Devala set aside his reservations and directed his attention to the future. 'Are there more of us? Enough of us to rise again? Where are they hidden? Jatavedas be praised! What I would give to set my eyes on true Firewrights, to live in their midst. But there will be time for that later. Has the uprising been planned already?'

'Well, there's the two of us... for now.'

Devala's joy ebbed as swiftly as it had risen. 'Two of us?' he repeated, incredulous. 'Say that a little louder, Sanjaya, and all it will get you is a cell next to mine, or the gallows. Two of us! Yabha!'

Sanjaya clucked his tongue in mild reprimand. He began to say something but stopped, reflecting quietly on his words. At length, he confessed, 'Despite the fact that I hate Govinda Shauri with all my heart, there is one thing – just one thing – that I have learnt from him. Rather, I had occasion to learn because of him. Men are like cows, Devala. It doesn't take a hundred men to herd as many cows. It takes just one. And so it shall be with us. The empire binds these fool kings together. Break this empire, and a man will no longer trust his own brother, a father will no longer trust his son. When that happens, they will turn to us. They will hate us and fear us and turn to us because they will hate and fear each other more. All they will believe in is us; they will feel safe only in the power that we can give them. And just one name, one whisper of the word "Firewright", will be enough to bring every one of them to his knees! Our name, Devala, our name! We will rule these men, these kings of Aryavarta by the power of our knowledge. *We* are enough.'

Devala squinted, unconvinced. 'And Dwaipayana, the Vyasa?' he asked. 'What makes you think he won't stop you – or the *two of us,* mighty force that we've now become?'

Sanjaya looked out of the slit in the door, taking in the scenery they passed by as if it were an everyday affair for him to ride in a prisoner's carriage with a condemned man. He turned back to Devala with the same casual air and said, 'Because I know the Vyasa's deepest secret, the one fact that can destroy him and the entire Firstborn order with him. For the moment, it serves our purposes better to keep this in confidence, but there will come a time when I will set this wild beast off its leash and leave it to wreak its bloody havoc. The Firstborn shall pay a thousand times over for what they have done to our kind.'

Devala considered the words briefly, before breaking into a delighted grin. He opened his mouth and curled his tongue back, letting the other man see the thin, reed-like blade hidden underneath. The device had been trained on Sanjaya all the while. Devala made a show of spitting it out, letting it wedge, harmless, in the wooden floor of their carriage. 'I wonder, Sanjaya,' he coldly rasped, 'which one of us is the more dangerous man.'

Sanjaya could not have been less perturbed or more cheerful as he said, 'I look forward to finding out.'

5

DHARMA, EMPEROR OF ARYAVARTA, RECEIVED WHAT OUGHT TO have been the delightful news of Devala Asita's capture with muted joy and the hint of a grimace. If the messenger who had brought him the missive was the least surprised by it, he did not show it as he withdrew. Dharma was left alone with an overwhelming sense of the one thing that bothered him beyond measure – irony. Indeed, his life was filled with it.

Many years ago, his unexpected, but not unwelcome, marriage to Panchali, daughter of King Dhrupad of Southern Panchala had brought him and his brothers out of their anonymity and into the line of inheritance to the Kuru kingdom. Dharma had thanked the gods and of course their preceptor and guide, Dwaipayana Vyasa. Never had he expected that the events that followed would lead him to the throne and, ultimately, to rule over an empire. The irony of it all surpassed by far the glory it brought, a glory that he lived with and ruled over, here at Indr-prastha, the capital of Aryavarta. He found no joy in the breathtaking visions of art and nature that greeted him at every step as he walked back to his personal quarters. His thoughts were far too despondent for that.

As a youth, Dharma had been only too aware of the politics that surrounded him. His father, Pandu, was the younger of King Vichitravirya's two sons and had come to power only because the elder, Dhritarastra, was blind. When Pandu had died, Dhritarastra had taken the throne and the question of succession had surfaced again – leading to inevitable tension between Dharma and Dhritarastra's eldest son, Syoddhan.

Many a time, Dharma had thought, no, he had *longed* to set aside his claim to the Kuru throne. But he had never dared mention

27

the notion aloud. His brothers and his mother would have been heartbroken and for their sakes Dharma had continued in the role that was expected of him, right to this day. Just as he had longed for a life of celibacy and frugality but had been thrown into matrimony for the sake of his brothers.

As Emperor, he had no interest in the affairs of government, in the endless disputes over water and land, or old, ridiculous feuds of honour between tiny fiefdoms that he had never heard of. The many nations were constantly scheming to edge up just another notch in Aryavarta's complex hierarchy. Much to his disgust, their kings commonly bartered loyalties, and formed and broke alliances at will. Dharma genuinely believed that his duty was to uphold the supremacy of divine law, the sacred precepts laid down in the scriptures. But the political was now imperative and the spiritual merely optional.

His brothers could not understand his agony, leave alone share his burdens. The four of them had been brought up to believe that Dharma would guide them, and were incapable of even temporarily adopting the role of a leader. They were exceptional, no doubt, in their own ways, but none of them had the acumen for government. Nakul was charming, but lacked humility. Sadev was both humble and as wise, some said, as Vidur – Dhritarastra's renowned royal counsellor and half-brother, and thus also their uncle. That may have proved to be his folly, for Sadev tended to avoid conflict at all costs. And Partha, of course, was dashing, brave and god-like. When it came to matters not connected with romance he was, however, notoriously indecisive. There was little argument against Bhim. He was brave, well-spoken and, above all, reliable. But Dharma had always thought of him as the strong, simple one among them, their protector and shield, never their leader.

The Emperor gnashed his teeth unwittingly as he confronted the thought that had irked him every moment in these past months. He, Dharma, was no better than his brothers. They were, at least, as strong as they were flawed. Each of them had their claim to distinction. But not he. The so-called flawlessness, the devotion to virtue that he was known for, meant nothing. And that meant he was nothing. For, all that he had he owed to the efforts of another. Govinda Shauri, Commander of the armies of Dwaraka.

Dharma tried hard to ignore the questions that sprang to his mind and the memories that surfaced in answer. Govinda's actions at the Kandava forest, Govinda during the imperial campaign, Govinda in Vidharbha, Govinda at the Coronation... With great effort, he drew his mind back from the inevitable question: *Why? What was in it for Govinda?*

For the longest time Dharma had believed that it was he who had convinced Govinda to take their side, tempting him with the thought of his bloodline sitting on the throne of the Kurus and eventually on the imperial throne – Govinda's sister, Subadra, was Partha's wife, and their son Abhimanyu had been declared as the heir to Dharma's throne well before Govinda had set out to consolidate Dharma's kingdom for him. It had been so easy to assume that Govinda had acted in his nephew's interests and, indeed, he often claimed that he loved Abhimanyu as his own son, a bond that Dharma had been happy to encourage. Now, the Emperor could not help but wonder if there was another explanation for all that had happened.

He dismissed the thought. It was best, he reasoned, that as Emperor he remain ignorant of certain things. He could not be held responsible for what he did not know. He was Dharma, the just and virtuous. It would remain that way. And he would continue to believe in Govinda's best intentions and, in turn, owe everything to Govinda. His empire, his throne and even his wife, Panchali. The last thought brought to his mind another memory that he longed to forget.

Two days after the coronation, as they had lain in bed still covered in the sheen of their lovemaking, Dharma had asked Panchali what she felt like now that she was the ruler of an empire. Panchali's answer had held neither awe nor romance. 'The Emperor is powerless, yet susceptible to blame,' she had said, 'and the empire is stable but weak.'

He knew she was absolutely right. Theirs was an empire of consensus, held together partly by the threat of force and mostly through diplomacy. He, as Emperor, was nothing more than an uncontroversial individual, the kind who neither enjoyed great support nor suffered acute enmity. The many nations of Aryavarta, the Emperor's vassals as they nominally were, found this to be an expedient arrangement. For the most part, their affairs were their own, but their problems were the Emperor's. Every niggling impediment could be referred to the Emperor and easily resolved at some cost to the imperial treasury, while every failure could now be blamed on him. Most of the kingdoms found their tribute a reasonable price to pay for such immeasurable conveniences. They found it to be an acceptable arrangement, so acceptable, in fact, that it had taken just about a hundred days for the new empire to become their way of life.

Uncontroversial, unremarkable, acceptable – the epithets in honour of mediocrity were endless. And Dharma was just that – a harmless, powerless, mediocre ruler whom no one took seriously. He had tried not to give in to the maddening thought, but within weeks of his coronation it had consumed him completely. The memory of Panchali's dispassionate assessment had made him want to take his own life simply to enjoy the anxiety and concern she would have displayed at losing him. Or perhaps, he noted, she would have been apathetic, the way she responded to most things these days. Panchali was no longer the fiery, outspoken woman she had once been. She had turned into a calculating diplomat. Silently, efficiently, she ran the empire. She took no credit for the things that went right, and ensured that her name was never mentioned anywhere by always acting through Dharma and his brothers, and the host of trusted diplomats who were her link to the outside world. Even in the presence of their closest companions, Panchali kept up the pretence of being nothing more than Dharma's intermediary, merely conveying the Emperor's orders and never giving her own. No matter what it looked like, though, he knew the truth as did many others associated with the royal court. Everything, from financing the armies, granting titles and collecting taxes to redistributing vassaldoms, setting up various industries and judging disputes, was in Panchali's care. Courtiers, courtesans, spies – they all served her with a loyalty he had not anticipated.

'You were raised to rule, Dharma,' she had once told him. 'You believe that loyalty, respect and obedience are yours by divine right as soon as you're crowned. It's quite natural; don't torment yourself so.'

'And what do you believe, Panchali?' he had wanted to know.

Hesitantly she had replied, 'I believe that these things must be earned.'

That day, Dharma had finally understood what it was he wanted the most – one chance to earn fame and bring glory upon his line. One chance to make Partha look at him with respect, to make Panchali yearn for him as women did for warriors. It was not a matter of vanity; it was one of duty. Destiny was an instrument of divine justice; the gods never blessed men with what they did not deserve. As far as Dharma was concerned, to doubt his merit to rule was to doubt the notion of Divine Order itself. He could not let that happen. He wanted the chance to irrevocably establish that Divine Order was everything, to prove that destiny towered over them all. He wanted to prove that he deserved to be Emperor of Aryavarta.

The need fuelling his quick, firm strides, Dharma entered the building that served as his private residence. Panchali smiled as he came in to the study. He returned the gesture with affection and a hint of desire in his eyes. Her years were yet to take a toll on her, and she had remained the shapely, attractive woman whose smouldering beauty had once drawn every king and prince in the realm to compete for her hand, the utility of having her father as an ally notwithstanding. Her dark skin reflected a golden glow from the huge bronze chandelier overhead, making her look like a fiery mirage. The silk of her red robes seemed to glide lovingly over her smooth skin, and her long hair rested in a heavy knot at the nape of her neck, highlighting the strong but graceful line of her shoulders.

Unable to resist her proximity, Dharma ran a finger over her full lower lip and then pulled her into a passionate embrace.

She protested, 'Patience! There's work to be done. Besides,' she teased, 'it's a short wait till nightfall…'

Reluctantly, Dharma let go of her and turned his attention to the scroll she handed him for his seal of assent. He frowned as he read through it. 'What is this?' he snapped.

31

Panchali said, 'As you can see, this is a decree removing all taxes and tolls throughout the empire on goods made by the Naga ironsmiths. The current tolls and taxes that the kings of the various nations impose are far beyond the capacity of individual ironsmiths and craftsmen. They have no choice but to sell their wares to the saamantas and vassal chieftains at a ridiculously low price, or else work as bonded labour in their forges. The vassal lords, on the other hand, can well afford to make the investment and reap the benefits tenfold, if not more. If we don't do away with the toll, our new empire will only serve to to make rich lords richer. It doesn't hurt the imperial treasury in any way – in fact, as a sort of inducement, we could even offer to reduce the levies we impose on these kings. The increase in charges paid by foreign merchants to the empire for the right to trade here will more than make up for any loss of revenue to us.'

Dharma stared at the scroll as he considered Panchali's words. He had no doubt that her simplified statement of the situation came more from her belief that he knew what he was talking about than a lack of understanding or analysis on her part. In fact, he would not be surprised if he found that she had already consulted with his advisors, even his brothers, before putting this proposal before him. Nevertheless, she had failed to see the basic problem, one that had nothing to with the wealth of the empire.

Drawing in an irritated breath, he began, 'You want me to remove taxes... No, wait, let me restate that. You want me to interfere in the internal affairs of one of Aryavarta's nations, at the risk of enraging all the monarchs in the realm, so that the Nagas can defy their lords and their rightful king Takshaka, to whom they owe allegiance by law and scripture? If this is a joke, Panchali, it's in rather bad taste...'

'Maybe we should have thought of that before moving the Nagas out of Kandava or walking on the roads they helped build in order to conquer the far reaches of our empire. Don't we now owe something to those who toiled for us? Aren't the Naga subjects your subjects too, Emperor Dharma?'

Forcing back his anger, Dharma tried to explain, 'No subjects will be served by destroying the moral and spiritual fabric of Aryavarta!'

'But…'

'Have you seen this?' He reached into his waistband and took out a small ring of black iron, which he threw on the table between them.

Panchali picked it up. Trying her best to conceal her excitement, she ran her fingers over the dark metal band and the rough engravings on the ingot at its bezel. 'It's a ring. Of no consequence, I may add.' She was intentionally disdainful. It served the purpose.

Dharma snatched it from her and, with an expression of disgust, slid it on to his finger. He fumbled with it a little, but finally managed to set it with the round ingot turned inwards, resting partly on his palm. Using his thumb, he pressed down on an indiscernible catch set into the band. At the same time, he curled his fingers tight, pressing on the ingot. A sudden flick of his wrist, and his palm was open.

Fire. It spluttered up as a small tongue of flame, an iridescent haze of blue coming from the ring itself. It lacked ethereal beauty, the floating appearance of what was known in legend as the dancing flames of Agneya, the so-called magical fire the Firewrights could invoke and hold in the palm of their hands. The mechanism used here was a poor imitation of the fine craft of the Wrights, but Panchali's eyes lit up. The ring was no less a marvel for her – a marvel of science without the illusion of sorcery. It was possible to see, explain and understand its function without relying on lores of celestials and demons.

'Hara be praised,' she finally gushed. Breathless and excited, Panchali held out her hand, asking to take a closer look at the ring, but Dharma moved his hand away, closing his fist tight as he did so. Panchali looked up at his face to realize that something was wrong. 'You don't look pleased, Dharma. Every era of prosperity has come on the wings of new inventions and discoveries, be they farming implements or wind-driven barges. Surely, this is what you as the Emperor dream of, to raise Aryavarta's fortunes back to the great heights of the Golden Age, and make it a land of progress and peace once again?'

'To consign these lands to the depths of Kali, the age of blackness, is not a dream, Panchali. It is a nightmare. This…this abomination is Wright-work!'

'What is it with you and this obstinate hate for what the Wrights created? Oh, Rudra forbid that we use Wright-work to light hearths in dark homes rather than burn down forests and fields for some noble conqueror! Hai!' She knew her sarcasm would hit a sore point by reminding Dharma of the times he had relied on Wright-weaponry to build the empire, but she didn't care.

Dharma stood his ground. 'What I did wasn't for selfish reasons and it certainly was not to challenge the Divine Order. I have always acted with the blessings of the Vyasa himself and if Wright-work was involved, it was merely a means to further the purpose, the righteous purpose of the Firstborn. It wasn't a profane attempt to harness the elements, the powers of nature, to suit human conveniences or to change destiny.'

'Destiny? Is it our destiny to never aspire to anything more than what our forefathers had? What about using the alloys that make up weapons like the Gandiva bow to create splints, or even surgical instruments that make incisions and blood-letting easier, more precise and painless? Or use those very same metals to make faster chariots and ships, not for war and conquest but for trade and travel?'

'I once found your innocence rather becoming, Panchali. You were young, and your idealism had ... a ... what's the word ... passion. Yes, you had passion, a fervour that was compelling. But you are the Empress now and I can't go on indulging your childish ideas. You're not a fool. You must learn to see what is best for you, for us, for Aryavarta ...'

'Which is?'

'Your ideas of so-called equality and prosperity will do nothing but erode our way of life. It will destroy the Divine Order that we replicate in the earthly spheres.'

'Do you hear yourself, Dharma? Your thoughts move like a blinkered horse ...' Panchali was incredulous. 'You sound like Dwaipayana, the Vyasa! What are you, his lackey?'

'I am true to what my teacher has taught me. We both serve the Divine, and we equally oppose the same evils. As for being a lackey, perhaps Govinda Shauri would like to hear these ideas of yours. Oh! I forget ... you told him never to set foot in these lands while you are

34

empress, or so I hear.' His earlier anger against Govinda took hold of him, and words he did not quite mean spilled out of him. 'Why did you do that, Panchali? Don't you *need* him anymore now that you are Empress? Or did you simply tire of him?'

'I told him to leave because I had to,' Panchali said quietly. She added, for lack of other words to explain, 'This is your empire, Dharma. *He* does not belong here.'

Her reply touched a chord, for Dharma shook his head mournfully. 'You think you've banished Govinda from these lands? When will you realize that he is far from gone? Govinda Shauri is very much here, *Empress*. He is inside you. I hear him in your speech, and I see the fire of his soul in your eyes. Did you know that once upon a time, in the days when the Universe was very young, the gods themselves inhabited the Earth, just as the other domains? It was over time that they took to the skies along with the celestials, leaving the Earth to men and the netherworld to demons. Maybe it is true, and maybe not, but it is reason enough, all these centuries later, to find prosperity by following a path of duty and virtue, to maintain the order that has been set. What the Wrights did was contrary to the Divine Order. No matter how great their utility, it does not justify a return to their methods or devices. And that is why things must be the way they are, do you understand? Panchali, trust me. I say this for your own good.'

'And what does your duty demand of you, Dharma?'

'My duty demands that I keep the empire intact and stable. If this means overlooking upheavals and conflict, so be it. My duty is not to a single individual or a group, but to all of Aryavarta. I can't remove taxes on these products as you ask.'

To his disappointment, Panchali was neither convinced nor intimidated by his rhetoric. 'As you wish, Dharma,' she said. With an elaborate and unneccessary bow she left the room.

Dharma stared after her till she disappeared from his sight. His jaw was set in uncharacteristic resolution and a vein throbbed in his temple as he willed himself not to call her back. *Aryavarta*. This was an empire of the Firstborn, of the faithful and devoted. There was no room here for heathen heretics, no room for Firewrights or their legacies. This, he noted with sullen determination, was *his* empire.

A SLEEPLESS PANCHALI GAZED DOWN FROM HER TERRACE – ONE of the tallest in the city – at the wonder that was Indr-prastha or the White City, as it was now known outside Aryavarta. Visitors marvelled at the way the city's man-made structures blended tastefully with both the natural undulations of the land and the varying hues of cultivated gardens and wild forests.

From where she stood, Indr-prastha appeared like a wave-filled sea with crescents of smooth, shimmering white, and troughs of deep, soothing green. Each wave was a cluster of white towers of varying heights separated from others by well-planned verdure. Further away were the walls that bound the city in a perfect square. Creepers and ivy climbed up the sides of the walls in dark patterns to blend into the green walkways on top. Filled with their reflections, during the day, the waters of the still, clear moat surrounding the outer side of the wall sparkled like a green jewel. Yet, the city's pleasant form was not without function. The clustered arrangement of buildings allowed for parts of it to be held even when others might be breached, the verdure served as gathering space for armies, the creepers and walkways along the city walls hid sharp metallic spikes, and the placid moat had been lined with tiny but deadly barbs that could well be mistaken for fallen leaves or moss. Indr-prastha was as deadly as it was lovely, and not even its many residents knew of its dark secrets as they went about their incessant activities.

It was still some time to dawn, but the bustle of life and light had merely slowed down, not stopped. Lanterns lined the sides of the major roads like golden pearls, and even the smaller pathways were dimly lit at the least. Even in the deepest night, the city remained safe for an endless tide of visitors and the citizenry that welcomed them with open arms. Indr-prastha never slept.

The empire never sleeps. Those bound by servitude must always remain awake, Panchali reminded herself, running a hand over her eyes. Of late, she felt constantly on the verge of tears, which was uncharacteristic of her. She told herself that it was because she was tired and overworked, stifling the tiny voice inside, which she knew spoke the truth. She had betrayed and been betrayed. But what haunted her was that she did not know to whom she owed the greater loyalty and, thus, who it was she had so miserably failed.

Soft footsteps made her turn. She smiled at the bearded scholar who approached her. He looked exactly like his older brother, but not entirely so. Dhaumya, royal priest in the court of Emperor Dharma Yudhisthir, had a kindness in his eyes that Devala the Firewright completely lacked.

'Is it not too late for a man of renunciation to be out and about, Acharya?' Panchali said.

'Too late, yes, Mahamatra,' Dhaumya replied, 'but not too early. My day begins early, for I must tend to the gods before I can tend to the affairs of men…and women. I saw one of your attendants was up, and she told me that you were too. I don't suppose you want a sleeping draught?' he joked as he came to stand next to her.

Panchali raised an eyebrow. 'Haven't you filled us all up with that stuff already?'

'There's always room for more.'

The two laughed and a comfortable silence fell between them.

'Tell me, Acharya,' Panchali said after a while. 'What do I still not know about the conspiracies around me?'

'Conspiracy is a strong word, Empress. Besides, haven't you already guessed all there is to know?'

'I've had my suspicions, many of which have been confirmed. The question is, dare I take the last step and ask you a question?'

'In my opinion, you should.'

'Are *you* a spy, Dhaumya?' Panchali's manner was commanding and matter-of-fact, as only a ruler's could be. Neither condescending nor overbearing, neither soft nor imposing, she was deceptively simple in her speech.

Dhaumya chuckled. 'A spy? Surely, you don't suspect me of treachery and intrigue?' he asked.

'Not at all. I leave those things to our common acquaintances. Of you, I expect intelligence and delicate but incisive action. I expect great loyalty to the one you've decided to serve, though perhaps even he knows it not.'

37

'And who might such an ignorant master be?'

'A stubborn gwala? For argument's sake, let's call him Govinda. Now, what would you deem your actions?'

'My duty, Empress,' Dhaumya said. 'A greater duty than the one I may have to any master. The duty I owe to the truth, just as you do. To truth and justice.'

Panchali nodded at his graceful win. She asked, 'Does that make me your enemy now?'

'Because you defied Govinda? Because you think you thwarted his plans?'

'Aren't these sufficient reasons?'

'They are good reasons, yes. But not sufficient.'

Panchali laughed at the wordplay. It felt good to share what lay on her mind frankly and with a touch of humour. She found herself opening up. 'The Emperor refuses to remove the taxes on goods produced by the Nagas... I'd thought that I could get Dharma to agree... Not only did he oppose it, but he also did so most vehemently. He still associates science with Wright-work.'

'Hmm.'

'Hmm?'

'Give him time, Panchali. Now that Devala has been found and arrested, the Firstborn will slowly begin to see that there is no one to fear. Soon Dharma will realize this too, and not too long after many will begin thinking the same way. They will reach out and aspire to greatness and glory, and that will require science to fuel it. When that happens, Aryavarta will rise beyond its former splendour to heights we've never dreamt of. There is,' he added philosophically, 'immense virtue in fearlessness.'

Panchali considered the scholar's quiet confidence even as old words echoed in her mind: *You think power and might lies only in armies and brute force? Prosperity can be power too.* Out loud she said, 'You expected this, didn't you?'

'I did. Or rather, I should say...'

'Govinda did,' Panchali finished. 'I feel like a fool, Dhaumya. I still don't know whether I did right or wrong. Govinda said he dreamt of an empire built on the might of the Firstborn and the Firewrights, both. But is that not treachery or, at the least, foolishness? Tell me, please, what have I been so blind to? What have I failed to understand?'

'I normally wouldn't dare respond to that question, especially when it's posed by a monarch,' Dhaumya jovially began, 'but in your case, I'll trust in our long acquaintance and share my thoughts with you.' He paused, thinking, and then continued, 'Panchali, all of our scriptures can be condensed into one simple principle... One above all.'

'The notion of a supreme maker, the power that was there even before existence came into being...'

'Precisely. Now, I have no complaints about the statement; in fact, I shall accept it for what it is. But when you think of the body of philosophy that stems from this one principle, there are issues we can't ignore. The scriptures it has spawned are all creations of mankind – earthly creations, if you will. They weren't set down by this supreme power, but by the seers of old. I suppose one could call them hymns of information and adoration. We sing in praise of the Supreme, and we also speak of the greatest act of this Supreme Being – the act of creation, a creation that encompasses Swarga, the celestial realm, Earth, and Patala, the netherworld. From this principle, we derive the notion of Divine Order, of life on Earth mirroring the dance of all Creation. And there lies the problem. The moment we are ready to accept the notion that existence is divided into inferior and superior beings, a hierarchical system that is divinely orchestrated as the pinnacle of perfection, we start believing in domination and hierarchy as being moral and righteous. We submit to the gods and to those chosen by the gods. Rather than question this system, we use the notion of divine predestination to explain things – which is precisely what the Firstborn do. They believe in a world based on this Divine Order, and their role in it as ensuring it remains such. Even if it means believing in things that not everyone agrees is just and fair...'

'The world as we know it wouldn't make sense unless Ahalya were turned to stone...' Panchali said, speaking to herself.

Dhaumya regarded her with kindness, guessing rightly where she had heard those words. 'Yes. You understand, don't you? These ideas, these irrevocable conceptualizations of good and bad are so deeply embedded within us that no one stops to ask why we are bound to our fate, what makes it unchangeable. Our rulers and our gods are all impervious to scrutiny. We put up with niggling inequities and blatant violations presuming that there must be a divine purpose or higher power that is beyond our comprehension. And then we reinterpret and redefine our past and present to fit in with the balanced view we have of the world. History, science, scripture – nothing remains untouched.'

'Then nothing is constant?'

'Nothing, except change. Evolution is not spurred by perfection and luxury, but by struggle. Today's rulers were once rebels and revolutionaries.'

Panchali shook her head. 'It sounds far too much like the notion of destiny. The inevitable, inexorable fate that rules us all.'

'Would you say that a pebble thrown upwards will fall to the ground, because it is destined to fall? To say that it will fall is nothing more than an awareness of cause and effect … Rules we construct, and keep refining …'

'We? You mean the Wrights?' She fixed Dhaumya with a steady gaze. 'That's what you are, aren't you, Dhaumya? A Firewright, just like Govinda Shauri.'

The scholar met her eyes with quiet confidence. 'That word no longer holds the meaning it used to, Panchali. Not since my brother began calling himself that … But to answer your question, yes, I did train briefly with them. Not in warcraft, mind you, but in medicine. Atri Angiras was a master of healing, as was Agniveshya, his student.'

'And here I thought you were a Varuni. Firstborn by training and birth, both,' Panchali said, an indisputable hint of accusation in her tone.

Dhaumya took no offence. 'I was. And I still am. But I am one of those that the Firewrights of old – true Wrights as they called themselves – considered a rebel,' he said. 'Don't you see, Empress? I am as much the product of Govinda's dreams as your empire – an empire built, as you mentioned, on the might of Firstborn and Firewright both. It was Govinda who took me to the Firewrights,

40

as he did others of the Firstborn. It was he who convinced them that it was the way forward, that the only way to take politics out of science was to share their knowledge with those they sought to keep it safe from. As much as the Firstborn and Aryavarta's own Emperor might begrudge it, the fact remains that the Firewrights are the very foundation of the empire. Their knowledge, now passed on to the people of Aryavarta as craft and skill, will fuel the future.'

'By Rudra, I'm so tired of this pandering, this unshakeable faith in Govinda's benevolence! Do you think I'm such a fool, that I can't see who or what he really is?' Suddenly aware of the rising pitch of her voice, Panchali forced herself to calm down. She took a deep breath before saying, 'Maybe he meant well, once. But I cannot trust him anymore, not after all the intrigue and manipulation. He believes that the ends justify the means, but I can't agree with those methods. Nothing has sanctity in his eyes anymore. He will stop at nothing.'

She looked at Dhaumya to find that his face bore the cross expression of a brother disappointed with a younger sibling. 'What more must he do to prove himself to you, Panchali?' he hoarsely demanded.

'I...'

'Why do you doubt him? Do you know that few have understood me ... or him ... the way you have? Yet, it would seem that few have misunderstood us both so badly. But that means little now. He is gone.'

Panchali felt a sourceless pain fill her at that statement. 'Do you think he will return?' she asked, dully.

'No. He won't. He cannot.'

'He never planned to, did he? It tore me to banish Govinda from Aryavarta right after Dharma's coronation, yet I did ... But it had nothing to do with what I said or did, isn't it? He was going to leave us all anyway.'

'Yes. He had to. Your husband may find it convenient to live in denial, but it won't be too long before those who don't start putting one and one together and realize that Govinda is a Firewright. And because of his own actions they won't stop to ask whether he is any different from the power-mongers of old.'

'He doesn't *have* to do anything, Dhaumya. Govinda Shauri never did anything he didn't want to. He believes in choices, not compulsions, so let's say it as it really is. Govinda chose to leave.'

'Because he thinks it's best this way.'

'He presumes too much.'

Dhaumya sighed and turned his palms upwards in a gesture of submission. 'For what it's worth, he has asked me to watch over you on his behalf. I shall try to fulfil that duty as best as I can.' He placed a hand on her head in blessing and continued, 'Jatavedas, the refulgent Agni, shall light your way, Empress. Be strong.'

With that, he walked away.

Panchali turned back to the view before her. A city that was silent, even lonely; a small, fragile whiteness against the mighty earthiness that was Aryavarta. She felt the confusion that had long cloaked her grow into a strange melancholy, turning finally into sheer despondence. There was, however, something familiar about the feeling. Govinda had made her his puppet, using her to weave his web of politics over Aryavarta. From the day he had turned down her affections, citing political imperative, to the day he crowned her Empress and left her behind he had always been one step ahead of her. It was important, he had told her, for the Vyasa and everyone who knew or suspected him to be a Firewright to believe that he was no longer a part of the empire's affairs. And for that he would leave everything – and everyone – behind.

Panchali tried to turn her mind to the promised glorious future of the empire – *her* empire. But reason failed her and the attempt proved futile. All she was aware of was an excruciating pain at the thought that Govinda would not return.

7

'NO! STOP! PLEASE...!'

Syoddhan, the crown prince of Western Kuru, lay on the cool marble floor, his hair and clothes dishevelled, begging for mercy and reprieve. It would have been a cause for worry if he did not

42

occasionally break out into laughter as he wilfully lost the wrestling match. The bout finally ended with Syoddhan reaching out and pulling his five-year-old nephew, his sister Dussala's son, to his chest. His own son Lakshmana was nearly sixteen and far too old for such juvenile pleasures, and when the blissfully exhausted child rested his head on his uncle's broad chest and fell asleep, Syoddhan lay back on the floor, enjoying the pleasant weight of his nephew's little body on his own, one hand gently patting the boy as he slept.

The bustle and murmur on the other side of the doorway told him that everyone had taken their places and the visitor they had gathered to meet had arrived. He decided to let them all wait. He wanted a few more precious, blissful fragments of peace and affection before reality intruded. Without quite realizing it, he was already frowning, as he ran his mind over what lay ahead.

Syoddhan had never shown much ambition, even though his father had tried desperately to inculcate the quality in him. His brothers, however, oozed the quality. It was just as well that he was the eldest, Syoddhan noted. He was forty-six years old but still a prince, while his father remained king of Kuru. Few others, his brothers included, would have been as patient as he had been. Dhritarastra, Syoddhan remembered, had once used the argument that his remaining king was the only way to keep the Kuru throne from passing to Dharma. The excuse was no longer valid, but Dhritarastra still held on. For his part, Syoddhan did not mind. His father's childishness inspired only pity in him, not anger. He knew how much it had hurt the blind king to be denied his right to the throne as the elder son and then be given the crown once his brother no longer wanted it.

The sleeping child stirred, bringing Syoddhan out of his reverie. He looked down at the boy with affection, pondering the hackneyed line about outgrowing childhood innocence. *We are all creatures who have once been divine and will, one day, become one with the divine. Our tainted humanity is but the present, and it shall pass. And that's why some things have to be protected, have to be fought for.* He closed his eyes again, trying hard to use the tranquillity of the moment to think things through. A medley of images flitted across his mind, drowning

43

out the many tensions that lay coiled within. He was alone now, with nothing but his own thoughts.

Ever since Dharma's coronation as Emperor… Syoddhan stopped himself short. It was not, he grimly reminded himself, a day to be remembered as a joyful occasion. On the contrary, it was the day his dearest friend Shisupala had died, no, the day he had been *murdered* by none other than Govinda Shauri. Shisupala had very nearly made public Govinda's terrible secret. From the destruction of the forests of Kandava and Ghora Angirasa's death to the long-ago obliteration of the Firewrights near Mathura, which had set a young Govinda on his path to power – all of it was nothing but a carefully orchestrated farce to deflect attention from the truth: Govinda Shauri was a Firewright, and one who had no qualms about using their knowledge to his gain. After all, which man possessed the will to destroy a source of power when it could be harnessed instead?

And for that ambition, Shisupala paid with his life. Memories of that day would never leave him, Syoddhan knew. He had managed to keep his temper in check for the duration of Dharma's coronation to the imperial throne, but hardly had the proceedings concluded than he had set out to find Govinda and exact his vengeance. He had not, however, expected to find Asvattama barring his way.

'You'll regret it,' Asvattama had cautioned. 'You do this now, you pave the way for Dharma's downfall and the empire's with it. Whatever complaint you have against Govinda, don't make your cousin, your blood, pay for it.'

'My cousin?' Syoddhan had spat out. 'What about my friend? What about Shisupala?'

'What about duty and honour and glory? Much as you may hate Govinda and what he has done, killing him now will only serve to destroy confidence in Dharma's empire. Let it go, Syoddhan, for now, at least.'

By then his close friends and advisors had clustered around him, adding their voices to Asvattama's.

'He's right, Prince,' Sanjaya had said. 'Think about what will happen if news of Govinda's death comes back to this hall. Things will descend into chaos, at least half the monarchs in here will get slaughtered, and where will that leave Aryavarta? Bereft of our kings what will happen to the people?'

'Do you counsel me to abandon my duty to avenge my friend? A scholar and a Suta telling a warrior of the Kurus to turn from a fight?'

'No,' Asvattama had said. 'I am telling you to follow a higher duty. It surprises me that the Suta here understands such a noble thing. Looks like there is still hope for him ...'

Asvattama's characteristic snideness had restored sanity to the occasion. Syoddhan had agreed, but reluctantly and not without a sense of guilt that continued to haunt him still. He sighed, grappling with his emotions as he tried to assuage his conscience. But no matter how he looked at it, what Govinda had done to his dear friend was wrong. He could never completely let it go.

With that thought, he stood up carefully so as not to disturb the sleeping child in his arms and signalled for an attendant to take the boy from him.

Syoddhan strode down the marble-floored corridor with its gold-trimmed pillars and the omnipresent elephant motif – the mark of his great ancestor, King Hastin, the founder of the city. Always prosperous and proud, the Kauravas had spared no expense in making their palace ostentatious and awe-inspiring, to the extent of being excessive. Now that a prince of Kuru sat on the imperial throne it was all the more reason for Hastina to shine, to take her place as sister-city to the imperial capital, Indr-prastha. But neither Syoddhan nor his father could think of their beloved home that way. Hastina was the heart of Kuru.

He stepped out from the corridor and into King Dhritarastra's private audience room. The room was meant for conversation and diplomacy, rather than a formal gathering of an audience. The seats, including the King's throne were arranged in a cosy circle. The throne was empty now, in Dhritarastra's absence, though Sanjaya stood, as he always did, right next to it. Also noticeably absent was Asvattama. Syoddhan found himself wishing that he had not taken Sanjaya's suggestion to send Asvattama to interrogate the captured

Firewright, Devala. But it was an important task, and Asvattama was the best man for it.

With that resolution Syoddhan turned his attention to the visitor, who stood up to greet him, an act of kinship rather than one of ceremony. Jayadrath, the king of Sindhu, was not only a friend but also Dussala's husband. Syoddhan would have preferred a more suitable match for his darling little sister than the middle-aged Jayadrath, but the king came from a line of distinguished royals and had an uncontested claim to the Sindhu throne. Though nearly twenty years older than Dussala, he was an accomplished warrior and statesman. That had been Dussala's only condition. She had demanded a man who was in no way lesser than her eldest brother, in stature or deed.

Looking around, Syoddhan smiled, this time with genuine pleasure, at his dear friend, Vasusena of the kingdom of Anga. His eyes moved on to rest on another man, one he welcomed with equal fondness if not familiarity – his maternal uncle, Shakuni. Thin and angular in build, Shakuni was the youngest of Gandhari's brothers, and not much older than Syoddhan. He sported a long beard, and had the habit of smoothing it out whenever he was in contemplation, which was often. This made him seem much older than he was. That, and the way he enjoyed being hailed as 'Uncle'. At that instant, though, Shakuni did not respond to Syoddhan's silent greeting, instead gazing into the distance, lost in his thoughts. Syoddhan knew better than to be taken in by his uncle's pretended abstraction. He was as wily as the red foxes of Dakshinavarta – a quality that the giant of a man seated next to Shakuni completely lacked.

Dussasan, the third of Dhritarastra's sons and second in line to the Kuru throne, sat up straight as Syoddhan glared at him. It was but a few muhurttas since morning and, already, the second prince reeked of inebriation and indulgence. Dussasan had inherited all of their father's ambition but none of his dignity. For this, Syoddhan blamed himself as much as he did his father. He knew well that Dussasan's first drink of the day had been consumed in none other than their father's chambers when the two men had got together, as they regularly did, to rant about how Dharma, the son of an

46

impotent napunsaka, ruled over the empire that was theirs by right. Syoddhan had joined them once, in the very first days since their return from Dharma's coronation, seeking reprieve from the pain of Shisupala's death. He had left, shaken to the core, and never graced that particular gathering again. It terrified him still to think that perhaps such hatred as his father and brother harboured ran in his veins too, and that someday, despite his best efforts, it would rise to consume him.

With bitter fury Syoddhan wished, as he secretly had in his youth, that Yuyutsu – his father's second child but by a palace concubine – had been born of a queen instead. Not one to wastefully cling on to what could not be, he dismissed the wistful, childish notion as quickly as it rose and strode to his customary seat.

'So,' Syoddhan began, 'what's this about? Looks like a matter of considerable importance! Tell me, what did you want to discuss, Jayadrath?'

The answer came as no surprise to Syoddhan.

'Govinda Shauri.'

Govinda Shauri. The very name made Syoddhan cringe. He said nothing and tried hard to keep his temper in check.

Jayadrath sat back, obviously enjoying the situation, though that was not because he had caused Syoddhan discomfort. He was fond of his brother-in-law: both of them were of the old, true blood. His undisguised joy, however, came from knowing that Syoddhan's reaction signalled the beginning of many things. He continued, 'I was one of those who held you back from vengeance for Shisupala's death, and it was not without cause. I hold no goodwill towards Govinda Shauri, or even Dharma Yudhisthir, but it had looked to me that Dharma's empire was to our benefit. Prosperity, peace and a placid Emperor. Of course, the fact that Govinda was neither seen nor heard of in the realm after the coronation completely justified my advice.'

'Really? I would thank you for your counsel, but I suspect you have had cause to change your mind…'

'Yes. Govinda is still in Aryavarta. There was a report of a fight, in an inn…'

'Since when does the king of Sindhu take an interest in common brawls?' Shakuni interrupted.

'Since it coincides with what I see as the first act of tyranny by our new Emperor. Or should I say puppet Emperor? Your spies must have reported the happenings at Indr-prastha to you? Even as we speak, a scroll awaits Emperor Dharma's seal of assent. It is an edict that will remove all taxes and tolls on Naga-made iron goods, that will supersede Takshaka's sovereignity as ruler of his own people and interfere in *their* economic affairs. Takshaka will be the first to lose his authority, or even his crown. What's to say you or I won't be next?'

Syoddhan studied his brother-in-law carefully, though he kept his face expressionless. 'Is that what truly bothers you, Jayadrath? Or is your concern because you and your dear friend and ally, King Saubha of Salwa, can no longer prosper from trading in confiscated Naga weaponry, which, I suppose, King Takshaka is no longer pleased to allow…?'

'On the contrary, Takshaka's son, the late Prince Aswasena – who, you no doubt remember, also died at Govinda Shauri's hands – previously had the foresight to enter into arrangements with myself and Saubha, which we are willing to continue. King Takshaka understands that letting the common people accumulate their own wealth is not…well, it's not in the larger interest. If our saamantas and vassals can no longer control their commoners and slaves because that lot begins to grow more prosperous, they in turn will rise against us. Of what use is that? We can use these riches with wisdom and benevolence, for the betterment of our people, but it's sheer folly to talk of prosperity while our coffers remain empty. *We* are the people, the king is the kingdom! We were chosen by the gods, it's our destiny as kings to do what is good for the people. Unfortunately, it appears that those charged with protecting the Divine Order of things are the ones who now seek to destroy it.'

'So what do you want to do, Jayadrath? Go to war? Rebel against the Emperor? For what it's worth, Dharma is the ruler by consensus – our consensus,' Vasusena interjected, speaking as he often did, just to remind the others of his hard-won right to do so.

As a Suta – one who was not a true-blooded Arya as Syoddhan and Jayadrath were – Vasusena had little right to address Jayadrath by name, but for the fact that he too was a king and a proven warrior.

'I have no problem with Dharma or his empire,' Jayadrath replied. 'In fact, I began by reminding you all of the hopes I had – and still have – of it. But I will not wait and watch as Govinda acts through Dharma to destabilize each of our kingdoms and have our own people rise against us. And then he will place his lackeys on the thrones in our stead. An assembly of vassal dolls, ruled by a puppet Emperor. It takes a different mind altogether to conceive of such a long-term strategy, an immaculately planned one at that, and see it through into action. Govinda Shauri must be stopped! I am of the view that we should attack Dwaraka.'

'You think too much of him,' Syoddhan muttered. He threw himself back in his seat and sat glaring into the distance. Disturbing thoughts flooded his mind, jostling for the attention he did not want to spare – Shisupala, his handsome face lighting up with joy, his severed head, his bloody carcass being dragged away by Govinda Shauri. Images of the helpless, spineless Dharma of their childhood and youth, and of Dharma now, proud and radiant on the imperial throne as the throngs chanted his name. Gradually, the chants transformed into Asvattama's old warning against vengeance and rang dully in his ears. Syoddhan drew himself back to the present and, looking at his brother-in-law, said, 'What you suggest is impossible on two counts. First, we have no due cause to attack Dwaraka ...'

'That's ridiculous,' Jayadrath interrupted. 'Govinda Shauri is a Firewright. Rudra knows how many more of his kind he has trained, and what other secrets Dwaraka holds. We have all due cause!'

'If you're so sure that you can show due cause, why not accuse him directly? Why not have him charged with treason and heresy and brought before the Emperor?

Jayadrath shook his head, impatient. 'The moment you call a demon a demon, it has nothing left to lose. Wait, let me not be so dramatic. I'll put it this way: what happens when you corner a spy?'

'He denies it, of course.'

'And if you persist? If you present evidence?'

'They usually try to kill themselves. The good ones try and take you down with them.'

'Precisely. If Govinda is accused openly, he may unleash Rudra-knows-what Firewright horrors on us. Do you really think that man doesn't have an arsenal of Wright-weapons hidden somewhere? Or that Dwaraka is not protected by every device know to the Wrights? But as long as he thinks he is merely under suspicion, even that he is tolerated, he will hesitate. And that gives us the time we need to strike him down before he comes at us.'

'Which argument brings me to my second point. He is a Firewright. How do you expect to win against him?'

'You have in your dungeons the one man who can help us destroy Govinda.'

'Are you out of your mind, Jayadrath? You want to pit one unscrupulous Firewright against another? Devala's malice knows no bounds.'

'Neither does Govinda Shauri's ambition. What makes you think he will stop now, after all that he has done? Besides, I am told that Devala is one of those who calls himself a true Wright. In his eyes, Govinda is a rebel and a traitor. This natural enmity makes Devala useful to us. And as for Govinda Shauri ... don't you see, unless we act now ...'

A silence fell over the room. It grew thicker for the soft rustle of robes as Dussasan sat up straight again. Syoddhan did not miss the slack jaw and the wide eyes that told him that his usually arrogant brother was, for once, unsure of himself. Perhaps even afraid. Syoddhan felt his resolve harden at the sight of what a mention of Govinda's name had done to his brutish, ruthless brother. He let the feeling grow till it overshadowed the niggling reminder from an incorporeal, righteous part of him that the ends did not justify the means; that if he used Devala now, he would be no better than Dharma, or even Govinda.

Syoddhan sent up a silent prayer and said out loud, 'How?'

Jayadrath said, 'The sea. Saubha is ready to sail against Dwaraka with a huge mercenary navy, the likes of which none of us can even begin to imagine. They will set sail from my ports and head for the open seas. Then they will turn and round the cape near Dwaraka at the last moment. We should be able to catch the Yadus unprepared, if not completely unawares. Meanwhile, our combined troops will also march against Dwaraka by land. King Damagosha – Shisupala's father – will allow our men to move through the Chedi kingdom in the guise of simple travellers and let them congregate at his borders. That way, Dwaraka's spies won't have more than a day's notice of the attack. Ekalavya of the Nishadas has agreed to form the rearguard of the attack by land. His forces will take up positions in the Madhu and Nishada forests, cutting off the west completely. Not even Vayu, the wind-god himself, can pass through their forests without their assent. In similar fashion, Rukmi of Vidharbha will seal off Dwaraka from the south. You see, Syoddhan, there are many who will rally to our cause.'

'As are those who will rally to Govinda's,' Shakuni added. 'Your military stratagem is sound, Jayadrath, but I am forced to bring us back to Vasusena's original question: Are we rebelling against the Emperor? For, surely, Dharma will send his own armies to help Govinda, as will the Panchalas. Indeed, if the *Emperor* commands us to join him, we must obey.'

'Must we?' Vasusena joined in. Despite his own initial objections, he apparently was in favour of the proposal at hand. 'What if we … well, defy the Emperor, if not rebel against him?'

Shakuni dismissed the idea at once. 'It's the worst thing we can do. Aryavarta is now ambivalent, uncertain even. Open defiance would force the various nations to pick sides, and many will in these new times choose to side with Dharma. The Panchalas for one … their armies are strong, and who knows what that Firewright has taught them … '

'We need to divide Dharma and Govinda,' Syoddhan concluded. 'We need to stop the Emperor from acting when we attack.'

Jayadrath said, 'What if we use the Danava mercenaries who serve Saubha to mount a distracting attack on Indr-prastha? It might just give us the time we need to … '

'That is again tantamount to rebellion, Jayadrath. If we do that, we might as well send out rose-water smeared parchments to every corner of Aryavarta, inviting them to rally their armies.'

'Do you have a better idea, Syoddhan? Or are you just going to sit there and rubbish everything we propose?'

Syoddhan stiffened at his brother-in-law's tone. Then he sighed and said, 'No, I don't have a better idea. But I do know that what Uncle Shakuni says is right. Unless we find a way to stop Dharma, there's no point attacking Dwaraka.'

Vasusena said, 'What if we make sure no messenger gets through from Dwaraka to Dharma?'

'We could try. But I don't see how. Indr-prastha is not in our control, and even if we try and get a few spies in there, they won't be enough to intercept everything.'

'You're right, Syoddhan. Indr-prastha is not in our control. But Hastina is. Bring Dharma here; bring the whole lot of them here, including his dear brothers and the Empress and that troublemaker Dhaumya. Let them leave only once Dwaraka is razed to the ground.' He smiled and added, 'You see, I have an idea.'

8

ASVATTAMA BHARADVAJA FLICKED ABSENT-MINDEDLY AT THE spot of weapon-grease that had found its way onto his white silk antariya. Despite the luxuriant texture of his lower robe, he still tended to wear it pleated tighter than was common for everyday use, for he never really stopped being the warrior he was inside even during the most relaxed or ceremonial of occasions. It served to emphasize his long, powerful legs as he strode through the corridors of Hastina's palace.

If he cared to listen to the awed whispers that filled the hallways he walked through at Hastina, or even those in his own capital, of Ahichhattra, he would have known that he was considered an exceptionally handsome man. As it stood, all Asvattama was aware of, and that too in a vague way, was that he had inherited his maternal grandmother's flawless pale skin and her sharp features, both of which were highlighted by the jewel he always wore on his forehead. His towering height and straight, black hair were, however, undoubtedly his father's. That, and his skill with weapons. Few could defeat his father, Acharya Dron, in battle. Fewer still could match Asvattama, brought up by his father and his uncle, Kripa, to be nothing but an instrument of death.

Asvattama had learnt long ago not to dwell on the path that had brought him to Hastina, but as he made his way past the closed doors of King Dhritarastra's jewel-and-velvet audience room towards the blood-stained dungeons with their fetid smell of death, it was difficult not to reflect on the choices he had made and on the things he had done. He was, by any reckoning, a man who saw much, revealed nothing and remained the master of his own will. For his part, he found the obvious face of politics too distasteful and the more subtle forms too dishonourable. And so he tried to remain aloof, as only a powerful man could, his power made all the more potent by his air of detachment. Only he knew that it was merely an attitude. He was as political a creature as Brahma had ever created.

Fuelled by irony, or inevitability, the political imperative had come to dominate his life. He had been wrested away from the place he had known and loved as home, nestled in the snow-teased lower ranges of the Great White Mountains – the hermitage of the Bhargava-Angirasas in the furthest reaches of what was now Northern Panchala.

A hermitage of Firewrights. Not just any Firewrights, but those reckoned to be the best fighters in all of Aryavarta, famed even in the far reaches of the world. Asvattama had grown up not just listening to the stories of their great battles and mighty conquests, but also seeing them, living with them and being trained by them. In his blood ran the same love of battle they had possessed and the same indomitable pride. That pride had disappeared, torn out of their hearts the day Ghora Angirasa, the greatest of Wrights and the head of their order, had led the rebellion against their own order. The Firstborn had taken full advantage of these internal conflicts to destroy the Firewrights. Tired and defeated, Ghora had fled. Worse followed – Ghora's son Agnivarna, and his grandson Agniveshya had surrendered to Emperor Jarasandha. With the end of their line the Bhargavas had been all that was left of the Angirasas.

Asvattama had been a young man then, with no more of an identity than being his father's student. He had silently, humbly, listened to the hushed discussions that had taken up many evenings at the hermitage. Not once had he voiced his opinion or even betrayed the slightest emotion, though he had thought and felt much. At length it had been decided that to protect their future the Bhargava-Angirasas would throw themselves at the mercy of Bhisma of the Kurus. Stunned, and not ready to accept such an outcome, Asvattama had approached Dron in private.

The acharya had indulgently listened to his son and said, 'It's true that Bhisma killed Ugrayudha, the man who was once our benefactor and protector. But that was a different Bhisma – he was hardly your age then! You know that he later became a student under your uncle, Rama Jamadagni. Bhisma was trained right here, at this very hermitage!' With a sad chuckle, Dron added, 'One can say that Bhisma is our protector now. Such is his destiny, and ours. Who's to question divine will, my son?'

'But…'

'Vathu!' Dron had flared up in his characteristic manner. 'I was patient enough to explain this to you, Asvattama. But don't think you're man enough to argue with me!'

Asvattama had humbly apologized and withdrawn, but the damage had been done. The first crack had formed in his already-tenuous relationship with his temperamental father.

The next day Dron and Kripa had left for Hastina, where Bhisma had offered them both positions at the court. The two Angirasas had accepted and a new phase of life, at Hastina, had begun. Asvattama continued his training with Dron, at the same time assisting his father to teach the students. It was at Hastina that he had met Syoddhan, and the foundations of their friendship had been laid. Meanwhile, Dron's newfound friendship with Bhisma soon elevated the acharya to the position of a royal advisor, and his fame and power had grown immeasurably. Life had been honourable, if not happy. At the least it had been free of politics, for by then Asvattama had learnt to keep his mask of aloofness on at all times.

But his isolation had lasted only so long. The Great Scourge, the bloody hunt for Firewrights had reached a peak, and in its aftermath Asvattama's beloved motherland had descended into famine, for no Wrights were left to help its people.

Asvattama and Dron had done what they had to. They sold their own craft, their knowledge of astra-weapons, to those who would buy it, including the Kuru kings. In return, these kings and nobles turned a blind eye to the use of Firewright irrigation methods to revive the dying soil. Those who could not be bought, or otherwise persuaded, had had to face Dron's ire – including Dhrupad, the rightful king of what had been a united Panchala before Dron and Asvattama had conquered the northern half.

It was then that Asvattama had briefly let fall his guise of detachment. 'Maybe,' he had told his father, 'there is still hope. The Kurus see how useful our weapons are. The Vyasa knows that the knowledge of the old Wrights – the true Wrights – has saved our people from starvation and death. Maybe now they will all see that we are not evil heathens, they will see ... '

'Muhira!' Dron had been livid. 'Listen to me carefully, Asvattama. There is no *we*. *We* are not Firewrights. You and I are the best military strategists Aryavarta has seen in many generations. *We* are useful, and our utility allows us to do a little something for our people. Don't outlive your usefulness to the Firstborn by holding on to the wrong sympathies. You are either a Firewright or my son. Choose!'

Swallowing his conscience and with the understanding that his words would serve to hide more than one injustice, Asvattama had said, 'I am always your son and your student, Acharya. I am not a Firewright.'

But these days it was difficult to fully forget what he could have been. In a bid to ignore the unwarranted notion, he found himself striding faster. It brought him face to face with a jubilant-looking Jayadrath, who was stepping out of the king's audience room.

Jayadrath grimaced at the unexpected encounter. It quickly turned into a smile, which Asvattama returned with extreme politeness and no warmth whatsoever.

'Acharya. You were missed at our little gathering. We could have certainly benefitted from your insight.'

Asvattama did not overlook the sarcasm. He said, 'You are too kind, Your Highness. Unfortunately, it is Syoddhan's orders that keep me from enjoying your splendid company.'

'You're interrogating Devala Asita, are you not?'

'Yes.'

'Has he said anything... of use... yet?'

'I'm on my way to meet him.'

'Surely that ought to have been your first priority today?'

'I've been busy. As you may or may not know, Syoddhan has entrusted the upkeep of the palace guards to me. I train them, and I make sure they keep the royal family safe. Surely you agree that their safety is more of a priority?'

Jayadrath was about to retort, but hesitated. His tone changed completely as he said, 'As I said, you'd have enjoyed the conversation, particularly in your position as a teacher of the military arts... and we could have benefitted from your advice.'

'My father is the teacher, Your Highness. I merely assist him.' Asvattama's expression remained neutral even as he silently cursed Rudra, Hari, Yama, and any other gods who cared to listen, for the unwelcome conversation. With practised disdain he said, even as he moved away, 'You must excuse me. I have a prisoner waiting.'

Asvattama reached the narrow doorway that led into the dark, subterranean prisons of Hastina and set off down the stairs. He raised his hand in unthinking acknowledgement as the guards in the prison below fell to attention and saluted him, but his thoughts remained fixed on trying to read more into the instinctive unease he felt after his conversation with Jayadrath. Something was up. And that something could not be anything good.

Power, his mind raced. *Jayadrath wants the power of the Firewrights. As does everybody else. Dharma is too weak an emperor to keep everyone in their place. If any of the kings of Aryavarta should decide Devala is more useful alive than dead...* The realization made Asvattama clutch at the hilt of his sword. *Unless...* One sweep of his sword, and Devala would be dead and this whole matter settled. Or perhaps not. He dismissed the last thought. It was too much to risk. Asvattama did not count himself a man of passion but he certainly was a man of honour, and it would take nothing less than cold reasoning to outweigh his sense of justice. It was not for him to decide Devala's fate.

With the grace that came of such conviction, Asvattama walked into the dimly lit cell and waited for the guard to shut the iron door from the outside. He sat down on a worn wooden chair that was set against a small table and bent his right leg square, his hide-sandalled foot resting insolently on the left knee. Ignoring the man who was chained and manacled to the wall in front of him, he curled his open palms into fists, as though testing their strength, and studied his hands through half-lidded eyes. His long, dark lower lashes brushed lightly against his cheeks in a way that had driven even the most discerning of courtesans in the realm to fawn over him tirelessly on some occasion or the other. The fire in his eyes as he finally looked up would have had them screaming, terrified, with the same vigour.

Devala, however, was unafraid. 'You look lost in thought,' he drawled.

The statement, Asvattama knew, was a means to begin the conversation. With reluctance, he put his contemplations away and snapped in his characteristic fashion, 'Thinking is a luxury that only those of us with minds can indulge in, Devala. I'd hardly expect you to understand that…'

Devala studied his interlocutor with patience, like a hunter watching a deer, waiting for the perfect moment to release the fatal arrow. Timing his words to intrude on Asvattama's exact chain of thought, he asked in a soft voice, 'Was it painful?'

If Asvattama was taken aback, he did not show it. 'No,' he plainly answered. He allowed a touch of sharpness to take over. 'And you? Did you make it painful?'

'No,' Devala shook his head. 'He died quietly. By his own dagger, as a matter of fact – though of course the hand that drove it into him was mine. Agnivarna Angirasa… Your uncle, wasn't he?'

'My cousin. A few times removed. I called his father, Agniveshya Angirasa, "Uncle" though.'

'Aah yes, it was your uncle you killed. Well, fratricide, parricide, what difference does it make… He was a rebel. You only did what was right.'

'There's no need to compliment me, Devala. I assure you, I'm beyond seeking your approval,' Asvattama retorted. He remained unfazed by the accusations, partly because they were true, but mostly because he knew his actions were justified. There were many heinous things he had done, but he was yet to lose sleep over any of his actions. If Devala's only weapon was guilt, then Asvattama undoubtedly had the upper hand.

Devala gathered as much, for he affected a subtle shift in tone. 'Did he tell you?' His voice held genuine anticipation.

Asvattama looked visibly amused. He shifted, switching legs so that his left ankle rested on his right knee, even as Devala struggled to hide the true depths of expectation that lay behind his affected eagerness. 'He didn't,' Asvattama answered, 'though he admitted its existence. A weapon, he said, far more powerful than the Bramha-astra. A weapon of his own making…'

Devala struggled yet again to maintain a neutral expression, as he waited for Asvattama to ask the inevitable question. When it did not appear to be forthcoming, it struck Devala that he had no choice but to reveal something if he wanted anything useful out of the other man. 'I tried,' he confessed, 'I tried for many, many years. I followed every lead, milked every spy and used every ingredient available to replicate the poison Agniveshya had created when he had been living in the Kandava forest. My efforts yielded results, though not the results I'd hoped for. I discovered a powerful toxin, one that would vaporize and spread as soon as it was exposed to air. Your dear friend Shikandin can vouch for it. He nearly died as a result of my handiwork and suffered a great deal of pain too.'

The statement failed to incite Asvattama on either of its implied counts. Instead, he asked, as he might, if he were enquiring about the weather. 'What did you use? For the key ingredient?'

'The venom of the mottled black cobra.'

Asvattama snorted, disparaging. 'I could've spared you the trouble, then. My uncle found snake venom highly unreliable as a toxin.'

'Don't lecture me, Asvattama. Agniveshya called his weapon the Naga-astra.'

'And so you assumed it was made of snake venom? Muhira! You fool, he created it in honour of those who had protected him for years – Takshaka's people. And so he called it the Naga-astra. As for recreating it – that seems highly unlikely now that the Kandava forest no longer exists.'

'Thanks to Govinda Shauri,' Devala hissed. 'It makes sense. He destroys that which he cannot control. As did the Firstborn, whom you have so faithfully served. Not much difference between traitors, is there? You and I aren't very different either, you know. We are both true Wrights; we both wait, and we both hope and fear that there may indeed be plans that are made to succeed when all others fail…'

'I am nothing like you!' Asvattama said, rising to his feet, the sudden movement sending the chair he had sat on clattering across the stone floor. He left the prison without another word.

9

THERE WERE FEW THINGS, SANJAYA NOTED, AS WORRYING OR AS satisfying, depending on one's point of view, as watching a war-hardy man be truly horrified. And to see clear concern, the faint but undeniable tinge of fear in the eyes of a man such as Acharya Dron – now that was a heady feeling indeed. He had been a little anxious that Syoddhan's meeting with Jayadrath would go on for a while and he would not be able to be here on time. And then Vasusena had put forth his idea. It was brilliant, and elegant in its parsimony. It had taken Sanjaya self-restraint to not be openly effusive, and he had to remind himself that not everyone knew what he did about the supposedly lowborn warrior.

Everyone has a secret, Sanjaya thought. *It's what makes them weak. To know those secrets is to hold unfettered power in one's hand. The Firewrights knew that well, as did my mentor, the former Vyasa Dwaipayana. It is time to put this invaluable lesson to use once more.*

As soon as the discussion had concluded, Sanjaya had excused himself and made his way towards Hastina's dungeons, stopping only to check that his attendant had, inadvertently and in the most casual manner, ensured that Dron would be waiting for him. He had indulged in an unusual smile when the attendant reported that he had seen Jayadrath in conversation with Asvattama not too long ago, but thought no further of it and, focussed on the matter at hand. Tasks such as the one he was about to perform were precious, not only for the vital part they played in his plans but also for the sheer delight they provided.

Careful not to let thoughts of impending pleasure distract him for too long, Sanjaya shifted closer to the respected teacher and counsellor standing by his side, the subtle move creating an air of confidentiality and trust. Dron was a much older man but still a fighter to be contended with. No one, Sanjaya included, would want to put the acharya to the test. As a result, he chose his next words with great care, 'It might just be coincidence, Acharya. Just because your son had the wrong sympathies in his youth doesn't mean he still does. He's older now, and far wiser.'

Dron shook his head, his eyes fixed on his son as the tall warrior exited the well-guarded stairway to Hastina's dungeons. 'What business did he have there, if not his own?' he snapped.

Sanjaya did not reply, and in the silence they heard a palace guard snapping to attention and greeting Asvattama, who in turn made a casual enquiry as to the security arrangements for the new prisoner. Muffled by the distance, their exact words were indiscernible but the general import of their conversation was obvious.

'Why should he care, unless … ?' Dron allowed his imagination to suggest many conclusions, none of them palatable.

'Acharya, for what it's worth, the Vyasa – I mean, the former Vyasa – never did doubt your son or his loyalty. Neither have your benefactors, the Kurus, ever had cause to do so. Grandsire Bhisma knows that both of you have remained true to the Firstborn cause,' Sanjaya said, careful to lower his voice further.

'With all due respect to the *former* Vyasa and to the Grandsire, Sanjaya, I've known my son a lot longer than they have. I also know the tempestuous heart Asvattama hides behind that calm exterior. There are times when I think I should've slit his throat myself...'

'Acharya, please! There's no proof...'

'My honour won't take proof for an answer, Sanjaya. You've seen the sway Bhisma holds over King Dhrupad of Panchala simply because of what that fool son of *his* did. Am I to be reduced to the same state because my son is equally an imbecile? No!'

Sanjaya made to speak, but realized that Asvattama's conversation with the guard had ended and he was now walking away. He waited till the warrior was out of sight. Next to him, Dron let out a deep breath. Sanjaya placed a gentle hand on the older man's forearm, the way he knew Dwaipayana was wont to. 'Acharya, please ... there are few men I admire more than you and your son. And I know that even now you see what needs to be done to protect him, to protect your honour. But can you truly believe that your enemies would think the same way? King Dhrupad is more important, more powerful now than he has ever been, thanks to his alliance with the house of Dharma Yudhisthir. Do you trust that he won't manipulate the Emperor against you? One word of Asvattama's mistakes, of what he did before he became king of Northern Panchala, and Dhrupad will claim just cause to hunt you and your son down like rabid wolves!'

Dron turned, his dark eyes boring into Sanjaya. Gone was the anxiety of moments ago. It was as if he had suddenly remembered that he was royal preceptor to the Kuru kings, while Sanjaya was a lowly Suta, a half-born. 'Say whatever it is you want to say, Sanjaya,' he said coldly. 'Don't presume to advise me.'

'My apologies, Acharya. I only wish to point out that Asvattama is indispensable to Syoddhan, just as you were and are indispensable to Grandsire Bhisma. If Syoddhan and his friends rise to be the moral restraint on Emperor Dharma's reign, then Asvattama will be safe.'

'Are these your words, Sanjaya, or the Vyasa's?'

'They are not Vyasa Markand's – for these affairs are not his area of comfort or expertise. Which is why my former master – the Vyasa Dwaipayana – has still left political counsel to my care. And I believe, as he does, that power must have checks and balances. Syoddhan can be the balance. But for that to happen, he must grow and come into his own. There are those, especially at Hastina, who have held power for far too long. They may need a gentle hand to guide them towards letting go. Your influence in this would be most invaluable, and, if I may be so bold as to point out, to your son's benefit.'

'And who at Hastina is it you speak of as needing guidance? There are two old men here who would fit the description well. One fancies himself king and the other *is* king. Neither knows what it means to age with grace!'

Sanjaya did not reply in words, but let his expression show acknowledgement. He knew he had played the move well. Dron prided himself on letting his young students rise to excellence. Often, he drew attention to the fact that when he had won Northern Panchala from King Dhrupad, he had installed Asvattama on the throne of Ahichhattra instead of taking the crown for himself – unlike Bhisma and Dhritarastra, who hung on to the Kuru throne as Regent and king, respectively.

'Well,' Dron continued, 'I'll do what I can to prod the old ones to let go. At the least, I shall support Syoddhan's ventures. He will prove himself in no time!'

'Thank you, Acharya. I'm most grateful. This isn't a duty I could have ever hoped to discharge on my own!'

Laughing, Dron gave Sanjaya a benevolent pat on his shoulder before walking away.

Sanjaya waited till he was sure Dron was gone, before moving towards the stairway from which Asvattama had earlier emerged. He entered the dungeons, ignoring the sounds and smells, the omnipresence of pain, flesh and blood that came at him from its bowels. He was not a man of violence and he did not regret it in the least. He considered killing a menial function, one of many tasks that could be delegated and seen through successfully if one held true power. True power, he knew, came from the mind. It was this knowledge that had fed his grudge and his dream for all these years. The sense of undeniable superiority where it mattered had led him to aspire to use the Firewrights, to one day lead them despite never having been trained as one. He was determined to take what was rightfully his by sheer force, his kind of force.

He made his way to one of the smaller cells set in what could be considered the best corner, noting that the air was cleaner here, and it was just that much brighter. He found Devala inside, pacing, rubbing at his manacled wrists. 'Oh Rudra! Don't tell me they still haven't taken that off you! Guard! Guard! Come here at once!' Devala watched, a little curious, as Sanjaya had him unchained.

'It's bad enough we have to keep you here for a while longer,' Sanjaya continued, as soon as the guard was out of earshot. 'Chains aren't needed. It's not like you're going to do anything I don't want you to.'

Devala chuckled at the implied threat, but took no offence. 'It's all right,' he said. 'It made for a good show in front of that fool who was just here. Treacherous bastard! May he wander the earth an accursed being for a thousand centuries! Men like him deserve to rot alive, the pompous fool! He knows nothing, but pretends he commands us all. You should have seen the hunger in his eyes when I mentioned the Naga-weapon.'

'Hunger? The look in Jayadrath's eyes when he mentioned *you* was sheer gluttony! But getting back to Asvattama, don't underestimate him. You think that you've interrogated him? I assure you, he's the one who's interrogated you and you didn't even realize it.'

'His ambition is plain enough, Sanjaya. He wants power. He wants Agniveshya's weapon even more than any one of those sons-of-whores kings do. The bait has been placed. But I think he knows nothing about this new Secret Keeper. In fact, he was so blinded with anger by the end of our conversation that the conceited muhira did not even realize what I was talking about.'

Sanjaya frowned. 'I'm not so sure it's as simple as that. But yes, the bait has been well placed. Asvattama is ambitious, but he is far from stupid and his loyalties have always been divided. He served the Vyasa well enough, far too well, in fact. In any case, the seeds of his downfall have been laid. He won't last long.'

'How?'

'His father. The only thing more dangerous than not being trusted by the man who sired you, is being hated by the one you've sired. I should know. Be ready, you'll need to go to work soon. How long do you think it will take?'

'To completely refit an army? That will take months. But I can make modifications to any conventional weaponry within two or three days. Why, I remember, I had Sudakshin fire up a hundred small forges just to heat and remove the tip off all his men's arrows to create the crescent shape that keeps the skin open so that the enemy bleeds to death from just a flesh wound.'

'I can tell you now that you will be dealing with Danava mercenaries.'

'That lot is a pleasure to work with. Show them any gruesome way to kill and they pick it up like trained monkeys at a village fair. I'll equip them all right.'

'Good. Now remember, at no point should anyone suspect my involvement in this affair. As far as they are concerned, you are the last Firewright, yes? Don't worry… you will be treated well by Saubha. Still, be careful. Don't outstay your utility, or reveal all your tricks just yet. And don't be seen at Dwaraka. Your involvement must remain known only to those who think themselves either benefitted or condemned by it, for only they will have cause to keep it a secret.'

Devala nodded. He was still a little stunned by the turn of events. 'Are you sure this will work? How did you get them to agree to this?' he asked.

'Getting them to agree was simple enough. Jayadrath and his allies have much to gain if they can take Dwaraka down, especially in these newly prosperous times. The port of Dwaraka is the key to the future, to trade and wealth. He was very easily motivated, as was King Saubha, weeks earlier.'

'They have much to gain once Dwaraka is gone.'

'Who doesn't?'

'I meant economically and politically, not in terms of moral satisfaction.'

'That too,' Sanjaya affirmed. 'But to be on the safe side, I've personally ensured that Dharma's legislators have been putting forward proposals which are just ambiguous enough to seem incursive on the sovereignty of the more sensitive kings. But the gods smile on us, Devala – something in those edicts has inspired Empress Panchali to present a controversial proposal of her own ... To remove taxes on Naga iron-work so that their craft will spread.'

Devala's usually bitter expression softened. 'She's a good woman. Honestly believes in what the Wrights stood for. Unfortunately, she's also rather malleable, as Govinda Shauri knew well ...'

'It's a quality we can put to use, just as he did.'

'But this proposal, this idea of removing taxes on Naga-made goods – you must admit, it has a certain appeal. It's not too different from what Agniveshya had hoped for, or what I myself would have wanted had I been the one to teach the Nagas the metal craft of the Wrights.'

'I agree. But that is precisely the point. We were not the ones to teach them their skills, nor are we the ones now to hasten their rise. If the power of the Firewrights is to remain in our hands, Devala, so must their knowledge. Now, more than ever, the need for secrecy and caution is upon us. Only if we centralize all knowledge in the hands of a few can we control Aryavarta's destiny. We must make ourselves indispensable to Aryavarta's monarchs – the new generation of rulers, mind you, not these old dotards that were happy to let the Firstborn spit on them! Let the old die quietly. We will be the might, no, the masters of the new breed of kings that rule Aryavarta. And for this greater good that we will bring to this realm, sacrifices must be made. In this case, the Nagas will just have to continue to play the role they have for decades. I'm sure they must have got accustomed to being used by now.'

With a nod that served to acknowledge but not quite yield, Devala said, 'So, Dwaraka?'

'Yes, Dwaraka. I doubt we could stop that particular storm even if we wanted to.'

'And after that?'

'After that? Hunger and fear, my friend. Hunger and fear.'

'How do you mean?'

'Dwaraka will fall, after which it's only a matter of time before these great kings start bickering amongst themselves, hungry to call the might of the Firewrights their own while fearful of the powers their neighbours may wield. And then, our time begins. One by one, they will seek us out. And, soon, the sound of hammer against iron and the scrape of molten metal against anvil will fill the air of every kingdom in this so-called empire. Aryavarta will never be the same again.'

Devala sneered, 'Now who's making the mistake of underestimation? You misjudge Govinda Shauri.'

'On the contrary, it is you who underestimate Govinda Shauri. I, on the other hand, know what he is capable of. He's not an idiot. He was one of Ghora's best students, or so it was said.'

'Much was said, not all of it deserving.'

Sanjaya gazed indulgently at the Firewright before him. Devala's anger reminded him of his own, of how, in the past, he would openly question Govinda's intentions and competence only to have Dwaipayana indulge him with explanations. He thought back to those days, those long years of playing the obedient acolyte as he gently guided the Vyasa's hand, allowing him to let Govinda build this empire. An empire that Sanjaya would now use for his own purposes. The notion made him feel important, benevolent and wary all at once.

It was the first of the two feelings that led him to explain, 'Govinda's plan to create an empire and take control of Aryavarta was not a bad one, and it would be folly to think otherwise. He had the foresight to set into motion a mighty chain of events, one that ended with Dharma Yudhisthir occupying the imperial throne. But that was his singular mistake. He chose *Dharma Yudhisthir*.'

'He chose Panchali. If only she'd been born a man ...'

'Then he wouldn't have chosen her at all. In the name of Agni, stop thinking of Govinda as an idea. He is a man. All men have weaknesses. As for Dharma, once Dwaraka falls ...'

'But will it fall?' Devala still sounded unconvinced.

'My dear Devala, you astound me. Is it your own skill as a Wright you doubt or ...? You are going to help arm Saubha's forces yourself. How can Dwaraka not fall?'

'I doubt my mother's virtue when it comes to anything related

66

to Govinda Shauri. Call him a man, an idea, or whatever you like. I'd prefer to call him dead.'

Sanjaya considered the statement. 'You have a point. Dwaraka may be more vulnerable and easier to take down if Govinda is out of the way.' He was silent for a while and then said, 'Once you are done equipping Saubha's forces, find Govinda and finish him off. He has been wandering Aryavarta ever since the Coronation. Kill him before he reaches Dwaraka.'

'That's nothing. I know where the dramatic fool will end up, sooner or later. But, there is one last thing…?'

In answer to the unspoken question, Sanjaya said, 'Asvattama? He won't come after you. You'll be released on Syoddhan's secret orders, as it were, so he won't be a problem. Nor will the old pair of king and Regent. But still, remember to be discreet.'

'What about Syoddhan? I did not see that particular bull being so easily tamed with fire but, clearly, I've underestimated you.'

Sanjaya ignored the compliment, though he was hardly displeased. 'He still has his doubts, but once Dwaraka is his it will be too late for him to change his mind about us. Saubha and Jayadrath will present arguments that Syoddhan cannot refute – not if he wishes to rule. And in the same vein, if Saubha and Jayadrath wish to remain persuasive forces, they will need us and our weapons. Either way, Aryavarta will be ours.'

Devala grinned maliciously at the thought. 'Well done! Rational and methodical. I like that in a man.'

'Of course I'm rational and methodical. I'm a Firewright.'

10

THE TEMPERAMENTAL SUMMER BREEZE WHISTLED THROUGH THE trees on the verdant hillside and sang over the water of the nearby stream. Occasionally, it came forth as a forceful gust, picking up just a touch of spray from the foam-flecked surface and landing as drops of sunlight on the grassy banks. Satisfied, it ebbed for a few moments, allowing birdsong to occasionally fill the air, till it decided it was time to resume its performance and rushed back to the trees and the water.

Govinda Shauri smiled, enjoying its cool, playful touch. He ran his fingers lightly through his dark, wavy hair, pushing it off his face with a contented sigh. The grass he lay on felt soft and scratchy on his bare back, tickling a particular spot along his spine. He could smell the freshness of the forest around him. In the silence, welcoming and comfortable, he could hear the forest breathe. Drawing in his fill of the crisp air, he revelled in a sea of simple, acute sensations. These forests, these lush glades and the sparkling river – this was where he had played as a child, fought and loved as a man, lived as a cowherd and a prince. This was the heart of Aryavarta, the land that he loved and revered.

This was where he had become who he was.

A Firewright.

Govinda was not one to indulge in reminiscence, for it got in the way of his dispassion. He simply remembered, his mind bringing to life images and scenes in a clear, ordered fashion.

He had been about eighteen when, disillusioned with his new life as the Prince of Mathura, he had sought out the Sramanas, a sect of dark mystics. Following their ways, he had tested his body and mind to the limits of endurance, fasting for days on end, standing in the rain and the sun without so much as twitching a muscle, daring to lie on the ashes of cooling pyres embracing the bones of the dead. He had imagined his own death time and again, till it held no fear, no fascination, just an unruffled acceptance of mortality, oblivious to individual existence. He had been alive, but hardly sentient. He breathed, he ate if fed, and he never slept.

Finally, his teacher had led him to a village. This village.

Here, there had been laughter. He could hear it now, the fearless laughter of a child, and in his mind he followed the sound through the village to find himself at its furthest boundary, on the river's edge.

A girl sat thoughtfully on the bank, watching leaves and flowers float by on the current, whirling through eddies and dancing over rocks in a show fit for an empress. A bustle of excitement went through the calm little hamlet of thatched huts, as two figures slowly entered the village. The adults left their huts and thronged around the duo, and the girl ran to join the chattering group of children that stood on the fringes of the crowd of adults. Their vision completely blocked by the crowd, the children stood ineffectively on tiptoe, hoping for a glimpse.

'Is Great-grandfather back?' her brother, a lanky boy, asked. 'May we see him, Father?'

A young man stepped back from the crowd. 'Not yet, little ones. He is very tired. He's been living a life of harsh asceticism in Dakshinavarta.'

The boy gasped. 'With the Sramanas?' he asked, a little fearfully.

'Yes, with the Sramanas. He has not eaten for a long time and his body has gone through much hardship. He needs to rest. You won't disturb him, will you?'

The two children had assured their father that they would not. The man was about to leave when the boy asked, 'Who's that with Great-grandfather? That man?'

'His student.'

The memory moved from morning to afternoon. The initial excitement in the village had died down, helped by the hazy stupor of the summer day. Few dared venture out in the blazing heat. Only the most enthusiastic of children, who intended to take full advantage of the fact that most adults were indoors, and in all probability, asleep, were about. He saw *her* then, smiling softly in a lazy reverie, curled up in the shade of a tree by the river.

Moments later, he realized, the girl was up and frowning at a small group of her playmates who were stealthily approaching the hut where the Sramana rested. Her brother was not with them. She ran over to the group.

'What are you doing?' she asked.

The boy leading the group grinned conspiratorially as he realized her reluctance. 'We just want to take a look at the other man, that's all.'

'He is a disciple and a Sramana. Treat him with respect. Leave him be,' she said.

'He isn't a Sramana. Your great-grandfather has brought back a wild man from the southern jungles.'

'I'm going to find father,' she said, unsure of what was to come.

'Are you scared?' one of the other children teased.

'Of course she's scared,' the first boy went on, 'she's scared of the wild man.'

Her little hands rolled into fists. She knew she could not win a fight against all these children, but she did not care. The only dissuading factor was the inevitable punishment from her father. She decided not to throw the first blow and let her hands fall to her side. 'I'm not scared!'

'Then come with us...' the boy said.

She considered the offer and nodded in agreement. Grinning, the boy took her hand lest she run away. She glared at him in response and took a step forward.

As one, the children huddled into the hut. A shuffling sound came from its dark depths. One of the smaller children whined, terrified. The sound provoked a response. Something was approaching, but its awkward, angular movements were hardly human. With yells and squeals, the children made to run away, the boy in the lead included. He bolted for the small crack of light that indicated the doorway. The heavy curtain swung in his face and he flailed wildly, bringing it down and letting a wide beam of light tear into the darkness of the hut before he fled from the scene. The others followed him out, still screaming loudly.

Only the girl remained in the hut. As the strange creature approached, she slowly moved back a couple of steps, uncertain and confused. Her every move, every expression conveyed meaning, just as if she were speaking aloud. Govinda knew she was terrified by what she saw: The occupant of the hut looked like a normal man, but he could well have been a wild creature. His body was bare, except for the scrap of cloth over his hips. Long, matted hair fell unkempt over his face, and his cheeks were covered with an uneven, scraggly beard. He was tall and grotesquely emaciated. His bones jutted out, giving him the look of a human insect, especially when he moved, as he did now. He crawled on his hands and knees, to where she stood.

Children's voices shouted from outside, telling her that others had run to get help. But the girl did not care. He knew that she herself was lost in the Sramana's eyes, an ocean of endless life, of infinity. In that moment, the child understood the oft-repeated truth that learned adults around her longed to make sense of. In a hushed whisper, she said the words he would never forget. 'I am the Primordial Being, Existence itself.'

Govinda heard a guttural sound, a croak that was speech from vocal cords that had not been used in many months. Was it him? Or was it the Sramana? He did not know. For all he could see was the fire of compassion in the girl's eyes. He was lost in its light.

'Are you hungry?' she gently asked, and without waiting for an answer she took the Sramana's hand. 'Come, we'll find something to eat. But first, you must have a bath and offer your prayers to the Sacred Fire. We have rules here in this hermitage, you know,' she said the last words in a conscious imitation of her grandfather when he addressed new disciples.

The Sramana said nothing, but unsteadily got to his feet and let her guide him towards the doorway. She stepped out, but he hesitated, as did Govinda, fearful of the bright afternoon sun. The crowd that had gathered stared at them, aghast. The girl giggled at the sight.

'Come,' she urged. 'Don't be afraid. This is my family. I won't let them hurt you.'

The Sramana disappeared, becoming one with Govinda as he raised his head and let the sunlight fall on his face. With an exclamation of joy, her great-grandfather – thin, tired, but otherwise very much normal and clean – came forward to embrace him.

'I feared we'd lost you, my son,' the old sage tearfully confessed. 'I feared you'd never return from the dark paths on which you travelled.'

Govinda felt the girl's chubby little hand, soft and warm in his large, calloused grip. He stood straighter, taller, like he had awakened from a dream. He was no longer watching now, but could feel every sensation.

That night, Govinda had slept in the dormitory, with all the other students. As he lay struggling to sleep, he heard her voice through the darkness, as she and the other students cajoled her father to tell them a story. A strong voice finally began the narrative, and Govinda had listened, as spellbound as the children had been.

'Once upon a time,' the man began, 'there was a goddess whose beauty and grace, form and spirit, were such that all the gods and celestials desired her. Her name was Sri. Wherever she went, there was always joy and happiness, and so, Indra, the king of the celestials, convinced everyone that she ought to be his. That way, Indra argued, Swarga would always be the happiest place in the Universe. And so it was. But poor, unfortunate Sri, who brought everyone such great prosperity, was herself unhappy.'

'Why?' a boy asked.

'Because, little ones, whoever had Sri could be happy. But Sri didn't have anyone. She didn't have herself.'

Govinda remembered that he had been amazed at the simplicity with which the man had explained such a complex notion.

'And then,' the narration continued, 'Indra was cursed by a sage, and lost his throne. Suddenly, there was a mad scramble among the celestials, demons and even humans to become King in Indra's place. More importantly, to claim Sri, and become victorious and prosperous. The terrified goddess went into hiding deep inside the Ocean of Existence on which the weaver of illusions, Vasudeva Narayana, rests. She remained there for a long, long time. The war for Indra's throne was catastrophic. Many died, demons and celestials alike. Finally, a truce was declared between them and they decided to churn the Ocean of Existence to search for the secret Elixir of Immortality. Can you guess what they found?'

The young girl responded in a mesmerized whisper, 'Sri?'

'Yes, they found Sri. When they churned the ocean, she had to come out of hiding. Once again, a great clamour started, as each of the celestials and demons tried to woo her, abduct her, or claim her. But, you see, Sri was no longer the helpless goddess who had gone

72

into hiding. She had found someone who cared for her and wanted her to be happy. He had borne her through her troubles and seen her true form. Do you understand, children? Not once in all those eons did Vasudeva Narayana ever seek to own her the way others had. Instead, he made her a part of himself. And now, Sri decided, she'd never leave Narayana, no matter what, for Narayana would never forsake the eternal truth, the universal balance. Vasudeva Narayana made her the source of his strength. Where he is Eternity, she is Nature; where he is Purpose, she is Action; and where he is the Soul of all things, she is the Manifestation. The scriptures describe her as a dark-hued jewel that lies forever in his heart. Whenever the great weaver of illusions descends to Earth, Sri, with the power of fire and the fragrance of lotuses, is born too. Always.'

'Always,' the girl had repeated.

Her simple conviction stunned Govinda.

The next morning, shaved, bathed and looking a little less wild, he searched her out and found her alone, revising her lessons with a diligence that appeared excessive for her age. She smiled as he approached, but did not interrupt her revision with speech.

Govinda sat next to her, the silence between them comfortable. They remained that way for a while.

Suddenly, she asked him, 'They say you're a prince. It must be nice to be one… Prince Govinda Shauri…' she let the name roll off her tongue and continued, without pause, 'when I was a little girl, I used to wish I were a princess so I'd never have to do chores, or study so hard, and I could eat what I wanted and not be told to finish without wasting any of it.'

She shook her head in a precociously adult fashion, clucking her tongue at her own juvenile fantasies. 'But not anymore,' she concluded.

'And what do you wish for now?' Govinda asked, amazed at her propensity to speak on without a care in the world.

The girl had replied, with solemn sincerity, 'I want to know…' She eagerly began explaining, the act second nature to her, 'You see, all the knowledge in the world is still incomplete, because there are questions we haven't answered yet. What does existence really mean? The scriptures say we each are as wide as Brahman, Existence itself, and Brahman is as small as the tiniest celestial atom inside us. It is within us, and we're within it at the same time – but what does that mean in our lives, yours and mine? And even if I know everything there is to know, these questions still cannot be answered. Who knew these things, when I did not? How did it exist if no one knew it? All we ever learn is only that which can be known. What is the unknown? What is … ?' She trailed off, unable to explain what it was that she sought.

'I am the Primordial Being, Existence itself,' Govinda reminded her.

'That is just the beginning of the road, Prince Govinda,' she had said, eyebrows raised in an effort to look haughty and condescending. 'It's not the knowledge that matters, it's the knowing.'

And then she was gone, lost again in the formless weight of a life lived once, and then over and over again in memory.

Govinda hissed as the breeze whipped a lock of his wavy hair into his eye, the light sting bringing him back to the present. He stood up and walked over to the tree that had featured so vividly in his recollections, even haunting his dreams. The swing he had built for her had long been severed and discarded, but to his eyes the faint abrasions left by the thick hemp rope still remained on the branch it had hung from. Govinda closed his eyes, letting his mind fill completely with her image, her voice, her laughter. If there was a word in the languages of Aryavarta, Dakshinavarta, or even foreign tongues to describe what had been between the two of them, he did not know it. She was a child, he was her playmate; she was a student, he was the teacher. Sometimes, he recalled, he had been the student and she the teacher. It did not matter. He had loved her. And he knew, in a way he could not explain, that if only they had had enough time when she had grown to be a young woman he would have fallen in love with her.

Now, all of it was only memory. What had once been a village was merely strewn wreckage and debris, the sad remains of the Firewrights that *he* had destroyed. He looked down at his empty arms, remembering what it had felt like to hold her close and then to let her go. It had felt the same way when he let Panchali go on the eve of her wedding, when her fingers had slipped out of his grasp, leaving a void that could never be filled.

'Was it worth it?' a rough voice intruded on his thoughts.

Govinda could not help but feel a flicker of surprise as he recognized the voice. He turned to face the speaker and his malice. 'You know it was.'

'Liar! Nothing was worth losing her.'

'You should know…' Govinda carelessly dismissed, even as he took in the men silently forming a ring around him. Each of them was dressed in the non-descript black robes of those who did not wish to be identified and had a mask covering the lower half of his face. From the style of their robes and the designs on the hilts of the swords Govinda guessed them to be Danava mercenaries. Cut-throat soldiers available on hire, they were among the most feared warriors in the world. Despite their lack of allegiance, Govinda had no doubt they were effective – far more so than the three men who had met their demise at his hands in that drinking-house. Whoever had managed to get Devala out of prison had neither intended nor needed to settle for less.

11

'YOU SHOULD HAVE RUN WHEN YOU HAD THE CHANCE.'

Govinda's voice held no trace of the many questions on his mind when he replied, 'You think too much of yourself.'

Devala snarled in response, but let it pass as he took yet another look at the devastation around them. A different kind of anger, a simmering rage, steeped in visible sadness, filled him. 'There was life here,' he said. 'Life which you brutally tore from its roots. Nothing can bring them back, Govinda. Nothing will bring *her* back…not the way she was then.'

'Are you here to reminisce, Devala? In which case, we should light a fire, have a drink… Or we could just get down to the matter at hand.'

Devala spat on the ground in response. He turned to one of the ten men with him and said, 'Kill him.'

The mercenary, a man with grey eyes and sun-browned skin that had, from the look of his scalp, been pale once, was not a native of Aryavarta, and his behaviour served to affirm it. 'Kill him?' he questioned Devala's command with all the impudence of a man used to serving just one master: money. 'But Lord Sau...'

'He said you were to take your orders from me, or you will not see a coin from him,' Devala affirmed. 'Now kill him. And once you're done, take his head. It must hang over the gates of Dwaraka. On second thoughts, take the rest of him too... We shall let a limb hang from each entrance to his precious city. Dwaraka the many-gated, they call it... We shall have Govinda quartered to adorn each of them.'

Govinda's eyes darkened. Devala's arrogant words were enough to suggest that something was wrong, terribly wrong. But there was no time to be wasted in seeking explanations or engaging in arguments. He would have to settle things swiftly. Ten, no, eleven against one was in no way favourable odds, but Govinda knew better than to be intimidated. And being a veteran of such situations, he also knew better than to be complacent.

Before any of the hired men could move, Govinda pulled the slender dagger out from its sheath around his calf and hurled it at the mercenary in the middle of the cluster. Taking advantage of the instant of shock that followed, he drew out Nandaka, his sword, and threw himself at the remaining men. The way they came forward alerted him to the fact that they were toying with him, baiting him, though he could not explain how or why. As their swords met, he noticed the savage glee, the feral anticipation he had seen elsewhere in the eyes of victors, on the faces of men riding to bloody plunder. It filled him with a desperate strength. Dropping down on one knee, whipping his head out of the way as a spear whistled past his right ear, Govinda swung a double-handed stroke that rent the soft bellies of three men at one go. It was not a killing move, but the keen edge of Nandaka ripped through flesh and muscle, pulling out the mercenaries' entrails. With howls of pain, the men staggered back, their weapons falling from their hands as they clutched at their stomachs before keeling to the ground. It would take them a long time to die, but they no longer posed a threat.

Their companions, however, had learnt their lesson. They formed a ring around Govinda before he could get back on his feet. This time, though, they kept a wary distance and watched his every move instead of rushing in. Govinda guessed that they would now take it slow, moving in smaller groups, tiring him out and pushing him to make a fatal mistake. One opening was all they needed.

Govinda stepped on a sword one of the fallen men had dropped. Without taking his eyes off his adversaries, he slipped a foot under the length of the blade and flipped it up, catching it by the hilt. He now had a sword in each hand. Twirling both blades around with strong turns of his wrists, he quickly got used to his new acquisition, the weight and length perceptibly different from his own silver-white sword. Evening out his breath, he concentrated on every sound and the slightest trace of movement around him, keenly aware that Devala had not joined the ring of attackers. His focus paid off, for he became aware of the soft creak of a bow not very far away, the smooth draw ending with a reluctant jerk, a sign of added weight on the bowstring. Govinda felt a hint of satisfaction, though he was careful not to let it show. It seemed Devala's impatience would prove helpful.

The moment he heard the twang of the bowstring, Govinda moved, throwing himself sideways and down to the ground. He heard the distinct sound of shattering as the arrow hit the ground, barely finger-widths away from where he had been standing. Instinctively, he held his breath. He saw at once that this was a poison of a different kind. Barely had the first whiff of a purple-green smoke risen from the broken remains of Devala's poison-arrow than Govinda let out the breath he had been holding. He noted the positions of his adversaries and closed his eyes, pulling his torn upper robe in a band around his face to give his eyes added protection. After that he let the screams guide him.

Govinda thought it unlikely that Devala had many more poison darts at his disposal – the toxins being rare and time-consuming to make – but even a simple arrow could prove fatal at such short range. He heard Devala's bow swing again, but could do little other than try to let the mercenaries' bodies shield him from the arrows. Crouching down to form as small a target as he could, he thrust and cleaved with precise parsimony, each stroke bringing down an assailant who was already incapacitated by Devala's premature attack. Ironically, in doing this, he exposed himself further to Devala's aim. Govinda cursed out loud as he felt an arrow graze his calf and wondered if he ought to risk opening his eyes. Reasoning that it would serve him no purpose to go blind, he fought on using sound and instinct.

He stopped when he realized that his strokes were cutting through nothing but air and stood still and alert, panting hard. He had counted six men falling, which ought to have left one more mercenary. For all he knew, the man was already dead. But Devala remained in the fray, and Govinda now had no clue where he was. A little reluctantly, he tried to provoke the Firewright to speech. 'Neither patience, nor allegiance. You lack the skill to be a tyrant and the honour to be a hero. Now do you see why she rejected you?'

Devala's voice was a close whisper that made Govinda realize that he was now in more danger than ever. 'She rejected me because she loved you. And you betrayed her love, her trust. You used her and threw her away as you do with everyone, Govinda. Of all your crimes, this has been the worst. And, by Hara, you will pay for it. Everything that you've built will fall. Your precious city, your people, shall lie ravaged and broken, the way her spirit was ravaged and broken when you betrayed her! And you shall die right here. Right here, where it all began and ended.'

Govinda felt the rush of air before he heard the stroke. More by reflex than calculated precision, he brought up his blade in a counter. A choked cry of pain escaped him as the blade missed his neck but rent his unprotected forearm, cutting deeper as Devala pressed down with his entire weight. Despite the agony, Govinda twisted his wrist around, trying to cut Devala's sword-arm even as he pushed himself up off the ground, at the same time slashing with his other sword. He heard Devala cry out in pain, and felt the pressure give as the other man stumbled back. Govinda straightened up, dropped his borrowed sword and pulled at the cloth over his eyes. Blinking as the glare of the light hit him, he steadied himself on his feet, ready for Devala to strike again. The full-body form of combat that often served Govinda so well was of no advantage here, for his adversary equally bore the marks of Firewright training. Yet Devala stepped back. Govinda understood as he saw the spreading stain on the man's robe. Devala was hurt. In a sudden move, Devala hurled his sword at Govinda and turned around to run as fast as he could. At his whistled signal, a powerful brown stallion emerged from the edge of the woods, slowing down to a trot only to let his injured master clamber on before taking off at a gallop.

'Balahak!' Govinda called out to his own horse, but even as the silver-white steed came thundering up the slight slope of the riverbank with a neighed response, he knew that giving chase was not a good idea. Devala could easily lead him into a trap. Worse, with their equally matched horses, the chase could well take a day or two, time Govinda could not afford to lose. This was not over. Not yet. From what he had gathered, an attack against Dwaraka was certainly in the offing. Indr-prastha, too, could be in danger. Govinda dismissed the last thought. For all his rage and anger, Devala would not willingly harm Panchali. It was Dwaraka, then, that was in immediate danger. As he had expected – rather, as he had planned – Dwaraka would pay the price for all that he had done.

With a sigh, Govinda remained where he was, letting Devala disappear out of view, while Balahak paced around, restless. *I've made my choices,* he reminded himself. *There is no such things as coincidence, and no such thing as irony. There is only cause and consequence, and there is no room for regret.* He ran his hand over the rough bark of the tree, *her tree,* careful not to let his blood taint its innocent verdure.

Sheathing his dagger and his sword, Govinda strode towards Balahak. He had wandered enough. It was time to go home.

12

DAWN.

The crystal spires of Dwaraka turned from a luminous gold to pure fire and then cooled to shine soothingly silver, the colours bleeding into the great ocean below.

Every morning, Balabadra, Govinda's brother and head of the Council that governed the affairs of Dwaraka, would stand on the terrace of his mansion and take in the glory of the city that he and his brother had painstakingly built. He would look over the shining prosperity, the proud beauty that was not just Dwaraka but also her people. Often, he would reach out to wrap an arm around his wife, Raivati, grateful for her companionship on the journey that had brought them here. Always, he would send up a prayer, thanking the gods for this, their bounty.

But not today.

A muhurtta and a half ago, the guards at the seaward watchtower had sounded the alarm. A great host of battleships, all of them flying the colours of the Salwa kingdom, was headed for the island-city, their sails full with the morning wind, the mighty wood and metal of their hulls shining like jewels in the sea. As they drew closer and settled into formation, the ships seemed to line the entire western horizon. Balabadra had hardly taken stock of the situation when the watch on the landward tower began a great clanging of gongs. A huge army was advancing towards Dwaraka through the marshlands in the north. Balabadra quickly assessed the situation. A part of the invading forces must have docked their ships much further north, outside the territories of the Yadu nation, and made their way down across the treacherous – and therefore less guarded – swamps. A scout's report that the enemy had no elephants, but more than made up for it in the sheer number of their infantry and cavalry, confirmed his suspicions.

Balabadra turned at the sound of approaching footsteps. Yuyudhana, his cousin, strode on to the terrace.

'I bring bad news,' Yuyudhana began. 'The scouts report that another array of chariot-rigs and cavalry is making its way in from the east, crossing the river at our border with the Chedi Kingdom. I guess this is Damagosha's revenge for…' He trailed off, not wanting to say in words what Balabadra also knew well. King Damagosha of Chedi was out to avenge his son Sishupala's death at Govinda's hands.

'So it's not just Saubha…'

'No,' Yuyudhana said. 'The armies are mainly Saubha's but Danava mercenaries add to their numbers. And of course this attack requires the complicity of others…'

Balabadra nodded. 'Do it. Activate the defences.'

'Completely?' the question held strain. 'That is a risk. Dwaraka can outlast any siege. It was designed that way. But if we keep a path open, if we try to hold the plains and the bridges…I am not saying that it is wrong, but… Have you considered this carefully?'

With a sigh Balabadra said, 'I have. We shall trust in the Emperor and the righteousness of his empire. Leave the main bridge open. Mobilize the forces to defend. Call the cavalry in, the women included. Have them ready.'

'But…the Council?'

'I will address the Council right away, but you know how they won't decide a thing before they are done cursing Govinda and blaming him for all that is happening. Kritavarman has been shouting abuses since the first ship was seen…'

Yuyudhana turned to go, but looked back. 'And you? Do you not blame Govinda?'

'Do you?'

'We are under attack. Is it too much to ask that our Commander be here?'

'He is. In Govinda's absence, you are the Commander. That is clear. Go now. We don't have much time.'

Dwaraka's unparalleled defence mechanisms were called into action right away. The sluice gates on the River Gomati were closed, cutting off the flow of water to the city's huge storage tanks in case the enemy should attempt to poison them. All but one of the wooden bridges connecting the island-city to the mainland were burned down as the impregnable city prepared for a siege. The harbour, too, went up in flames in a bid to keep the enemy's ships out. Still, the terrifying hordes descended on them from land and sea.

Trapped between the enemy's army and navy, Balabadra knew it was only a matter of time before the city fell, unless the Emperor, or their Panchala friends, came to help. He had made a choice to place his faith in the empire for no reason other than that it was of his brother's making. His faith would now be put to the test.

Taking a deep breath, Balabadra called out to Raivati to fetch his armour.

13

SYODDHAN'S INVITATION TO VISIT HASTINA HAD ARRIVED AT Indr-prastha with its own royal escort, as would benefit a scroll of such importance.

Though pleased at this overt display of ceremony, in his typical fashion Dharma had not shown it. He had dismissed Bhim's suspicions with a wave of his hand and all the conviction that came of being Emperor. 'It's only fitting that our cousins entertain us first, before the rest of Aryavarta shows its regard for the empire. It would be most impolite to refuse, would it not? What say you, Sadev? You're the diplomat among us.'

'You are right, Agraja. But a state visit…a visit from you, as Emperor, has its own formalities. One does not simply call on a brother on a whim.'

Dharma had said, 'Then all the more reason to show that I remain his brother, even though I am now Emperor. I am as brother and father to all Aryavarta, am I not? Or do you think me a tyrant, a self-centred overlord? My position is a burden, brother, a great and honourable burden of duty. I bear it because I must, because it is my destiny to do so. Surely, you cannot expect me to stop being the man I am because of it?'

Dharma's brothers had received his righteous declaration with practiced acquiescence. They knew their place in Dharma's world, as Panchali knew hers. They were the pillars on which the Emperor stood, a man raised to great heights on the shoulders of others. But pillars and shoulders had no voice, and so they remained silent, even as Dharma functioned as their head and heart both. It had always been this way, a bond forged through love and respect, and an acceptance that the elder was always meant to lead. If anything, becoming Emperor had convinced Dharma all the more that this was how it was meant to be. It was, therefore, with quiet certitude that the four allowed themselves to be treated as nothing more than Dharma's servitors, though that in itself commanded respect. Each one was entertained at Hastina by one of Syoddhan's brothers, and all of them bore it without complaint, their personal likes or dislikes for their cousins notwithstanding. Panchali remained Dharma's near-constant companion, except when he chose to indulge in pursuits that were considered an essential mark of royalty, particularly among the Kurus. She asked no questions when he did not come to her bed at night, and made no mention of it the following morning. Not that she had much of an opportunity to, for the rest of her time was spent in the company of the royal ladies of Hastina. While she entertained most of them out of courtesy, her visits to Syoddhan's mother, Queen Gandhari, and his wife, Bhanumati, were enjoyable enough. In all, quite to her surprise, she found the entire visit turning out to be an undeniably pleasant affair.

On the fourth evening of their stay, Panchali found herself involved in an interesting conversation. Dharma was with her, as were Syoddhan and Asvattama, who remained a frequent and welcome visitor at Hastina. Panchali was glad to see him, just as she was glad that Vasusena was not around. She knew that despite the passage of time Vasusena had yet to get over his perceived shaming at her wedding competition. He could never look at Panchali without grimacing, while the hatred in his gaze made her flinch.

The final member of the group was Shakuni, Syoddhan's uncle, though he looked no older than Dharma. Shakuni was a man of varied learning. In keeping with his comparatively liberal Gandhara roots, he did not share the patriarchal Kaurava view of women and social hierarchies, and took pride in flaunting it – with the result that Panchali had no lack of stimulating conversation. Neither did Dharma.

The topic that had them engaged in debate that evening was, Panchali knew, an old favourite with her husband: Dice. Shakuni passed around the pair he owned for each of them to examine. The dice were exquisitely light, made of a dazzling white metal, and fell to the ground with a metallic clatter that was pleasing to the ear.

'Dice has been considered a game of chance. Is it true that there's not much skill involved?' Panchali asked.

'On the contrary,' Shakuni said, 'dice is a rather philosophical game … In fact, I'd say that one's beliefs determine whether it is played as a game of chance or of skill.'

'Oh! Please do go on.' Panchali took a seat in anticipation of more conversation. Dharma hesitated and then sat down next to her, while Syoddhan and Shakuni took a throne-like chair each. Asvattama, continued to stand, genially waving away Syoddhan's gesture to sit.

'It all depends on what you see as cause and consequence, Mahamatra,' Shakuni explained. 'If the fall of the dice is the end result, then we must ask why they fall that way. Those who believe in chance, in fate, will argue that it is predestined, and we are just tools, or a means for the dice to be cast. I'd reckon Emperor Dharma here subscribes to this view.'

'Indeed I do,' Dharma emphatically said. 'What happens to us is the will of fate, of the gods. Even if there is means or skill involved in the throwing, that itself becomes a predestined causality.'

'Or,' Shakuni said, 'one may believe, as Syoddhan here does, that the fall of the dice is completely the result of human skill or the lack of it. It may be that you can't predict the way the dice will fall, but an unskilled player ought to know that he is unlikely to get the outcome he seeks. It is a game of probability, of inevitability …'

'He knows that he doesn't know …' Panchali muttered to herself.

'Exactly!' Shakuni confirmed.

The loud exclamation made Panchali come out of her brief abstraction. She asked, 'And if the fall of the dice is not the consequence?'

'Ah! If that is not the consequence, what can it be? Can it be the cause?' Shakuni said in a dramatic whisper. He chuckled. 'And that is why I always win, Mahamatra.'

'I don't understand...' Panchali said.

'Now, now! Don't force him to reveal his secrets and tricks,' Dharma said.

Shakuni waved his hand in disagreement. 'A skill may seem like a trick, or even a sleight of hand, to one who doesn't know how it's done. But I have nothing to hide. The rumour goes that these are magic dice and they follow my command, but there is no magic. Very simply, these dice were cast using the lightest of iron alloys, one that allows for skill on a throw to determine the outcome. Nothing surpassing this metal has been crafted since...'

Panchali shook her head, again confessing that she did not comprehend.

Asvattama spoke now, an occasion unusual enough to surprise Dharma and Syoddhan both. 'These dice? They are Wright-work, like the imperial sceptre. Made from the bones of an Angirasa scholar. No need to explain what that is probably a metaphor for,' he sardonically added.

'Unless the scholar was an exceptionally hardy... or bony... man,' Panchali quipped.

Asvattama, Syoddhan and Shakuni roared with laughter, while Dharma looked aghast. He forced a polite look onto his face, but his voice was laced with derision. 'Amazing how we still allow these unsanctified artifacts to be treated with such reverence... Once, the Wrights polluted our entire realm with their supposedly magical silver-white metal. Now, it's the heathen Nagas and their black ironwork, their life-sucking arrowheads and other such nonsense,' he declared with gravity.

'Come now,' Asvattama said. 'It would be a pity to forget history. It was the restrictions we imposed on the Nagas' ironwork, the subjugation we had kept them under these past decades, which has made their weaponry both rare and valuable. If the Nagas begin to trade freely throughout your dominion they would no longer need to push their craft as something elusive, steeped in dark magic and all that. They can sell their products simply and openly for their own gain. But they are now under a different form of subjugation – one that uses economic forces instead of political or social sanctions – and that might again lead to what you call pollution, and science being lost. It's imperative now, as you well know, *Emperor*, that the Nagas be encouraged to trade, to share their craft. At the very least,' he added, 'it would save us the trouble of another bloody scourge in the years to come.'

'And over time,' Panchali added, 'popular demand determines how the craft moves forward – why make arrows and other weapons, if there are no wars? Instead, we can turn our attention to devices that make life more productive for the common people. Instruments that may help us grow more crops, or perform effective medical procedures… Imagine!'

'There are no maybes,' Syoddhan said. 'We could certainly do much. The library at Hastina is a treasure trove of knowledge that becomes mere arcanum with disuse. To put knowledge together with method would create a whole universe of possibilities. You're right: Imagine. We can do so much, if only we have the courage to…' He stopped, aware that he was leaning forward, eager, as was Panchali. He was also conscious of a thought that had never occurred to him in all these years, but had just taken hold. What if…? What if it were he who had married Panchali, won her hand? Would he now be Emperor? He would have been a good one, taken Aryavarta forward in the obvious direction. Yet, it was not he, but Dharma, a feeble, prejudiced gardhabha who lorded over them all.

With silent self-recrimination for what he considered purposeless, blind ambition, Syoddhan turned his attention back to a hopeful-looking Panchali, forcing himself to note and then to ignore the becoming spark in her eyes.

Dharma, however, was growing more discomfited by the moment, more so because he felt compelled to condone this mild but open heresy. He directed his words at Panchali and allowed a rough note to enter his voice, one that he could not assume with any of the others in the audience. 'You presume, my dear, that these tales of heathen magic are nothing more than fantastical creations aimed at creating sensation. What you forget is that there is a greater duty, a higher morality that binds us Aryas; a duty to wipe out all that espouses an unsanctified way of life. The correct, accepted way is one that reflects and recreates Divine Order on earth.'

'Divine Order doesn't fill a man's stomach when the rains fail, or pestilence sweeps through the realm, killing king and commoner alike, Dharma,' Syoddhan pointed out.

'My dear Syoddhan, if Divine Order were truly recreated on earth, why would it not rain? Or why would the lands be cursed with pestilence? That is precisely the point. It is not for us to defy destiny, but merely our duty to protect the way of life that submits to it. Anything that subverts the Divine Order – be it called magic, heresy, or science – is to be fought and destroyed. There is no room to question our ultimate allegiance to the gods themselves!'

Sitting tall, Dharma quoted,

> 'With civilization comes law,
> A remedy for flaw
> And both law and social norm
> Must weather every storm.

> 'When the innocent quail
> Know the law has failed.
> When rulers forgo what is right,
> Know that evil shall delight.

'There. Did I get that right, Panchali? You are so well versed in these tomes. If only I too had the time to read and study as I wished ... But I cannot, and it is one of the many ways in which I must pay for my destiny. But I cannot defy it.'

Panchali made to argue, defiance a lifelong instinct. Yet, wisdom prevailed and she held her tongue. Dharma wanted – no, needed – to establish his moral and temporal authority, given especially their current company. She was merely an instrument and this was yet another part she had to play. She nodded, admitting the Emperor's point without really apologizing for her own and said, 'Well, it's late, and I'm sure you have many things to attend to. Chivalrous warriors that you are, I know you won't admit you're bored of my chatter, so I'll excuse myself while you're all still awake ... '

Panchali left the room, providing the others with an opportunity to close that part of the conversation. Her graceful exit drew a look of appreciation from Syoddhan, but he said nothing.

'I should go too,' Asvattama said. Unlike Panchali, he saw no reason to accommodate Dharma and felt himself to be in rare danger of losing his temper.

'Stay ... ' Syoddhan urged, only partly out of courtesy. Asvattama's presence was not required to keep Dharma's attention diverted from the outside world, though it did make it a less onerous chore.

Asvattama shook his head. 'I'm needed back at Ahichhattra ... I'll return in a few days. Why don't we all hunt together then?'

The men exchanged farewells and, with a polite bow, Asvattama left.

An uncomfortable silence followed his departure as the three who remained found themselves at a loss for conversation. 'Well, cousin,' Syoddhan eventually said, 'what shall we do now? I for one wouldn't mind a game of dice, given all this talk of it.'

Dharma's voice was unusually cold. 'Yes. We shall play dice. They say that a man who turns away from dice is a man who turns away from battle. Let's test our mettle, shall we? Let's see if your wagers can match your uncle's words.'

'How do you mean?'

'Do you dare play to conquer, Syoddhan? Dice truly is not very different from war. It may well prove why one man is an emperor while another remains just a prince. Destiny.'

'Surely you jest?'

'Jest? But of course! Just as you were jesting when you spoke of courage. It is not courage to defy destiny. It is folly.'

'Folly is sitting down to a game against Shakuni. He is an exceptionally skilled player ... '

'Well, then you should have no problem staking even your kingdom on the game. For my part, the wealth of the Emperor is boundless, and more bountiful than the wealth of virtue that is mine.

I am Dharma, and by my word and deed I remain virtuous, free from sin. The gods must reward me, as they always have, irrespective of whether you call on probability or magic... And that, Syoddhan, is the truth of who I am. It is not men who have made me Emperor, but the gods themselves. It's time all of you understood that. As for talk of courage and folly... Well, it was you who proposed that we play. I have agreed. It is now up to you.'

Syoddhan stared at Dharma, unsure whether he ought to take up the challenge or simply walk away, disgusted as he was. What gave Dharma the right to behave the way he did? Was this what Govinda Shauri had done; was? Was Dharma's soul now so corrupt that he had forgotten his basic duty as Emperor? Syoddhan made to speak out, but stopped himself. If Dharma took offence, if he left Hastina now, it would put all their plans at risk. He had, over the past few days, made sure that Dharma had received nothing but the most harmless of missives. The one messenger who had brought tidings of troop movements in the west – a fact that required nothing but observation in the normal course of events – had met with an unfortunate accident. But all this was possible only because Dharma was in Syoddhan's palace, under his influence. If he were to leave... Syoddhan could not afford to let that happen. Gritting his teeth, he readied himself to play his part. 'As you wish, *cousin*.'

He turned to Shakuni. 'Let the preparations be made, Uncle. Gather all the emissaries as well as the vassals, in attendance. The entire assembly shall witness this conquest, such as it may be, of Hastina. The game commences tomorrow evening.'

'But... all right.' Shakuni left the room.

Dharma regarded Syoddhan with an amused, pretentious air. 'Well, I think I'll call it a night. I believe there are lovely ladies, exceptionally skilled at music, and other entertainment, waiting for me. Indeed, your hospitality is impressive, cousin!'

Syoddhan nodded his thanks, but said nothing. His thoughts lay elsewhere. Despite the fact that he ruled an empire, it was clear that Dharma's heart still desired Hastina. Would he truly ask Syoddhan to play the kingdom as stake?

It's just a game, he reassured himself. *A game of dice. What can either of us lose beyond a couple of horses and elephants and a few heaps of gold?* Yet, Syoddhan could not escape the sense of foreboding that shrouded his thoughts.

Someday they will speak of us, his mind raged, *of Syoddhan and Dharma. But whatever happens next, they will remember that I invited Dharma to Hastina, and I sat him down to a game of dice...* But that mattered not. There were greater issues at stake than what would be said of Syoddhan Kauravya in times to come.

With stern resolution, Syoddhan turned his mind to the west. Saubha and his armies would have reached the gates of Dwaraka by now. A day or two more was all they would need. By then, the city would surely lie in ruins. In the depths of Syoddhan's imagination, Shisupala's handsome face delighted at the sight of foul vultures and carrion crows picking and tearing away at the remains of Govinda Shauri.

14

SCATTERED RUINS WERE ALL THAT REMAINED OF WHAT HAD ONCE been Kampilya. Now the city had shifted westwards, closer to the river, and grown into a sprawling trading centre, while its original location was but a small cluster of rubble and stone, a dot in the vast moonlit fields between the city's walls and the Great Road. Though used on occasion by travellers to rest or by lovers seeking privacy, for the most part the ruins remained deserted. The people of Southern Panchala tended to avoid the crumbling structures altogether – the result of a healthy wariness of snakes and other avoidable occupants of the area, coupled with a less wholesome but more colourful belief that ghosts and spirits too resided there.

Shikandin cared little for either kind of inhabitants as he made his way into the dark heart of the broken structures, leading his horse beside him. The bright moonlight made a torch unnecessary. Besides, a torch would attract attention, which neither he nor the person he was to meet wanted. The distinct smell of horse and bridle-leather told him his visitor had already arrived and he turned as he heard slow, measured footsteps behind him. Silhouetted against the night sky that shone through the nearly roofless ruins was a tall figure, wrapped in a black, shroud-like cloak. The man reeked of danger, an animalistic power that Shikandin found comfortingly familiar. The visitor, he knew, was in many ways not very different from him.

'Do you still have nightmares?' the man asked without prelude, his eyes taking in the subtle but unmistakeable glint of the silver-white beads Shikandin wore on his neck.

'No. Not since…not since Panchali and Dhrstyadymn…' Shikandin let the words hang between them, before adding, a hint of laughter in his voice, 'not since you stole half my kingdom from me…Chaura!'

Asvattama laughed softly at the accusation, well aware that it was true but delighted that Shikandin did not mean it with malice. He noted with satisfaction that the last time the two men had shared a moment of mirth had been before Panchala was split in two. Laughter had been all the more precious then, for terror and bloodshed had surrounded them in the last phase of the Great Scourge, when all of Aryavarta had turned against the Firewrights. The terrible things they had seen had left scars in many ways. He was glad to know that Shikandin had found some relief from his haunted past. Asvattama said, 'You love them very much, don't you?'

'As I would my son and daughter.'

'I think the affection is mutual. Panchali can't have an extended conversation without bringing you and Dhrstyadymn into it. I particularly enjoy watching Vasusena grimace at every mention of Kampilya.'

'That's a sight worth seeing, I'm sure. I take it the…erm… imperial visit is going well?'

'Tediously well and consummately boring, as most of these family gatherings tend to be. Speaking of family…'

Shikandin pre-empted the question. 'Yudhamanyu is well. He has grown up to be a fine young man. Makes me proud to be a father.'

Asvattama knew better than to say or ask more. He reached out to give Shikandin's shoulder a squeeze, earning him a warm smile from the man.

'And you?' Shikandin went on, as he lightly looped his horse's reins over a plant that grew from a fallen pillar, 'I don't suppose you'll ever marry?'

'It's too late. I'm a few years older than you are, as you well know. Besides, I seem to have built up an undeserved reputation for being celibate, among other things. It has its uses, so I won't complain too much. I do what I want to anyway.'

'Do you? Do any of us?'

'We can pretend to …' Asvattama said, with a light shrug. The statement dispelled the illusion of friendly, aimless conversation for he said in a grim tone, 'I have a very bad feeling about all of this.'

'Devala?'

'Yes. Why isn't the son-of-a-whore dead yet? I don't see what the Vyasa gains by keeping him alive.'

'Is it the Vyasa who's keeping him alive, Asvattama?'

'Point well made. I fear that the Vyasas, old and new, no longer retain the power and influence they once had over Aryavarta. A development to a good end, no doubt, but …'

Shikandin nodded. 'So, someone else's influence is instrumental in keeping Devala alive … What could this person want?'

'What did anyone ever want from the Firewrights? Power.'

'Weapons?'

'But of course!' Drawing in a deep breath, Asvattama confessed, 'Devala asked me about the Naga-astra – the all-powerful toxin Agniveshya supposedly created after the fall of the Firewrights, during his years of hiding.'

'Was he trying to tempt you, do you think?'

'He knows better. He was trying to find it.'

'Find it? But that would imply …'

'Precisely.' Asvattama knew he did not have to explain as Shikandin's brow furrowed into an unusually deep frown. He continued, 'If it weren't for this bastard, whatever weapons remained would soon become relatively obsolete. In any case, in a few years from now it will all be redundant. Aryavarta will be one united economic entity, and any weaponry that has been found or invented will only make us stronger against foreign invaders. Internally, we'd be bound by forces far stronger than Firewright weapons or Firstborn morals. I swear, Shikandin, we should have killed Devala the day we had our hands on him. We should never have let him be taken alive! But now, he or whoever it is that's behind him wants whatever weapons may still be out there… An ambition that is best fulfilled now, while the Firstborn are weak.'

Shikandin considered the analysis briefly, before declaring, 'Yes. It is also an ambition that *you* can fulfil as well as any other man.'

'You mean… find whatever Firewright weapons are left?'

'Yes. Why not?'

Asvattama slowly shook his head. 'No, Shikandin.'

'Why not?'

'Because I don't trust myself. I don't trust what I could become if the power of Hara himself came into my hands. I'm just a killer, an assassin, and a good one at that. Don't tempt me with power. I lack your nobility to resist it.'

'You underestimate yourself,' Shikandin declared, forceful. However, he did not press the point. Instead he concluded, 'So we do nothing.'

'We do nothing. Especially since…' Asvattama did not finish, but knew that Shikandin had understood. It was the best decision they could make in the current ambivalent situation. A situation both men suspected they would have to soon get used to. A situation that he did not like in the least. 'It could have been you,' he said.

'What could have been me?'

'You, Shikandin. You could have been Emperor of Aryavarta. The house of Panchala comes from the blood of Pururavas and Yayati. Your claim to the throne by blood and deed is as strong as Dharma Yudhisthir's. In fact, if it weren't for you, I know Dharma could never have conquered the east. Did you never wonder why…'

'And what has my brother-in-law done now to irk you so?'

'Don't change the topic, Shikandin. I asked you a question.'

Shikandin showed neither affront nor regret. 'And I answer: *I* would not have served the purpose. Dharma is Emperor by consensus. Whatever he thinks of himself now, he will soon see that the only way to remain Emperor is to do what serves the larger interests of the realm, not just that of his conscience.'

'If I didn't know better I'd call you muhira. And not just any fool, but one blinded to ineptitude by his own wisdom. I said I lack your nobility to resist power. I am not the only one.'

'All men have a weakness.'

'And most have the same one.'

'As do I…'

Asvattama smiled, the edges of his eyes creasing to reveal warmth that few had seen in him. 'Someday, Shikandin, I will tell you what I think your weakness is. But not today.'

'In that case, you had best leave now. The road is well-patrolled, and though I have no doubt of your skills, I don't want to lose any of my soldiers in an unnecessary scuffle.'

'But of course! I'd sooner be taken for a spy and arrested than be seen fraternizing with you, you old crone!' He gripped Shikandin yet again by the shoulder. Shikandin clapped him on the back in return and walked with him a few steps to the horse that had been tethered outside. Without another word, Asvattama swung on to his steed. He was soon gone, a silent shadow vanished into the night.

Shikandin stood as he was for a while, listening intently. Then he mounted his horse and made his way back towards the city.

Silence fell once again over the ruins as the soft thud of hooves on grass faded away. A sigh that was almost a sob tore through the heavy stillness. Assured that he was alone and could not be heard, or uncaring that he might be, Dhrstyadymn fell to his knees in the shadowed corner that had hidden him all this while. Not a word of the conversation had escaped him. Indeed, every word was etched in his mind, stirring questions too painful to answer. He was oblivious to the sharp shards that cut into his knees as he crumpled into a heap, relishing the sting on his palms as jagged debris cut into the skin.

My brother! My brother!

Never had he believed the rumours that had floated around the palace, the hushed whispers hinting at Shikandin's dark deeds, at actions that had irrevocably stained King Dhrupad's honour. He had always thought their father's anger against his brother was undeserved, and used every opportunity he got to try and prove his brother innocent. Now he wondered if it truly were so. What else was he to think after having heard and seen what he had?

What did anyone ever want from the Firewrights? Power.

Dhrstyadymn shuddered at the thought of an ambitious Shikandin – it felt unnatural, even frightful. There was no doubt he had been denied his right, been treated unfairly at many a turn – but to resort to treachery and deceit of the worst order? Shikandin had only to ask and Dhrstyadymn would gladly give him the throne, no matter what Dhrupad had to say about it. But to join forces with Asvattama? To find Firewright weapons? And to what end? Rebellion? Patricide?

The last thought made Dhrstyadymn retch silently. He had no idea how long he remained that way, before finally pulling himself together and forcing himself to face facts. If things did come to that, he reasoned, if he had to protect his people, his family and their kingdom against an attack… Could he? He felt anger – wide, undirected rage – swell up within him as a sense of being completely alone fell over him. Not just he, but his kingdom, his beloved Panchala was on its own. For all his talk condemning the Firewrights, Grandsire Bhisma of the Kurus had not balked at learning from them or taking the best of their weapons. His grandchildren too had been trained by Dron and Asvattama, not to forget Acharya Kripa, Dron's brother-in-law. Rumour had it that Vasusena of the Angas had also acquired Firewright weaponry. And Panchala? Panchala had nothing, except a fearful king, a traitor of a prince and, worse, an inept muhira of a crown prince!

An ambition that is best fulfilled now, while the Firstborn are weak.

The words continued to haunt Dhrstyadymn as he slowly trudged across the silver fields to the city he had called home for as long as he could remember.

15

IN ALL THE YEARS THAT VIDUR HAD SERVED THE BLIND KING
Dhritarastra of the Kurus as minister, advisor and companion, he
had taken the utmost care to never impose on the ties of blood that
bound them. He could not, for they were not equals. Though they
shared the same father, Dhritarastra was born of a queen, whereas
Vidur was the child of an unknown serving woman who had died at
childbirth. Or so he had been told as a child by Bhisma Devavrata,
then Regent of Kuru and its effective ruler. Bhisma had also ordered
that despite his unequal birth he be brought up in the same manner
as his royal half-brothers.

Vidur had soon developed a reputation for great intelligence
and wisdom, and the young boy quickly learnt his place in the larger
scheme of things. He was not a prince, but a kshatta – the polite
term used for sutas, those of his kind. The same acumen had made
him Dhritarastra's constant companion over the years and, more
importantly, the blind king's eyes. It was a role Vidur had played
with consummate discretion, never transgressing the bounds he
had set for himself in childhood. He had, thus, earned Dhritarastra's
affection and implicit trust. Now, for the first time in all these years,
Vidur wondered if he might impose on the privilege and proffer his
opinion, though unsolicited.

'Is this all right?' Dhritarastra's voice cut in on his thoughts.

The king stood in his private anteroom, adjusting his robe
before a mirror that he knew to be there as a matter of habit.
Dhritarastra often behaved as though he were a sighted man, partly
from a childhood kindness to spare others the discomfiture of his
condition, and partly to prove that he was in no way incapacitated
by it. Indeed, the other two men in the room – Grandsire Bhisma,
still the titular Regent of Hastina though no longer its effective
ruler, as well as Acharya Dron – ignored the king's question as
rhetorical. Vidur, however, stepped forward to adjust the pale blue
silk over his half-brother's broad shoulders. Barring his blindness,
Dhritarastra was a splendid specimen of Kuru manhood: wide-
chested and well-muscled, with a ruddy face and an excessive but

not unpleasant tendency towards the hirsute. A strong chin sat well on his square jaw, the mark of King Hastin's line that Syoddhan too displayed. Nature's mockery was not lost on Vidur. He and Dharma looked nothing like their great ancestor, while both Dhritarastra and Syoddhan did. Yet, none of them was truly of Hastin's descent. In them all ran the blood of Krishna Dwaipayana, once Vyasa of the Firstborn.

When the young prince Vichitravirya had met his untimely demise, Bhisma Devavrata, bound by his vow to never take a woman or the Kuru throne, had sent for Dwaipayana. As the situation demanded, the assistance rendered had been extremely direct, to the point that neither Dwaipayana nor Bhisma had ever attempted to conceal the fact that Pandu, Dhritarastra and Vidur were all Dwaipayana's sons.

Vidur was not a man to believe in curses or boons, but he was briefly tempted when it turned out that the lack of progeny would haunt the Kuru line yet again – Pandu was, to everyone's dismay, incapable of consummating his union with his two wives. This time, the resultant niyoga surrogacy, though not denied in fact, was never admitted in detail. No one quite knew who had fathered Dharma and his brothers beyond the metaphorical allusion to gods and their boons – a strategy Vidur had heartily approved of, hoping that it would help seal the legitimacy of Dharma's eventual claim to the Kuru throne. He had not accounted for Dhritarastra's fecundity or his ambition, both of which had led to strained relations between the monarch's many sons and Pandu's five. And now, after all these years and the building of an empire, trivial sibling rivalry was raising its head.

Vidur made up his mind to speak. 'My King…'

Dhritarasthra interrupted, 'Do you know, Vidur, you sound exactly like my dearest wife Gandhari did this morning. It makes me wonder if, like her, you too are going to counsel me at length to stop this evening's entertainment. A pity, since I believe Syoddhan entrusted the arrangements to your care. Things are coming along well, I hope?'

Vidur inclined his head, the action both answering and ignoring the question at once. 'It's more than entertainment, Your Highness,' he said, 'and the queen remains as wise as she has always been, so we would all do well to heed her words.'

'She is as persistent as she is wise,' Dhritarastra laughed, though it sounded more like a rasping cough. 'So much so, that I had to rely on Grandsire Bhisma here, as well as on Acharya Dron, to rescue me. I do hope their presence is enough to dissuade you, Vidur. I don't want to go through all that again.'

'Your Highness …' Vidur stopped short as Dhritarastra frowned, the gesture all the more pronounced for the vacant stare that accompanied it.

'My son is a patient man, a very patient man. He is a loving and dutiful child who is content to thank the gods for the long life and reign that they have blessed me with, instead of resenting them or me for it. The least I can do, Vidur, is to allow him these small adventures that please him so. It is but a game, a dice game. What sort of a father would I be if I were to deprive my dearest son of meaningful pleasures?'

'My king, with all due respect, a dice game is not meaningful in the least.'

'All the more reason to allow it then, don't you think? Why fret over such trivialities? At best a few coffers of treasure and a few herds of cows and horses will be lost or won. At worst, my children – and I include here my brother's sons – will drink themselves into oblivion, bed a few courtesans and leave the game forgotten for other pleasures. And you want me to forbid that? You think too much, Kshatta!'

'But …'

'Enough, Kshatta,' the irascible Dron interrupted. 'This is no longer a matter for us old men. Dharma is Emperor of Aryavarta. Syoddhan is his brother. These lions among men are more than capable of making decisions for themselves. Ours is the task to watch and applaud, to share in their joy and laughter. It is not for us to decide what must be done.'

'But …'

'He is right,' Bhisma added. 'It is time we learnt to gracefully accept the honour these youngsters still show us, and leave them be. Let Syoddhan do as he wishes.' The subtle implications of the statement carried far more finality than the words themselves.

Vidur allowed his gaze to rest lightly in turn on each of the three men. He did not fail to notice Dron's defiant glance, or the Grandsire's patronizing smile. Dhritarastra's face was set in a careful expression of apathy that Vidur knew was the king's attempt to conceal ambition. 'In that case,' he said, 'I shall go see to the arrangements right away.'

The royal assembly of Hastina was, even in these times of prosperity, a marvel that could only be described as excessively lavish. Those who stepped into the hall could not help but raise their gaze upwards each time they entered. The high, vaulted ceiling was painted to rival the blue of the clearest skies, and a series of precisely placed skylights allowed for the sunlight to colour the hall in the shades that nature was disposed to don. Against this tapestry of light were set the images of gods and ancestors, great men who looked downward at the mortal occupants of the hall. They were meant to be a constant reminder to those who sat on the Elephant Throne of King Hastin.

And now, the grand legacy of King Hastin comes to this… Vidur dismissed the thought and squared his shoulders in resolution. He briefly observed the on-going preparations for the dice game. A multitude of activities was underway – from laying out the seating to decorations and lighting – for the Kurus had no qualms about playing through the night. Sharing a few words of instruction and encouragement with the attendants overseeing the arrangements, Vidur made his way to the slim, pleasant-looking man who stood against a pillar, watching.

'Don't tell me you condone this travesty?' Vidur began as he neared the man.

Dhaumya shrugged. 'Dice? I have no love for it. But I have no principled argument against it either.'

'Dharma insists that it was Syoddhan who proposed a game and that to refuse to play would be cowardly. I tried speaking to Syoddhan for the few trasenus he would suffer to hear me. He agrees that he

99

suggested a friendly game, and this...' he waved his hand at the elaborate arrangements around them, '...was Dharma's idea. As a host, Syoddhan was bound to honour the request. My brother will not heed my warning, and the only person who shares my concern is Queen Gandhari. Unfortunately, this once, she is as powerless as I am.'

'It is not like dice has never been played here before, or that it shall never be played hereafter. I don't understand why you are in such a state.'

'Even when you know what sway it holds over a man like Dharma?'

'He is compulsive...'

'Compulsive?' Vidur's eyes took on a faraway glaze. 'Compulsive may be one word, and an apt one for sure. But it is not enough. No one knows Dharma better than I do, Acharya... Not his mother, not Panchali, and not you. Perhaps not even Dharma himself. His ambition is of the most dangerous kind, for its existence is neither suspected nor admitted. He is Emperor, but he wants more.'

Dhaumya said, 'What more could he want?'

'He wants to deserve his title.'

'He can deserve it by ruling well. Really, Uncle Vidur, you make the Emperor of Aryavarta sound like a child.'

'I make him sound like a man, Acharya. And a man he is. He wants to believe that what is his is so because he has earned it by his own deed, or because he was destined to it by a greater power. And that sense of self-respect is really not too much to ask for, if you think about it.'

'It's not self-respect; it's sheer self-indulgence. And, frankly, I care little about it at the moment. There's something else that has been bothering me,' Dhaumya said with a frown.

'Oh?'

'Panchali tells me we are missing a report, and the man who was supposed to bring it.'

'A report?'

'Yes, she had instructed that a daily summary of all administrative reports be delivered to her … to Emperor Dharma, that is, here at Hastina. Yesterday's messenger has not arrived as yet.'

'But today's has?'

'Yes. His material was the most mundane, but our interview with him was not. He said that he and his possessions, including the scroll he carried, were subject to inspection. Possibly, the other messengers too were so searched.'

'It is unusual, and not the most diplomatic of behaviours, but certainly not cause for suspicion? Unless you think that … Surely the scrolls were sealed?'

'They were,' Dhaumya confirmed. 'In fact, Panchali insisted on receiving written messages for that very purpose. These may be days of peace but she knows, as an Empress should, that such times are cause for more caution, not less.'

'She is a wise one,' Vidur noted with a dash of affection.

'Dharma is a fortunate man.'

'All the more reason for him to be careful.' Vidur frowned. 'I don't like it,' he repeated, this time with far more vehemence.

Dhaumya shook his silver-grey hair out of its loose knot and decisively pulled it back, securing it with a scrap of ochre cloth. 'You're right,' he said, 'I don't like it either. And it's time I did something about it.'

'What … ?'

'For one, I'm getting out of here. I shall find Shikandin, or send a message to Asvattama. By Rudra, I'd feel so much better about everything if either one of them were here.'

In a sad, hushed whisper, Vidur declared, 'I'd feel better if Govinda were here.'

Dhaumya stiffened and then forced himself to relax. His eyes held warm memories but his voice was cold as he said, 'There is no point speaking of those who are gone; of those who had best stay away. Trust in those who remain. Trust in our Emperor and Empress …' He left the hall, making his way directly to the stables.

With a heavy heart, Vidur turned back to supervising the preparations for the evening's festivities.

16

THE HYENAS LOOKED UP AT THE SOUND OF HOOVES, BUT DID NOT retreat. The carcass was just a day old, far too succulent to pass up. Cackling, the bold leader of the pack buried its face back into the young soldier's flesh. An arrow whistled over the animal's head, grazing but not wounding it. With a yelp, it fled into the depths of the woods, its cronies close behind.

Govinda felt a pang of pain at the sight of the disfigured soldier, but he knew better than to take his anguish out on the hyenas. They were merely following nature's dictates. A seasoned soldier, he ignored the flies and maggots and pulled the arrow sticking out of the fallen soldier's back. The shaft was short and made of black iron, a common metal in Aryavarta, but it was the vane that told him more. A huge feather, curved nearly like a horn, was attached to the end of the arrow by means of thread and wax. Spitting out an expletive, Govinda cast the arrow aside. The curved feather, with its brown, white and black markings was from the wings of a gorgeous, graceful eagle native to the mountains of Kyrghis, far to the north of Aryavarta. The thread, on the other hand, came from the land of the Danavas, even further away. *Add to that sweet beeswax from their mountains and, of course, iron from Aryavarta*, he mentally noted. His face grew grim as the implications jumped out at him. More Danava mercenaries.

When Govinda had left Central Aryavarta, right after his encounter with Devala, he had headed south-west, through the wooded lands of the Nishadas. He found the entire route abuzz with troop movement. It made him fear the worst and yet he had hoped for the best. While it was the prerogative of every ruler to move troops in whatever manner he pleased within his own borders, the extent of the present deployment was still enough to merit mention in the daily reports of imperial affairs that Dharma would receive. Even if the Emperor did not find anything suspicious or significant in these events, Panchali would ask questions and that might just spur Shikandin or Partha to investigate. However, Govinda had considered the possibility without optimism. If his friends tried to help, they would walk right into the cordon that the Nishada and Chedi forces had set up, sealing the west off from the rest of Aryavarta. It had been one thing for a lone traveller like him to slip through, largely unnoticed, but it would be impossible for even a division of men to get through without a fight. Now, finding Dwaraka under attack from a mercenary army explained everything.

Letting the mercenary's tell-tale arrow fall from his hand, Govinda briefly retraced his path before cutting away from the main road, into the woods. Instead of taking the direct route to Dwaraka, he headed up one of the smaller promontories that dotted the shore north of the island. Finally, he could see the blue of the sky beyond the last line of trees on the cliff. Dismounting, he surveyed the scene before him. The rocky hill fell in a sheer cliff right into the ocean, to his right. To his left, in the distance, the Raivata mountains ran parallel to the sea. The gentle green slope eased down on the seaward side to form a huge cultivated plain dotted with creeks and lakes. Golden sands fringed the plains and natural dunes offered protection from tempestuous sea winds. Shoals of rock dotted the seascape, leading to the huge outcrop that extended out into the sea.

Dwaraka! His magnificent city was surrounded – like a mighty lion cornered by jackals. A large fleet of ships waited, anchored on the open sea at a distance from the city. Closer to land, two of the huge vessels swayed on the lashing waves, wrecked or abandoned. Govinda smirked. Few knew how to navigate through the series of sharp ridges that were hidden in the waters of the channel between the port and the city.

On the landward side of Dwaraka, however, the situation was one of concern. Govinda stiffened at the sight of the bodies and debris that littered the plain, chilling evidence of the war that had been fought there. Both the outpost atop the last mountain peak on the Raivata range as well as the one on its foothills flew the enemy's ensign – the flag of Saubha, king of Salwa. The pastures and the homesteads on the plains had been burnt down and the occasional storage tent showed that Salwa forces now occupied the land. Well beyond the verdant terrain, just where the beach began, a barricade of sorts had been set up. A wooden pole defiantly flew the pennants of the various tribes of the Yadu nation, but it did not appear likely that it would remain there for long.

Govinda watched as the huge force advanced towards the barricade, the last post on land still under Dwaraka's control. The earth seemed to shudder as the enemy marched out of the soft grassy plains and onto the deceptively hard, packed sand. The Yadu soldiers at the barricade did not move. They were waiting. The sand gave way without warning and many of the enemy soldiers fell headlong into the deep pits that had been dug underneath. Confusion reigned briefly amid Salwa's forces as Dwaraka's archers began shooting at those still advancing towards them.

Moments later, the gates opened, letting a group of men out across the single bridge that led to the mainland. At the same time archers appeared on the turrets of the city's walls and began letting loose their arrows. Clearly, Balabadra had kept a passage open in the hope that the Emperor would come to their aid. But Govinda knew Dharma would not. No one would. Saubha would have rallied the Nagas and Nishadas to his aid, along with Chedi and Vidharbha. Dwaraka had been isolated completely.

And right now Dharma is probably presiding over some diplomatic assembly or the other, blissfully unaware of what is going on here…

Govinda imagined Panchali frowning over a parchment or listening intently to administrative reports, an expression of graceful indifference on her face. Pushing the image out of his mind, he led Balahak ahead. If he could make his way down the cliff, there was a chance he could race along the sand and across the bridge while the barricade still held. Once that too was conceded, there would be no way across to the island city except by boat.

The path was little more than a goat-trail, and it was with difficulty that horse and man made their way down the hill. No beast other than Balahak would have so trustingly followed his rider down the treacherous, slippery path, nor could any man other than Govinda have commanded such faith. Even so, the two soon reached a small ledge and could go no further. Below them, the cliff angled inwards all the way down to the sea.

Govinda gently patted the stallion on his haunches and swung back into the saddle. 'Ready, my friend? Now!' he commanded, urging the horse forward in a short burst of speed. Then rider and horse leapt off the ledge.

They hit the cold, frothy waters with a hard splash. Govinda held on tight, his arms around the horse's muscled neck, as their weight dragged them both deep into the water. Balahak kicked his powerful legs in an attempt to surface, even as Govinda slithered off and began to swim alongside him. The currents were powerful, and Govinda had to let go of the reins and use both his arms. He kept his head up, out of the water, and constantly called out to Balahak, shouting encouragement and instructions. Eyes wide with fear, the horse managed to battle his panic and stay at Govinda's side.

Just when he thought his strength had finally run out, Govinda realized that Balahak was wading. With a shout of effort, he kicked hard, willing himself to swim the next few feet against the tide's incessant pull. Finally, he felt his feet skim the ground and a little later he was on the shore. He gave the snorting, heaving Balahak a moment of rest, but that was all they could afford – the barricade had fallen and the few men that remained had drawn back to the bridge.

Govinda urged the stallion on at a gallop, riding into the thin gap that divided the two warring fronts. He was now close enough to see the carnage, hear the cries of rage and pain. As he drew near, he realized with a shock that more than half the elite Yadu forces known as the Narayaniya had already fallen, and the rest were hopelessly outnumbered. Those who remained had formed a human wall, protecting a person or thing that was being carried back towards Dwaraka. Looking towards the tower over the city gates, he caught a glimpse of Balabadra's horrified face. It made him fear the worst, only to have it confirmed as he neared the scene – Yuyudhana and the second of his adopted heirs, Samva, were together carrying the bloody, listless form of Pradymna, his elder son.

A shout went up from the city walls as Govinda was sighted. It made the enemy hold back for an instant even as it gave the Yadus a renewed surge of strength. Govinda swiftly turned Balahak onto the narrow bridge and then slid off as the horse came to a stop.

Drawing his sword, he raced back to the foot of the bridge, where the Narayaniyas were valiantly holding off the Salwa soldiers. He threw himself into the fray with a vengeance.

'Father!' Samva shouted after him.

Yuyudhana swung into action at once. 'Samva! Take your brother and get back inside. Tell Balabadra to close the gates,' he instructed, hauling the limp Pradymna across Balahak's back.

'But...'

'Go!'

With a nod, the youth complied. Immediately, Yuyudhana turned his attention to the other men on the bridge, calling for them to retreat. Balabadra and the other archers stood with their bows at the ready. The first of the enemy soldiers was now on the bridge. Govinda fought on, stepping back slowly, hoping to give those still on the bridge enough time to get back into the safety of the city. Yuyudhana yelled, urging him to start moving back. It was only once Pradymna was safely inside the city that Govinda complied.

The path was covered with blood, still warm as it oozed out from the bodies of the dead. Govinda slipped, landed on his hands and knees, but quickly got up again to parry an attack by a Salwa lancer. He disposed of the man and looked down at his palms, coated with blood and pieces of flesh, the sight stunning him into inaction. Yuyudhana ran forward and dragged him for the last few feet. They had hardly stepped through the gateway when the heavy iron doors were swung shut behind him. The whistle of arrows filled the air, followed by a loud crash and many screams. Balabadra and the archers had set the bridge on fire.

Dwaraka was now completely under siege.

17

WHEN BALABADRA CAME DOWN FROM THE COMMAND POST AT THE gate, he found Govinda gone. Anxiously, he set off along Dwaraka's streets looking for his brother. Debris littered his path and haggard and tired faces could be seen everywhere. The city and the sky above it glowed with light – not the orderly, colourful artistry of a planned celebration but the red, primal glow from bonfires lit by those who were simply glad to be alive for one more night. People huddled with loved ones around the circles of light, singing sad songs or sharing old reminiscences. Some soldiers found escape in the arms of bewitching courtesans, others in sharpening their swords. There was a dull weariness underlying their activities. For what it was worth, Balabadra realized, his people did not despair. This was the sombre, unsullied tiredness of those who would fight to the last. When they fell, it would not be for lack of courage or hope.

Balabadra made his way to the infirmary, where Pradymna lay still and pale. Rukmavati and Samva sat by his side, their faces drawn in grief and fear. Govinda had already been there, he was told, leaving with a simple nod of his head when the medics told him that Pradymna might not last the night. The news made Balabadra frantic, and he continued his search of the city with renewed vigour.

Faint notes of music drew him towards Sudharma, the Hall of Justice that was the heart of Dwaraka. Through either a stroke of luck or some brilliant secret in its construction, the structure remained undamaged. Its crystal walls were, however, stained with soot and grime, adding a poignant steadfastness to the building. Balabadra peered inside. At first, its vastness looked empty. Finally, he spotted a forlorn form huddled in the darkest corner. He walked up to Govinda, who sat leaning against a sculpture of Varaha, the boar-unicorn form of Vishnu, lifting the Earth from the waters that threatened to destroy her. Balabadra chuckled softly. He should have guessed that his brother would be here.

From the sea came the first manifestations of life, and then came land, and all creatures including humanity, Balabadra reflected, *but who made the sea, and what was the first form of life, the Hiranya-garbha or entity of creation? It is that force we name Varaha and worship. This force is what we search for all of our lives.*

Next to Govinda sat a little boy, one of the simple farm-dwellers who lived in and cultivated the plains between the sea and the Raivata mountains. The boy played soft, sad notes on a reed flute like the ones the brothers had used years ago as children herding cows. For an instant, it seemed to Balabadra that the Govinda he saw sitting there was also just a boy – an innocent playful child – and not the great warrior who had set Mathura free and built the nation of Dwaraka against all odds. He felt a lump in his throat as he wondered where and how that mischievous boy had been lost. *Is it my fault? I'm his elder, yet he's the one who leads us all. Why haven't I protected him, as I should have?*

The music stopped.

Govinda looked up at his brother. He had never cried in front of another person, not even as a child, and he would not do so now. But Balabadra saw the sadness in his dark eyes. In an instant it was gone, and Govinda was as tranquil as always. Balabadra studied him, then turned to the little boy. 'Go find Raivati. Tell her I said you'll be having my rations of tonight's meal … and all the sweets you can eat.' The boy grinned at that, his simple delight both incongruous and refreshing in their precarious situation. Balabadra gently ruffled his hair and sent him off with a light pat before sitting next to his brother, his back to the wall.

It was Govinda who broke the silence. 'Have you seen this?' He gestured to the arrow that he held in one hand. His voice was filled with admiration and amazement, as he went on, 'Our enemies have outdone themselves. It's quite impressive – it contains a small vial of a special kind of powder, right at the tail. When the arrow burns all the way down it ignites the powder, causing an explosion. Of course, even Devala hasn't been able to solve the problem of how to ensure that the flame doesn't go out as the arrow flies against the wind. The Firewrights have designed these arrows using a mix of powdered sulphur and rock oil for generations now. It's still the flaming tip that's the problem.'

'Devala? But …'

'He was captured. And now he is free.'

'You should have killed him yourself!'

'So I'd originally planned. But it would have defeated the purpose. Devala's capture was meant to reaffirm the power of the Firstborn, of the Vyasa, after what happened at the Coronation. But he was taken to Hastina, instead of Indr-prastha. I don't know why.'

Balabadra was far too taken aback to respond. Govinda did not notice. He continued, 'Do you think I did the wrong thing? Was I selfish, Agraja? Were *we* selfish when we rebelled against Kans? Were we thinking only of our imprisoned parents, ourselves, our family? Did we really think about the people?'

'We did what we thought was best, Govinda. We never meant to end up at Mathura, or even at Dwaraka. I didn't think things would go this way.'

'You're right. I didn't think it would go this way either. At each stage, I just thought of it as a task to be done. I'm not even sure I thought, really,' Govinda admitted. 'The first time we were brought to Mathura... I assumed that sooner or later we would go back to our village and life would be as it was.'

'You mean back to your romancing and unabashed flirting with the women of our vraja,' Balabadra said.

'It was you they were all crazy for! I just tried to console them, as best as I could!'

The two brothers savoured their memories in silence.

Suddenly Govinda asked, 'Do you remember... when the Naga Kaliya chief attacked the herds?'

'Hmm...'

'We were just gwalas, cowherds, all of us. But we stood up to him, we fought him and his warriors. Why? Where did a bunch of gwala boys find such courage?'

'We fought for our own, Govinda. We fought for what was ours, for what we believed in. That is what everyone does. It's not just the two of us.'

'And Aryavarta? To whom does the Empire belong? Why don't we, why don't the people, fight in the same way for the empire?'

'What empire do you want us to fight for? The only empire we – all of us in Aryavarta – have known is a fragmented sense of nothing. At the end of the day, nothing changes. We are many nations, subjects of many kings, no matter what glorious titles we give them. We are divided by borders and loyalties, we are fragmented and powerless... Or so we've been, till now.'

'And now?'

'Now, it might be worth fighting for.'

They sat for a few more moments, again in desolate silence. Slowly, Balabadra stood, and pulled a tired Govinda to his feet. He walked towards the door, assuming that his brother would follow.

'Agraja…'

Balabadra turned to see that Govinda remained rooted to the spot. With a sigh, he retraced his steps. 'Yes, Govinda?'

'Tell me the truth, brother. Have I failed?'

Balabadra sighed. 'No, Govinda. You haven't failed. You've done right by Aryavarta, by the empire. But… and you must know this… Dwaraka will pay the price.'

'But why? Because of who I am? Because I'm a Firewright? Or because I brought them down?'

'Govinda, please…'

Govinda ignored his brother, needing to hear himself speak. 'What was supposed to be the fall of the Wrights was a way to break them, break everyone away from their obsession with the past, with astra-weapons and poisons and destruction. Both Ghora and I, we thought that if we shook the order to its core the Wrights would once again, as a matter of survival, turn their skills to tools of prosperity instead of weapons of war. And Aryavarta would accept them. After all, knowledge doesn't grow in isolation – society grows alongside, driving and being driven by it, by economics as much as politics. But…'

With a sad smile, he confessed, 'I used to think that my mistake was that I had desires of my own, desires that weren't dreams of something greater and good – wanting to go back to the vraja, wanting to live my own life… I've wondered if, had I been less selfish, things may have gone differently, all those years ago. Perhaps the Wrights would have lived, perhaps *she*…'

Govinda stopped mid-sentence. Acutely aware of the fact that he had revealed more than he wanted to, he went on, his voice even, 'But, like all mistakes, it was fine if one learnt from it.'

'Maybe, Govinda,' Balabadra gently said, 'it was a lesson learnt in excess. You know for a fact that many of our own kinsmen have doubted your intentions… They haven't always believed that you acted objectively. To be honest, you've even tried my patience and trust on occasion!'

'Why? I don't understand what they fear so much...'

'Tyranny.'

'Tyranny? But how does a rule of and by the people become tyranny? I dream, I hope, that one day all of Aryavarta will be as Dwaraka, a united realm where the people are their own sovereign. How is that tyranny?'

With the soft, practised patience of a man who had explained things before and knew he would have to do so yet again, Balabadra said, 'To those who would lose their power, Govinda, it may well be one and the same. These kings cannot comprehend might divided among many. They cannot comprehend a society that does not follow the Divine Order, a hierarchy of power. So they assume that if you wish to supplant Divine Order, it must be for your gain. They would not dare leave Dwaraka standing.' A trace of irritation crept into his voice. 'I know this is something that you stubbornly refuse to get into your head, that you'd rather stick to your idealized notions of the inherent goodness of human beings and all that, but surely the Secret Keeper would have anticipated this?'

Govinda smiled, the first mention of the unnamed, unknown leader between them in years becoming a moment to relish and regret. Balabadra had never asked him, even once, who it was that Govinda had laid their hopes on, who it was for whom Dwaraka would now fall. The realization of the overwhelming trust so many had placed in him hit him hard. They had believed in him, and he had done nothing but let them down. But the fault was his, and Govinda could not let the Secret Keeper be held to blame instead. He said, 'He did. He advised me to leave Aryavarta at once to prevent Dwaraka being attacked.'

'Why didn't you? Where in the name of the Brahmi bull's backside have you been all these days?'

'I was waiting for them to find me.'

'But why?'

'Do you really not know, Agraja? In all these years, in all the plans I have made, there is one fatal flaw, a loose thread that can cause the entire weave to unravel. You saw how the fear of the missing Ghora Angirasa took hold of everyone, including the former emperor Jarasandha and Vyasa Dwaipayana. It was only his death, his indisputable and violent death, that set off the chain of events that led to the formation of Dharma's empire. In the same vein, if I simply disappeared, if I'd left Aryavarta, it would have been of no use. I have to fall. Otherwise the notion that the Firewrights remain would drive the kings of Aryavarta to mutual distrust and suspicion, and the empire would splinter in a matter of months. I couldn't let that happen.'

'Can't you?' Balabadra's tone held unrestrained ire. 'I don't suppose you considered the fact that to some of us you are far more important than these ideals. Your own life may not matter to you, Govinda, but surely the heartache you cause us does?'

Govinda sighed, and met his brother's accusatory gaze. 'You have to understand, I chose this option over others because I thought it to be the best one.'

'What do you mean?'

Govinda said, 'Dharma Yudhisthir was not my first or only choice for Emperor. A stronger man might have allowed me to stay in the shadows and fade quietly into obsolescence. I considered many choices, from then-emperor Jarasandha to Vasusena of Anga. But it had to be a Kaurava.'

'Because of the Firstborn? Because of the Vyasa?'

'Yes.'

'In that case, you should have backed Syoddhan,' Balabadra grumbled, making no effort to hide his affection for Dhritarastra's eldest son.

'I almost did. I really like him. But it was neither practical nor prudent. Short of turning him against his own father, there was no way of making him king of his own land, leave alone Emperor. Once that happened, his reign would have been fraught with rebellion and civil war with his own brothers. Besides, I didn't dare let Panchali near that lot – Dussasan and the others. Well, so much for my objectivity… And as soon as I realized Dwaraka was under attack…'

Balabadra began to understand the enormity of what his brother had done. Gently, he said, 'It's not too late, Govinda. It's never too late.'

'Too late for what?'

'To be human. To admit what you feel. To let yourself care and love and...'

'But I don't.'

Balabadra knew his brother was not a man to show extreme emotion or lose his equanimity, but to remain so unaffected under these circumstances seemed to him inhuman. He stepped up and grabbed Govinda by his shoulders. 'What's wrong with you? You've really started believing in your own prattle about selflessness and letting go, haven't you? By Govardhan, don't you see what sort of a man you've become? Not a man even, a monster, a thing that believes in its omnipotence. How can you be this way?'

'Omnipotence? Time is the only omnipotent force, Agraja. What you see as my selfishness is nothing but an acceptance of my place in the larger scheme of things. What you deem arrogance is just awareness, self-awareness. Like many, you too think I want power. I want nothing and, yes, that is power. I can't help it, and I don't care to. Being understood is a luxury I don't need any more.'

'Does nothing move you?'

Govinda hesitated. Though he willed it not to, his mind went back to his last conversation with Panchali.

'No.'

'But...'

'Nothing can move me, at least not while there remains work to be done. It is for posterity to decide whether I have been right or wrong.' He cleared his throat and said, 'Now, how many ships do we have left?'

'The whole fleet, except one,' Balabadra said shortly. He remained terse. 'We used her as a decoy...'

'That's more than I had planned for. Excellent! Here's what I need you to do, right away. If we move our ships at night, it'll confuse Saubha and his sailors. Take ten of the vessels and sail them around the northern cove. They won't stop you. The wind will be against them now, and they won't risk getting the men to row without having some idea of what we've planned.'

All Balabadra could manage was a disbelieving stare. Slowly, he found his voice. 'No! No, no, no! Govinda, you'd better not be thinking what I suspect you're thinking… In the name of Yama's black bull, no! It's too dangerous.'

'To whom, Agraja? There's nothing left to grieve for, nothing left to lose. Don't you see? My purpose here is served, and I'm ready for whatever may lie ahead, even the end. As for Dwaraka, all I know is that I shall not let this city fall!'

'And Aryavarta?'

Govinda took a deep breath. 'The Secret Keeper. The Secret Keeper will take care of everything. The task that remains, the last part of Ghora Angirasa's plan, is one that the Secret Keeper alone can fulfil. I'm finally free, for there is no more use here for me.'

Balabadra's eyes glazed over with numb acceptance – a sense of acquiescence that he ought to have been used to by now but was not. With a silent prayer, he let go of all thoughts of the future. There was no other choice. Whatever happened, he doubted that either of them would ever leave Dwaraka again, alive.

18

MORNING RAYS GLINTED ACROSS EVERY LINE AND FACE OF Shakuni's dice, setting the silver-white metal afire. At that moment, Syoddhan could almost believe that they had come alive, demons that served their master's command to fall as he wished, no matter who cast them. Yet, it was not Shakuni, a man filled with love and loyalty for his nephew, who made the air feel malevolent. Syoddhan knew that his uncle had harboured no ill will when he first sat down to play. It was the stakes that had changed it all.

'Syoddhan?'

He started as he became aware of Shakuni's voice. Slowly, he looked around him, aware that every friend and ally of the Kuru kingdom present in the assembly hall was waiting for his response.

His own brothers seemed jubilant, as did Vasusena, for much had been won. Sanjaya's face showed no discernible emotion at all.

Across from Syoddhan, Dharma sat with his eyes raised to the ceiling of the great hall. The gods still looked down on the assembly as they always had, but none were inclined to descend to the Emperor's aid. Quelling the urge to reach out and shake his fool of a cousin out of his crazed stupor, his self-righteous sense of potency, Syoddhan sought out Dharma's brothers instead. Partha pointedly ignored him and surveyed his surroundings with an air of affected superiority. Bhim was brooding. The twins were grim. All of them stood, arms crossed in a posture of servitude, upper bodies bare, as a sign of respect.

Dharma played his brothers as stakes… Syoddhan repeated the words in his head hoping that the sheer absurdity of what they conveyed would make them false. *How had it come to this?*

At first, both he and Dharma had wagered simple baubles – jewellery they wore, or gold they had on their person, a newly acquired stallion, then two. But as the night progressed, Dharma had grown bolder. Bolder? No, it wasn't boldness, but a need, a yearning of sorts. A hunger Syoddhan had not seen in years. Not since he and Dharma had been young men. The scene remained vivid in Syoddhan's memory, as did the conversation that went with it.

'Agraja, tell them to stop!'

'Relax, Syoddhan. I have ten gold coins that say Bhim is going to land a blow to Dussasan's face in… Oh, there. He does it as we speak.'

'What's wrong with you, Dharma? I brought you here to stop them fighting, not gamble on them!'

'Don't be so scared, Crown Prince! Gambling is a warrior's art, just as fighting is. Our very lives are games of risk and reward, and… He's down, he's down! Well done, Bhim! Who's next? What say, Yuyutsu? Care to wrestle Nakul here? Wait, let's make it more exciting… Sadev, blindfold Nakul, will you… I bet twenty coins that he will still win! Well, Syoddhan, what have you to play with? I'd hate to make a wager you cannot meet.'

'You cannot do this, Dharma.'

'What do you mean I cannot, Syoddhan?'

'You cannot be so callous with another's life, not even your own brother's. You don't own them.'

'I own nothing, Syoddhan. I am just an ordinary man. It is because of the love my brothers hold me that they will follow my every command, no matter what I ask of them. They don't have to do a thing they don't want to.'

'You know they won't disobey you. That is not how things are. We are brought up to believe that it must be thus, that hierarchy is the sacred manifestation of Divine Order. But that is no justification for you to do, as you like. One of our brothers could die as a result of your stupid wagers.'

'Divine Order? No, Syoddhan. My brothers obey me out of their love and free will, as do the people… Oh yes, the people of Kuru. I command nothing, I own nothing. Yet, my dear Crown Prince, it is me they want as king, and not you…'

That day, Syoddhan had seen a spark in Dharma's eyes, a spark not of something good but of an insanity that was beyond good and bad. At first he had thought it the madness of a common gambler, the intoxication that he knew could take the best of men at times. But as the years passed Syoddhan understood that the intoxication was of a unique nature. Some men became drunk with power. Dharma was the first man Syoddhan had seen who could become inebriated with morality, the satisfaction of being right and good. He believed that the force of destiny guiding his life was not a cause but the consequence of his piety. And a gambler he remained in chiefly one thing: Dharma believed that he would, sooner or later, win. It was destiny.

And so, after he lost his lands, his jewels, all his possessions, he had played his nations, his empire and his people as stakes. And then, one by one, his brothers.

But he does not own them! Syoddhan's fury, delayed till the moment by his sheer astonishment, finally overcame him. He looked at Bhim, Partha, Nakul and Sadev, and it made him sick to see how they had accepted their fate without protest. Just as Vidur, Bhisma, Dron and Kripa had accepted the outcome of the gamble without protest. Their regret was apparent, but none of them had raised the smallest objection.

Once again, Shakuni's voice intruded on his reflections. 'Syoddhan?'

Syoddhan turned to his uncle. Trying his best not to show how shaken he was, he said, for no reason other than to speak, 'What was the last stake, Uncle? What did we win?'

Shakuni looked puzzled, but answered, 'Dharma Yudhisthir. He staked himself.'

Syoddhan stared at Dharma. His cousin, no longer the Emperor of Aryavarta, sat lifeless. His eyes were blank; he had become incapable of thought or emotion, regret or despair. *He is a corpse now*, Syoddhan thought. Or worse, a hollow, wooden image of a man who had never known life. *And this is the man Govinda Shauri put on the imperial throne? Yabha!*

Rage coursed anew through Syoddhan and he made to rise from his seat and put an end to this mindless game, to walk away from it now as mad wagers made in excess, a brotherly squabble of little consequence within and beyond the household. He froze halfway.

Slowly, like an unreal spectre come to life, Dharma's fingers moved. His eyes did not see, nor did the rest of him shift. Filled with energy of its own, his hand edged towards the dice, reaching out to lightly touch the cold white metal. His eyes lit up, as though he had drawn life from the accursed dice. He pulled his hand back, sat straight and fixed his opponents with a confident look. 'I stake Panchali.' As the dice rolled to a stop, Dharma hung his head.

It took a while before Syoddhan finally stirred. He felt devoid of sensation or emotion. Slowly, the beat of his own heart filled his ears, the throbbing a meaningless rhythm, as were his words and his actions. He turned, without really knowing that he did so, to one of the many attendants around them. He said, 'Go, bring Panchali here. Dharma Yudhisthir, the man who was supposed to rule us all, has just condemned his wife to slavery. I shudder to think what would have become of this realm if he had remained

Emperor. Go now. Bring her here and let her see for herself what her husband has done.'

19

THE SUN WAS SEARING DESPITE THE EARLY HOUR, ITS STRENGTH leaving little hope of cloud or rain. A hot wind blew in from the north, dry and stinging. One by one, five huge galleys cruised out of the safety of Dwaraka's harbour. Each carried a crew of three hundred oarsmen and another hundred fighting men, as well as a large supply of armaments. The sixth and last ship alone was much lighter and less heavily manned than the rest. Govinda stood on its deck, his light metal and hard leather chest armour gleaming under the bright sun, his curly hair dripping with perspiration, as his captain, Daruka, brought the ship into position. The six vessels were now arranged in the shape of an arrowhead, with this, the flagship, as the tip of the formation.

All of Dwaraka had gathered along the city walls and on its towers to watch what would be the final battle for their city. If they lost, there would be no hope left. Salwa's soldiers, now thronging the beaches, reminded them of that with their taunts and rude jeers.

'We're in position, Commander,' Daruka informed Govinda. The warrior nodded in response.

And then they were off. Hundreds of oars creaked in unison and cut the choppy waters with a loud splash. The arrowhead of ships slowly began to move north-west, against the headwind and towards the open sea.

King Saubha had astutely positioned his fleet as close as possible to the placid waters of the gulf off Dwaraka. They waited just ahead of the long-shore currents that ran from north to south, parallel to the coast, but were still close enough to use the tide to move his ships in and out of formation. The fleet loomed like a floating wall, the bare masts making the vessels look ominous, like the skeletons of dead ships. The northern wind was too strong for the Salwa navy to use their sails this close to shore; the wind would drive even the largest galley onto the treacherous shoals. Vayu the wind-god, it seemed, would favour neither side.

'They're expecting us,' Govinda dryly commented as the enemy ships began raising anchor.

Daruka eyed the formidable array from his post at the ship's wheel. 'Commander,' he pointed out, 'King Saubha must already know that ten of our vessels left the harbour last night ...'

'He surely does ...' Govinda distractedly said as he took a look over the side, judging the depth by the colour of the water. He placed a light hand on the wheel, adjusting their course. 'Hold this line,' he instructed. Behind them, the other vessels of their force too veered, using the flagship's wake as a guide.

Govinda went forward to the bow of the ship and surveyed the scene before him. Saubha's forces, comprising over thirty vessels of navy and pirate origin, were arranged in the arc-shaped attack formation preferred by large navies. All they had to do was to encircle the smaller Yadu fleet and methodically sink each vessel. At sea, nothing determined the outcome of a battle as much as the size and strength of the navy. Occasionally, smaller navies would use decoys or set traps in the hope of averting an inevitable rout. One such trick was to lure the enemy fleet to form a tight circle around a few ships sent out as bait and have another fleet of ships attack from the outside. Govinda hoped that this was exactly what Saubha was expecting them to do.

It was.

Torches went on Saubha's flagship, in a signal to the others of their group. The vessels began manoeuvring and the arc split into two, right down the middle. Anticipating that the ten ships Govinda had moved during the night would inevitably spring an attack, Saubha was dividing up his huge force. A group of ships, most of them of Danava make, heavy and massive, veered hard and to the left in a quarter-turn. They were now moving due east, directly towards the mouth of the gulf.

King Saubha's command ship, however, was all set to engage Govinda's fleet. The mighty Salwa war-craft, which had earlier been the centre of the arc, now veered right and forward. More vessels came up alongside to form a straight line. All of them pulled in their oars.

The ships were little more than empty husks, bobbing up and down on the waves. Suddenly, as though pushed by a powerful but invisible hand, the entire line began bearing down on the Yadu ships at great speed. Saubha had moved into the longshore drift. He planned to harness the powerful current to ram down and sink Dwaraka's feeble fleet. A cheer rose from the shores as Saubha's army realized what was happening. Once this was over, Dwaraka was theirs to plunder.

Saubha's flagship was closing in fast, set to smash them on the side.

'Commander … ?' Daruka hesitantly ventured, when Govinda did not give the expected order to take an evasive course.

Dwaraka's vessels were fairly hardy, but not heavy enough to take the impact of a direct collision. Their ships would most likely keel over and capsize, or simply break into two and sink. Daruka normally would not have dared doubt his commander, but he had watched Govinda as Pradymna had been brought in from the previous day's battle and knew that Govinda would undoubtedly conceal his own grief to keep up courage and morale among their troops.

'I'll take it,' Govinda said, turning and walking to the ship's wheel. He grabbed hold of it as Daruka let go and began issuing instructions in loud shouts. 'Tell the rest of our ships to drop anchor. Keep them on alert to cut and run.'

The captain felt reassured. At least, Govinda was not going to be reckless with all their lives – the five ships behind them would come to a quick stop, requiring King Saubha to change his course if he still intended to run them down. If the others then cut free of the anchor instead of pulling it in, and ran, there was a chance they could evade the first attack. But to what end?

Govinda continued, answering the unspoken question, 'Stand by to raise oars on one side. And ready the sails…'

Daruka's jaw dropped, utter surprise defying his well-trained stoicism. They were going directly into the wind, which was blowing against them. Not only would they have to turn the entire ship around with just the oars, but with a wind as strong as this, even the smallest miscalculation – a little too loose, too soon – and the whole ship was doomed. Even if they succeeded they would still have to get control of the ship, wrestle her rudder, as it were, swiftly enough to avoid colliding into one of their own ships that would be anchored behind them.

Finally Daruka found his voice. 'Yes, Commander,' he said, and left to carry out the orders.

The sound of the oarsmen rowing dimmed as the other five ships dropped anchor. Soon, they were left behind a fair distance. Ahead of them, though, Saubha's flagship was hardly ten lengths away. A few stray arrows shot into the sky fell into the water between the two vessels. The ship was still out of range, but Saubha was taunting them. He had no wish to put his archers to work. He wanted the satisfaction of physically crushing Govinda.

Govinda held his course till the ship's wheel jerked hard, nearly wrenching itself out of his hands. Gripping the wheel tight, he shouted out to Daruka, 'Now!'

Instantly, the rowing stopped. Oars were lifted out of the water and pulled in, but it took a short while for the ship to lose its momentum completely. In the uncanny stillness that followed, a sense of despair settled over the men. Then the ship began to move slowly turning around without sail or oar, like some possessed being. A few of the men cried out in alarm, fearful despite their natural bravery. Daruka knew full well how this was possible, how it was happening, but that made it no less astonishing. He now realized that all this while they had been rowing directly into a strong rip tide or reverse current, which headed away from land. The moment they had stopped moving forward, the current began to make the ship heel, or swing around. The captain ran forward, as it struck him that this was no accident. *Govinda must have known. He must have expected this.*

Govinda was bent over the wheel, every muscle in his body tense as he fought both ship and sea. As the vessel swung around with the current, the force of the tide hitting squarely on one side would make her tilt over. When that happened, the ship's rudder would

121

get lifted out of the water and they would lose control of the craft. To avoid that, he had to let the rudder catch the current and use its force to stabilize the ship. The warrior instinctively adjusted his footing, balancing himself as the stern of the ship began to lift clear of the water. Buffeted by the waves, the rudder squirmed and twisted against the forces of nature, held in position by nothing more than Govinda's entire weight against the ship's wheel.

Daruka made to help, but Govinda shook his head. 'Get … the … men … astern,' he grunted through clenched teeth.

'But …'

Warning shouts rent the air, drawing everyone's attention. The second group of Salwa's ships had been taken unawares by the reverse current. One had capsized, while another two had crashed into each other. One more was keeling over precariously, its mast touching the water. A few of the vessels had tried to navigate out of the current and were now caught in an undertow, which was dragging them towards the crags and shoals. Two of the enemy craft, however, were being pulled right towards them by the drift.

'Mih!' Daruka swore under his breath, and began calling out orders, getting the men into action. Together, they scrambled to the end of the ship, trying to weigh it down. After what was a long and tense interval, the tilting slowed down, almost stopped. It was, however, only a matter of time. The rudder was still out of the water.

Govinda knew it was now or never. His arms had gone numb with exhaustion, a welcome relief from the spasms he had borne for a while, but now he needed to use them. He flexed his fingers as best as he could without letting go of the wheel, welcoming the pain that shot through them as sensation returned. Breathing deep, he focused on the wheel in his hands until he could feel its every move, the pull of the tide and the embrace of the sea. Then he knew it was time to let go. 'Daruka!' he ordered, 'hoist the sails!'

As the wind filled the silk and linen canvas with the force of a storm, it drove the ship forward as though it were nothing more than a piece of wood. But only for an instant. Thrown ahead by the wind, the vessel hit the water evenly. With a perceptible jerk, the rudder sliced through the waves. Govinda was ready. He quickly spun the wheel around, getting the rudder to turn, steadying the ship in the current. The huge craft moved around completely, set to glide with the wind and the unexpected tide. Finally, filled with the power of the elements, the craft proudly rode the waves.

Cheers of celebration rose from the deck and turned to cries of war and victory as they cut effortlessly through the sea, heading straight for Saubha's command vessel.

The hunted was now the hunter.

20

IT WAS NOT UNCOMMON FOR A MENIAL IN THE SERVICE OF THE princes of Hastina to feel fear. Dussasana and many of his brothers were not known to tolerate failure, and anything that displeased them was often deemed as such. Yet, the kneeling messenger had never quite felt as terrified as he did now.

Panchali remained expressionless, but her voice was hoarse and cold. 'What senselessness is this? What do you mean I have been wagered and lost?'

The messenger shifted uncomfortably, aware that it was the sheer ridiculousness of his statement that still kept him safe in the presence of the Empress and her guards.

'Dh … Dharma Yudhisthir commands you to … to …'

'That is *Emperor* Dharma Yudhisthir.'

'Mahamatra … He … he is no longer … He … he … wagered his crown and lost …'

'That's impossible. The imperial crown is not a bauble to be wagered.'

'Mahamatra … that is what has happened. He first began with his personal possessions. Once those were lost he … he began to wager the tribute due from your … from the empire's vassals … at first for a month or a year, and … and then in perpetuity. When that was gone, he began to wager … wager armies, then other tradesmen. And …'

Panchali smiled, as though reassured. 'I don't know who asked you to play this trick on me, pratikramin. As a joke it is not in good taste, but I know the fault is not yours. Now, tell me, who is this prankster?'

To that, the attendant could only respond with a horrified stare.

As the first tinges of doubt crept in, Panchali began to argue, with herself as much as with the menial before her. 'But … he can't wager people! It is madness to wager his treasury and lands and property, but he has no authority to wager people! No one stopped him?'

The man before her looked stricken at the suggestion. 'Mahamatra, he was the Emperor …'

Panchali quailed – not at the statement, but at the honest conviction with which it was delivered and accepted by those around her. 'And so he staked me? He had nothing left to stake?'

'No … no, Mahamatra. When all his four brothers were lost to slavery, he then staked himself … Only then did he … ' the attendant began sobbing. The chilling and pitiful sound rankled in the always-festive surroundings of the women's palace.

With great effort, he pulled himself together to deliver the last part of his message. 'He also sends word for your ears alone, Mahamatra. He bids you to come as you are, distraught and begging for mercy, to the assembly. He has asked me to say that as he is your husband and lawful master, he orders you thus … ' the man broke down completely, unable to speak.

Panchali did not know whether it was compassion or cowardice that had driven him to tears, and she didn't care. Drawing in a deep breath, she made her decision. 'Go back to the assembly,' she directed the messenger. 'Go back, and present my message to Dharma Yudhisthir, to Prince Syoddhan who gambled with him, and to the entire assembly that ruled this wager as lawful. Tell them … Tell Dharma Yudhisthir that I am Panchali Draupadi, and he had no right to stake me.'

It felt as though she had hardly sent the messenger back, or perhaps she thought it so for the shock and horror she felt, but Panchali was still standing where the pratikramin had left her when she heard the knock at the door. Her sairandhari looked at her, uncertain. 'Mahamatra?' she said, the question in her tone conveying concern.

'Open it,' Panchali said, but before the girl could act on her orders, the door splintered apart. The two eunuch guards posted in every royal woman's chambers at Hastina stepped in to intercept the intruder, but immediately moved aside.

Dussasan stood in the doorway, a hungry expression on his face. 'You had a question for the assembly, had you not, my dear? I've been sent to escort you there, so that you may ask it in person.' He sprang at her.

Panchali wasted no time on protest or plaint. She elbowed Dussasan in the stomach as hard as could and he doubled over with a grunt of pain. She had hardly reached for her sword when he grabbed hold of her by her hair. She grimaced at the pain, but said nothing.

Dussasan twisted her around, making her face him. 'Slave!' he cackled. 'You whore! Come, you are ours now.'

'This is madness! How dare you? Let go of me!' Panchali demanded.

'Hush, my dear,' Dussasan said, unaffected. 'You've been duly wagered and lost by your husband. You're now rightfully our property, a slave to the Kuru princes.' He caught her face in his thick fingers and forced her to look at him. The action prompted her handmaidens to gasp, but the same sway of authority that had led them to accept their Emperor's untenable stakes without question now kept them from questioning a prince's deeds, no matter how vile. They stayed silent and still, their eyes fixed on the floor.

Oblivious to them, Dussasan bent his head and ran his thick tongue up the side of Panchali's neck and face. She squirmed. In response, Dussasan trailed his thick fingers over her thigh, cupping her from behind to pull her close against him. He forced his fingers against her skin, howling with feral delight as they came away stained red with her monthly blood.

'They say an insatiable woman like you is all the more desirable when your season is upon you ... like a wild animal in heat.'

Panchali let a defiant screech escape her, as she struggled against Dussasan's hold. It only served to spur him on. His gaze leaving no doubt as to his future plans, he taunted her, 'If you'd been any other slave in this palace, I'd have taken you right here, right now. The things I want to do to you ... ' he left the sentence unfinished. With a chuckle he added, 'But who knows, you might enjoy my ... special attentions ... insatiable as you are! We shall see. For now, *slave*, come along. Your masters are calling for you. Come now, *whore!*' He began dragging her out of the door and towards the assembly.

Panchali fought hard against his hold. She kicked, she slapped and scratched – but to no avail. Dussasan slammed her against the hard walls of the corridors and threw her to the floor, using her long hair to keep his hold on her. When that did not suffice to stop her struggling, he kicked her in the stomach and grabbed her again by her hair. Overcome by her own desperation and helplessness, she felt herself going numb. Her limbs felt heavy, and she could not struggle any more. Afraid that she would faint, she focussed on the raw, burning sensation on her legs from being scraped across the stone floor. Then, just when it seemed she had got used to the pain, she suddenly felt the cool smoothness of marble and heard the hum of conversation. Panchali looked up despite the painful grasp that Dussasan still had on her hair. She was in Hastina's hallowed assembly hall.

Each and every elder, every vassal, every ally of Kuru, was present and their eyes were on her and her alone. She was painfully aware that her robes had come loose and clung, disorderly, stained and wet with her own blood, to her thighs. Laughter, mocking and derisive, punctuated the air. Vasusena pointed, not at her but to her body. He clapped his hands in glee and cried out, 'Look at the slave! Look at the whore of the Kaurava clan!'

The words seared through Panchali, filling her with a bitter strength, stoking her fiery spirit out of its submissive resignation. She looked into the crowd around her, searching out, one by one those who ought to have known better. But neither Dharma nor his brothers could meet her eyes. She noted that Syoddhan was staring at her aghast, his mouth hanging open. He briefly looked away to glare, furious, at Dussasan, but the younger prince, consumed by his brutish power, remained oblivious to it. At that, Syoddhan turned back to Panchali, his eyes holding a helplessness that she understood far too well, as she did the controlled horror that she saw in Dron's eyes, and Bhisma's, and in every gaze that fell on her.

Fear and ambition rule us all. Fear and ambition... Oh Rudra, how has it come to this?

And then, Vasusena was speaking again. 'Panchali! You are to proceed immediately to the attendant's quarters of the king's palace. There, you will change into the white hemp robes of a slave-woman and cast off all your jewels and begin the menial duties assigned to you.' He paused, and pointedly added, 'You are now a slave to the Kuru princes. You were wagered by Dharma Yudhisthir and lost. That is the law.'

Panchali rose to her feet with effort. She turned to look at Dharma and his brothers. The five of them stood with their arms crossed in subservience, eyes downcast in shame and submission. Her own gaze fixed on Dharma, she said, 'And whose master was Dharma Yudhisthir to make such a wager?'

The assembly erupted in a roar, and indistinct murmurs of disbelief vied with cries of anger. Panchali knew that many of the abuses and admonition were directed at her. Shakuni and Vasusena called for silence and after much gesticulating managed to get the assembly to comply.

'You dispute that Dharma had a right to stake you?' Vasusena asked as soon as he could make himself heard.

'Yes.'

The chaos resumed. Now, even the elders, Dron, Kripa and Bhisma looked offended. Dharma's head drooped further still. Shakuni stood up and gestured to the assembly to take their seats. Once again, the hall fell quiet and all eyes turned towards Panchali, who continued, unperturbed. 'We speak of our role, our duty as the rulers of Aryavarta, to ensure that Divine Order is replicated here on this earth. And the greatest function that comes of that duty is to ensure that justice is served; a function that the Emperor of this land swore to discharge without fail. Unfortunately, neither the Emperor nor the Empress of Aryavarta are in a position to preserve that oath,' she punctuated her words with a sarcasm that was as soft as it was scathing. 'So it is, that I call on the rulers of Kuru, in whose jurisdiction this matter now lies. I call on the famed justice of Emperor Bharata's line and submit to the authority of this royal assembly – now in effect a court of law.' Her speech was more than many could take.

'Slave!' Dussasan cried out. 'You're a slave and a whore and, by the gods, you will give us brothers as much pleasure as you've given those five eunuch cousins of ours!'

With an enraged cry, Bhim launched himself at Dussasana. It took the combined efforts of Partha, Sadev and Nakul to hold him back. Dharma did not stir. His inaction infuriated Panchali far more than Dussasana's abuses had, and though she tried not to let it show her face was strained with wrath.

Shakuni stepped forward, eager to break Panchali's confidence in his own subtle way. 'So, you maintain that you are not a slave?'

'Yes,' Panchali affirmed.

'Because Dharma had no right to stake you?'

'That is correct.'

In a voice filled with mock astonishment, Shakuni said, 'But you are his lawfully wedded wife, are you not? Doesn't the husband have the right to stake his wife? Or do you admit that you are not his wife alone? For if the case is that you are wife to his brothers too, as some suggest... But then, we return to the question of whether a woman of... err... such distinction deserves any protection at all...'

The statement was met with much crude laughter and applause.

Panchali ignored it all. She said, 'I am wife to Dharma Yudhisthir. However, the moment Dharma's enslavement began, he ceased to have the rights accorded to free men... including rights as a husband over the *property*, if one should tastelessly call it so, that is his wife. Whether you deem him my overlord by virtue of his position as Emperor of Aryavarta, or as my husband, when a man has lost himself, he has no one left to command and nothing left to rule over.'

'That is of no consequence,' Vasusena roared from his seat. 'The wager was made, clear and loud. It was accepted by Dharma without objection. The stake was then declared lost, and that too was accepted by Dharma without objection. You were accepted by the princes of Hastina as their property and sent for. Again, Dharma did not object. When the one who made the stake has conceded you as lost and the winner has accepted you as newly won, what question then of the propriety of the wager?'

Panchali shook her head. 'The gambler may dream in his sleep and in the course of his dream believe that he's playing at dice. He might proceed to lay a wager as he wishes, and even concede the stake as lost. Yet another may dream that he has won at dice and claim the stake as his rightful due. In the sane light of morning, however, neither is the stake relinquished, nor is it claimed. Such is the case here, for a wager made without authority, no matter how unambiguously declared, accepted and admitted, is simply not a valid one. I await the assembly's judgement. Grandsire Bhisma, you have always led this gathering in delivering justice. I ask you, what is your decision?'

Throwing herself on to her knees, Panchali awaited justice. Bhisma's expression, however, was far from cheering. By and large, the elder remained impassive, but there was that particular way he thrust his chin up, as though irked at being involved in such sinfully human affairs. Panchali was familiar with the posture, for she had seen Dharma adopt it often enough, as she did the words that went with it: *It is fated. Destiny is willed by the gods, and we are all powerless against it. It is fate that you must suffer. Let the gods do as they will.* Panchali had no doubt that similar thoughts were going through Bhisma's head.

Finally, Bhisma stood up. 'My child,' he said, 'morality is a subtle thing, and what is considered moral often depends on the situation. Laws are crafted so that we may live noble, honourable lives. Your question isn't an easy one to answer.' Clearing his throat, he declared, 'If anyone here can answer you, my child, it has to be your husband, Dharma, the very embodiment of justice. For he alone can truly say what authority he has, or had, over you, and whether or not you are now a slave. It is for Dharma to speak and set you free.'

In the expectant quiet that followed Bhisma's declaration, Dharma said nothing. Dharma said nothing at all.

'Well then,' Vasusena's words cut through the void that surrounded her. 'Dharma's silence speaks for itself. Dussasana ...'

All sound died, replaced by an ominous stillness. Panchali

knew that stillness. It was the soundless anticipation that filled the air when a sacrificial animal was brought in, the eager calm when humans, for a short while, believed they were no less than the gods, for the power of life and death that was in their hands. It was the instant before the axe fell, blood splattered in wanton worship and the crowd rose with a roar to celebrate the raw might they held as though each one had struck the killing blow with his own hand, the unmistakeable tumult of life that was a blood sacrifice. And then, like animals at a feast, they would pounce on her to consume her alive, her body left bloodied in more ways that one. She tried to look into their eyes, to find reason, but there was none left in them to find. A mob, no, a pack: a feral pack that worked as one to serve the singular command of brute instinct.

It was all she could do to not bleat in fear as Dussasan advanced towards her. His eyes held an inhuman pleasure and his face was contorted in evil satisfaction. Yet again, Panchali tried to resist his grasp, only to be thrown painfully to the ground for her efforts. She tried to edge away. He mocked her feeble defiance, pretending to tease and bait her. Slowly, deliberately, he raised his leg and brought his foot down on her thick, flowing tresses. Pain shot through Panchali as he pinned her down, but she tried hard not to show it. As far as she could, she would deny this animal its sadistic pleasure.

But the hunter was not done. His eyes were locked on hers, his gaze that of a predator paralysing his prey. Enjoying every moment of Panchali's torment, he leisurely bent down to grope at her flesh, in the process grabbing hold of the single length of cloth that covered her body. Then, his breath heavy and ragged, eyes bulging with the anticipation of ecstasy, Dussasan pulled at the cloth.

21

'MIH!' DARUKA CURSED. 'THESE MEN ARE NOT GOING TO GIVE up without a fight, Commander.'

'Then a fight is what they will get, Daruka,' Govinda replied, his eyes fixed on Saubha's flagship as he remained at the wheel.

Saubha's archers rained down a torrent of arrows, catching those on the Yadu warship who failed to take cover in time, or were not in a position to leave their posts. Their cries of pain and dying prayers made Govinda's eyes blaze, though he neither turned around nor offered help. Before their bodies hit the deck, he knew, another one of his sailors would take their place. Each man now fought, not for glory but for their city and their loved ones.

'Get the oarsmen to abandon ship, right now!' he commanded. 'And as many of the crew as we can spare. Get our ships to pick them up.'

The orders left no room for doubt. Daruka gave the signal and the men lowered themselves into the sea. At the same time, the anchored ships sent out rowboats. Keeping well beyond the reach of the current, the soldiers on the boats threw out ropes to the men as they treaded water against the current. Realizing that a collision was inevitable, a few of the Salwa soldiers, too, began to abandon their vessels in fear, taking their rather dismal chances with the raging tides.

'Look at them scurrying to hide like rats!' Daruka gleefully noted.

'You know what needs to be done now, Daruka?'

'Yes, Commander.'

'Go on, then…'

Bowing to his commander, the captain made for the sheltered space below the deck. There, he thrust a few oil-soaked torches into the glowing embers of a brazier. Then, as an afterthought, he kicked the brazier into the depths of the hull, which was now empty of oarsmen. He understood why Govinda had insisted on carrying as few men as possible on this ship. Making his way back up to the deck, Daruka called out to the crewmen for help. Three of them rushed to take the torches from him. The flames spluttered in the strong wind, but did not go out. Acting quickly, the four of them moved to different parts of the ship, setting the sails and the dry wood on fire. Like their own vessel, the men knew, nearly every part of the enemy's ship was easily flammable. Fire ships were an old and dreaded means of naval warfare. They seldom failed to destroy their target, especially when piloted by willing and brave men till the last.

An alarm rang out on board the Salwa command vessel as the enemy realized what was going on. In a desperate attempt to avert the attack, King Saubha's men relentlessly launched arrows at the burning ship. Many of Govinda's crewmen fell, pierced by the black-tipped arrows, but the fire ship did not swerve from its course. Govinda kept his place at the wheel of their infallible weapon, the faithful Daruka at his side. Propelled by the mighty northern wind, it smashed through the side of King Saubha's craft, and remained wedged there.

Govinda held on to the wheel with one hand, and with the other kept Daruka from falling down from the impact. The two men watched as the fire spread across the two vessels caught in their ghostly embrace. Barely moments later the towering mast of the Yadu ship fell, shattering as it hit the other vessel's iron-clad stern. Like bolts of lightning, burning shafts of wood shot out across the water. The Salwa navy's close formation now proved to be its downfall. Fuelled by the wind and the debris, fires began to break out on many of the vessels.

The task done, Daruka readied to abandon ship but realized that Govinda was standing rooted at the wheel, staring across the mangled decks of both ships at a group of similarly unmoving men about thirty feet away. The war was over, but one battle remained.

'Commander...' Daruka called out, hoping to defray what he considered an unnecessary altercation.

Despite all their naval preparedness, Saubha and his men were in no position to swim to safety. Trusting in their ships, they remained attired for intense battle, clad in a shining array of mail and metal, grotesque masks covering their faces. To Daruka's eyes, they appeared veritable monsters. Saubha himself was discernible by his large helmet, shaped in the form of a snarling beast, some strange mythical being from legends native to Salwa. It broadly resembled a bear, though its maws were longer and extended outwards at the king's chin, making it look like he had teeth of shining black metal. Horns rose long and sharp over the bear's head, forming a diabolical crown. The armour on Saubha's body matched the visor, and spiked shoulder plates and claw-like protrusions from the gauntlets on his arms and hands gave him the look of a metallic monster. Slowly, the king removed his helmet to reveal his face, repugnant not for its features but for the malice that lined every bit of it.

Govinda defiantly met his enemy's gaze, uncaring that time was running out. To remain on board the floundering vessel was to face certain death, either by burning alive in the spreading flames, or drowning as the sinking debris created whirlpools impossible to swim out of.

'There's no way they can swim with all that armour, they'll just drown. Commander ... let's go!' Daruka shouted.Govinda ignored him, and drew his sword.

Saubha rushed forward, his own sword drawn, a fearful yell renting the air. Govinda's actions mirrored Saubha's. The two men met over an uneven, smouldering surface formed by the wood of both ships mingled in eerie conjugation. Smoke and flame added a curtain of confusion; screams of pain and terror filled the air. But neither of the two commanders seemed to care.

Daruka stood ready, his own sword drawn, but none of the other soldiers came forward. This was, he realized, a different sort of fight. Saubha knew he was going down. And he wanted to take Govinda with him. The thought only made the captain worry more. King Saubha's feared reputation as a ruthless slayer was a well-deserved one, and he would be all the more vicious if he had no concern for his safety. In fact, if he kept Govinda engaged long enough, both of them would burn and drown together.

Saubha knew this. He prowled around, biding his time. He was fast on his feet and used his curved, whip-like sabre to good effect, keeping his opponent out of striking range but still engaged. Daruka cried out in alarm as Govinda rushed in recklessly. For a while, all the soldier could hear was the soothing rhythm of the waves against the shattered hull of the ship, punctuated occasionally by the whiplash sound that meant a dodge or the clang of metal hitting metal.

Saubha drew first blood. He aimed for his opponent's neck, but Govinda deflected the blow. Relentlessly, Saubha whipped his sword round to catch him on his upper arm, inflicting a deep gash that began to bleed profusely. He stepped back, satisfied, and once again the two men began circling each other, oblivious to the flames and smoke around them.

Sensing that his opponent would be weakened by the loss of blood, Saubha moved in. His next stroke came down hard. Instinctively, Govinda brought his sword up in a double-handed counter. It was just the opportunity King Saubha had been waiting for. He pulled out a thin dagger, coated with a distinct, brown liquid, from a secret compartment set inside his metal gauntlet. A smile curving one side of his mouth, he struck hard to drive it in between Govinda's ribs. In an instant, his delighted expression changed to one of panic. Mortal terror filled Saubha's eyes as he realized what had happened. He had stepped in close to stab Govinda, but it was a bit too close.

Govinda had switched his sword hand and used his now-free right hand to grab Saubha's wrist and pull him in closer still. Saubha tried to thrust the smaller, poisoned blade in where he could but the pain in his arm from Govinda's grip was unbearable. Not one to give up so easily, Saubha slashed wildly with his curved sabre. But at this proximity, the thin whip-blade was no match for the unyielding Nandaka. Govinda deflected Saubha's attack and in a left-handed sweeping thrust caught him from the side, finding a gap in his armour between his shoulder and chest plates. The white metal blade ran clean through the king's chest and stayed wedged in his flesh. Saubha looked down at it, his mouth stuck in a disbelieving, idiotic grin. He staggered back a few steps and fell.

Govinda wrapped his fingers around the hilt of his sword and pulled it out of the dead king's body, sending a spray of blood and fine flesh through the salty sea air. He would have thrown himself at the rest of Saubha's warriors, who stood paralysed with awe and fear, but for Daruka's insistent calls.

'Commander! Now! We need to get off the ship *now*!' The captain pulled at Govinda's arm, gesturing wildly to another wayward Salwa ship that now bore down on them, no longer under the control of its crew. The two men had hardly climbed over the edge of the deck, when the vessel ran into theirs. It turned out to be a blessing in disguise, for the impact of the collision threw both Daruka and Govinda into the water, well away from the huge swirling eddy that was created by the three battleships sinking in unison.

The two men watched the ensuing chaos as they treaded water, waiting for the Yadu rowboats that were already heading in their direction. Their plan had worked

'There's just one thing...' Daruka said 'Where are our other ships? The ones you moved during the night? The ones Saubha thought you'd bring back in a surprise attack?'

Govinda managed a tired, but irrepressible grin. 'Under water, in the cove north of Dwaraka. Saubha saw the ships leave the habour and assumed that I was just hiding them there. He planned to turn the trap against me with his naval formation. But I didn't hide those ships, I sank them.'

Daruka laughed out loud at the matter-of-fact declaration. By sinking the ships, Govinda had created an artificial barrier that had the same effect as shoals and sandbars had in nature. As the natural flow of the landward tide was barred by the submerged wreckage, it pooled near the shore eventually becoming a narrow but strong rip tide that flowed *away* from land, into the sea.

Amidst the clamour, the shouts of victory and the desperate cries of drowning men, the destruction by fire and water, the two men looked fondly over the waters at their beloved crystal city. Trumpets and horns blared from the towers of Dwaraka, and thousands raised their voice in a united war cry. Spurred by the victory on sea, Balabadra and Yuyudhana were leading what remained of their soldiers against Saubha's landward forces.

'What...?' Daruka frowned.

Govinda said, 'I told him to. There is no way those mercenaries will fight without their paymaster, nor will the Salwa soldiers fight without their king. Once they are gone, the rest of the forces – Damagosha's men and the others – will scatter and disclaim all involvement. The blame for this will fall on Saubha and his ambition alone.'

'So... it is over?'

'Yes,' Govinda replied, with a content sigh, 'it is over. Dwaraka is safe.'

22

DUSSASAN'S TOUCH SEARED, VIOLATED. PANCHALI FELT ANGER
prick the back of her neck and she pulled her shoulders back in
instinctive defiance. The sensation lasted for just a moment and then
fell heavily to the pit of her stomach, turning into a cold, clammy,
desperate trepidation that became an incomprehensible sorrow.
She no longer felt his touch, no longer cared where he touched her.
The pain inside her was incorporeal and endless, as though the most
sacred part of her being, the core, which held love and hope and
happiness, was being ravaged into a bloody pulp.

It did not occur to her to beg for mercy. She felt her rage to fight
tamed into numbness by shock and fear. She willed her hands to
move, her legs to kick and her voice to scream, but they did not.
Thoughts swirled through her mind. Words, voices, images – she was
racing through them, in search of something. Some meaning, or an
anchor. Lucidity came in torturous bursts, and she realized that the
screaming in her head was not against her aggressor but against her
own sense of helplessness and despair, the petrified stillness that had
taken over. Her being was hers, every pore of it, to always own and
give as she wished. And that was precisely why Dussasana wanted
it. His was not an act of lust. It was an act of dominance.

Pleasure was something any one of these men could easily have
in greater measure and at a lesser cost. Dussasana hungered for
power, as did Vasusena and the rest. Over her body, her will, and
over those they considered the owners and protectors of her being.
To take her was to destroy Dharma, his brothers, the empire; to burn
to cinders their hearts and will and reduce them into tiny specks of
shamed subservience. It did not matter that she was not anyone's
to own or protect. She was no longer a woman, a person, a human
being. She was simply the embodiment of everything they wanted
for their own, a thing – not unlike the land they wished to conquer,
to plunder in the name of right, duty and morality in perverse proof
of domination. Like soldiers in the heat of battle, like hyenas that had
scented blood, the entire hall seemed to her a mammoth, slithery
creature of legend, with many sharp-fanged heads but a single body

and collective will driving it. She was no longer aware of Syoddhan or Vasusena, or the crazed Dussasan, the silently acquiescent Bhisma, submissive Dharma or maddened Bhim. There was neither friend nor foe, just one fell, foul creature, a mindless mob that sought to affirm its own being.

Some things are defined only by their property to destroy another. Every antidote is defined by its poison.

She could not remember where she had heard those words or who had spoken them. It was strange that they came to mind at a time such as this but she knew why they did. It was because she felt now what she had felt when she first heard them – a debilitating fear that left her with no strength to fight, no will to protest, given the futility of it all. She remembered fire and screams, though the screams were not hers, and she remembered thinking that to be burnt alive was far better than to survive, that pain lasted longer and did not always bring death at the end of it. And that was what it had come to – the thought of one doom being better or worse than the other, because doom was all that was left to come. For that which gave meaning to the world as she knew it had collapsed, utterly and completely.

Kings and queens, wise courtiers and acharyas of great learning, and those of no station at all, but still people, living, sentient beings, had all failed and now looked on in mute awe as one of their own dared to do what ought to have been unthinkable. There had been law, a system beyond the folly of human beings and their fickle minds, but that too had failed, as had the ultimate fibre of life as ordained by Divine Order – morality. She had called on the noble keepers of the empire to deliver justice, but they had failed her. Dharma had not spoken a word, and by their laws she was a slave.

While Panchali weaved in out of the universe in lightning bolts of thought, time expanded, and the single action of Dussasana pulling at her robe spanned many lifetimes. Instinct told her to resist, reason told her to submit.

This is not justice, her inner voice railed. *An unjust law is no law at all; an unjust monarch is no ruler.* The realization made Panchali more despondent than before. She felt surrounded by the empty blackness of a soul in despair, stripped of every hope, every joyful feeling she had ever known, of any sense of calm and contentment. Her fingers, which had clutched reflexively at her robe, were weak and lifeless, and she let go. Like the slow, inexorable movement of the planets, Dussasan kept pulling. She did not know if she was smiling but felt as if she did – a sad curve of the lips that was worse than tears.

Is this what death feels like, she asked herself. The cool marble of the floor was soothing against her cheek. It reminded her of the spring winds, cool and laced with the heady smell of jasmine. Then she was elsewhere. She did not want to open her eyes, and look, lest she still find herself here and not there. As her senses took over, she could smell the fresh grass, its own crisp scent mingling with that of the heavy pollen that dotted its blades. The wind blew soft but incessant, now whispering, now singing in tune with the music of the birds. She waited for her pulsing heartbeat to ebb, listening to it with a vague sense of curiosity. Gradually, it seemed to slow down and fade. Panchali waited for it to stop, certain that it would soon fade away. All that was good and happy, dreams of an empire, of glory and prosperity – all of it would shatter into tiny invisible specks and disappear forever.

There is nothing left to fight for, she heard herself say, though it was in another time and another place.

A voice replied, *Then there is nothing left to lose… It is time to rise.*

Panchali felt a detached sense of surprise as she recognized the voice, though she had no recollection of these words having been spoken. The words brought with them the sensation of another touch, quite unlike the filthy hands that groped and squeezed at this shell that no longer felt like her own body. That touch had been strong but gentle, as respectful fingers had picked up a ragged cloak and wrapped it around her in a promise of protection and hope. That touch, she knew, was from before the fire that had made her who she now was: Panchali Draupadi, Empress of Aryavarta. As was the warmth that had coursed through her body, thrusting life into it as though against its will. Her body heaved as she took a great, long breath into her near-extinguished lungs and blood began to pound once more through her veins. She remembered his eyes – his dark, infinite eyes, filled with love. She felt his warm breath on her skin, as he placed a soft kiss on her forehead.

A single name screamed through her head and spilled from her lips, bringing her crashing back to reality.

This isn't death. This is life.

Her consciousness returned as though she had been in a dream, falling headlong only to wake up before she was smashed into nothingness. She realized that Dussasana was no longer pulling at her robe, and had stepped away from her, letting the garment slip from his hands. It had fallen to cover her bare shoulders and back, the soft silk forming a loving cocoon. Then she became aware of the silence around her.

She did not understand what had happened, what she could have said or done that might have turned the earth over in a moment. Her eyes met Syoddhan's and she was stunned by what she saw there. He looked as though he had just been slapped hard on the face, the force enough to make him lose all hold on the present. And in his eyes she saw how it was that he saw her, as though he were trying to remember where it was he had seen her before. But it was not quite her he was trying to place but the conviction, the subtle confidence she exuded as if she wielded the very power of the Universe. Through the haze that briefly surrounded them both, she gradually became aware that Vasusena was speaking, instructing Dussasana once more, to take her to the pleasure-quarters. But it did not happen.

'Vathu! Enough!' Syoddhan called out, speaking for the first time since Panchali had been dragged into the assembly.

A hush fell over the entire hall. Bhisma's grip on the arm of his seat tightened, and Dhritarashtra sat forward. Dron and Kripa remained as they had all this while, staring into the distance as though the events around them were of no immediate concern. Sanjaya was the only one to show obvious emotion, the act as unusual as its content: unfettered contempt. It only served to fuel Syoddhan's newfound resolution.

139

'Mahamatra,' he said, his respectfulness surprising many in the audience, 'let even one of Dharma's four brothers endorse your claim. Let even one say that the stake was not valid and that Dharma isn't their master. I swear to you, all shall be as before.' He then turned to Dharma and his brothers. 'We can end this now at one word from any of you. One of you, any one of you, can set Panchali free if you as much as question Dharma's right to stake her. Or even if Dharma himself admits that he was at fault and ought not to have staked Panchali, I'll accept it.'

A tense silence followed.

Trying hard to contain his earnestness, Syoddhan tried yet again to appeal to Dharma, willing him silently to stand up just this once, to come forward and accept his part of the blame. 'Dharma...?' Syoddhan prompted, promising himself that for what Dharma would say now he would forgive all his cousin's past silences, the many instances since their youth when Dharma had failed to rise to his rightful defence and led them all down the path of antagonism that had brought them to this juncture. But Dharma remained resolute.

Unexpectedly, it was Partha who stepped forward. He said, 'I...we... We have always been loyal to Dharma, and so we remain. Dharma was our master as he began to play. But...' He took a deep breath, and fixing his gaze on Panchali, continued, 'whether he remained master of anyone or anything after losing himself is doubtable.'

Murmurs ran through the audience. If Panchali was relieved, she did not show it. Syoddhan breathed out hard and looked to his father. Vidur was already whispering in Dhritarastra's ear, vehemently waving an eager Sanjaya back.

The king stood up and all conversation subsided. He addressed Panchali, 'Come here, my daughter. Come closer.'

Silently, expressionlessly, Panchali complied. She did not bother to adjust her clothing as she stood up, or attempt to cover her body further as she moved forward. Dhritarastra continued, 'Ask of me anything you desire.'

Panchali did not hesitate. 'Father, I ask that you set Dharma free from slavery,' she plainly stated.

'So be it,' the king ordered, raising his voice over the murmurs that filled the court He then added, 'My heart isn't yet filled, Panchali. Ask of me another wish.'

'I ask that you set Bhim, Partha, Nakul and Sadev free from bondage so that their mother and children may not suffer.'

'It is also done. Ask for more, Panchali. Ask now, for your own sake, what you will.'

Panchali looked at the old king with an expression that was haughty and innocent at once. The blind king remained unaware of her stance and waited to hear her words.

'Thank you, Father,' she said. 'I fear that asking for one more gift is but avarice on my part. I already have my freedom. It was never taken from me. I need nothing more.'

Dhritarastra was all affection. 'Go in peace, my daughter. Take back all that was lost, including your realm. Forget these tragic events, and do not hold it against your cousins. Remember always that you are all my children, you are Kauravas bound by blood. Let there be peace and prosperity in the empire. Go now, return to Indr-prastha and rule again as Emperor and Empress.'

Dharma gave a discreet sigh of relief and looked uncertainly at his brothers. They refused to meet his gaze, each one of them lost in their own private nightmare of fury, shame and regret. A soft babble of conversation filled the air, a mix of disappointment and reprieve. The rustle of people standing, of moving, of the general conclusion of things was a soothing melody. In the middle of that meaningless rustle of activity, Dharma smiled.

Syoddhan flinched at the unexpected reaction. It turned to contempt as he saw Dharma glance longingly at the dice, the board, and the remnants of the game, unaware of his cousin's gaze on him. The spark in the reinstated Emperor's eyes was neither lust, nor ambition, for even those Syoddhan might have condoned. Dharma looked at the dice with nothing short of reverence, as if they had the power to redeem his soul.

Syoddhan glanced at Panchali and found that she too was staring at Dharma. In her eyes he saw acceptance, even understanding, and it spurred his own. For all his talk of destiny and fate, Dharma Yudhisthir could not bring himself to accept that once again his empire had been given to him by another. He would either win it on his own, or lose it all. But Syoddhan had no pity left in him, not for the creature he saw in front of him. He said, 'One more throw?'

Dharma nodded. Yet another silence fell over the assembly. His brothers stood dumbfounded. Panchali watched, expressionless.

'Identical stakes, this time. Even and identical stakes, for one throw.'

Dharma nodded again. 'And the wager?'

Syoddhan's voice held the pride of a man ready to die a warrior's death, a man bound by honour to the way of life that they all stood for. A man who could no longer let Dharma Yudhisthir rule. 'The empire. We play for just the empire. And the right to be known as Emperor of Aryavarta. The loser must retire into exile.'

'I agree.'

Shakuni reached for the dice, but Syoddhan waved him back. His eyes fixed on Dharma, he picked up the dice and passed it over for him to throw. Shakuni made to protest, but decided against it. This, he realized, was his nephew's destiny. Fame or dishonour, Shakuni was merely an agent. It was Syoddhan who would be praised, or cursed, for millennia to come.

When the dice fell, Syoddhan did not look down at them at all. He said nothing. No one did. Even the loud Dussasana could not bring himself to break the tense silence.

'Kali...' Dharma tremulously said the word.

Kali.

The single dot.

The ultimate losing throw.

After what felt like a long time, Dharma rose from his seat. He silently bowed to the assembly and walked out, his brothers behind him.

Panchali followed the five men, the outline of her feet leaving red stains on Hastina's white, marbled floors.

23

THE GATHERING STARED AT GOVINDA LIKE A CROWD AT A RAGING
bull, not knowing whether to run for their lives or fall with unified
strength on the frightening creature and destroy it. Govinda's eyes
were transformed. What was once infinite bounty was now barren,
not the bleak barrenness of drought but the charred, blackened
devastation of burnt prosperity, as though the endless ocean of
eternity had collapsed in on itself, leaving an empty, formless void
filled with pure, molten, wrath.

Govinda neither looked at nor spoke to any of them. He no
longer cared for Dhaumya's relieved greeting or the description that
had followed of what had transpired at Hastina and since. He paid
no attention to the many questions that came at him of what had
happened at Dwaraka, or the answers that Balabadra and Yuyudhana
gave. His eyes roved over the gathering, searching for the only face
he wanted to see.

In the three days it had taken him to reach Vyasa Markand's
hermitage in the heart of the Kamyaka forest, where Dhaumya had
brought the six exiles, much had changed in the empire he had built.
Treaties had been recast and alliances remade. Allegiances had
been sworn anew, titles given and taken. The heart of Aryavarta had
swiftly shifted to Hastina, the hallowed seat of ancient rulers of the
realm and rested, tenuous, in the hands of an old king and a prince
yet to be Emperor. It was, everyone knew, only a matter of time that
the prince would claim the throne. Without doubt, Syoddhan was
the most powerful man in all Aryavarta and wise enough to know
its perils. He had left Indr-prastha, with its armouries, armies and
treasury, in the hands of the man he trusted the most. Neither
enemy nor ally would dare covet Indr-prastha while Asvattama
Bharadvaja served as its regent, and a quiet peace hung over the
famed White City.

In contrast, what ought to have been a serene hermitage,
refuge and home to scholar-seers, was abuzz with activity. The
visitors were not many, but were of a nature that had thrown the
settlement's placid routine askew. A horse whinnied; Govinda

recognized the dark steed as Shikandin's but bothered neither with beast nor man, not even when Dhrstyadymn called out to him or when Yuyudhana went forward to grip his dearest friend's hand in a silent pledge of support.

'Govinda!' Partha's voice held many sentiments – hope, apology and plaint.

'Govinda?' The question was Bhim's and held its own agonizing answer.

'Govinda, where have you … If only …' Sadev began, and it was clear he spoke for Nakul too.

Dharma said nothing, but stepped forward. Govinda ignored him and walked on through the hermitage. He ignored the clusters of people, his eyes searching instead among those who sat alone.

He felt her presence before he saw her. She came up to him, a cool, soothing breeze that enveloped his pain. Panchali smiled and took his hand in hers. His eyes filled with agony. He tried to speak, but could not find any words that would do.

When she spoke, her voice was soft, but it cut through the oppressively heavy moment. 'I keep trying to remember the first time we met, Govinda,' she said. 'Maybe it was many lifetimes ago. The point is, I can't. I can't remember how it all began, and I think I've known you ever since I existed and there was no first meeting. But I feel that you were there even when I didn't exist. The very thought of you was a warm cocoon of safety, Govinda. It made me feel clothed and covered, no matter how many times I was stripped naked by Vasusena's harsh words and Dussasana's ugly hands. By Rudra, how much affection you must hold for me.'

She laughed softly and went on, 'See now, how the mighty have fallen. We bowed to kings and seers, and hailed them as gods on earth, gave them unimaginable power over our lives. But what about the benevolence they owed us?' She paused, as though hoping the silence would be filled with an answer, then resumed. 'What we call corruption, the failed strength of the noble, is nothing but a system of power without responsibility. A man, an emperor, saw it fit to wager those he was sworn to protect. A court of kings sat in judgement, but declined to pass its verdict. Honestly, I ask you, why then do we need to be ruled? Am I not better off fighting for myself? I've asked myself time and again how it came to this, and I can find only one explanation, however difficult it may be to accept. It isn't the gods who have failed, it is us humans. Nothing moves us anymore; nothing moves us enough to question what is just ...'

'Panchali ...' Govinda began, but faltered. He tried to reach inside himself, searching for the fount of dispassion, the beatitude that he had wrought himself into a long time ago. He had selflessly given up all that he could ever have or want even before he wanted it. Nothing could affect him, or hurt him, for he had neither purpose nor meaning of his own.

For the sake of all that exists, the Primordial Being sacrificed himself. From him came all existence. I am the Primordial Being, Existence itself.

Those words had defined Govinda's life, taught him that nothing was more precious, or sacred, than the willingness to give up one's own self. It had made him who he was, showed him what to aspire to. He had denied himself the essence of being human, an imperceptible but acute torment that no one had noticed or understood. Except for Panchali. *And that is why*, Govinda told himself, *she is your greatest sacrifice.*

He tried to remember the decisiveness with which he let her marry Dharma, let her serve his purpose in building this empire, let her draw the Wrights out of hiding. But he could not. He could feel only passion, as it flowed through him, filled him with life, with strength, though he had tried for years to smother it. To his own surprise, Govinda realized he was enraged, and was forced to admit the anger that had smouldered in him ever since he had heard of the dice game and what Panchali had endured.

He took both her hands in his, uncurling slender fingers that she had rolled into tight fists. Her palms were red and welts showed where she had dug her nails in deep. He stroked her palms over and over, as though with this action he could erase her terrible memories. Or, perhaps, erase his own guilt, the burden of knowing that he had failed.

What Panchali said next cut him to the core. 'You raised me to the greatest possible heights, Govinda. But you too staked me, used me, for what you thought was a greater cause. Look what has become of your precious Empress now ... Or, this is what I deserve for charging you to never to set foot in these lands while I reigned ... This is what was needed to bring you back. And you had to come back, to see what has happened to the glorious empire you left, your promises and dreams of a spectacular future ...'

The tears she had fought back since Hastina now spilled out of her being. 'Before he staked me, Dharma had gambled away our citizenry, and their property, their lives. Such was the empire that you created! Why didn't anyone stop him? Why didn't anyone say that this sovereign had lost his power over the people as soon as he abandoned his responsibility? Why don't we protest now, to say that the Kuru court had no authority over us once they refused to judge the plaint before them? And why do we sit here now, bemoaning what we've lost, instead of asking whether anything was lost at all?

'Aryavarta looked the other way, when I was treated with such impunity. Husbands, fathers, brothers, friends, and sons – some have many protectors, but I had none,' Panchali admitted. 'I didn't even have you, Govinda ... I don't have you, for you won't admit you care. How can you honestly claim equanimity when your blind dispassion keeps you from doing what you were meant to do as a simple human being? As a fellow human being, as your friend, and as one whom you respect as an individual, don't I deserve at least a touch of indignation on your part? Doesn't the basic compassion that makes us human inspire you to anger, not because of who I am, but because of who you are? Is this the empire you dreamt of, for which you treated me so callously? Fourfold and many times more did I deserve your protection; but even you weren't there when I needed you. You weren't there when I needed you the most. What am I to you, Govinda? Nothing at all?'

Govinda stared at her, his expression inscrutable. Specks of a strong sun had reddened Panchali's bronze cheeks. Her eyes were deep pools of mystery that could turn into fire or a benevolent twinkle. He saw her as the earth, as life itself, full of compassion and bounty. She was all that was good, alive, and beautiful. Creation, the spirit of nature, existence, all that he loved, every creature, every leaf and blade of grass, every drop of water, every atom, endless potential, the reason for reason. He reached out to the vastness of the Universe around him, drawing in its energy, finding meaning and succour. Time, since the beginning of existence, flashed through his mind as a single thought. He could hear his own heart beating, feel it as the source of the life that coursed through him, and it amazed him how that one tiny sensation could engulf all his senses. Closing his eyes, he let himself revel in the sensation as it coloured the Universe, becoming one with a myriad other emotions. He lived through aeons, he saw universes come into being and shrink into nothingness, stars that existed just for moments, and moments that lasted forever. He lived as every being, every sentient creature through all of eternity, feeling all their hopes and fears, their despair and euphoria. Familiar and unfamiliar faces were all his own as he expanded, filling everything there was and everything that could ever be.

Taking Panchali's face gently in his large hands, Govinda looked into her eyes, willing her to understand his newfound clarity. His voice was hoarse as he told her, 'I am you, just as you are me. I am the primordial being and you flow through my body, course through my veins as the life-force that gives meaning to the manifested and the material. I am Existence, and you are the Earth. Together we are life and death, creation and destruction, we are the cosmos. We are complete. No one can understand the difference between us, for one has no meaning without the other, but together we are meaning and nothingness both. We are all there is.'

Panchali felt complete. It was all that mattered.

24

DHARMA FELT A SHIVER RUN DOWN HIS SPINE AS HE WATCHED the exchange between Panchali and Govinda, undoubtedly private even though it took place in the middle of a throng. An indescribable emotion took hold of him. Slowly, he let himself notice what he had seen many times, but always ignored – the warmth in Panchali's eyes, her unspoken words and the omnipresent affection, well-restrained by the bounds of propriety. The silence in her suffering tugged at him, even as its uncharacteristic presence in her nature filled him with doubt. He had always respected her as a woman of good conscience, but as he studied her now, it seemed to him she had acquired a quality that was undeniably Govinda's. She had become one with something larger, her heart opening wide to embrace as much of humanity as she could.

The silent change in Panchali had its impact on Govinda too. Squaring his shoulders, he completely ignored Dharma's presence as he called out, 'Shikandin! Dhrstyadymn! Rally your men. We attack, five days hence. We take back Indr-prastha and then deal with Syoddhan and his friends at Hastina. If we send word now, we should have reinforcements from Dwaraka. Samva can lead them here.'

Dhrstyadymn snarled in delight, as Shikandin responded with grim anticipation. A reluctant Bhim, however, pointed out, 'Govinda, Syoddhan has appointed Asvattama as Regent of Indr-prastha. Do you really think we can win it back from him?'

'We will win back this empire. We will win it back from Yama himself if we have to,' Govinda declared. He turned to look at Dharma for the first time since he had arrived, his eyes holding a disdain that was completely absent from his voice. 'Before long, Dharma Yudhisthir will be Emperor, once again.'

'He's right,' Sadev added, 'there are men in the armies of Indr-prastha still loyal to us. We should rally them first. Also whatever personal forces we have are deployed outside and not under Asvattama's control. We can do this. We can win everything back.'

'Panchala's armies are already on high alert,' Dhrstyadymn said. 'That should be enough for now, but let's send messages to the east and to Dwaraka as well, if you have men to spare at this time.'

Shikandin affirmed, 'For all we know, there won't be any need to fight. I suspect if Dharma steps up to reclaim his throne, it won't be denied him. We need to get him to Indr-prastha, from where he can send a call rallying the vassals. As Govinda said, Dharma will be Emperor once again, and soon.'

'No, he won't,' a tired voice interjected. Before any of them could retort, Dharma stepped forward, his eyes on Panchali as he spoke. She stepped aside to let him come face to face with Govinda. In a lower, but determined voice, Dharma repeated, 'No, he won't. I won't, Govinda. I won't ignore what has happened. My empire was meant to be lost. The gods wished it so. It was an empire of unrighteousness and darkness, built on treachery, blood and the work of heathens. It is best that it remains lost, and I...I shall fade into nothingness for my mistakes. We – Panchali and my brothers – we shall remain in exile and seek forgiveness for our sins through penance.'

Govinda said nothing, but the others stared, incredulous, even as Yuyudhana voiced their common thought. 'You are out of your mind!'

'Mind your words, Yuyudhana!' Dharma snapped.

'Why? You're not an emperor, and you don't want to be one. You won't even fight for your honour, to claim what is rightfully yours!'

For a short while it looked as though Dharma would retort, but then, with a deep sigh, he took a step back. 'You're right,' he finally admitted. 'It's wrong of me to take offence. It's wrong of any of us to take offence,' he said, gesturing to his brothers and Panchali. In a tone that made it clear he would brook no argument, he added, 'I thank you all for coming to our help in these difficult times. But I must ask you to return to your homes. It is not for me to comment on whom you owe your allegiance to now, but I hope that together you all will build the glorious, pious and righteous realm that I had dreamt of. Please, for the love you hold for me, for the allegiance you once owed me as your Emperor, whether I have deserved it or not, I ask you to return to your homes. My reign is over. The empire stands but the Emperor has fallen. This is the end.'

Dhrstyadymn sprang forward, equally ready with word and sword, but Shikandin placed an unyielding hand on his chest and forced him back. A confused Yuyudhana looked from the two men to Govinda and then reluctantly began walking away. It served as a sign of sorts to all the other assembled, for slowly, with mumbled words of commiseration, even discontent, they began to disperse.

Balabadra stepped forward to place a hand on Govinda's shoulder. 'Come,' he added, for emphasis.

Govinda nodded, but did not move. He looked directly at Dharma. 'Why?'

It required an obvious act of will for Dharma to restrain his rage. His voice quivered with the effort to not shout or even lunge at Govinda, as he seemed about to do. But the impulse passed and Dharma met Govinda's piercing gaze with recrimination. 'Do you really dare ask me that question, Govinda? Don't you know? Don't you know that of all that has been wrong with my reign, my empire – why, my very life,' he spat through gritted teeth, 'there is no greater stain than the one you've left on it? It is *you* that the kings of Aryavarta wanted to destroy, not me, though I deserve no better for having trusted you!'

Yuyudhana responded by drawing his sword from his scabbard. The ring echoed through the glade as many others gripped their weapons, some to stand by Yuyudhana, and others against.

'Please ... ' Dharma looked around, appealing for peace. He turned back to Govinda and said, 'You have done much for me, Govinda, and I have loved you as a friend, a brother even. But I cannot, and will not, let it be said that Dharma Yudhisthir the righteous, Dharma the just, the heir of Dwaipayana in the house of the Kurus rose to might on the wings of the Firewrights. I thank the gods for taking away from me what I should have refused in the first place. At least they leave me with my honour.'

The fury in Govinda's eyes had subsided. He considered the statement with a neutral expression, as though Dharma had asked him if he thought it was likely to rain. 'You speak to me of honour, Dharma? Then it shall be so: I swear that mountains may break, the skies fall, the earth shatter, or even the oceans run dry, but what I say now shall bear true. Upon *my* honour, I'll change Aryavarta as you know it. I promise you all, the world will remember Panchali, her valour and her dignity; that she dared to hold the gods, and you *honourable* kings and queens of these lands accountable when no one else did. Those who have hurt her, who have failed her, shall pay. The bones of men will mingle with dust and their blood will fill the core of this earth such that it tells her story for millennia to come. And Panchali will, once again, be a queen over all kings!'

'You will change nothing,' said Dharma, defiant. 'You can change nothing. Leave now, Govinda. Leave before I spit on the ground where you stand.' His voice cracked as he added, 'And if I had even a tenth of the authority that I once wielded, not as Emperor but as the least of the loyal vassals who served the interests of the realm and respected all about our way of life that is just and divine, I would have ordered you to be arrested this instant. As it stands, I am lord of nothing but my own self and can give no orders. But there are others, even among those you count as your own people, your own friends, who will not be as tolerant.' As a sense of doom hit him with finality, Dharma finally hissed out the words he had tried to hold back, even though it burnt at his very conscience. 'You have no place here, *Firewright*. Leave. Leave us to our destiny.'

'Destiny? Hah!' Rage, hatred, joy, desire – all fused into one sense of being alive till Govinda exuded a raw, terrifying energy. Yet, for all his fiery authority, he wrapped his arms around Panchali in a tender, protective embrace. 'There is no destiny but what we make of it. Come, Panchali. Come with me. Enough is enough!'

Panchali shook her head. 'No, Govinda.'

Govinda dismissed her refusal as petulance and smiled. 'Come.'

She shook her head again. 'You don't understand. I said that you weren't there when I needed you the most. Do you not understand? The world will already tell my story for millennia to come. It is up to you what they will say.'

And with those simple words, it was over. Govinda understood, and the weight of comprehension crushed him. He had let Panchali down before, but she had always been his sacrifice. This time, it was apathy, betrayal, failure, folly ... a senseless sacrifice, an offering made in vain. He had no words to convey the unbearable grief that took him, twisting him beyond redemption into a lifeless creature that he had never known he could become.

At last, Govinda Shauri realized what force it was that had ended the dice game, stopped Dussasan mid-act and brought the entire assembly of Hastina to a stunned silence. It was the very same force that had stained Dharma's conscience, shattered his pride, and reduced an Empress to exile. In her moment of excruciating agony, when she had lost sight of all hope and meaning, Panchali had let just one word fall from her lips ...

Govinda.

25

THOUGH HE DID NOT SHOW IT, SANJAYA GAVALGANI WAS A HAPPY man. If an omnipresent observer had even suggested as much, Sanjaya would have denied it, because he preferred to think of himself as far too disciplined to indulge in personal pleasures while there remained important tasks to be completed. Or, as in this case, two important tasks that were connected in mutual fulfilment, like the fragile balance of a jeweller's fine scales. *One by one*, he reminded himself as he came into the former Vyasa's presence. *One by one*.

Diminished. That was the word that came to mind when he saw Dwaipayana. Sanjaya knew well that conflicting emotions – guilt, rage, pain, self-recrimination – had left the old scholar in this state. Yet, above all, ruled a poignant regret mingled with pride. Dharma Yudhisthir, the man on whom Dwaipayana had pinned all his hopes, had failed. Yet, Dharma Yudhisthir, Dwaipayana's beloved grandson and moral heir, had succeeded. He had done that which Dwaipayana himself had been unable to: He had spurned the might of the Firewrights, cast aside the tainted empire that Govinda Shauri had built for him, on sheer principle. Sanjaya knew that this one act alone was enough to compel Dwaipayana to forgive Dharma his every transgression and excess and hold him up as the beacon of morality. It was the only way the former Vyasa – or Veda Vyasa, the compiler of the great books of knowledge, as Suka had now taken to calling him – could maintain his own moral integrity in the face of all that had happened. As far as Sanjaya was concerned, Dwaipayana's situation was entirely to his benefit. Now, more than ever, the Veda Vyasa was under his control. Now, more than ever, Dwaipayana would rely on Sanjaya to keep his biggest secret safe.

Appearing very much like a man who could not be cheered even by the hearty mountain air, Sanjaya walked up to the two men – one sitting on the threshold of the hut, the other standing next to him. Dwaipayana looked up from his mournful huddle as Sanjaya approached, but spoke no words of welcome. Next to him Suka looked alternately unconcerned and worried. It struck Sanjaya that if at all the younger scholar cared about the situation, it was for reasons far more trivial and selfish than any of them might have anticipated. All Suka wanted was to be left alone. Sanjaya relished the prospect of fulfilling that particular wish someday, quite literally. Right then, however, he had to deal with Dwaipayana.

After a brief, awkward silence, Sanjaya hung his head, looking shameful, and said, 'I've failed you, Acharya. Forgive me.'

'After all that I've lived for …' Dwaipayana began in a tremulous voice, ' … after everything that the Firstborn have struggled to do … One miserable dice game … A chain of events started by a single, stupid act … Look where it has brought us! Hai!' Suka placed a comforting hand on his father's shoulder, at which Dwaipayana forced himself to calm down. He turned back to Sanjaya, 'Who can understand the workings of destiny, my boy?' he said. 'Don't be so harsh on yourself.'

Sanjaya nodded, even as he observed the silent exchange of glances between father and son with interest. Not once had Suka shown Dwaipayana's zeal, his commitment to the Firstborn order. He had been happy, even relieved, it was said, when his father had passed the title of Vyasa to the elder Markand. Such lack of ambition was something Sanjaya had never been able to understand or come to terms with. One day, he promised himself, he would spit in Suka's face. He would spit in the faces of both the Vyasa's heirs who had taken from him his rightful due. But this was, he knew, not the time for such ruminations. He had a task at hand, one that he could not compromise. 'Acharya,' he softly began, 'I *will* keep my promise to you. I *will* see your blood, Queen Satya's blood, rule Aryavarta. The glory of this line shall not fade.'

'The glory of this line?' Dwaipayana cried out, enraged. 'Muhira! What glory do you speak of, Sanjaya? The glory of my two sons – the

153

blind fool and his impotent brother? Or that of my grandsons – one a gambler, the other a malicious beast? For years I have kept the records of our times, preserved the history of Aryavarta, and now the history of my line, Queen Satya's line, has been besmirched forever. If Dharma is held up as the noble, righteous king that I had expected him to be when I helped him become Emperor, it makes Syoddhan an evil, greedy demon. And if history speaks of Syoddhan as the reasonable, honest man he is, it leaves Dharma as little more than a cheap gambler. What would you have me choose as my legacy? And if I make the wrong choice … then what? Sanjaya, my ultimate failure is not even that my grandsons behaved like common gamblers. My ultimate failure is that such events, such great events swept across the face of Aryavarta, and yet the Firstborn knew nothing, did nothing. Morality was lost and faith was broken and the Firstborn … They were good for nothing but a few words of prayer and blessing when all was done and broken! Did we not know or did we not care? We are broken!'

'Please …' Sanjaya said, earnest, his eyes glimmering with tears of raw emotion. 'Trust me to do what I must. Let me take care of this. Acharya, you've taught me much. The least I can do is repay you by putting those precepts to good use, as best I can.'

'But how …? What can you do? What can anyone do?'

Sanjaya looked once again to Suka, hoping for words of support or reassurance to the weary Dwaipayana. The scholar, however, stood by his father, expressionless, as though he were nothing more than a serving boy waiting for orders. What kind of a man could remain so unambiguously apolitical? Fighting back instinctive disgust, Sanjaya reminded himself that Suka's malleability was an advantage. He said, 'These sordid affairs need not occupy you … or Suka here. There are things best not known to you. You're both men of the gods, while I remain a man of the world. Do not ask me for details, but simply know that what is done is done for the greater good. You have my word. A Kaurava shall rule this empire, now and forever.'

Dwaipayana remained quiet, his eyes showing doubt. Sanjaya persisted, his voice low, even though he knew that the elder alone could understand his veiled words. 'You've carried more than your fair share of earthly burdens, of *terrible secrets*. There is no reason why Suka, or anyone else, should inherit this load. Let me deal with this. Let me make the choices you are not in a position to make. There is yet another tiger that can be tamed to our use...Asita Devala, the prisoner...'

'Are you out of your mind, Sanjaya?' Dwaipayana snapped, a little harsher than he had intended to. His heart raced as he studied Sanjaya's face and the pang of disappointment that crossed it, and he could not help but wonder whether some day the courtier might discover the horrible secret that he hid away in his heart. And if that were to happen, would Sanjaya have the strength and the loyalty to preserve such a terrible secret? For if Suka ever found out...Dwaipayana looked at Suka, who returned the gaze with even certitude. He knew it would destroy his son if he ever found out who his father really was. And that brought him back to Sanjaya. *What choice do I have but to trust him*, Dwaipayana silently admitted. *My hold over Aryavarta weakens. The Firstborn's hold weakens. We need Sanjaya.*

'Can I rely on you to act in the interests of Aryavarta, Sanjaya? It is not enough if Syoddhan rules in Dharma's stead. You must counsel him towards peace. You must use your political craft to set things right. The realm cannot be compromised. Divine Order cannot be forgotten.'

'I shall do as you command, Acharya.'

'And what about...the tiger that I failed to tame? What about Govinda Shauri?'

'He is of no consequence. At best, he is already dead. At worst, he soon will be – either by his own hand, or that of one of his kinsmen. It's been just days since he has returned to Dwaraka, and already the Council has asked that he step down as Commander. Without Govinda at the helm of affairs, the Yadus will inevitably regress to the infighting and squabbling that has been their lot. They don't matter to us anymore.'

'All right, then. Go with my blessings. Varuna protect you, my son. Aryavarta is now in your hands.'

Sanjaya bowed, glancing at Suka as he did so. His heart nearly quailed at what he saw. Like a simple-minded child whose broken toy had just been mended, Suka was smiling.

26

THE SECRET KEEPER WATCHED THE SCENE UNFOLDING IN THE heart of the hermitage with well-veiled satisfaction. For a moment, personal affection reared its head and he wished that things had not come to this. The lapse lasted for just a fraction of an instant before trained rationality took over. He had *had* to do what he had done. Govinda knew that as well as he did.

Your greatest strength is also your biggest weakness.

The Secret Keeper remembered the day Ghora Angirasa had told him that. Govinda had been by his side. It had been a long time ago, and felt longer still. He had been young then, and full of optimism, too much so to believe that Govinda could ever become weak. But it had happened. Finally, the man had broken under the great burden of them all: guilt. Panchali's refusal to come with him, her confession that in her great need it was his name she had called out – it had destroyed him in a way no one had expected. The same dispassion, the detachment that had once made Govinda the most efficient and strategic thinker in all of Aryavarta, had left him bereft. Govinda had not, and could not contemplate a world where sacrifice was in vain. He had given up everything for a cause, but when the cause itself was lost he had nothing left to hold on to. Nothing in his world made sense once that rule had been broken.

Nothing except pain.

'Do you want to leave Aryavarta?' the Secret Keeper had asked Govinda soon after he had returned from Kamyaka to Dwaraka. Or rather, he had asked the man who had once been Govinda, for the shadow that had stood in front of him was a vacant corpse, a shrivelled soul.

'Do you want me to?' Govinda had said, at length.

'No. I think it's best you stay here, where the rest of Aryavarta can see you, so they know that you are...'

'That I am...?'

It had hurt the Secret Keeper to say the next words. 'They must see that you are harmless, Govinda, that you have been conquered and tamed and are no longer a threat to any of them.'

At that, Govinda had laughed, cold, mocking, bitter. He had said, 'Bring them here and tell them to spit in my face. I deserve it. I deserve that and more.'

'I would, if it served any purpose. All I need now is for you to let the Council try you as a Firewright and sentence you as they will.'

'To death?'

'No, not death. You need to stay here, alive, a symbol of the Firewrights' complete defeat. Only then can I fulfil the ultimate task that was left to me, Govinda. Forgive me, my friend, but even the affection I hold for you cannot get in the way of that.'

Govinda had said nothing more. The Secret Keeper had sat with him in silence for a while, before leaving him to his misery. The scholar's own path lay towards the future, and he had no time for regret or repentance. True, men like Govinda came once in millennia, but the Secret Keeper was a practical man. He would make do with the resources he now had in hand: Sanjaya.

The Secret Keeper did not completely understand why Sanjaya acted as he did, but that did not make it difficult to predict what he would do next. Using Devala's power, Sanjaya would support Syoddhan's rise, a rise that would be built on the downfall of Govinda and Dharma. It was not the most desired outcome, but the Secret Keeper had planned for it nevertheless. Govinda's empire had depended on peace and commerce to bring about prosperity and, with it, the resurgence of the Firewrights. Syoddhan's empire would be one of equal prosperity and resurgence, but be built on strife and mutual distrust as the various nations of Aryavarta fought to outdo each other. But it was the only way forward.

The Secret Keeper felt age hit him anew as he remembered that once Ghora Angirasa, too, had made such a choice and failed. But then, there had been Govinda. Now, there was no one.

We are on our own. Govinda is a spent force. His time is over. With a sigh, the scholar turned his attention to the four-year-old acolyte tugging at his robe with all the endearing impatience of childhood. *The future is what matters. One man for an empire. That is a very, very good trade… even if that man is Govinda Shauri.*

Part II

Part II

1

SYODDHAN KAURAVYA OPENED HIS EYES AND STARED INTO THE darkness. Twelve years as Aryavarta's virtual ruler had done little to dim his trained instinct. He slept uneasily on most nights, that was if he slept at all. His dreams were nightmares of wakefulness, memories of a day twelve years ago that still came to him, heavy with silent accusation. The day he had rightfully won this empire from Dharma Yudhisthir in a travesty of a dice game. The day Panchali had been dragged into the assembly hall of Hastina...

He dismissed the thought and strained his ears in the darkness, trying to decipher what had woken him. All he could hear was his wife's even, content breathing, and feel the warmth of her cheek as she slept with her head on his chest. He smiled at her in the dimness and, with a light touch, smoothed back her dishevelled hair – the result of their slow, passionate lovemaking, a ritual celebration of the deep bond they had shared over the years. It was an affection he had come to cherish, for it had nearly been lost.

After the dice game, as Dharma and his companions had left Hastina as exiles, Dussasan and Vasusena had made their departure as difficult as possible, following them to the city limits, shouting abuses and jeers. Syoddhan, however, had left the assembly hall and directly made his way to his quarters. He wanted to make sure that his wife, Bhanumati, heard the news of what had transpired from him, first.

Bhanumati had been aghast. She had sat rigid with denial while he had sobbed quietly, his head on her lap, like an errant boy. 'What if it had been me?' she had asked. He had not known what answer to give but had realized that things would never be the same again between them. And so he had set about trying to make things all right the only way he had known how: by being a good ruler to the people of Aryavarta.

It had not been an easy task, but slowly the realm's prosperity had grown, healing even the destruction from the war in the west, till people from nations far and near said that Syoddhan's rule was no less than the golden age promised by Dharma Yudhisthir. Just as, over time, Bhanumati had healed and grown to love him once again. As had the people of Aryavarta – all but those who ought to have loved him the most. It was the price Syoddhan had paid for Aryavarta's prosperity. The stronger and more affluent the nations grew, the more they began to distrust and fear their neighbours, and the more their rulers prepared for war. None was more eager for battle than his own brothers, and none more apathetic to that fact than his advisors – Grandsire Bhisma and the acharyas Dron and Kripa. Yet, their advice for him in the face of the nations' aggressive weaponization was far from ambiguous.

'Fight fire with fire,' Bhisma had said, with obvious reference to the use of Wright weaponry. Dron had remained impassive as the Grandsire had continued, 'What the others have, you must have too, and more. It is what once made the Kuru kingdom the greatest nation in all Aryavarta, even up to my father's time. Enough of politics. A warrior's honour lies in battle. A nation's peace lies in its strength. Be the strongest, Syoddhan. You shall never want for peace.'

Partly convinced, partly concerned, Syoddhan had complied. It had not only changed the face of Aryavarta, but had also elevated him above the rest. Strife, when it came, was in clusters and pockets, for his overwhelming strength and influence was enough to maintain a kind of peace. Domestic boundaries and borders were sometimes adjusted, entire territories sometimes acquired. But the empire remained as it was, a huge pond that subsumed a stray ripple.

In truth, the situation made Syoddhan fearful. He knew the limits of his influence and power, as well as the fact that the empire itself was not a creature of loyalty. It was then, and only then, that Syoddhan envied Dharma. More specifically, he envied Dharma his brothers. Among his own, Syoddhan felt alone. His brothers seemed strangers,

162

creatures that he could no longer recognize or understand. It had taken him a while to see what the unstated tension between them was. He had created a bigger, stronger empire, which his brothers could not dream of taking over in a single stroke – of war, dice, or otherwise – as he had done with Dharma Yudhisthir.

From the news that came in about the recent exiles, Bhim, Partha, Sadev and Nakul had taken to their lives as forest dwellers, without demur. *Five, forged into unshakeable oneness. That is what had helped build the empire. That was Dharma's greatest strength, and it is my biggest weakness.*

Once, in a fit of frustration, Syoddhan had confessed to Bhanumati, 'Perhaps Dharma was a better Emperor.'

Her response had been vehement, 'He was not! And certainly not a better man. You would never stake your wife at dice, nor watch while she was molested.'

He said nothing, but flinched at the memory of Panchali's terror in Hastina's assembly hall and the fact that he had been a mute witness. When he looked at his wife, Bhanumati's eyes had finally held forgiveness. At length she had said, 'You are a better Emperor, no doubt. But Dharma Yudhisthir had Govinda Shauri.'

Govinda Shauri. It was a name Syoddhan hardly heard any more. Yet, it was a name he remembered often, and with mixed emotions. He wondered what it was that had made Panchali call out Govinda's name in her moment of utmost helplessness and greatest need. Had it been a token of surrender? A plea for help? Or a final whisper of affection with what he imagined must have felt like her dying breath?

And what sort of a man was Govinda Shauri, who had sought no vengeance? He had simply faded away, leaving Panchali behind to live as a commoner, a woman of no importance, in the forests of Kamyaka. *But that had not been without cause or consequence,* Syoddhan noted. *As soon as the puppet falls, so does the puppeteer.* And so, the further Dharma had receded into the oblivion of exile, the more Govinda descended into infamy, while he, Syoddhan, had gained legitimacy and support over all of Aryavarta.

It had worked well. Syoddhan had seen at once that to leave Dharma alone in anonymous seclusion was useful at many levels, but Dussasan, who had made the most of his new-found fame as the Emperor-in-fact's brother and soon acquired an air of superiority and assumed the title of second-in-command, had not understood the reasoning. Vasusena and Shakuni had prevailed on the younger prince to be patient, though he remained reluctantly so.

The fault, Syoddhan knew, was his own. He had, over the years, freely shared his criticisms and complaints against Dharma, but never his reasons for them. It had served only to breed in his brothers unfettered hostility and hatred for the sons of Pandu. In the past decade the hatred had become his own, serving as vindication and validation both. He threw himself heart and soul into running the empire the way he believed Dharma ought to have run it and into becoming the man he believed an emperor ought to be. But nothing he did, and no amount of rationalization or probing, had helped him answer the question that had haunted him for most of his adult life. He just could not fathom what sort of a man, really, was Govinda Shauri.

Weary with the futility of his introspection, Syoddhan gently shifted his wife off him and turned, curling uncharacteristically into a foetal position, as he would never have done but for the privacy of darkness. The action saved his life.

2

SYODDHAN WAS OUT OF BED AS SOON AS HE HEARD THE DAGGER whiz past his ear, in the instant before it plunged into the soft pillow by his head. His eyes locked on the outline of the intruder and his hand reached out for the sword that always remained by his bed. But he need not have bothered. The assassin did not see the dark form creep up behind him, too silent to be a shadow, too fearsome to be a ghost. The killer got no chance to make even a sound as the sliver-like blade went right through his throat, severing his vocal cords, the blade precisely placed so as not to draw a hideous spurt of blood. Before he could crumple and hit the ground, the dark figure moved again, twisting the blade completely into the assassin's torso to kill him instantly before easing the body down to the floor.

'Who ...' Syoddhan began as he wrapped on his lower garment.

His rescuer silenced him with a nod at the still-sleeping Bhanumati. Syoddhan realized that his wife was naked under the sheets, but the other man neither noticed nor cared. To Asvattama Bharadvaja, everything was an element on a battlefield – friend, foe, inconsequential victim and incidental bystander. Silently, Asvattama hoisted the dead man over his shoulder and made for the door. Syoddhan followed.

'Who ... ?' Syoddhan repeated once both men had stepped out into the room adjoining his bedchamber.

In response, Asvattama pushed back the cowl covering the dead man's face.

'Him?' Syoddhan was incredulous. 'He's always been loyal!'

'To you or your brother?'

'Which one?'

'Do you really need me to answer that, Syoddhan?'

'But ... why? Why would my brother do this?'

'Why not? There is rebellion in the east. One also hears rumours of invaders on the western frontier.'

'One always hears rumours of invaders on the western frontier.'

'True. But often a rumour is excuse enough. Your brother thinks your position is precarious.'

'And you? Do you think it to be so?'

'Yes, I do. You've done a rare thing, Syoddhan. You've given your vassals *and* their people enough to be happy about. Usually, it's one or the other. Such success is bound to have its price. In this case, too, many people have become powerful, too soon.'

'I am one of those people, am I not? My death would have suited many, you included. Is that why you let this assassin through? If you knew I was in danger, why didn't you just have him arrested? Why did you wait till the last instant?'

If Asvattama found the statement offensive, he gave no indication of it. Matter-of-fact, he said, 'I wanted you to have irrefutable proof,

Syoddhan. I've warned you before that not all of your brothers are to be trusted. Now, you know as well as I do who sent this assassin. As for making an arrest ... I have the contingent of your royal guard waiting. I'll personally escort the real criminal to ...'

'No!'

'Syoddhan ...'

'He's my brother. They all are. I cannot arrest them for treason, Asvattama. What would you have me do next, execute them all? I cannot do it!'

'With all due respect, Your Highness, there is no room for fraternal affection in these matters. You brothers are divided in their loyalties. Some have ambitions too big to be constrained by their affections. Others have no ambition, but they lack courage. They will follow whoever takes the reins of power without dispute, whether it is you or one of their other brothers. You must act now. The man who sent this assassin cannot be ignored.'

'Acharya, you have your orders,' Sanjaya's voice interrupted, artificially soft and sweet.

Asvattama did not bother to turn around. 'Stay out of this, Kshatta. A servant should know his place, and it certainly is not in the middle of a conversation between two monarchs.'

'Servant I may be, and I am gladly one – but so are you. You stand here tonight in your capacity as Prince Syoddhan's vassal and commander, and I as his minister and advisor. This conversation concerns me as much as it does you.'

'Really? And what advice do you intend to give your liege-lord?'

'Actually, Acharya, I was going to agree with you. Indeed, there is no room for fraternal affections in this situation. It is time Prince Syoddhan assumed the title that goes with his power and settled these affairs once and for all. It is the best way to quell dissent – both within this palace and outside it.'

Syoddhan was astounded, but the feeling soon gave way to visible sadness. 'You speak of dissent like I'm a tyrant or usurper, Sanjaya. By law, moral and convention, by any means we hold to in Aryavarta, Dharma Yudhisthir lost his empire to me. The former Vyasa, the current Vyasa, Grandsire Bhisma ... why, Dharma himself admits that there is no questioning the legitimacy of my acquisition.'

'And what of his brothers? And the next generation? Your father was lawfully installed as king of Kuru, but did that stop Dharma from staking his claim? From portioning this great realm into two? And the tribal uprisings in the east? You cannot ignore them as sporadic events. If Dharma, or even one of your brothers, takes it upon him to ally with them, it might give their cause legitimacy. Before we know it, we will have war on our hands. If you want to avoid that, you must make your claim absolute.'

'How?'

Sanjaya set his face into the appropriate expression of resignation, as though it pained him to say that which duty demanded. 'Kill Dharma Yudhisthir, Your Highness. Make an example of him, and your own brothers will learn the meaning of loyalty. We should crush this fraternal rebellion right away.'

'No,' Syoddhan's tone suggested he would brook no argument, but Sanjaya persisted.

'I know you find it heinous, but it is for the greater good. What would you rather choose, Your Highness? The death of one man can save the lives of many, including his own brothers and his wife. Once Dharma is dead, his brothers pose no threat to anyone, nor will they be of use to your enemies. You can even bring them here, or let them be housed in comfort at Indr-prastha as your dependants. The alternative is to risk civil war within the Kuru kingdom, for sooner or later your dear brother – yes, the same one who sent tonight's assassin – will mistake your kindness for weakness.'

'Another man would never have dared speak to me this way, Suta,' Syoddhan hissed. 'In case you did not hear me, I said "no". And if my brother thinks that letting Dharma live for twelve years, when I could have had him killed within this very city, shows my weakness and not my strength … Well, I suppose that explains why he can never can be king. He's an idiot.'

'Your Highness …'

Asvattama interrupted, 'He is an idiot. But that doesn't make him any less dangerous, Syoddhan.'

'Asvattama! Don't tell me you agree?' Syoddhan was shocked.

'All I know is you need to do something. I shall leave it to you to decide what will be done.'

Sanjaya nodded, eyes downcast, as though honoured to find support from Asvattama. He said, 'Send Jayadrath. Vasusena and Devala are still needed in the east... And once that is done, Your Highness, it will be time to think of your coronation... as Emperor.'

Asvattama's voice dripped sarcasm. 'My, my, Suta. You are the best prime minister these lands have seen yet. And, who knows, you may soon enough become an imperial counsellor...'

Sanjaya accepted the remark as a compliment with the restrained arrogance of one who knew he would be much, much more.

3

THE RAIN BEAT AN INCESSANT RHYTHM AGAINST THE DRY ground, pushing the fragrance of wet earth into the air. Dhrstyadymn lay awake on his reed mat, listening, breathing, but finding no relief in sleep. His body ached from the numerous blows he had received from the flat of Dron's sword and he longed for rest, but his mind was awake, going over the morning's sparring session again and again, trying to identify his mistakes. He found it difficult to concentrate – but then it had been difficult to do anything with certainty since the day he had left Panchali behind in the forests of Kamyaka.

Dhrstyadymn had ridden straight home to Kampilya, eager to rouse Panchala's massive armies and lead them in an attack against Hastina. But his father, Dhrupad, had been ready to make an agreement with Bhisma, Grandsire of the Kurus. Panchala would swear allegiance to Syoddhan. Panchala would not go to war. And Panchala would continue to pay Syoddhan's empire the tribute it had paid Dharma's. In return, Dhrupad would finally get the one thing that had been denied him all these years: His son, the heir to the Panchala throne, would train under Acharya Dron.

Dhrstyadymn had found the conciliation unacceptable for more reasons than he could count, the fact that they had been compelled to forsake Panchali not the least among them.

It was Shikandin who had pacified him. 'Do you know why our father asks that you be trained by Dron? Because, like every other ruler in Aryavarta, he is now going to build his armies and his forges, both. Like every other monarch, he will be driven by ambition and the need to survive, to be stronger and mightier than his neighbour. To avoid war, we will all have to begin to prepare for it, every day and every moment. And for the same reasons that men like our father once gave when they hunted down each and every Firewright during the Great Scourge, we will now squabble and conspire to get our hands on every piece of Firewright weaponry that may, somehow, have been left behind. We were fools, all of us ...' Reluctantly, he added, 'Perhaps Govinda too.'

The admission had mollified Dhrstyadymn a little, but not completely, given his concealed misgivings about his brother. 'What about Panchali?'

'Trust me, the best way to keep her safe is to do what is required of us. Syoddhan has no reason to bother with her or that spineless bastard Dharma unless *we* give him cause to. Panchala's assurance of loyalty is essential, not only for our kingdom's safety but also Panchali's. That's why I ...'

'You counselled this? You agreed to this shameful, despicable peace?'

'Yes. Not directly, though ... You know our father would rather stab himself in the eye than ever listen to my suggestions. I had his advisors put it forward in a way that he would find palatable.'

Words had failed Dhrstyadymn. He could only ask, defeated, 'What do you want me to do?'

'Go to Hastina. Train. Train hard. Rudra knows what lies ahead.'

'And you?'

Shikandin had smiled. 'Some of us have been fighting this battle while you were too busy being born. I'll look forward to reliving those good old days.'

And now it had been more than a decade since Dhrstyadymn had seen his brother or his sister – the two people he loved the most in all existence. In his first few years as Dron's student, he had spent all his time at acharya Dron's training hermitage on the outskirts of Hastina, living as one of the disciples, going through the routine of menial chores and lessons. All that had changed the day a messenger had come from his father, requesting him to return at once to Kampilya. He had rushed home to a quiet and brooding palace. An air of melancholy hung in the air – but not quite.

'Shikandin's dead,' Dhrupad had informed him, not appearing any the sadder for it. Satrajit – commander of Panchala's armies and Dhrupad's son by a concubine – had later explained that nobody had heard from Shikandin in a little over two years, and that had led Dhrupad to decide that his inconvenient son was dead. There had been no mourning, no state funeral, no loud wailing or sacred rites to mark the elder prince's passing. It had been as though Shikandin had simply ceased to exist. The queen – Dhrstyadymn's mother and Shikandin's birth mother – had refused to see her son or speak to him.

Hurt and shaken, more by what he suspected was Shikandin's continuing treachery than Dhrupad's lack of emotion, Dhrstyadymn had, for the first and last time that he could recall, refused to obey his father's wishes. He insisted that he would not ascend the throne just as yet. He did, however, take on greater administrative and ceremonial duties, as Dhrupad ordered. In his heart, he remained a shattered man, torn between his life as Dron's student, his belief that Shikandin was alive and his constant worry for Panchali. The thread that tied it all together was a complicated one that he dared not unravel as yet, but every night, before he slept, he thought of Govinda Shauri, his failure and his betrayal.

Dhrstyadymn tried his best to understand it, but he could not. And so he would wake to yet another day of learning every martial method, every strategy and move that Dron had to offer. He did not know whether Govinda was friend or foe, but if ever they met in battle, he wanted to have what it would take to kill him if he had to. It was why he continued to come back to the hermitage whenever he could, year after year, to learn more than any student of Dron's ever had. It was, he also knew, why Syoddhan encouraged and welcomed him, and made sure that acharya Dron did the same.

To be fair, Dhrstyadymn had found that Dron was a true teacher, a man who shared what he knew with little distinction between enemy and friend. A student was a student, and remained as such till he defeated Dron himself in a sparring contest. Of course, the students all knew that none of them was Dron's match on a battlefield. But here, on the training ground, the acharya occasionally let a student win. It meant that he had deemed the student ready. And Dhrstyadymn was far from ready.

During his training sessions with Dron he received more blows and cuts than any of the other students, grown men like him, who sought to learn the most advanced fighting skills or even dedicate their life to fighting as an art more than an activity. Dron now also took in princes from countries that were much further away, including Gandhara and beyond, where the people had fair hair and blue eyes. Dhrstyadymn had once casually wondered what the women of those countries looked like, but soon had little time for such leisurely thoughts. Every day, the acharya urged him on, cheered him, taunted him and admonished him to do better, but every time they duelled, Dhrstyadymn remained defeated and went home to a disparaging father who was only too happy to remind him of the heavy burden he carried. He regretted that he would hear it all soon enough, for Dron had instructed him yet again to return to Kampilya.

Rising from his mat, Dhrstyadymn walked out of the dormitory he shared with nine other students. Standing in the middle of the courtyard, he let himself be drenched by the torrential downpour. Every raindrop that touched him stung and cooled him, stoking and extinguishing the fury and self-hatred that seethed within. Arms outstretched, eyes closed, head turned upwards in eager welcome, he gratefully received the rain, willing it to wash away his doubts and dismay. Under the cover of the storm and darkness, he let his tears fall, mingling with the downpour.

He cried for his brother, who stood in the shadows of doorways in the very palace he ought to have ruled, a stranger peering inside his own home from the uncertainty of the threshold, humiliated by his father and hated by his son. Was that why his brother had turned into a traitor? He cried for his sister, and the strange bond between them – for neither he nor she knew of their origins or the life that may have once been theirs. Foundlings both, they had slowly grown to become Dhrupad's children. At that thought, Dhrstyadymn finally cried for himself, for the life he had lost and the destiny he had never been able to find. He felt, at best, like a ghost – always present but incorporeal, there but of no consequence. Through all that had happened, he had been nothing more than an angry witness who neither protected nor avenged.

Dhrstyadymn stood that way till the rain stopped. Only when the weight of his being returned, dragging at him like wet robes, did he move and open his eyes. He started, uncomfortable, as he noticed the tall figure watching him from the sheltered awning of a hut. No doubt, Asvattama had been standing there for a good while. Dhrstyadymn peered through the night, trying to read the man's expression, but his face was completely hidden by shadows. He stood with his arms crossed over his chest, and all Dhrstyadymn could see was that the skin of his long, slender fingers was ghostly pale in the moonlight.

Unsure of what to do next, Dhrstyadymn settled for a polite bow: Asvattama was as much a teacher here as Dron and deserved respect as such. In response, Asvattama crooked a finger and beckoned him to approach. As Dhrstyadymn walked towards the hut, Asvattama lit a small lamp and set it in a stone alcove. Laying out two reed mats, he sat down comfortably on one and gestured to the other. Dhrstyadymn complied, bearing the other man's silent scrutiny with patience.

Finally, Asvattama said, 'I don't know if you've seen it yet, but you have a gift, a rare gift. Your mind...the way you think... You can look beyond the battle, you can see the whole battlefield. Men like that are rare, and those that possess this ability make the greatest commanders. But...'

'But?'

'Your anger is your strength. Right now it controls you. You will have to learn to control it.'

Dhrstyadymn looked at Asvattama like he did not quite care. He said as much. 'Your father has instructed me to go back. He said he would send word when he is ready to teach again. I have a feeling it won't be very soon.'

'And you'll wait? You didn't strike me as a man who could hold his curiosity and vengeance for years. Whatever happened to the angry young prince you once were? Or are you turning your rage into motivation? That's not a bad idea, really, but it could do with some improvement.'

True to the first allegation, Dhrstyadymn stood up at once. 'I don't have to tell you anything!'

'Sit down, Dhrstyadymn,' Asvattama commanded. 'Till such time as you leave this place I am still your teacher and you will do as I instruct!'

His eyes blazed defiance, but Dhrstyadymn did as he was told. Asvattama reached out, letting a drop of rainwater fall off the leafy thatch and on to his palm. Displaying the drop to Dhrstyadymn, he asked, 'Tell me, what is this?'

'Really?'

'If you don't want to indulge me, then obey me.'

'A raindrop.'

'It looks like any old drop of water to me. Where is the rain?'

'Mih! What the…' Dhrstyadymn began to argue, but stopped short as he understood what the acharya was saying.

'Yes, you're beginning to see. Warriors are like raindrops. Our meaning goes beyond one command, one act and one victory. We fight *for* something, Dhrstyadymn, for a belief, a principle that we stand for. When you do that, it does not matter who is killed or who kills.' Asvattama twisted his palm lightly, letting the raindrop roll playfully over his palm. He said, 'When this drop fell, it simply fell. It did not stop to consider where it fell from or where it would land. Its true nature is falling and so it fell. Its true nature is not being a drop, it is being rain. And that, young man, is also why you find the rain so captivating – because you have much to learn from it. Far more than my father or I could teach you. If you ask me, you're done here. Anything more you need to know lies within you.'

'Acharya…'

Asvattama stood up, forcing Dhrstyadymn to scramble to his feet out of courtesy. 'You may not like me, Dhrstyadymn. But you know what I'm saying makes perfect sense. It makes sense because you and I have an important thing in common. It is strange in itself, but persuasive enough to bind us. Both of us sit on thrones that rightfully belong to your brother. Both of us watched, helpless and angry, as his crowns were taken from him and placed on our respective heads… I can't forgive myself for letting it happen, and I know that you can't either. But it is up to us whether we will let it haunt us forever, or choose to use the chance, the power that has been given to us, to do what is good and just. Shikandin made his sacrifices willingly. It is up to us whether we will honour them or not.'

'But… I… He… How do you know all this?'

'We are old friends. As for how that happened, this is not the occasion for such tales. Someday, we shall sit together, the three of us, and you shall hear two old men talk of their youth. But now is not the time. I suggest we get what sleep we still can. Oh, and for what it's worth, in my authority as a teacher I declare your training at this hermitage over. I don't suppose you mind missing the ceremonial sword-giving ritual and all that? The children find it exciting, but I'm hoping you won't insist on it.'

Dhrstyadymn smiled. It felt new, as if he were doing it after an immeasurably long time. 'I don't mind at all, Acharya. But you will still bless me, won't you?'

'If I do, you will owe me guru-dakshina – the payment due to me as teacher. Are you sure you can afford it?'

'Anything you say, Acharya,' Dhrstyadymn was sincere, as he bowed low.

Asvattama placed a warm hand on his head and spoke a blessing over him. He said, 'In that case, here is what I claim of you in my right as your teacher. Trust your brother, Dhrstyadymn. Shikandin is one of the strongest men I know, but even the strength of the greatest man can fail if he loses hope. Your brother needs you; he needs you to believe that he is not a traitor to his people.'

'Shikandin is alive?'

'Don't you know in your heart that he is?' Asvattama sneered, far more like his usual self than the warm teacher of moments ago. 'He's alive. I don't agree with what he is doing, but I don't want him or his friends to die for it. Head east, you'll find him soon enough. Move fast. He has trouble headed his way, though he doesn't know it … yet.'

Dhrstyadymn nodded. 'Thank you, Acharya.'

Asvattama waved his hand, dismissive, and turned his attention to the skies as though his exchange with Dhrstyadymn had been nothing more than an intrusion. This time Dhrstyadymn knew better than to take it to heart.

<h1 style="text-align:center">4</h1>

THE HEAT FROM THE FORGE WAS OVERPOWERING, BUT VASUSENA appeared not to care. He was dressed in a simple cotton lower robe, a far cry from the royal vestments he wore as a matter of entitlement. Yet, as his wife was fond of telling him, he looked powerful and regal in such simplicity. He often snapped at her when she said so – not because he disagreed with her but because he agreed. Given a choice, Vasusena would have gladly remained the simple son of a charioteer in the Kuru army and his loving wife. Such a life would have been devoid of the best joys he had ever known, though being king was not one of them. He was, however, grateful for many other things: his fame and honour as a warrior, his doting wife, a princess of the Kashi kingdom he had married for love and not politics, and his friendship with Syoddhan of the Kurus. The last to him was the most precious treasure of them all.

Over time kingship too had become less irksome but he had made it a point not to let it overwhelm his inner simplicity. He was known among his people as a just and generous king, a reputation that he had earned by never denying his humble origins. Yet, in the dark silence of the night, as he lay under silken sheets on a gem-studded bed of gold and wood, he admitted to himself that he hung on to his confused sense of identity, the contradictions, for a reason – neither was the truth. He was, by birth, neither the king of Anga nor the son of a charioteer. He was more. Far more.

In the aftermath of Dharma Yudhisthir's fall Vasusena had become a less tormented man. His wife had declared him positively congenial to live with, and for the first time in past years he found himself forming a strong bond with his son, Vrishasena. He did not want to admit it, but he felt that he resented the world around him less now that Syoddhan held the reins of power. He was a man Vasusena respected, loved as a brother and was proud to serve. Dharma had deserved none of those affections.

And Panchali?

Vasusena had never quite forgotten his humiliation at Panchali's wedding contest decades ago, not even despite the explanations and evidence Syoddhan had subsequently offered to suggest that they had both been drugged and so compelled to fail. Since that day, he had let his hatred and disgust for Dharma and his brothers flow over to Panchali. She had become, in his mind, the symbol of all that had been wrongfully taken from him and handed to an undeserving, incompetent man like Dharma. If she had married Partha, or even a good man like Bhim, Vasusena would have made his peace with it. But no. It was Dharma who was recognized as Pandu's eldest son, declared as heir to the Kuru throne, married to Panchali and finally elevated to the role of Emperor. A man who had probably never held a sword the way it was meant to be held, who knew nothing of consecrating its sacred blade with the blood of his enemies. Dharma was nothing. What had happened to him was well deserved and Vasusena coaxed himself into feeling proud of his role in seeing the man fall.

With a muted growl, he spit on the sandy floor of the forge, earning him a disapproving look from the young man who was working on a sword under Devala's critical eye.

'Show me that,' he commanded the youth. With a glance at his master, who nodded, the apprentice complied.

Vasusena took the tongs the apprentice held out, the red-hot blade in its embrace. He held the blade up at eye level and looked it over before returning it to the youth. 'You're striking it on the wrong edge. If you keep hammering at it here,' he pointed, 'you won't make it keener. You will only cause more stress down the centre.'

The apprentice regarded him, sceptical, not convinced that the king knew what he was talking about. He snapped to attention as

Devala shot him an angry look. 'He's right, you idiot. I shall make sure that when war comes, that blade finds its way to you. Then, when it breaks on the battlefield, you might learn the meaning of respect.'

Vasusena chuckled and moved away. Devala followed him. The two men made their way out of the large, bustling forge and emerged into the sunlight. An attendant came up bearing a large silver basin filled with rosewater for Vasusena to refresh himself.

Devala watched him with open curiosity as he wiped off the sweat from his brow and chest with a cloth dipped in the rosewater. 'You know your blades.'

'As does every good warrior. You can't quite use a sword unless you know how it is made, how it is meant to kill.'

'I think it's more than that, Vasusena. There's a rumour back at Hastina that you were trained by the Jamadagnis, the best of the Firewrights. Is that true?'

'You mean the best of your kind, Devala?' Vasusena retorted.

Devala hesitated, but Vasusena went on. 'Did you expect me to believe that anyone else was capable of setting up a forge such as this one, and the many more like it throughout the Anga-Kashi-Kosala regions?'

Devala laughed. 'All right then, let us speak as men should. You trained under Bhargava Rama, didn't you? I must point out that that would explain how Anga became what you just referred to as the rather expansive Anga-Kashi-Kosala region.'

'I did. It seemed a good idea at that time.'

'To conquer the east?'

'To train under the Firewrights. I was a very young man when it happened. I'm older now, if not simply old, and hopefully the wiser for it.'

'You regret it?' Devala asked.

'Not, not regret. But...let's just say that I went to him for the wrong reasons – rage, ambition, a need to prove who I was. Or, to be more precise, to prove to myself that I was indeed worthy of the truth.'

'And the truth was?'

'None of your concern,' Vasusena snapped. He added, 'No offence.'

Devala held up his hands. 'None taken.' In a bid to change the topic, he said, 'We need more guards around the forges, Vasusena.'

Vasusena frowned. 'I thought the whole point of placing the forges in the middle of these godforsaken woods was that no one would know of their existence. Still, I suppose it doesn't hurt to be careful. I'll ask my commander to send out more contingents as soon as we get back. They should be here by tomorrow evening.'

'Good. I, too, plan to leave right away, but I think the men we have will do till the reinforcements get here.'

'You're not coming back to the palace?'

'No. I need to go to the other forge to oversee those new arrowheads. The last batch was not etched deep enough to hold sufficient poison.'

Vasusena mulled over the observation. 'You really think there will be a war, Devala, like you told that young one back there? I'd say Dharma is getting quite used to a life of idle retirement. Why still talk of war?'

'With all due respect, Vasusena, I said nothing about a war against Dharma. It took us more than five years to set up these forges and a few more to train the men who work in them. But since that has happened, your domains have grown nearly twice in size, have they not? You are next only to your dearest friend Syoddhan in stature and might. Even Jayadrath, I hear, is often referred to as the Vasusena of the west. Surely, it is too early for us to get complacent. I don't expect effusive gratitude, but...'

'It is deserved. Once again, I'm sorry if I offended you.' With a polite nod, Vasusena climbed into the waiting carriage. He waved as it set off in a gentle trundle and then settled back against the cushions, enjoying the cool breeze.

Devala wondered abstractedly how such a genial person could turn into a self-obsessed, arrogant man the instant he set foot in Hastina. Deciding that it was none of his concern, he let his thoughts wander to other things as he continued to watch the small contingent till it was out of sight. After that, Devala made his way back into the forge.

5

SHIKANDIN LET THE TENDER BRANCH FALL BACK INTO PLACE without a sound and stepped further back into the thicket in which he had concealed himself. He stayed within earshot of the forge as he planned his next step, trying to decide between attacking at once and waiting until Devala had left. The primal temptation to avenge himself against Devala had only grown stronger with every passing day of these last years. Still, Shikandin had the patience of a tree. He decided on the second option. Much as he would have liked to kill and gut Devala right there, it made more sense to let him go and then track him to the other forge he had mentioned. That way Shikandin would save valuable time in finding the other workshop and razing it to the ground.

His decision made, Shikandin retreated deeper into the forest till he found a tree with low, overhanging branches. He settled himself under their cover, intending to rest till moonrise. A new weariness had crept into his being, and Shikandin did not understand if it was the natural effect of age or the more subtle but dangerous frustration of fighting what felt like a never-ending battle on his own.

It had been easier in the initial years of Dharma's exile. Devala had begun, quite logically, by trying to rebuild the old forges that had been left in the outer reaches of the Kashi kingdoms, the main ones having been destroyed by Shikandin and Govinda during the imperial conquest. The old forges that remained were already weak and in many cases not easily usable, and it had been a fairly easy task for Shikandin to create problems for Devala without attracting attention to himself. The newer constructions, such as the one not too far away, required more careful planning. It was not that Shikandin was afraid of injury or death. But, if he were caught alive, or if other evidence were presented to link him to these acts, it would not bode well for his father and his siblings. Syoddhan's cronies would insist that this was treachery, a crime that was not only punishable with the traitor's execution but was also adequate justification for annexing the said traitor's territory. That was not a risk Shikandin could take. On pain of death, he would have to keep his involvement in the destruction of these forges, and the other sundry attacks on Devala's men and materials, a secret.

It was a slow, tedious effort. But then so was building forges and workshops. In all, it had settled into a languorous rhythm of creation and destruction that Shikandin had got used to. Feeling reassured, he turned his mind to more trivial thoughts, stirring only when the smell of the forest told him that it was night.

The guard, a capable Anga soldier, neither heard nor saw the attack. In fact, the man died swiftly, his last sentiment one of surprise that a wild animal possessed the ability to strike in such precise strokes to sever a man's neck.

Shikandin rolled the soldier's body under some bushes and went on to his next target. The guards were stationed in a circle around the forge, with an additional sentry constantly on the move, making impeccably timed rounds. It was, Shikandin noted, far too predictable to be effective, and it did not take him very long to bring down the eight guards and the sentry. Within the forge, he had observed, there was just one guard stationed by the door. Still, there remained the possibility that the men working within might offer resistance as well. Shikandin had already spent half the day trying to choose between warning the workers, who were innocent, even unwilling participants, and treating them as the enemy, undoubtedly the safer option. Finally, he made up his mind.

Propping the dead sentry up by the eyehole in the door, Shikandin knocked hard on it. The guard within looked out, exclaimed loudly and made the mistake of releasing the locking mechanism. Before he could realize his mistake, Shikandin had him in an arm-lock and held a dagger to his throat for added effect. The guard offered no resistance as they went down the stairs into the underground cavern that formed the main area of the forge.

The structure had been dug out of the earth and the mud walls had the fragrant moisture of fertile earth that could still yield verdure if allowed to. Shikandin supposed he could get the cavern to collapse in on itself... But then how would he get out? He had much more to do, and dying here was hardly a worthy sacrifice. First things first, he reminded himself, as he walked into the heart of the forge.

'If you don't want this man hurt, get out now!' he ordered the astounded workers within. They did not look very sympathetic toward the guard, which made Shikandin all the more glad of his decision to let them escape. But before he could say another word, the workers were talking animatedly in their own, accented dialect, gesturing to Shikandin and to their own necks. Only then did he realize that the white metal beads he wore blazed with a life of their own by the light of the forge.

One of the workmen stepped forward. 'What do you want with this forge?'

'That's none of your concern. Get out. Now.'

The man moved, as if to comply, but stopped and looked around at his companions. 'We can destroy this for you. We can make sure it will never be of any use to anyone, again.'

Something in his eyes made Shikandin believe him. 'All right,' he said, 'but quietly. No explosions.'

'We are not fools. We know a true Firewright when we see one. Unlike that liar Devala…'

Shikandin started to protest at the declaration, but then decided it would be best to say nothing at all. He nodded, and began to back out through the doorway.

'Wait!' the man commanded. 'Leave the guard behind. He has been especially good to us. We would like to repay the favour.'

At this, the guard began to scream and struggle, leaving no doubt about the nature of his kindness towards the workers. Still, he could not extricate himself from Shikandin's grip. 'Please… Please don't… Please take me with you… or kill me. Please, I beg you.'

In response, Shikandin shoved him roughly to the floor and made his way up the stairs, into the clean air of the night.

He stayed hidden in the forest till well past daybreak and then went back to the site of the forge. All that remained was scattered debris and a small but deep pond that had not been there before. The workmen had used the underwater source that had served to cool and power the forge to submerge it. Shikandin saw their tracks leading away from the place, the footprints telling him that their departure had been slow and celebratory. He picked up a fallen branch and used it to muddle up the signs they had left behind so that they would not be followed. Then he set out for home.

As tired as Shikandin was, he could not help but smile as he led his horse out of the dark thicket and into the large glade that ran all the way up to the banks of a gushing stream. Right at the river's edge was the place he had called home for the last many years. Truly, it was home to him more than Kampilya had ever been. The village consisted of a simple cluster of hutments, a stone-lined pond that was constantly replenished with fresh water from the river and a small patch of cultivated land. In itself the settlement meant nothing and if ever one asked its inhabitants where they lived, they would name their tribe as their home. No matter how many times they moved, Shikandin found that its essence always remained the same. It was home, and he belonged there.

A distant shout went up as the children of the village noticed him. They stopped their play and ran up to greet him. Shikandin let his grin widen at the sight of the bedraggled bunch. For all his pain and weariness, he had not forgotten to pick fruits and berries for them. The youngest of the crowd, a girl, squealed as he picked her up, swung her around and placed her in the saddle. Others, too, began clamouring for a ride and he obliged, lifting two more of the smallest ones on to his horse's back. The older children ran around him, asking questions and telling him news of the village in the scattered and unpredictable way that he found so delightful. As a group, they made their way towards the village.

Shikandin had hardly stepped through the gate in the low reed fence that ran around the landward side of the village when a young man came up to him. They exchanged no words, but Shikandin felt better just looking at the strapping young fellow. He let the youth take the reins of his horse and then reached out to pull a bundle off the saddle.

'Here. As promised.' He handed the bundle of berries to the eagerly waiting children before making his way deeper into the village.

Men and women called out to him as he passed by. A few enquired casually whether he had had a successful expedition, his activities as natural to them as any other task he might have been on. He answered them in brief but gave no details.

The hut that was in a sense his was situated close to the river. It was one in a cluster of four, each with its main doorway facing in a different direction. This not only ensured privacy but also made it easier for the inhabitants to gather to the settlement's defence when attacked. For all their rustic simplicity, Shikandin knew these forest dwellers to be brave warriors and clever craftsmen. He found the meticulous organization of the settlement no less impressive than any of Aryavarta's greatest cities. Every detail had been thought through and arranged for, from stone hearths that let the smoke quickly billow out of every hut to well-placed washing areas that allowed waste water to drain into the ground instead of flowing directly back into the river. What made it all the more becoming to him was the complete humility with which these men and women held their knowledge, believing it was a sacred trust they were honoured to keep.

Shikandin peered into the empty hut and let out a tired sigh. He began pulling off his armour, grunting softly at the mix of pain and relief that coursed through his limbs. He was not hurt, but every muscle in his body felt sore.

'You're getting too old for this.'

He did not turn at the familiar voice but drew in a deep breath instead, relishing the smell of jasmine that had been hers right from his youth.

'I'd show you exactly what this old man is capable of,' he teased, 'except…'

'Except?' The woman set down the pot of water that she had been carrying and came to stand facing Shikandin.

'Where's Kshatradharman?' Shikandin asked.

'Playing. That's what children his age do. Didn't you see him on your way in? In that case, he's probably wandered off into the forest… He's started doing that a lot these days.'

'He's growing up.'

'But you don't grow old, do you?'

183

In response, Shikandin reached out to cup her face in one of his dirt- and blood-stained hands. She did not flinch, but leant into his touch. It made him feel healed and clean. 'Guhyaka ...' he said her name softly and pulled her close. Not all aging was bad, he noted, enjoying how her body had changed since he had first met her. He had been barely seventeen and she around the same. She had altered his life in ways he had not understood for a long time, yet, when he had come back to her after so many years he had found her no different. The hard life of a forest-dweller meant that she was still slender and her limbs taut. But her hair now held much grey and her body had been agreeably rounded by childbirth. At that thought Shikandin placed a hand on her waist, letting it slide down to her wide hips.

She giggled, childlike, and stepped back into the darkness of the hut, pulling Shikandin in with her. He drew the heavy hemp curtain over the door as he stepped in.

Shikandin woke up with a start. He could not remember what he had been dreaming about, but it had not been pleasant. He reached out for Guhyaka's familiar body next to him. She was not there. He sat up on the reed mat that was their bed and listened in the darkness.

'Should we wake him up? He'll want to go.'

Shikandin recognized the young man's voice. He got up, wrapped on his lower robe and stepped out of the inner room of the hutment into a small living space. 'Go where?'

The young man turned. 'To the shrine. It's a full moon tonight.'

'What ... has the sun set?'

'It will shortly.'

'Then I'd better have a bath, and quick.'

Guhyaka stepped up to help Shikandin unbraid his long, matted hair.

'I'll go see to the hot water,' the young man said as he left the hut.

Shikandin said, 'It's time we find him a wife, since he can't seem to manage that task on his own.'

'Which is hardly a shock, considering he is your son ... He doesn't realize that most of the young girls in the ten tribes around us have their hearts set on him and that he's been consistent in breaking them all.'

'Can you ever forgive me, Guhyaka?'

'For what?'

'For breaking your heart, my love. I should never have left you.'

'You didn't have a choice, Shikandin. Besides, it was a long time ago. I know why you left. I know why you came back. I have no complaints against either decision. You did what you had to. I understand that. *He* understands that.'

It had been a bittersweet moment for Shikandin to come back to Guhyaka after many years to find that she had a child. He had not asked her, even once, whether Uttamaujas was his or not. He simply had not cared. Guhyaka was his. In his heart, he knew she had always been his, and he hers, though neither a rite nor a word had bound them together. In the same vein, as far as he was concerned, he was the boy's father. As Uttamaujas had grown into youth, his resemblance to Shikandin had become more apparent. Now, the young man – barely a couple of years younger than Yudhamanyu – stood as tall as his father and shared his green-brown eyes. Uttamaujas wore his hair shorter and it tended to curl a little, like Guhyaka's. If ever he grew it enough to wear it in braids, as Shikandin did, age would be the only factor telling the two men apart at first glance. By contrast, Kshatradharman, who was barely nine, took after his mother, though the entire village proudly declared that he had his father's brave heart, as did his brother.

Guhyaka said, 'He wants to go with you, you know... On your... expeditions.'

Shikandin shook his head. 'It's too dangerous.'

'You trained him, Shikandin. Uttamaujas is a good fighter.'

'He is. But I can't risk it, Guhyaka. If anything were to happen to him or Kshatradharman... or to you...'

'It would break your heart... as it would break mine if anything were to happen to you,' Guhyaka pointed out. 'Yet, this is what we must do, Shikandin. You know that. Come now, it will be moonrise soon.'

Shikandin sighed and made his way out of the hut and to the

bathing area behind it. He did not fail to notice that Uttamaujas had already cleaned his cast-off armour and polished it till the metal shone.

Moonrise brought the forest alive in a medley of light, shadow, sound and smell. Shikandin walked barefoot on the mossy ground, Guhyaka on one side of him, Uttamaujas and Kshatradharman on the other. Around them, other villagers walked in silence or in hushed conversation with their own families, cherishing the companionship of loved ones. Shikandin felt one amongst them in many ways. In fact, he had traded his usual robes for the knee-length sheath that the men of the tribe wore on such occasions, and he had allowed Guhyaka to wrap many strings of beads around his wrists, each one with a prayer for his life and well-being. He turned to her to find that she was looking at him with unrestrained affection. On impulse, she reached up to run her fingers along the wrinkles around his eyes and trace the line of his strong, firm jaw.

Shikandin bit lightly at her finger and she pulled it back with an embarrassed look at Uttamaujas, who pretended he hadn't noticed.

The moment filled Shikandin with peace and guilt. A part of him was glad to be here, away from the larger world, from the wounded realm that was Aryavarta, and his own, scarred life as a prince. Yet, he felt guilty that he could find peace and happiness when Panchali was suffering as she was, that he could think of beginning a new life when so many old bonds and duties remained to be fulfilled. But how could he turn away from Guhyaka, who had accepted him as he was, without question; from Uttamaujas, who had treated him with the love and respect that Yudhamanyu had never shown; and from Kshtradharman, who had given him a glimpse of the innocence and childhood he'd never known.

Shikandin pushed all such thoughts out of his mind as ahead of them a small stone shrine gleamed in the moonlight. His hand went, in an instinctive move, to the Wright-metal beads around his neck. He felt that every man, woman and child in the village was looking at him, but he knew it was just imagination. With an effort, he brought his hand down, forcing it to fall at his side.

One by one the villagers went down on their knees before the stone shrine, their eyes closed and heads bowed to the ground in prayer. All except Shikandin. He knelt down with the others, but his eyes remained on the single pillar. Its surface still bore the dark scars of fire. Uttamaujas had been right, Shikandin had not wanted to miss this gathering. It was the only time he could stand in front of the shrine without wanting to break into tears, without hearing the screams of pain from the past. It was the only time he dared look upon the spirit within the stone and ask for forgiveness for all that had happened and all that he had failed to do.

It began to rain. One by one, the villagers made their way back to the settlement, those most content with their lives the first ones to leave and seek the dry sanctuary of their hutments. Shikandin and his family were the last to leave, but it was not for lack of happiness. They walked back in silence, uncaring of the rain. Shikandin hoisted a sleepy Kshatradharman on to his shoulders and wrapped an arm each around Guhyaka and Uttamaujas, who gave him an indulgent smile, as though he knew he were old enough to protest against the excessively paternal gesture but cared for his father enough to allow the transgression.

That night, Shikandin slept with the contentment of a man who had everything to lose and knew it. His last waking thought was of his sister.

6

'AAH! I HATE IT WHEN THAT HAPPENS,' PARTHA SAID, SPITTING vehemently on the mossy forest floor.

Bhim snorted, partly amused and partly in derision, and continued to skin the dead deer with relative ease. 'The greatest archer in all Aryavarta, they call you, and you can't skin your kill without getting blood and bile in your mouth. Stop pulling at the hide, muhira, you need to let it slide off!'

'I'm an archer, not a butcher, Bhim. I don't care how long I do this, I'll never get used to it.'·

The statement brought on an unintended silence as both brothers thought of a conversation that had begun on many occasions, but had not yet been concluded. They worked together in silence until where there had been a deer there was now meat, ready to be cooked. They took a bath in the pond nearby before sitting down under the shade of a tree, far enough from the smell of raw flesh.

Partha spoke first, 'He must have a plan.'

'What makes you say so?'

'Govinda Shauri always has a plan!'

'Doesn't the fact that he has made no move tell you that he has no plan...that he has failed? It's over, Partha!'

Partha smiled. 'What is faith, Bhim?'

'You tell me.'

'It is believing in a man who has lost faith in himself. I know that even if I were to ever lose my will, my courage, Govinda would never lose faith in me – his faith in anyone, in humanity. That faith has kept him going, and it keeps him alive still. But he has lost faith in himself and so he can do nothing. He doesn't trust himself, so he refuses to act. There is no plan. This is what it is, what it has been for years now. *He* is our ruler.'

'Syoddhan?'

'Why not? You have to admit he is doing an admirable task of running the empire, even though he has not taken on the title of Emperor. He can't even impose edicts, but he still gets the other vassals to do what is needed by sheer force of reason and diplomacy. Of course, the price he pays for that is allowing the militarization of all of Aryavarta, but frankly I don't see a problem in that. We are safer than before. We are more prosperous than before. And no one knows that better than us – common people as we now are. He's good. He's really very good.'

'Maybe that's why Govinda has done nothing. He knows this is best.'

'Hah! For all your doubts, you too want to believe this is yet another of Govinda Shauri's complicated plans, don't you?'

'You have your way of keeping faith in him; I have mine.'

Partha did not argue the point. Bhim, he knew, was right. This was a matter of faith and there was no single way to keep it. Just as there was no right way. For all they knew, Govinda was gone, truly gone.

Yet again, Bhim broke the contemplative silence. 'Did...did you ever think of him as a brother, Partha?'

'Govinda?'

'Syoddhan.'

'Not really. I wonder why... He's older than the both of us and it should have been natural, I suppose, to treat him the way we've always treated Dharma. I don't know why we never did. You were with him at Kashi, Bhim. You trained under Balabadra at the same time as he did. Surely you'd know him better.'

Bhim hesitated. 'Can I be honest? I'm not sure I've quite admitted this even to myself, but I found Syoddhan easy to get along with. I guess the only thing I didn't like is that whenever there were others around, especially one of his brothers, he used to pretend that this so-called rivalry between us was a big thing. But I've spent enough time in relative solitude with him to know he's not like that at all. I'm not saying I like him – his behaviour is, in my estimation, hypocrisy. I think I've just learned to dislike him less since...since I've realized that I may not have been too different. Everything I thought and felt about Syoddhan and his brothers was what I had learnt to believe, as Dharma's brother and Pandu Kauravya's son. Never did I question why things were that way, and whether it was right.'

'I think that's a mistake all of us have made, but...' Partha trailed off and waved a hand in welcome as Nakul and Sadev walked out through the foliage on the far side of the pond and made their way to where Partha and Bhim were seated.

'Fruit?' Nakul asked. He tossed a red-orange mango to each of them before biting with relish into the juicy pulp of a third.

'I thought you were supposed to be shooting down jungle fowl,' Partha said, frowning at the twins with all the authority of an elder brother.

'Nah!' Nakul said. 'We found this particularly inviting mango tree. And we had to pick the herbs Bhim wanted to flavour the meat with. Don't worry...I'm sure Panchali will shoot down enough fowl for you.'

Bhim laughed. 'You make me feel like we haven't aged a day, Nakul. You still act like a teenager.'

'I didn't know there was a particularly grown-up way of eating fruit, brother.'

'There he goes again with that sharp tongue of his. I tell you, some things never change.'

'It's in our blood. Grand-uncle Bhisma has looked exactly the same for the last forty-odd years that I've seen him. Unless he's changed in these past eleven … no, twelve, is it not … years?'

'I doubt it!' Partha said, a dash of acrimony creeping into his voice. He found it impossible to think of Bhisma without thinking of the dice game and all that had been said and done.

'Twelve years … We say that like it's nothing.'

'It was nothing when we built the empire. That took us nearly twelve years too, if you remember. Days, months and years, moving forward, fighting, negotiating, planning and executing. Yet we didn't begrudge a single day or a single muhurtta of that time. I did not see my son for those years, nor did most of you see your children. It didn't hurt then, but it does now. I wonder why.'

'Fighting and conquest are easier,' Sadev said, speaking for the first time. 'What we are doing now, this is the difficult part.'

'Why do you say that, Sadev?'

'Because we don't know what it is we are really doing, brothers. Or do you? Tell me, is this waiting? If so, whom are we waiting for? Is this hiding? Who are we hiding from? Or is this is our way of living, and I certainly hope it isn't because I'm beginning to think death is better than this meaningless existence. Ten years? Twelve? At times, it feels like just ten days have passed, I find myself inexplicably happy, and a part of me wishes against all reason that life could be this way forever. But there are other times when the pain and rage make me want to … Never mind!' He passed the back of his hand over his eyes, wiping the dark thought away. 'We want a meaning to it, Partha. If you'd died during the campaign, would you have regretted it?'

Partha shook his head, resolute. 'Never! I'd have been proud to die in a greater cause.'

'And what cause was that?'

'Why, the empire. Our brother's empire.' No sooner had the words left his mouth than he came to terms with what he had known all along. Partha sighed and let his head fall back to rest against the rough bark of the tree behind him. He closed his eyes and tried to empty his mind, but found it difficult to do so. Things had changed, and he hated that they had changed.

Bhim said, 'Maybe it's not just an empire or a kingdom, or even our honour we've lost. We've lost faith; we've lost our belief in the one thing that made us who we were. We've lost faith in Dharma Yudhisthir. Now it seems there's nothing left to fight for.'

'It wasn't just Dharma we fought for then,' Partha argued. 'We fought because we believed in the dream of a united empire, and that dream was not Dharma's. It was Govinda's.'

Nakul countered, 'And where is he now? At the end of it all it turns out that he was the least powerful and the least principled. Where has he gone? If he believed in that dream so much, why didn't he stand up to Dharma and say, "Well you good-for-nothing Emperor, you've pretty much thrown away everything I gave you so why don't you just sit in this hermitage and play with your silly notions of morality while I go ahead and be the man you should have been…" I'm sorry…' he added, noticing his brothers' stunned expressions. 'I'm sorry. But really, I wish someone had said that to Dharma. I wish I had said it… It's taken me so long to even put it into words.' Throwing the pip he held in his hand into the lake with as much vehemence as he could muster, Nakul began striding around the clearing, trying to work off his ire. His brothers watched, pensive.

It was Sadev who said, 'Did you ever wonder what *she* fought for… and fights for still?' He had no need to use her name. They all knew whom he spoke of.

'Every single day,' Bhim replied even as Partha nodded.

'Perhaps it's time we fought for the same reason, brothers. Perhaps it's time we fought for ourselves, for what we know to be right.'

'The drama is all very fine, Sadev,' Nakul interjected. 'But what can we do? And how does one decide what is right?'

Sadev did not reply, but held up a cautionary hand, squinting his eyes at the thicket behind him. 'Someone's coming.'

The four brothers ceased conversation at once and listened. The sound came again, unmistakeable – the irreverent rustle of leaves that suggested that not only was someone approaching fast, but also that he or she did not care to hide it. Sadev's hand moved towards his sword, as did Nakul's. Partha and Bhim continued to remain seated, but their stance grew more alert as the rustling drew nearer. When their would-be aggressor burst through the foliage, it was difficult for all four of them not to break into laughter.

A small boy, hardly six years of age, his ochre robes and shaved head still bearing the sheen of newness, charged into the clearing at a run. The four brothers recognized him as the youngest and most recent induction into the group of acolytes at Vyasa Markand's hermitage.

The boy came to a stop, and doubled over, gasping, 'Horses... men... forest...' Then he ran off even faster than he had come, partly because he was too overawed to stay in the presence of the four warriors, but mostly because he wanted to boast to his fellow students about being just feet away from their distinguished neighbours and, yes, they were every bit as imposing as they had appeared from a distance. His excitement lightened the air for a short while and Bhim chuckled out loud while his brothers smiled. But the moment passed.

'The Vyasa's guests? Or have they come to see us?' Sadev said.

Partha stood and reached down to give Bhim a hand. 'Only one way to find out. Let's head to the hermitage. The last I saw, Dharma was there, deep in discussion with the Vyasa.'

It was Nakul who said, innocuously enough, 'Where's Panchali?'

7

PANCHALI FROZE AS SHE WAS – ON TIPTOE, FINGERS STILL RESTING gently on the fruit that hung from a branch overhead. She had been about to pluck it when the sensation hit her; the feeling that her skin was crawling, but on the inside, as though her flesh had come to life and sought to break free of her body, which was strangling it from within. Only once before had she felt this way, the discomfort acutely different from the cold instinct of being watched or hunted that her brothers had taught her to recognize and trust. This was disgust, the sense of being made of all that was repulsive and unclean. This was how she had felt at Hastina, on the day of the dice game.

Letting go of the fruit, Panchali dropped to her haunches, the need to conceal herself taking over completely. She forced herself to breathe, inhaling deeply to calm herself, to find the part of her that had been taught to remain unafraid and strong, even in the face of death. But she could not. For it was not death that she feared. From the day she and the five brothers had been on what Dharma proudly referred to as their exile, she had been unable to sleep without nightmares, terrifying visions that ended in her waking up screaming. She never remembered them and could not understand why they continued, even though she was safe. Dharma's brothers had taken to staying awake by turns at night, outside the hut she and the former emperor shared. Dharma himself had nothing for her but blame. All that had happened was her fault. She had refused to heed his advice. She had refused to beg for mercy. She should have, Dharma insisted, known better.

Finally, lonely, weary and at her wits' end, Panchali had confessed her feelings to Shikandin. 'I am not a child, and I do not remember what I believed when I was one. But there are times when I feel like … like the darkness of the earth and of Patala – the underworld – have become one, and there are demons crawling out of that forsaken pit. They are coming for me, Shikandin. Those demons are hunting me down.'

Her brother had understood only too well. 'It's not just because of what happened, Panchali. It's because of what has changed.'

'What has changed?'

'Your world. Your view of it. Your belief in it. The things you had to endure – you knew them as things that happened to other people, things that you heard of, felt horrified about and moved on from. The fact that it *could not* happen to *you* was the only thing that justified life as you knew it; justified the way the world was. But not anymore,

Panchali. Not anymore. Nothing about this world feels right anymore and that, my dearest, is the most frightening thought of all.'

Despite her own terrified realizations, she had said, 'Have you ever known such fear, Shikandin?'

He didn't reply immediately, but played with the blade of grass in his hand. After a while he said, 'Once you've seen the darkness inside human beings, once you've seen what we … those around us, those we may have known for years, become capable of in a moment of bleakness, it is impossible not to be afraid. It's not just women who are hurt that way. Worse things have happened in Panchala's dungeons than blinding or starvation.' After a brief pause, he had added, 'I once knew a woman who used similar words as you, Panchali. She too spoke of demons from Patala, who crawl out of their pit when darkness falls. She said what frightened her the most was not that the creatures would feed on her flesh, but that they would ravage her soul, mark her and scar her forever because to do so was to shame and scar all those who loved her, and so constantly remind them who was more powerful.'

'Who was she?'

To that question, Shikandin had not replied. And he had not come to see her ever since. Rumours of his death came in from Kampilya, as did one last message from Dhrstyadymn, who apologized for not being with her in her need. And then she had been left alone, in this world that was no longer her own, to fear a fate worse than death.

Panchali focused her thoughts on her brothers, on their smiling faces, and tried to will courage back into her body. Slowly, she reached for the sword she wore on her back only to realize she was trembling so badly that she could not draw the weapon. Her breath came in ragged gasps, and she was crying, whimpering like a child, for the only emotion that now stayed was the one she had learnt over these past years: Shame. Shame that she was a woman, a weak and frail object that needed protecting and so served as a man's weakness, a thing, an object – a plaything in fact. *She should have known better.*

'Tsk, tsk….' A man stepped out from behind the trees, followed by another and then many more.

Panchali did not dare look up or meet their gaze. She flinched when the man bent down and cupped her face in his fingers but was far too terrified to scream.

'A beautiful woman like you should never have to cry this way, Panchali. You should never have to suffer like this. You deserve to lie naked on the finest silk sheets and have fragrant oils rubbed into your lovely skin and be pleasured by the best of men. Instead, you live here, in the forests, with five ... Well, I don't suppose I can call them men now, can I?'

At that comment the entire group burst out laughing. Panchali wished only to curl herself up to mimic the safety of the womb, but the man would not let her. Instead, he forced his palm underneath her chin and lifted it upwards to get her to her feet. 'Oh, I can imagine, Panchali, how *unsatisfied* you must be ... But if you came with me, you'd be a queen in my bed ... The great Jayadrath's queen. And you would not need to settle for me alone, you know. My sons are young, strong men, and they'd be happy to give you more ... after I'm done with you ... every day. Isn't that so boys?'

Something in his voice made Panchali look up for the first time. She saw that it was indeed Jayadrath, whom she recognized from his many visits to Hastina at the time she had lived there, as well as his sons, who were now grown men. At least two of them were still young enough to be her children, yet the look in their eyes was hardly filial. She saw the same look on the faces of the rest – sundry courtiers, guards and soldiers.

Demons. Shame. Primal instinct coursed through Panchali. Before Jayadrath or any of the others could react, she stepped away with a jerk and set off at a run.

'Get her!' Jayadrath commanded, at which his soldiers went after her on foot. He and his sons remained as they were, laughing, exchanging lewd comments about how exciting it was to watch a woman run.

The words rang in Panchali's ears as she raced through the undergrowth, trying to will her senses back into order to craft an escape route. *When the women ran. Demons from Patala.*

Had she not known? Was this how it always was? During the

imperial conquest, had Partha and Bhim laughed while their soldiers had ravaged women and brutalized men? Had Nakul and Sadev raped women old enough to be their mothers and young enough to be their daughters? And her brothers? And Govinda? If that was the reality of the world around them, then how had she not seen, not known all these years?

Images rushed through her head as her feet pounded on with increasing force. The days she had ridden through fields and forests, believing that men and women bowed their heads out of love and adoration for the princess of Panchala? Was that which she had taken for respect, merely fear; was it merely what was left when self-esteem was brutally removed? *Is that all we were as the rulers of this land?* Darkness pressed in from all sides, and the world shrank, shrivelled into nothingness even in the full light of day, because it knew it could no longer exist. Jayadrath's soldiers closed in from behind.

A loud whinny and a crashing sound came through the undergrowth. Panchali slowed down, startled, and it was just as well. A war chariot drew up ahead, effectively cutting off her escape. She stumbled, and the soldiers were on her.

'Hold her down!' Jayadrath instructed as he leapt off his chariot. His eldest son, Suratha, was with him; the others soon arrived riding horses of their own. 'I said, hold her down. Oh, one fiery bitch you are, aren't you, Panchali?'

Panchali struggled and kicked, but to no avail. One of the soldiers held her arms down over her head, while two others pinned down a leg each. Jayadrath laughed and knelt down by her head, while Suratha began stripping off his armour, piece by piece, and handed it to another man nearby.

'Don't take too long now,' one of his brothers cautioned. 'Leave time for us to take our turn. And then we need to find Dharma and kill him. Who knew we'd come upon such an amusing distraction in the forest?'

'Oh no, my son!' Jayadrath said. 'This is not just a distraction. This is important. We will kill Dharma Yudhisthir, yes, but it is what we will do to the lovely *Empress* here that will strike terror in the hearts of men and women, king and commoner, everyone, everywhere. Her screams will ring loud and long in their ears and each time someone thinks to challenge us, our might, this memory of what we did to her shall change their minds. Death is only so powerful, my boy. If you want to be a ruler, you must know how to make them fear, really fear you. Isn't that right, Panchali... *Empress of Aryavarta*?'

Panchali stiffened at his words and began to struggle again as a hand fell on her robes. It was the prince, now naked of his armour and clothing. The leer on his face sent rage coursing though her and she found a little bit of the courage that had failed her all the while. As the prince began to lower himself on to her, she wrested her right leg free of the guards grip, brought her knee up and drove it hard into Suratha's groin. He doubled over in agony.

'Hah!' Panchali let out a cry of satisfaction, but it was in vain.

'Bitch!' Suratha slapped her, over and over, the force of his strokes knocking her head from side to side. Huge bruises formed on each of her cheeks and she began to bleed from the mouth. Still not satisfied, the prince stood, cursing against his pain, and began to kick her in the stomach and on her head. Panchali let out a gluttural scream as the back of her head struck the rocky ground. She stopped struggling as her vision blurred and spun in eddies of colour, before turning to black oblivion.

8

'EMPTY YOURSELF. SEE THAT YOUR MIND IS NOT YOU, THAT THIS body is not you ...'

Dharma Yudhisthir drew in a deep breath, and complied as best as he could. Vyasa Markand was a patient, pious man, and Dharma was happy to be under his instruction, but having Dhaumya around unnerved him.

'Let go of judgement...'

Let go of judgement, his mind countered. *Then how will one know right from wrong? And if one cannot, then would there be any meaning left to life?*

'...of what you think of others, and of what they think of you...'

Then how can one decide the greater good? How can one define what was righteous and just?

Dharma opened his eyes. 'Acharya...'

Markand, a moderately plump, good-natured old man, with a round face, was all attention. 'Yes, my son?'

'Acharya, I do not understand. Is it not right and wrong that define who we are? How can we embrace righteousness if there is no higher morality, a divine law against which we judge all our actions?'

Dhaumya interrupted, unusually scathing, 'I thought you believe morality to be relative? Why then this search for absolutes, *my prince?*'

Dharma frowned. He was used to Dhaumya's regression to his old, and hence less alienable title, but the tone in his voice was new. 'It is not my place to believe, Acharya. It is my place to follow what the gods prescribe. I ask the question in all sincerity.'

Unaware of the tension between the two, Markand continued, in his genial way, 'And a good question it is, particularly for one whose name is Dharma: righteousness. And it arises because you contemplate a situation where morality and Divine Order are against each other ... else, by rational argument, that which is natural law must always be moral, isn't it?'

'Such a situation cannot exist?'

'Alas, such situations do come to pass, particularly when the forces of evil are at play. But then, when the world as we know it is suspect, it is no longer a matter for us men but a matter for the gods. It is for them to descend – to destroy evil and restore Divine Order, and make law and morality the same.'

'And if it should be time for morality to change?' The query came from Dhaumya.

'Then the gods will change it. They will recreate Divine Order as is appropriate, as they have done in each age. Barely one yuga ago, morality required that we speak the truth and that it must be the whole truth. In this age truth simply means the absence of falsehood. It is neither complete nor unambiguous.'

Dharma said, 'And so morality is both subjective and absolute! Grandsire Bhisma was right.'

Markand nodded. 'The Grandsire is a wise man. As are you, Dharma Yudhisthir.'

The compliment pleased Dharma and he was about to break into a wide grin, but instead set his face into an expression of placid composure as his brothers approached.

Bhim began the conversation without prelude. 'Have you seen Panchali?'

Dharma replied, 'She was hunting, was she not? Why, what happened?'

'One of the disciples reported horses and men, in the forests.' Bhim turned to Markand, 'Do you have visitors, Acharya?'

'No, and I am expecting none. This is most strange.'

'We have to find her,' Dhaumya rose to his feet at once. 'I'll come with you.'

Bhim nodded. The others looked eager to begin the search. Dharma, however, remained seated. 'Come back here with her, when you find her,' he casually instructed. 'I would love for her to hear the Acharya's explanations on morality and its imperative. She will surely find it fascinating.'

Bhim thought he heard Sadev mutter under his breath, but was not sure. It could have been, he reasoned, just the wind.

Nevertheless, Dharma said, 'On second thoughts, I'll come with you.'

In retrospect, Dharma could see that it was destiny. He was meant to go in search of Panchali. He was meant to be there when Nakul, who was gone ahead as a scout, came back filled with rage and incoherent ramblings about Panchali and what Jayadrath and his men were doing to her. He had been needed, to stop his brothers from running headlong into danger, instead, suggesting kindly but imperiously that an ambush was better – a fact which Sadev grudgingly admitted and Partha endorsed. And now Dharma knew that he had been destined to what lay ahead, the ultimate test of who he was, as a man, a righteous man. But first there was Panchali.

'That's it. They're in position. Come on,' Partha whispered, as the call of a jungle fowl came through the air. 'Nakul said there are about twenty of them. Taking them down should be no problem if we have the element of surprise to our advantage, but we need to make sure they don't have time to react and hurt Panchali or hold her hostage. So get to her, and get her out of there, Agraja. Get your wife out of there.'

It struck Dharma that he ought to find it offensive that his brother was commanding him, but he reminded himself to make allowances for the stressful nature of the situation, and Partha's genuine zeal to rescue Panchali. 'All right, Partha,' he said.

Another bird cry came through the air. 'Go!' Partha urged and set off at a run, an arrow notched to his bowstring.

Dharma drew his sword and followed close behind, moving to his left so as to circle in better on their quarry. He stumbled out from behind a small thicket into a clearing that was just as Nakul had described it. Already, Partha had brought down four men, including the naked man hovering over the prone figure that Dharma realized, with a shock, was Panchali. More men fell, caught in the arrow-fire from all directions as Bhim, Sadev and Nakul closed in.

Just as Partha had warned, Jayadrath went for Panchali. He tried to swing her inert form over his shoulder and retreat, but before either he or Dharma could do anything further, a wide-eyed figure clad in the ochre robes of a scholar jumped out of the foliage with a bloodcurdling yell that was completely uncharacteristic of his kind. 'Let her go!' Dhaumya commanded. 'Let her go before I curse you and seven generations of your ancestors. Let her go!'

The declaration failed to have the desired impact in full, but the unexpected move served its own purpose. Jayadrath stood as he was long enough for Dharma to reach him.

'Now, Jayadrath! Let her go!' Dharma pointed his sword at the king for emphasis.

Jayadrath took a look around him. One of his sons was dead. About fifteen of his soldiers and courtiers were down. The others were nowhere to be seen. With a frown, Jayadrath lowered Panchali and let her fall to the forest floor with a thud. The impact seemed to bring her to her senses, for she moaned and her closed eyes twitched. Immediately, Dhaumya was at her side.

'You bastard! You animal!' An enraged Bhim advanced on Jayadrath, who responded by pulling his sword out of its scabbard.

'No, Bhim!' the injunction came from Dharma. 'Don't! He is, after all, Dussala's husband, and she's our sister. Just because he does not know the meaning of nobility and respect, we should not forget who we are.'

'She's Syoddhan's sister, not *ours*!'

'Bhim!'

'But, Agraja...' Partha stepped forward.

Dharma ignored him and turned to Jayadrath. 'I will let you leave here alive, Jayadrath, so that you may reflect on how sinful, how depraved your activities have been. If a lesser man had committed these heinous acts, then by morality and law he would be dead. But you are a kinsman and a king, you are Arya... I trust that you will see the error of your ways. Go now, and remember forever that you owe your life, not to me but to the principles of righteousness and Divine Order, our Arya way of life that compels me to show you mercy. Go!'

No one was more surprised by the sudden declaration than Jayadrath. He still did not sheath his drawn sword, but began edging towards one of the horses, tethered to a shrub. The five brothers kept their eyes on him till he was gone. They turned around to find Panchali, revived, watching in silence.

'How could you let him go?' Bhim was beyond himself. 'We should have gutted him alive. And that son of his, the one who...' He glanced at Panchali, not daring to ask the question whether they had been in time, or not. Her eyes answered, telling him that it did not make any difference, for something inside her had been destroyed anyway, that it was but part of an ongoing horror that had begun many, many years ago.

Out loud she said, 'Dharma did the right thing, Bhim. Killing Jayadrath would have put us in a difficult position. All of Aryavarta would have held us accountable for his death. By leaving him alive, the problem is now his. He cannot speak of what happened here without explaining what he was doing here in the first place, and that he cannot disclose. Dharma did the right thing...though not for reasons I find right.'

Dharma beamed. His eyes held unfettered affection for Panchali, but it was to Dhaumya he addressed his words. 'See, Acharya. Morality is indeed a subtle thing, both subjective and absolute at the same time. But what is important is that we never act against it.'

No one cared to counter his statement, and Dharma took their silence for enlightened acceptance. He stepped forward. 'Come, Panchali, let me carry you back.'

She shook her head. 'It's all right. I'm fine. I can walk.'

Dharma shrugged his shoulders as if to say 'as you wish', and began making his way back towards the hermitage. His brothers fell in behind him, Bhim the last to follow.

Dhaumya helped Panchali to her feet, trying hard to keep the many things he wanted to say and ask within him. Finally, he settled on a topic that he hoped was trivial enough to be neutral. 'The brothers said one of the disciples told them about Jayadrath and his men. How would a child know…?'

'Because I've taught them to be on the lookout, Acharya. I teach the youngest and newest ones every year.'

'For how long have you been doing this?'

'Ever since we've been here.'

'What are they watching out for, Panchali? Who was it you were expecting? Enemies such as these…? Or are you waiting for a friend? Because if you are…' Dhaumya faltered. 'My dear child, if you are waiting for him to come, he won't. He won't. Don't you see? He has lost all hope. It is useless to wait for him.'

Panchali looked up into Dhaumya's face. It looked familiar through the blur of her tears, not as the face of one she had seen all these years but a memory she had almost forgotten. She thought she had heard him tell her stories that had made her laugh but had also made her ask questions. There had been one tale, in particular, about a princess in a desert, and a vulture. No, that story had been told by an older man, a much older man she could not identify, though his image flickered in her mind's eye. She tried to remember, but it only brought the darkness spinning down again to hit her hard, and she gave up.

'Panchali?'

'It doesn't matter, Acharya… Govinda Shauri *is* hope.'

202

9

'GOVINDA!' THE NAME ESCAPED HER LIPS IN A GASP, HER BODY taut with ecstasy, fingers digging into a strong, sweat-stained back.

Govinda Shauri smiled, but it was merely a curve of his lips. His eyes remained as they had been for twelve years now, like a mighty fort gone to ruin: haunted when empty, pitiable when filled.

'Govinda!' the woman cried out again, clutching at his shoulders as if by doing so she could bring their naked forms any closer. Govinda closed his eyes and let his body surrender to pleasure, finding relief not in his being's release but in the sharp ache it left behind in his heart. All joy was torment, all desire was punishment and all pain was penance. Yet, he felt no closer to forgiveness.

Sitting up as the whirl of sensations faded, leaving behind nothing but the dull throb of reality, Govinda looked out of the window at his beloved city. Dwaraka, the western jewel of Aryavarta, shone with muted grace by the light of the moon. It was late. All lights except those that burnt incessant – flares that lit the city gates and its roads, and the huge torch that blazed at the mouth of the port as a warning to approaching ships – had been put out for the night as the city's residents slept. The fateful events that had shaken their lives over a decade ago were now a part of a past that would not fade with time, partly because the people of Dwaraka had changed since and partly because the empire around them had transformed. All lights but Govinda's own. Darkness had always soothed him and so he denied himself of it. Now, lights always shone in the tallest turret of Dwaraka, which had been home to Govinda Shauri since the day the city had been built.

That he was still allowed to live in it was an act of kindness and residual gratitude. In truth, it was a luxurious imprisonment, partly determined by the Council of Representatives that governed the Federation of Yadu Nations, and partly assumed by Govinda himself. No nation in Aryavarta could have a Firewright for its Commander, or even as one of its leaders, and after Dharma Yudhisthir's public denouncement that was what Govinda undoubtedly was and unequivocally identified as.

In a perverse way, Govinda felt relieved. He finally had an identity, an allegiance. He had not bothered to counter or question the assertion, facing without demur the trial that the council had put him through.

Yes, he was a Firewright.

No, he had not trained any others.

No, his children did not know.

No, his brother had not known either, but had suspected as much and counselled him to keep his loyalties where they ought to lie.

When asked whether Dwaraka had been built by Firewrights, Govinda had simply said, 'No.' His inquisitors had, very wisely, refrained from asking whether any Firewrights had been involved in designing, planning and overseeing the building of the city. No doubt they had been all the more glad of it in the decade since as the many nations of Aryavarta raced to build their arsenals and armies.

Thus satisfied, the Council had concluded the trial by asking Govinda whether he intended to act as a Firewright in times to come. He had replied, 'I do not intend to.' With that the Council had divested him of his post as Commander of Dwaraka's forces and left him to his own devices, though he knew his every move would be supervised.

Govinda had since lost track of when his imprisonment had been handed down as a sentence. To him, it was self-imposed; a punishment he deserved. He stayed in his chambers, drinking, reading and writing. If he emerged from his rooms, it was to visit his horses. Occasionally, he would ride along the seashore, always staying within sight of Dwaraka's watch tower, so that he could be spared the ignominy of an escort, and he refused even the company of his closest relatives.

In the initial years of his seclusion, Balabadra and Yuyudhana, and even Pradymna and Samva, had tried to draw Govinda out of his dark melancholy. His sister, Subadra, had been persistent in her efforts to restore normalcy to Govinda's life. He, on the other, hated the sight of her as much as he loved her, for he could hardly look at her without thinking of Partha, of Panchali, and of all that had happened. At first he had accepted her company because to be reminded of his failure was a punishment he forced himself to endure. But her kindness and love threatened to be a balm for his wounds and he roughly told her never to see him again. Not her, and not the one person who could still make him want to look for hope within – her son Abhimanyu, the boy he thought of as his own.

Subadra's tearful exit had finally brought Balabadra and Pradymna back to his doorstep, this time commanding and cautioning him where they had earlier cajoled.

'What's the point?' Govinda had protested at first.

It had taken them a long time to understand his complete withdrawal, and the moment of realization came only after a hysterical Pradymna had shouted at his father asking him when exactly he was planning to get around to doing something about Panchali's plight, the state of affairs of Dwaraka and his own increasing despondence.

'There is nothing to be done,' Govinda had declared.

His response had infuriated his son further. '*Nothing to be done?* I suppose not, given that you hardly have time to spare, what with all the women who are in and out of this place. Really, Father, does blood even flow to your brain anymore, or...?'

'Pradymna!' Yuyudhana said, reprimanding. 'Is that how a man speaks to his father?'

'Is this how a father behaves? He's bedded more women in these past two years than a whore entertains customers. What does that make him?'

Govinda had sighed, running a hand through his silver-gray hair. The rest of his appearance remained as it had always been, except for his eyes. They had lost all their light. To look into his eyes now was to see darkness so plain, so hollow, that it felt like the end. Not the cataclysmic end of all things but a hopeless, meaningless, finite end as though to cease living with the promise of death removed. To see his father this way was more than Pradymna could bear.

'Why?' he shouted. 'Why in the name of every god have you become like this? Dwaraka is not what it once was, Father. Your beautiful dream, your democratic island on the sea is crumbling and turning once again into a rubble ruled by a bunch of squabbling princes. We need you, we need you to set things right. How can you ignore us now? How can you be so cruel?'

Pradymna's outburst had drawn a quiet response. 'Don't you see?' Govinda had said, 'This time, I don't have a plan.'

The simple declaration sealed in his own acceptance as much as everyone else's. Govinda Shauri had failed. Govinda Shauri was defeated. All that was left for him to do was to spend his life flitting from pleasure to meaningless pleasure, never quite forgetting his pain. He was useless, a spent force, a lamp that burnt dim. Yet, in his mind, the flame of guilt and self-loathing blazed with a fury. Govinda spent the next ten years as he had the first two. Day and night he grappled with the regret and the pain of what he had done, and the terrible consequences of his actions that *she* had faced. But he would not allow himself the simple joy of saying her name, not even in a secret whisper.

'Who is she?' The woman next to him asked, pushing her tousled golden-red hair off her forehead.

Govinda frowned, wondering if he had spoken out loud without meaning to. He said, 'What makes you think there's another woman, Philista?'

'I know there are many other women. As does all of Dwaraka. And frankly, I don't care. But this woman, she is different. She is special. You don't think of her with desire or lust... even affection is too worldly a word to use for what I see in your eyes, Govinda. Whoever she is, this woman is as much an idea as she is a person.'

In response, Govinda turned to rest his head in the crook of Philista's neck. She shifted, taking his weight on her shoulders so that he was comfortable. He trailed his fingers on her bare skin, but his eyes looked into the distance. At length, he said, 'Yes, she is special.'

Philista laughed. 'That much was obvious from the beginning. But what is bothering you? Is she in trouble?'

'She has been a homeless exile for the past twelve years, because of me.'

'You give yourself too much importance!'

'It's true. It's as the philosophers in your Yavana *agora* always say: guilt is a rather conceited indulgence.'

Philista knew better than to argue or affirm. Instead, she took simple delight in studying the man in her arms. Glancing at Govinda again, she realized that he was still staring into the distance, completely unaware of her ruminations. She frowned and ran her hands through his hair in silent reassurance. He stirred, smiling up at her.

'Why did you leave her? What if she's in trouble?'

Govinda sighed. 'I could say I had no choice but the truth is, I did. And the choice I made was to leave her. As for why… It's because I failed her. She trusted me and I failed her. I used her time and again, claiming it was all for a greater cause that was far more important than one individual, even her. But I did not achieve what I'd hoped to…'

'And what do you hope to achieve?'

'Peace. Glory. Stability. Not for me, Philista. For my homeland. For Aryavarta. And then beyond, for peace and glory grow when shared.'

'How can a realm be peaceful or glorious if it can hurt those you care for so much?'

'Believe me, I've asked myself that question many, many times.'

'And the answer?'

'I don't know.'

'Perhaps that is what you search for among the stars. I've seen you, you know, staring endlessly at the night sky, looking for something.'

'Perhaps. But some answers must be found elsewhere. I knew a bunch of old men once, like your uncle and your teacher. They used to say that infinity lies not in the skies, but within.'

'Do you believe that?'

'I'm a man of knowledge, not of faith. I prefer to know things and arrive at conclusions through reason. Faith – that is not for me.'

'All right. What *do* you know? What drove you here, away from her, when she needed you to be with her?'

Govinda cleared his throat as he settled back against the pillows, his hands tucked under his head. 'I know that if there is change, if the system – or the "State" as your people call it – can be turned into an instrument of justice and equality, if it can do right by those who come after us, then it is worth giving up those we care about for the cause.'

'But if wrong was done to her … if she was harmed …'

'Do you know why our ancestors – yours and mine – invoked the gods for everything? Why both our lands have a rather large and admittedly temperamental pantheon of divinities which is a part of every aspect of our lives? It was because those wise old men wanted a way of life, a system, based on forgiveness and benevolence. Perfect gods don't teach patience, kindness or the other virtues we need as human beings.

'Before you ask me what that has to do with this situation, let me explain: The State or system is the best and possibly the most benevolent aspect of what is, admittedly, a flawed design. It is meant to defend and protect, but also to be defended and protected. If, however, the system begins to place its own existence, its own defence and protection, over that of its people – those it is meant to defend and protect – then it has failed. That is what I know. But it doesn't help me to understand how an edifice can come to this; how it can hurt the very people it is supposed to protect.'

'And so, you have given up? Because you cannot understand the world as it is? Because you cannot understand why you failed?'

'How can I fight that which I do not understand? I have tried. My efforts have brought nothing but pain to those I care about. Either what I fight for is not worth it, which is something that I cannot bring myself to accept, or …'

'Hmm?'

'Or, I am not the right person for this. The greatest folly of the fool is that he does not know the limits of his folly. And that makes him a dangerous man. *Dio*, as your uncle would say, this system is flawed, or I am. Either is reason enough to …'

'To …?'

'To give up. Which … you never do. Must I complete every sentence?'

Philista said, 'Yes, if you wish me to continue thinking of you as a rational man.'

'Can fools ever be rational?'

'I don't think you are a fool, Govinda. But there is, as you say, a flaw. But not so much in the system as in your reasoning.'

'What do you mean?'

'Remember, you once explained to me the notion of kala, or time, in Aryavarta. You told me that the manifested world was cyclical in nature, with interregnum of dissolution or inexistence between every cycle of creation or destruction?'

'So I did… Go on.'

'In that case you would also remember how I explained to you the uncanny parallels between our concepts of time – Kronos and his consort, the serpent Ananke, hold in their circular embrace the primordial egg that was the origin of the cosmos and all creation. Not unlike what your people call Hiranya-garbha – the primordial womb with a golden egg within.'

'My, you've been paying attention,' Govinda teased.

She gently swatted at him. 'What did you think I was, a dumb Yavana girl with half a brain whom you could charm with your sweet talk? Anyway, you're getting me off the point. I meant to say; we also have another concept of time. I don't know its equivalence in your pantheon or scripture, but we call it Kairos and it holds a sense of many things: opportunity, potential, crisis. Essentially, it thinks of time not as a temporal unit but as linked to the context and the events within which it is placed. The gods' concept of time, some call it, but…' she stopped as next to her she felt Govinda stiffen and then relax.

'We call it Pralaya. The beginning of the end, of dissolution. It happens when Vasudeva Narayana, he who sleeps on the Eternal Ocean, wakes.'

Philista turned on her side. She placed her hand on Govinda's bare chest, enjoying the way it rose and fell with each breath. Her fingers traced one of the scars that ran across his body before gently threading into the smattering of fine hair. 'Then it might be time he woke.'

'It's not a flippant event. The world as we know it is destroyed when he wakes.'

'And what is wrong with that, Govinda? If the world has shown me nothing but despair and pain, I would much rather it were destroyed, if only in the hope that it might be a better…as you say…more benevolent place when it is made again. It is what I would want if I…if I were she… Ask yourself what she would say to the gods… or the State or system. When the State can no longer protect the weakest and the most powerless, it is time for change. Even if that change is Pralaya.'

Govinda did not answer, nor did she press the issue. They lay there for a long time, the smell of their mingled sweat forming a pleasant cocoon in the still night air. Time and space blurred in thoughtlessness, or as close to it as Govinda had ever been in years, when a loud knock, insistent and impatient, came at the outer door.

Govinda slid out of bed and put on his clothes. He walked out of the bedchamber and into the adjoining sitting area, pausing at the doorway. 'There is one more meaning to Pralaya, Philista. It also means revolution. And I have no stomach for that, not anymore. It's time for you to go back to Elis. Tell Pyrrho that there is nothing more I can do. Once, my dreams of glory and progress had been not just for Aryavarta, but the whole world. I'd thought he and I, we could help each other… that our nations could work together… but when I can't even protect those I love, what talk of dreams and glory?'

'But…' Philista began.

Govinda did not react as he stepped out of the door, his tread heavy and resigned.

Philista stared at the space where he had been, then threw herself back against the cushions and closed her eyes. Fighting the instinctive jab of pain she felt at the thought of what might follow, she made up her mind.

Not once in the past years had Govinda ever locked the door to his rooms from the inside – it would not, after all, be incarceration if the prisoner could keep his holders out. Balabadra would have been well within his rights to have had the bolts removed or, even now, to enter the room as though he owned the premises, which, in fact, he did. But he waited for his brother to let him in and wave him towards a seat, which he declined. Finally, not knowing how else to delay the inevitable, he related, in as few words as possible, the news of Jayadrath's attack on Panchali.

In the silence that followed, Govinda crumpled, falling to his knees. His head bent to the floor, and every line in his shoulders was taut with the effort of restrained emotion. His fingers clawed into cold stone, the veins on his hands bulging, threatening to burst.

Balabadra could not tell whether the emotion was fury or pain, for he could not see his brother's face behind the veil of curly silver-grey hair. He decided it was best to leave him alone, and turned away. Govinda called out, 'Agraja...'

'Yes, Govinda?'

Still on his knees, eyes gazing at the stone floor, Govinda said, 'There is one place they can hide. It's probably the most dangerous place in all of Aryavarta for them, but that ironically might be what makes it safe. No one will think of looking for them there. Please, for Panchali's sake, not mine, get word to Dharma... even Dhaumya... Please...'

Balabadra considered the request. 'I can speak to Vidur. That's all. Will that do?'

'Yes.'

'What do you want me to tell him? Where should Dharma and the others go?'

'Home. Vidur will understand. Tell him to take them home.'

10

THERE WAS NOTHING ABOVE THEM BUT THE BLINDING, BLAZING sun, shining down with a vengeance on the dry, hard stone path under Dharma's feet. Once, he had heard, these lands – the land of his ancestors, of the great queen Satya – had been the heart of a great empire, verdant beyond measure and prosperous beyond envy. Now they lay barren and ignored by all but the most desperate of people, who sought refuge here. And in the aftermath of Jayadrath's attack that was exactly what Dharma and his brothers had been – desperate.

211

Dhaumya had seen the event as an unambiguous sign that Syoddhan had finally tired of their being alive, which meant they were now in great danger. It had been a worried Vidur who had sought them out and counselled them on their only option. Dharma had eventually agreed, with a reluctant obedience, to go into hiding to the one place that was part of Aryavarta, yet not. Matsya.

The rest of Aryavarta considered Matsya a lawless land, for the rules it followed were its own. Even during the imperial campaign, Dharma's armies had not set foot in Matsya, nor had its people bothered with the events around them. The nation acknowledged no emperor and paid no tribute, but traded the precious gemstones found within its harsh earth with foreign nations through Trigarta – the north-western neighbour that was both its greatest enemy and biggest ally. Matsya depended on Trigarta for access to the outside world, just as Trigarta depended on Matsya for the levies it paid for such access. For the rest, Matsya relied on itself. Its people were as hardy as the dry scrub desert that surrounded them. Equally robust and even more impressive were the huge herds of resilient cows that survived in the harshness of the desert, providing sustenance and wealth to the many nomadic tribes that wandered the lands beyond its capital, Upaplavya. Matsya was rich, yet it was poor. Matsya had nothing, yet it was everything that Dharma needed it to be at this point in time – the perfect hiding place.

Matsya had once been the seat of emperors, the imperial capital of Aryavarta, till the Wrights of old and its leaders had turned the land into a desert. In the aftermath of Matsya's fall, the Firstborn had finally stepped forward to cleanse Aryavarta of the Firewrights, and the Great Scourge had followed. Dharma was filled with pride at the outcome. His ancestress, Satya, had played an important part in that cleansing. Her womb had borne Krishna Dwaipayana, the greatest Vyasa of all time, the man who had finally rid the realm of Firewrights. And for its transgressions Matsya still paid the price, serving as an example to all Aryavarta, its isolation reminding them that the Divine Order was its own keeper. Today the nation existed only in name. It was the Virat Confederacy, named after the man who was now its Chief – a city-state formed around an oasis set in the middle of a harsh, impassable desert that served to both isolate and protect. Matsya was an island of uncivilized brutes amidst Aryavarta's great nobility.

At that thought, Dharma felt emptied of all pride. No matter how dramatic the story of Matsya and its princess, it did not make him feel any better about why *he* was here. Vidur had explained to him at length. 'My son, only ashes can hide a spark. We've always looked down on Matsya, called its people uncouth and ignoble. Where better to hide the Emperor and his family?'

'But is that justified?' he had asked. 'Matsya is what it is; they place no faith in the precepts of righteousness and Divine Order that guide all of Aryavarta. Isn't that why the Firstborn have never sanctified its rulers – who remain merely chiefs and never become kings?'

'And the chiefs of Matsya accept this practice. Does that not mean they accept our larger notions of righteousness? Besides, the rulers of Matsya were once emperors of Aryavarta. Those now in power relegated themselves to being simple chieftains because they hold the throne in trust for those who actually have the right to rule. Or such is the story, for times have changed, and the true heirs are no longer welcome in Matysa. And that, my son, is why it is the perfect hiding place for you. But under no circumstance must anyone know who you are. That would be most dangerous. You see ...'

By the time Vidur had finished with his explanation, Dharma had not known what to say or do. 'Trust me,' Vidur had reassured him yet again, 'it's the best place for you to hide yourselves in the guise of commoners.'

Now, as they neared the unprotected borders of the desert, Dharma realized that they were not the only ones crossing the barren lands in search of refuge. They fell in as part of the long, straight line of people trudging along an unseen trail. Women, men, entire families, ostracized because they did not fit into Aryavarta's conception of Divine Order and hierarchy and so thrown out of the realm, now sought refuge in the one place that would still have them, that still found use for them, no matter what their faults.

As the six of them mingled with the other refugees, becoming yet another indistinct, grime-streaked, forlorn huddle in that mass, Dharma prayed for the strength to accept what fate had brought him.

The shame of their situation hit him all the more when, walking next to him, Panchali said, 'What sort of an empire could turn its backs on so many people – on the elderly and on children? Perhaps it was an empire worth losing.'

Dharma was about to reprimand her when Sadev, who was a few steps behind them, gently said, 'Let it go, Panchali. We have enough problems of our own. We're still in great danger, more so than we have been all these years.'

He was right. No sooner had they entered Upaplavya, the main settlement of the Matsya nation, than they attracted attention. Despite their unkempt appearance, the guard on duty, who was responsible for admitting refugees into the city and guiding them on where to go next, jested with his fellow soldiers and other passers-by: 'Five men and a woman … If I didn't know better, I'd say you were that mockery of an emperor, Dharma Yudhisthir, and his brothers. And that would make this lovely lady here wife to you all, I suppose?' He punctuated the implications of the statement with a hand on Panchali's arm, which she swatted away.

The action prompted a hiss of disapproval, which provoked Bhim to lunge forward aggressively. The soldier's companions drew their weapons, and Nakul and Sadev too stepped forward. A horrified Dharma looked from them to the soldiers, unable to find the words he needed to intervene and settle tempers. He turned to look at Panchali only to realize that she had stiffened, and was holding her breath. Bhim, too, noticed and he stepped in front of her protectively. Panchali did not protest, but gave Bhim a glance of gratitude.

A crowd was beginning to gather at the sign of trouble, and just when Dharma had helplessly resigned himself to the terrible consequences of being recognized, Partha stepped forward. 'Are you calling me a man?' he challenged the guard in voice unlike his own, though not completely lacking the deep tone of his gender. 'You must be blind, calling this skinny thing lovely when *I* am standing right here in front of you!'

The brothers exchanged looks as the crowd around them broke out in guffaws, and the situation turned in an instant from tense to light-hearted. The soldier grinned and said, 'You? Well, then, why is … err … a lady such as yourself dressed like a man?'

Partha said, 'For my own safety, of course! Hai! With men like you around, is a pretty young woman safe? I won't sleep in peace till I am in the care of a household and well-employed!'

The guard laughed again. 'Don't worry, my dear. You are safe among us. As for employment, make your way to the palace kitchens. Take this skinny friend of yours with you. They can always do with more eunuchs and serving women in Queen Sudeshna's rooms.'

Flashing the guards a brilliant smile, Partha took Panchali's hand in his and began walking away with an alluring sway of his hips.

'And you?' the soldier's attention turned to Dharma, as Bhim stepped back to let Panchali pass. 'What is your trade?'

'I'm a scholar,' Dharma proudly declared. 'A learned man and wise counsellor. I once served in the imperial palace at Indr-prastha.'

'Palace. Follow the eunuch. Tell the chief attendant that I sent you. He said our chief needed a jester or entertainer. Tell you what – you get yourself the position, I'll buy you a drink. The chief attendant will owe me for finding him the right man … Move on, and now let's get to this hot-tempered fellow here and see what use he will be.' The soldier turned to Bhim.

'But …' Dharma began to protest at what he considered a demeaning assignation, but the crowd behind him was swelling and the soldier merely pushed him through.

Over the course of a painful year Dharma, or Kanka as he was known, had managed, with a shrewd display of political acumen and emotional reticence, to rise from the position of being an entertainer to one of Chief Virat's advisors. Despite his new found status, the Chief often called on Dharma to fulfil the original duty to which he had been appointed to play dice with the ruler. To Dharma, it was like sheer mockery, not only to be reduced to such a task but also because Virat hardly played as a monarch ought to. He was only too happy if Dharma won the game, provided it had been played with skill on both sides.

Dharma did not know what tormented him more about Matsya – the heathen absence of hierarchy, or the fact that he and his companions were a part of it. He learnt to deal with his discomfort in the only way he could. He ignored it. He ignored Nakul and Sadev, who had taken the names of Granthika and Tantripala, clad like servants in short, dirty antariyas, rubbing down horses and tending to cows. He tried not to notice how their fair skin had been scorched dark by the sun, their cracked lips and the soles of their feet that were always blistered and bleeding. He ignored Bhim, now known as Vallabha, bruised all over from wrestling man and beast alike for Chief Virat's pleasure and perpetually soot-stained from cooking in the palace's dreary kitchens. He ignored Partha, who was still pretending to be a eunuch named Brihannala and doing a fine job of it. And there was Panchali, now Malini the handmaiden.

Dharma felt crippling anguish every time he saw her, though it was not because he regretted Panchali's suffering. He understood her loneliness – the result of her assumed identity – but there was little that could be done about it in the initial months. She had little reason and hardly any occasion to meet Nakul and Sadev. Indeed, in the first couple of months of their stay in Matsya, she had seen none of the five brothers save for Partha and, on occasion, Bhim. Even Dharma had been unapproachable in his earlier function of a courtier and entertainer, but as he grew to become Virat's advisor it became less suspicious for the two of them to be seen in conversation.

Even so, Dharma found that he no longer enjoyed Panchali's company as he once used to. Her refusal to see the truth about their situation made him feel more distant from her than ever before. He believed that pain was a sign of penitence, of sacrifice, of adherence to the purest morality – provided one accepted the pain, bent down to the greater forces that wove one's life into a tapestry of sorrow, and understood that it was a part of the Divine Order. He knew that Panchali believed that her pain was undeserved, a sentiment he found completely self-centred. He could not fathom how anyone could fault the forces of destiny and insist on one's own innocence. Nothing happened that was not part of something greater and it made sense that each individual merely suffered the consequences of their actions.

That, and the fact that he alone carried the burden of Vidur's words, the great irony of what could be and what was.

As a result, he was not taken aback in the least when Sadev's proclamation came true and trouble finally did find them.

11

'WHO IS THAT MAN?' IT WAS A QUESTION OF NO REAL SIGNIFICANCE, mere curiosity, in fact.

Panchali was using the excuse of admiring the horses on the exercise grounds to speak to Granthika and Tantripala for the first time in the many months since they had all come to Matsya.

Nakul-Granthika said, 'That is the General.'

'The General?'

'His name is Keechak, but no one calls him that. He's the head of Matsya's armies and also Queen Sudeshna's brother. Of course, if you hear the rumours going around you'd think he's the ruler of all Matsya. He was away these past months, though I'm not sure where.'

'You have to admire his discipline,' Sadev-Tantripala, added. 'Hardly half a day off the travel trail, and he is at his post checking on the war horses.'

The two brothers snapped to attention as the General approached. Panchali bowed, her face carefully set into the unsmiling yet not unfriendly ambivalence that gave the impression of aloofness without being offensive, and stepped away from the horses. Keechak gave her a curious look and a small smile before falling into conversation with Granthika and Tantripala about the horses and other livestock. Panchali discreetly slipped away, and thought no more about the encounter till Queen Sudeshna sent for her the same evening.

Panchali entered the room to find Sudeshna in conversation with the General. She felt a little wary at running into him again, so soon, but reasoned that it was not unusual given that he was the queen's brother.

'Malini, come,' Sudeshna beckoned her closer and gestured to the usual seat Malini was accustomed to take. Panchali glanced at it and then at the General, wondering if it would be appropriate for her to sit in his presence. Sudeshna noticed and laughed. She turned to Keechak and said, 'She has been here for ages now, but still isn't used to the way things are done.'

The General laughed. Then he stood up. 'A person's worth is not judged by their station, Malini. But if it makes you more comfortable, please remaining standing. I take it you like horses? Do you ride well?'

The abrupt change in the line of conversation caught Panchali off guard, but she managed to answer that and the rest of Keechak's questions in a matter-of-fact way. After a while the General excused himself, saying he had a task to attend to.

'Sit, Malini,' Sudeshna commanded. This time, Panchali complied. Sudeshna said, 'My brother likes you, Malini. He would like to see you again. May I arrange it?'

Panchali was astonished at the nature of the request, as well as the mild way in which it was conveyed. She declined in equally polite terms. 'Forgive me, Mahamatra. But I fear it would be inappropriate. Please excuse my inability to agree to this suggestion.'

Sudeshna was taken aback by the response but said nothing, letting Panchali go without any show of rancour.

As Panchali discovered in the women's quarters in the next few days, her refusal had come as a shock to most. The General was disgusting neither in form nor in behaviour, and a different woman in a different situation would have not been averse to the attentions of a man who was as powerful as he was pleasant. But Panchali was not such a woman, and she persisted in her objections, no matter how many times Keechak or his sister presented his case. Soon, it became common knowledge that the war-hardened General was, simply put, besotted with Malini the handmaiden.

The General's proclaimed interest served one advantage. It quelled the rumours that filled the palace about the passionate desire Malini and Vallabha the cook, who had come into service at the same time, had for each other. It also put an end to Queen Sudeshna's comments in the privacy of the women's chambers, where she often teased Panchali with bawdy descriptions of the rumoured mutual seductions – gossip that only brought Panchali dislike from her fellow handmaidens, many of whom openly professed their attraction for Vallabha.

Keechak's confessed attraction also helped to deflect interest from Bhim-Vallabha's rising popularity with Chief Virat and the soldiers of Matsya. Over the months, Bhim had progressed from being a mere wrestler and martial sportsman, to training many of Matsya's captains in advance fighting techniques. In Keechak's absence, particularly, Virat had come to rely heavily on Bhim – a development, which Dharma had been happy to encourage in his position as counsellor. Upon the General's return, Bhim had astutely avoided attracting attention by relegating himself to his kitchen duties alone. The rumour that Vallabha was no longer in Malini's favour – if so he had ever been – served to let him resume his training duties and avoid offending Keechak.

Barring these advantages, the General's undiminished interest in Panchali was, to her, an inconvenience. As his persistence and proclaimed passion moved rapidly towards a dangerous situation, Panchali confessed her fears to Partha.

'Be patient, Panchali,' Partha-Brihannala advised. 'We are safer than we have been in all these years. Dharma's influence, Bhim's strength … all these have made Matsya a comfortable, if not amiable home for us.'

'And you wish me to add my body to that list?' Panchali retorted.

'You're not the only one making sacrifices here, Panchali. Look at me! Neither man, nor woman …'

'But still a human being! Which is more than what I feel like. I can't Partha. Besides, there won't be much favour left if the General forces himself on me and satisfies his wishes. And if I give in to him willingly, there won't be any safety left us either. Rumours will spread beyond Matsya, and Syoddhan will find us. Is that what you want?'

Faced with the dilemma, Partha alternately considered asking Bhim and approaching Dharma for advice. Panchali understood his vacillation. There was a part of Partha that still looked obediently to his eldest brother for instructions and advice. Another part of him knew it would be futile to bring the problem to Dharma's attention.

Finally, Panchali directly approached Dharma. Dharma said, 'He's made it obvious that he likes you, but has the General sent for you? I mean... has he ordered you to his bed?'

Panchali shook her head. 'No. But you know he will. Dharma, please... I can't take this anymore!'

'Ah, my dear! If only that were excuse enough! This sad destiny is ours to suffer! We can't afford to do anything, Panchali. Anything that is out of the ordinary, even to the least extent, must be avoided. If Syoddhan finds us... I'm sure you understand.'

'What do you mean?' Her voice held a trace of sharpness.

Dharma winced at her tone. Nevertheless, he patiently explained, 'Today, we're little more than commoners. If fate has it that we live as the servile, we can't fight it.'

'And? Doesn't it once strike you that the commoners, this servile class that you've been relegated to, *deserve* better? Aren't some things just wrong, whether they are suffered by peasant or king? What sort of Emperor...'

'Don't you dare speak to me in such a tone, Panchali. Unlike you, my principles are immutable. Divine Order is paramount. I don't spit on the system the moment it ceases to go in my favour. I remain faithful to it – whether as slave or as king! Where was all your anger and concern when you ruled these lands as the Empress?'

'True,' Panchali admitted. 'I deserve it. Everything we took for granted, everything we assumed was permanent, has been taken from us. You, an emperor, must serve as the chief's fool, advise him on his pursuit of duty and righteousness. Partha has been rendered impotent, Bhim's might is now a source of entertainment for others, and Nakul and Sadev must tend to herds that are not theirs. Just like commoners. By Rudra, we all deserve it. You're right, I'm no longer an empress and...'

'No, you are not an empress,' Dharma said through gritted teeth, desperately trying to keep his temper. 'You once were, but you are not one today. This is the life destined for you, and you had best make your peace with it as we all have.'

'And if the General...?'

'Then I suggest you satisfy his needs, as would every other handmaiden in this palace.'

Panchali stared at him for a while, and then spun on her heel and walked away.

Furious as she was with Dharma, Panchali did not see where she was going until it was too late. The impact made her lose her balance, but she felt an arm go immediately around her in support. She tried to push it away, but in vain. The General was a big, strong man. With a cry of protest, she tried to twist out of his grip. He only held on tighter. Panchali squirmed as he pushed her against the wall and held her there with his body. He was genuinely confused by her reluctance. 'What now, Malini? We're alone. Why do you still pretend to resist me? Stop being such a temptress.'

'Please...' Panchali pleaded as the General placed his hand on the bare skin of her waist. 'Please listen to me.'

He showed no signs of letting her go. 'Ah, my sweet love,' he cajoled. 'A fine woman like you could have her heart's fill of riches and jewels, I know. But I can offer you much more... I can offer you that which a woman's heart truly desires.' Panchali turned her face away, even as the General placed his lips to her ear and whispered, 'I can please you in ways that you've never imagined, my dear.'

'You'll die for ever speaking those words to me!' Panchali snapped, her rage filling her with strength. She pushed hard at the man.

Keechak yielded and took a step back. He said, 'Really, Malini, you're the finest of them all. You could be a man for the iron will you nurse in your shapely body. I suppose I was right. You're not just an ordinary handmaiden. You're a special woman, a woman fit to be queen... My queen. Marry me, Malini. Let us do this the honourable way.'

Panchali closed her eyes, squeezing them tight against the tears that threatened. A mix of fear, fatigue, and the sheer incongruity of a situation where a man she did not care for seemed to value her sentiments more than the man she was married to, overcame her. She could hear Dharma's words in her head. *Just a commoner.* It was not the appellation that had hurt, but the insinuation that she meant nothing and was worth nothing. The feeling turned into words, and the vague hope that it may well be a way out of her predicament.

221

'Please, General,' she said, 'I'm hardly worthy of a man of your stature. I'm nobody, a servant, a handmaiden. Please just let me be…'

Keechak frowned. 'Since when is a handmaiden nobody, Malini?'

'General…'

'Where are you from?'

'I…'

'Where are you from? You're not from Matsya. You came in months ago seeking shelter and employment, that I know. Which part of Aryavarta do you come from?'

'I…the Central lands,' Panchali said.

'That explains it. Well, Malini. These are not the Central lands. Come with me.'

'But General…'

'Yes, yes! I know, I know. Come!' Keechak took Panchali's wrist in a firm grip and began leading the way.

She went along silently, her suspicions growing by the moment as he strode across the palace grounds, to a windowless structure at the far end. She had often wondered what purpose the building served but no one had been able to tell her. No one, not even the groundskeeper, was allowed near it. Rumour had it that this was the General's private dungeon, where he fulfilled his depraved needs for pleasure.

The guards on duty at the large metal doorway saluted their General, but failed to hide their surprise on seeing Panchali in tow. She was equally astonished by their reaction. *If this isn't where he takes his women… then?* She had no time to think further on it, for as she stepped through the door it was pulled shut behind them. It was pitch dark inside the building, except for a brazier on the far wall. Without warning, the General pulled Panchali back and into his arms. She began to flail about, but, as her eyes adjusted to the light, she realized that she had been standing precariously on the edge of a narrow flight of stairs.

'Careful.'

Panchali nodded and, extricating herself from his grip, began climbing down. The stairs levelled out into a small corridor, which led to a long, cavernous room. Unlike the one above, this room was well lit, not just with braziers, but with the light of three huge furnaces. Men working at the furnaces saluted the General and quickly returned to their tasks. Panchali was bewildered. Never had she imagined that a forge of such huge proportions remained in existence in Aryavarta, for the only one she had seen, an old forge hidden in the forests of Panchala, was just a fifth part of this one. Like the other, however, it was made of cold, dark stone, with the main chamber set within the earth. Despite the fires, the air felt cool, and a light breeze was blowing through the cavern. She wondered how it was that the forge was cooled in the absence of running water or an obvious air vent, but knew better than to ask. She turned to the General. 'Why have you brought me here?'

'To tell you that you are wrong. To show you that there is another way of thinking, a way that allows you and me to be together if we wish it, for no reason other than we wish it.'

'I don't understand.'

The General said, 'Malini, what you believe is what most of Aryavarta believes: that birth and gender and position are what decide our lives. It is the philosophy that the Firstborn have instilled deep into the core of Aryavarta, and they have done so at a terrible price. You see, they believed that destiny and duty sanctified all things. To them, inequality was not necessarily injustice. Things were determined by a greater law, a Divine Order, and as long as that balance was kept, all other things, including hierarchy, inequality and the unfettered power of those who ruled, were justified. But here you see a man who would be considered a suta as commander of this nation's forces. His sister, as much a suta as he is, is queen. How? Because here, in Matsya, lived those who believed otherwise ...'

'The Firewrights,' Panchali said before she could stop herself.

Keechak looked pleased. 'Yes,' he said, 'the Firewrights. The Wrights liked to pretend that they believed in equality. For what it's worth, they once did. Their belief was that all other inequalities – be they of social standing, wealth, servitude – came from a fundamental inequality in power. And their way of achieving equality was through knowledge.'

'Because knowledge would result in the dispersion of power from the few to the many. So, over time, inequalities would vanish.'

'Precisely. Yet you wonder why I admire you! You really are a clever woman, Malini. And so it was that till the Great Scourge began, Matsya was by far the most powerful kingdom in all Aryavarta. Once, our kings were emperors of the entire realm. Now we hardly dare to call them kings.'

Panchali did not look convinced. She said, 'But do you see the problem there? Knowledge itself becomes a cause of inequality, a source of power. Matsya rose by the might of the Firewrights. Matsya fell, condemned by its own ascent.'

Keechak's face clouded with anger. With visible effort, he willed his expression into neutrality and said, 'There's a saying I've heard: "Every poison is defined by its antidote." It is something my greatest enemy used to say.'

Panchali felt her heart begin to race, but she willed herself to reveal no emotion. Oblivious, the General continued, 'He believed that inequality was inevitable, that its existence is immutable. The only thing that can change is its form. He claimed that the search for equality was what defined humanity... I would have listened more closely to him had he not betrayed me and my people. But no. No one ever came to our aid, Malini. They used us – Firewright, Firstborn... all of them used us and cast us aside. They took our life-giving river, the Saraswati, and hid her underground. And then cast us out of their lives and minds forever, exiling us in our own home. But in their folly, their blind selfishness, our transgressors did not see what a terrible decision that was. Take a look at this.'

Keechak held out a sword, impeccably crafted, but heavy and made of dark iron. As she took it from him, it reminded Panchali of Naga weapons, except that, she realized, this sword was not beaten and forged, but rather cast from a mould and polished to a shine and keenness that Naga iron could not rival. It was lighter too, far lighter, and very well balanced. Panchali resisted the instinct to point the sword and look down its blade for a precise assessment.

The General said, confirming her suspicions, 'Of all the things that the Firewrights created, nothing was more important or powerful than what was called Wright-metal. It was easy to pour and malleable beyond imagination. But it was also strong and supple and light. And so, the Wrights began casting weapons out of these stone moulds ...' he gestured with his hands.

'So you use iron in their old moulds? Is that it?'

'Mih! If you do that, you'll only get the heavy, ugly things that the Nagas use.'

'Then how ...?'

'We found a way to temper iron.'

'You what?'

'Don't be so surprised, my dear. What other choice did we have? Cut off from everyone and everything, isolated from the rest of the world, we had to make do with the materials we found here, within our own borders. There was little to farm and much to mine, and we had time, Malini. We had all the time in the world. While the rest of Aryavarta has been playing dice, we have been working hard to find a way to temper iron with other metals to make it lighter, more malleable. We've designed new moulds to suit our needs, and those needs are far more important than swords and arrows.'

His voice hoarse with long-contained rage, Keechak said, 'The river dried up, and there was no rain. Matsya had been cursed by the gods. Many lost their lives, before we managed to build a new home for ourselves here again. And we have, by our sweat and blood, and with this metal! Not for war, but for survival.'

Panchali could not contain herself. 'What ... what do you mean?'

'We have found newer uses for this tempered metal. We use it for just about everything. It's all we have. Haven't you ever wondered how it is that you can bring me a full cauldron of hot water using those slender arms of yours? Or did you think yourself so strong? No, Malini,' he laughed. 'It is this metal – Kali. Iron but not quite, though one would never be able tell just by looking. And these workmen of mine can make more than pots and pans. In case you haven't noticed, we hardly have any lumber here in the desert. What do you think holds up our walls and roofs? We pack the mud and stone around bars made of this metal. Even an elephant couldn't break though the palace's walls.'

225

'But...' She stopped herself from asking the question, but the Keechak understood.

'Why then do we live as outcasts, suffer in this forsaken desert, while the rest of Aryavarta spits on us and calls us uncivilized brutes? We wait, we prepare, Malini. Our solitude has allowed us to deflect attention while we have built arsenals greater than the might of many kingdoms combined. Where the Wrights made one sword in months, I can now cast them in hundreds, in less than a week. No army in Aryavarta has the weapons that mine does. Those who betrayed us should not have made the mistake of leaving us alone and alive.'

Despite the cold feeling in the pit of her stomach, Panchali brought herself to look the General in the eye. 'I'm sorry for your suffering and that of your people,' she told him. 'And I see that you truly are a brave man and an honourable one. But that doesn't change my position – please understand...'

'Shh. Come here, Malini.' The General led her to the end of the chamber, where a small door was set into one corner. Panchali noticed it for the first time. Despite its unimpressive size, the door was made of heavy, black iron, and protected with chains and locks of the same metals.

Keechak removed a small bunch of keys from a chain around his neck and inserted them into the many locks in a specific sequence. The door gave way with a groan. He stepped in, bending down to accommodate his bulk into the tiny space, and gestured for Panchali to follow. The room was commensurately small, no more than a large cupboard. It had no light of its own, but the glow from the furnaces outside was enough to see by. On the walls were stacked bottles and receptacles of many shapes and sizes. Many were empty, others little more than broken shards.

'These are not of our making. They are things left behind by the Firewrights – their poisons and hallucinogens...' the General said. He walked over to a high shelf, where a few unbroken, dusty bottles were innocently clustered together. These, Panchali noticed, were not empty.

The General picked up two identical vials. 'You give me hope.

Not just for me, but for all Aryavarta. If only you would see beyond these webs that Firstborn and Firewright have woven around us ... I trust you, Malini. I want you to know what you mean to me. And that is why I share with you this, my biggest secret. Do you have any idea what this is? No, of course not ...' Laughing loudly, he went on to explain.

All Panchali could do was listen, her eyes widening further with every word.

12

BHIM HELD HIS BREATH AND SHRUNK BACK INTO THE SHADOW of a pillar as he heard the sound of footsteps punctuated by the melody of anklets. He relaxed as the figure that emerged through the darkness turned out to be taller and broader than the one he sought to hide from.

'Well? What's so important? Why all this secrecy?' The individual demanded in a voice that was completely appropriate to his feminine attire though incongruous with his person.

'Shh!' Bhim cautioned, pulling Partha into the darkness. 'Panchali is meeting the General here.'

'You're out of your mind, Bhim! How could you even think to say such a thing about her! She'd die before ...'

'How many times can she die, Partha? She's afraid, she's tired. Three nights ago, I saw her and the General walking across the grounds to that private palace or dungeon or whatever it is that he has. Today I overheard him talk of their plans to meet here, in the dancing hall. I know the fire Panchali is made of, but there is only so much anyone can take, especially when ... when her own family can do nothing to protect her.'

Partha frowned. 'I don't believe you. You, the cook, know things that I, the palace attendant, don't?'

Bhim sighed, annoyed at having to explain. 'The General was posturing in front of me. I was there to serve him a special dish, on his sister's orders. He took the opportunity to flaunt his conquest.'

Partha shrugged. 'I still don't believe you. But this much is certain: if the General comes here, if he as much as tries to touch Panchali…'

'And if she is willing? If she comes to him of her own free will? What would be so horrible, so wrong, if a woman left a man who cannot care for her, for one who truly does? How does that make her a bad person?'

'Vathu, Bhim!' Partha snapped, without regard that the other was older. 'Or has the kitchen soot finally clouded your brain? You've been listening to too much gossip.'

'Oh, shut up, Partha,' Bhim replied. 'You're just jealous that for once it's me the women want, not you!'

The accusation calmed Partha down. He turned pensive. 'Jealous?' he said. 'Yes, maybe. I don't know if I'm the most fortunate man in the world or the most frustrated. Just yesterday, one of the handmaidens asked me to bring her more bathwater – and while she was still in her bath. Whatever you may or may not be doing as Vallabha the cook, your little act is nothing compared to what I've got going on here…' he gestured to his feminine clothes, the vestments of Brihannala the eunuch.' With a sigh, he added, 'There are times when I don't know who I am any more. Not because I have been emasculated. Haven't we all, in some way? What bothers me is that I don't know why I do what I do…'

Partha fell silent as his sharp ears picked up the rustle of clothing and the jangling of bangles. He shrunk back into the shadows next to Bhim, who pointed silently first to Panchali and then to the large shadow that approached from another entrance. 'He's here, too.'

The dark outline of the General came into prominence as he lit a lamp and placed it on a pedestal nearby. He greeted Panchali with a warm smile. 'Malini… Tell me you are going to say yes.'

Panchali set her face into studied neutrality, her stance more confident and commanding than she had allowed herself to assume since she took on the identity of Malini the handmaiden. 'You're a good man, General.'

'But…?'

'No buts. We have other matters to discuss. You took a great leap of faith the other day, when you trusted me with your biggest secrets.

Now it is my turn. I ask for your patience to hear me out, for these are things that I myself did not understand till you told me what you did. I need you to trust me as you did before and listen to what I have to say before you make your decision.'

'Of course. What is it you want to tell me, Malini? You've always been mysterious, but I've never seen you this serious.'

Panchali took a deep breath and chose her next words with care. 'You said I gave you hope. You are not the first man to say that to me. Just as you are not the first person to hear what you said were your enemy's words: "Every poison is defined by its antidote." He... the man you consider your enemy... once said those words to me.'

Keechak started despite his assurances of patience. 'You know him?'

'I do,' Panchali said. 'I know him. But it was not till you spoke of him, not till you showed me what you did, that I understood what it was that he has done. He is not your foe, General. He never betrayed you. He truly believed that neither Firewright nor Firstborn had the complete solution. He believes in dualities, in the power of opposites. When he bound all of Aryavarta into an empire, he left Matsya an island. Why? Because where the empire would grow by having everything, Matsya would prosper, as it has, because it had nothing. Your skills with metal are unparalleled today, perhaps even in the world. He knew you would grow, and grow to become a society that valued all that he believed was good and just – equality, self-reliance, compassion... I shall be honest. I, too, once thought Matsya was a land of impoverished heathens. But I now see...'

'Stop the flattery, Malini. What is it you are trying to say?'

The General's sharp tone stirred the first traces of fear in Panchali. She wondered if she had been hasty. Brushing the thought aside, she willed all the conviction she felt to show through in her words. 'He never meant for Matsya to fall. He would never betray you. Your isolation was necessary, so that unlike the rest of Aryavarta you would turn your skills to the things that mattered rather than to making weapons. And you've done exactly that, don't you see! Soon, it will be time for you to share your knowledge with the rest of the realm, to guide them to more peace and prosperity than

229

anyone ever imagined. It is as you said: Matsya will rise. Matsya is meant to rise!'

'And how would you know?'

'Because I *know* him. I know what he thinks, what his plans are. His ultimate loyalty is neither to Firewright nor Firstborn, but to humanity. I too once thought he served no interest but his own, till...' She gave up, not finding the words to convey her emotions. 'Send for him, General. Let him explain. Govinda Shauri always has a plan.'

Many things happened in quick succession after that. Bhim and Partha hardly had the time to recover from what Panchali had said and done when Keechak, who had gone unnaturally still, suddenly threw himself at her. His large hands were around Panchali's neck before she could react.

'Why?' The General asked, shouting now, his need for comprehension alone keeping him from snapping Panchali's neck in two. 'Who are you? Why did you do this? Did he send you here? Did that traitor send you here?'

Panchali tried her best to keep calm. 'Yes,' she gasped. 'I mean... I think so. He wanted me safe. Just as he wanted Matsya safe. You must believe me...'

'There is nothing to believe.' The General tightened his grasp.

Panchali felt darkness sweep down on her as her breath tightened in her chest. A burning sensation shot from her throat to her stomach and she felt her knees buckle. Yet, for all her discomfort and the memory of all that had happened over the last years, she felt unafraid. She knew. She understood. There was still hope. There was still Govinda. She closed her eyes and readied herself to die. Hardly was she aware of the presence of someone behind her than she felt the pressure around her neck give. She fell to the ground, coughing hard

'Panchali! Are you all right?' She heard Partha's voice, and felt his hands, with familiar calluses from his once-life as an archer and marked by the more recent fragrance of turmeric and rose water, on her face. She opened her eyes, to a sight that ought to have terrified her, but did not. The General was on his knees, his red, contorted face held tight in the crook of Bhim's arm. His eyes were bulging out, blood pooled in them as tears otherwise would have, and more blood flowed from his ears, while drool dripped from his slack jaw as he struggled, ineffectively, to breathe. He tried to kick down Bhim, claw at him, but to no avail. The General was the stronger man, yes, but Bhim was impelled by his cold rage, the cumulative resentment and anger that he had suppressed for years.

Panchali had never seen Bhim like this: silent and contained, even during a fight. It frightened her to see this side of a man she thought she knew well. 'No, Bhim!' she called out. Her eyes sought out Keechak.

'General, please! All I ask for is a chance to explain.'

In response, Keechak mustered the last of his strength and spat at her. Panchali considered him for a moment longer, and then looked at Bhim. She nodded her head once. The two men remained frozen for what felt like a long time, though Keechak's eyes showed his desperate – and ineffective – struggle to escape Bhim's grip. Finally, Bhim moved, letting go, and the General slid to the floor, lifeless.

Slowly, Panchali got to her feet. Her eyes held certainty. 'Thank you, Bhim. And you too, Partha.'

'What … what is going on Panchali?' Partha said.

'I'll explain tomorrow. It's a long story.'

'Does it have something to do with the General's private palace?'

'It's not a palace. It's a workshop.'

'And it has something to do with Govinda?'

'Yes. He sent us here, I'm sure of it. Matsya was part of his plan, it always was. He sent us here only because we were in too much danger outside. That being the case, the General's death …' She shook her head. 'Tomorrow. We will speak tomorrow. Now, get rid of the body.'

Bhim said, 'We'll need to find an excuse, an explanation …'

'We'll find nothing, Bhim. We know nothing and so have absolutely nothing to say. Let the General's disappearance be discovered in due course and let rumours spread, as they will. If we try to intervene or misdirect, we will only attract attention to ourselves.'

'Still,' Bhim countered, 'we should at least tell Dharma before we do anything at all.'

'We tell no one,' Panchali snapped. Softening, she added, 'Dharma does what he believes right from his point of view, just as the General did what he believed right. And in the same way I can only do what is right. Your brother … his is a difficult path. He tries to remain truly committed to an ideal that is no longer relevant. Ten generations ago, he would have been the best of us all. Now, while he remains the same, the world around him has changed. It's not easy for him to live with that. More tomorrow. I need to think, I need to unravel this complicated web before we decide on our next step, otherwise ….' She trailed off, her brow furrowed in thought. 'Never mind that, I'd better get going before someone notices both Malini and Brihannala are missing from the Queen's palace. Bury the body and get some sleep, both of you.' She did not wait for a reply, but left the dancing hall.

Bhim and Partha exchanged a glance before stepping forward to dispose of the General's bloody, lifeless body. None of them noticed the figure in one of the dark corridors overlooking the chamber, standing still and silent against the wall, intent on their every word and action.

13

'IT'S A SIMPLE ENOUGH CALCULATION, SYODDHAN,' SHAKUNI WAS saying. 'These disparate incidents – the attacks on Vasusena's forges, General Keechak's death in Matsya – may not mean much. But taken together, they cannot be dismissed.'

Syoddhan pressed down on each of his fingers one by one as he paced the room, letting his knuckles crack loudly. The sound rang through the near-empty chamber like sneers, as if the pristine marble was mocking him, flaunting its unblemished whiteness as a reminder of the momentous events that had played out in this very hall. He put the past out of his mind and turned his attention to the issues at hand. The news of the strange events in Matsya had finally found their way to Hastina, where the announcement of the General's death, in particular, had been received with mixed emotions. To add to that, Devala and Vasusena had arrived bearing their own tidings, this time unambiguously disastrous. Many of the forges they had set up in Anga had been attacked and destroyed completely. Syoddhan had known better than to ignore these incidents and had called his advisors together to get their views. As always, the session was presided over in name by his father, King Dhritarastra – the man, he noted with a private smile, with the greatest ambitions of them all.

Aware that everyone's eyes were on him, Syoddhan stopped mid-stride and spun around to face the group. He said, 'I agree with you, Uncle. But I also think that seeing conspiracy where none exists is counterproductive. Dharma Yudhisthir indulged in such guile and political conniving. Where did it lead him? Men who build towers of sand cannot hope to live in them for long.' He looked at Devala as he spoke. It did not go unnoticed.

The Firewright said, 'I agree. And that is precisely why we must act. You see, the situation now is … shall we say … more comparative than competitive. It doesn't matter what your military strength is in absolute terms. Rather, it matters how much stronger you are, compared to potential challengers.'

'And who might such potential challengers be?'

'Anyone in Aryavarta, really,' Shakuni said. 'Any king or vassal prince who can craft the right alliances with the right people. Ambition is a vice in those who lack the power to act in its furtherance. In a warrior, however, it is the ultimate virtue. Which is why you must choose, you must decide what you will do, and do it quickly. You may think that the events in the east have nothing to do with the General's death. I agree they may not be related in cause, but the consequences are linked. The loss of the forges in Anga makes you weaker. Not considerably weaker, but weak enough that it may tempt another ruler … Say, for example, Susarman of Trigarta, may consider annexing Matsya. Admittedly, Susarman is hardly a match for you and your allies today, but that would change the moment he holds Matsya – enough for many of your vassals to go over to his side. You cannot afford to ignore the inevitable. Now that the General is dead, every man of some means in Aryavarta will think, at least briefly, of conquering Matsya. There are few who can do it, but the point is why should you not be the one?'

Syoddhan sighed, still not convinced. 'Why is Matsya so important? We don't even know what is there!'

It was Sanjaya who said, 'Neither does anyone else. Matsya may mean nothing, or it may be everything. No one knows, and it was our common ignorance, combined with caution, that had led all of Aryavarta to stay away from Matsya. But the empire ... it is like a pack of wild dogs, Your Highness. They wait, wary of each other, but as soon as one of them makes a move towards the meat, they will all throw themselves at it. And besides, you might be willing to trust in the loyalty of your vassals, but there are others to consider ...'

Indifferent to Bhisma and Dron's presence and eager to show it, Vasusena let out a crude swear. 'Yabha! Who in the name of an elephant's backside are you talking about?'

Devala said, 'What about Dharma Yudhisthir? And what about Govinda Shauri?'

'Listen to me carefully, Syoddhan,' Dron began in the tone of instruction that had now become a habit. 'You're now the strongest of warriors in all of Aryavarta and, by the values we hold sacrosanct, the only one fit to lead. Lawfully and morally either you or your father ought to become the Emperor of Aryavarta. But the fact remains that Dharma is your brother. He and the other four are Kaurava as much as you are, and as for Govinda ...'

Syoddhan favoured the teacher with a doubtful look. It bordered on insolence, but right then he felt little respect for his father's counsellors. 'Vathu!' he snapped. 'Enough! Govinda! Govinda! What's this constant obsession with Govinda? Why does everyone elevate him, as if he remains above these sordid affairs? All over Aryavarta, men long for power and title – scholar and warrior alike. Govinda is just one of those men. A clever man no doubt, but he's no different from the rest! None of us is! But, I no longer care to pass judgement on Govinda Shauri, or my cousin Dharma, or anyone else for that matter.

'Consider me a fool if you like, but I believe that we must live by the principles that we seek to embed in the fabric of society. This isn't just a moral stand, but a practical one. If we forsake principles to send a message, then that message itself is lost. We can't fight manipulation with more manipulation and intrigue; nor can we change a tyrannical system by resorting to coercion. Still ...' He took a deep breath and added, 'I won't risk civil war for this. Announce to the vassals that there will be a joint expedition to Matsya. We will begin by laying siege to the city-state and see if we can negotiate a surrender. Above all, I want Susarman's cooperation in this. If it is to happen, let it happen that way.'

Bhisma intervened, 'Consider the alternative too, Syoddhan. What if we refuse to invade Matsya? If we refuse to be yet another kingdom harnessed into submission by the Firewrights?'

It was Devala who answered, though he addressed Syoddhan. 'Then you risk being harnessed into submission by Govinda Shauri. Or, really, any man who is willing to seize the might that is Matsya. You cannot confuse the future of the Kuru kingdom, why even all of Aryavarta, with your affections for your kinsmen. Who in Aryavarta can exercise the restraint you and your grand-nephew here have shown? Really, would you trust anyone else? I have named Dharma and Govinda as your obvious contenders, but surely you can see that there are others too?' he glanced, discreet but meaningful, at Dussasan.

Bhisma followed the Firewrights's gaze. He began to speak, ostensibly in continuation of his earlier argument, but decided against it. Syoddhan looked at the two of them and then at his brother. The very sight of Dussasan, insolently sprawled out, languid and half-drunk, made Syoddhan feel strangely repulsed, and the thought of that drunken pig on any throne only increased his resolve to keep a firm hold over the empire. He drew his breath in with a hiss as he realized how the many threads came together. 'All right.'

'But what about Govinda?' Dussasan drawled.

Syoddhan ignored the drool that rolled down his brother's drink-slackened jaw and looked to Vasusena. 'Take care of it. Quietly. Don't involve any of the Yadus. I don't want Govinda's death laid at our doorstep. And take care of that problem in Anga, too. You said you suspected a rebellion by the forest-folk, isn't it? Well, deal with them in a way that affirms our control over the situation. I want you to bring your troops here to join in the attack against Matsya. Make an example of those foresters so that no one will think of giving us trouble while our attention is on the west.'

Vidur stepped in. 'This is both unnecessary and misguided, Syoddhan,' he said. 'I must protest. Dharma...'

'And I must insist,' Syoddhan said. 'You're notoriously transparent, Kshatta. You've always had a soft corner for Dharma, but now you are allowing your partiality to interfere with your duty as the royal advisor. It seems to me that all your counsel is designedly contrary to my interests. It certainly doesn't become a man of your reputation to manipulate me this way!'

'The task of a counsellor is to provide advice, irrespective of whether it draws fame or disfavour. I realize that my words are no longer pleasing, nor welcome to you. But, forgive me, it's my duty to say what I must. Nothing is ever gained by forsaking compassion and virtue. My advice cannot change to please your tastes. If you order me to leave, I'll obey without hesitation. But, if I speak, my counsel remains the same.'

'Then, Kshatta, you'll no doubt understand if I choose, as a simple policy, to never heed a word you say. Particularly when my teacher and my grandfather both agree that my chosen course of action is the one I'm duty-bound to follow – whether it brings desirable outcomes or not.'

'As you wish.' Vidur inclined his head politely.

Syoddhan nodded and strode out of the room. All the others followed him, except for Vidur.

'Your Highness,' Vidur began, as soon as he was alone with the king. 'You know Syoddhan will listen to you. If you forbid him...'

'Ah, brother! I know your advice to be for the best but, alas, I'm at the mercy of my tempestuous son and his noble ambitions. He is every bit a warrior and believes in the virtue of conquest. At times, he may appear over-eager, but like you he always has our nation's glory at heart.' Dhritarastra sighed again, for added effect. 'You're lucky, dear Vidur. You don't know what a father must suffer for the love he bears his son.'

Vidur said nothing. He knew Dhritarastra's comment could not be further from the truth.

14

SANJAYA GAVALGANI SMILED IN HARD-WON SATISFACTION. AFTER all these years, things were now in place, just where he had meant for them to be. One last detail remained, one last man to be settled into submission. But there was no room for mistakes. He had to let the man make the first move. So, Sanjaya waited patiently till Vidur sent for him. He then made his way to the older courtier's study briskly enough to show respect yet in a leisurely enough manner to show confidence. As he strode down the corridors, Sanjaya found himself thinking of his childhood, here in this very palace at Hastina. It seemed appropriate to indulge in a little reminiscence, for today would be a very big day.

Sanjaya had known neither his father nor his mother. He had been brought up with the Kuru princes, as one of them – at least for a while. But a suta could be treated as a prince for only so long. He was merely the son of Gavalgana, King Vichitravirya's charioteer. Or so they had told him.

As a young man, Sanjaya had once searched through the palace's old administrative records. Nowhere did he find as much as a salary payment to Gavalgana noted nor any mention of where and how the charioteer had died. Sanjaya had often thought it a joke that the name Gavalgani literally meant 'king of bulls'. It was ironic. The bull, the sacred emblem of Rudra himself, was also the insignia of the Firstborn.

He waited at Vidur's door for the attendant to announce him. Entering, he greeted the older man with a silent bow. 'Sanjaya!' Vidur welcomed him with warmth. His cheer faded as he noticed the aura of cold composure that Sanjaya exuded. 'Well, you've been expecting this encounter, haven't you? In that case, you also know what it is I plan to say ... '

'Yes. I have expected it, and I do know what you'll say. But, I doubt if you've expected what I'm going to tell you ... or ask you ...'

Vidur looked perplexed, but said nothing. He gestured for Sanjaya to sit, but remained standing himself.

'Why?' Sanjaya asked, after a while.

As Vidur remained silent, Sanjaya chuckled sardonically and said, 'I know everything. I just want to hear your feeble explanations, before I tell you how you've destroyed everything with your folly. Now tell me – why?'

'Because ...' Vidur tried, but could not speak further.

Anger flashed across Sanjaya's face and he strode over to where the older man stood. In a low, sad tone, he asked, 'Is it because you wanted the fame of giving up your own flesh and blood? I can understand why Grandfather did what he did, but how could *you*? And now look at how they treat you, trample all over you, call you "Kshatta" and "Dasi-putra"! How can you bear it, when those who should be scraping at your feet treat you as their slave? Shame on you!'

Vidur felt a twinge of disappointment, but forced himself to ignore it. 'Because I'm not ashamed of who I am, Sanjaya. I *am* a dasi-putra. Whatever else I could have been, I'm happy to be Vidur, the kshatta. That is who I believed I was for many years, just as you've believed yourself to be Sanjaya Gavalgani.'

Breathing out hard, Sanjaya subsided, touched by the other's man's simple confidence. 'It's not you I'm angry with, really,' he ventured.

'I know,' Vidur replied, 'but I must also confess that I don't see what it is you really want.'

'I want justice. Is that so difficult to understand?' Sanjaya felt tired, impossibly tired. On impulse, he went down on his knees in front of Vidur.

'Father ...' he tentatively said, the longing visible in his eyes.

Vidur stiffened, and then, with a nod, he yielded. He helped the kneeling man to his feet and embraced him as he had longed to for many years now.

'Ah, Sanjaya! This has been the most painful secret of them all to keep. How many times I've longed to call you my son, to embrace you with pride, but ...'

'But … ?' Sanjaya asked, as he stepped back from his father's embrace.

'My father, your grandfather … Dwaipayana … feared that it would condemn your generation, as it had condemned mine. Already, the strife between Pandu and Dhritarastra had been passed on to their sons. To acknowledge you – it would have led not just every Kaurava, but also all of Aryavarta into civil war. Surely, you of all people know enough politics to see that?'

'And you let him convince you?' Sanjaya rhetorically questioned. With a groan of resignation, he sat down on a cushioned stool and buried his face in his hands. 'What madness is this!' he finally remarked. 'I can't understand what shred of dignity remains for us, with all these lies and the deceit. A man knows neither father nor brother, leave alone his lineage or right.'

'Dignity lies in doing what is right and good in the time that we hold, my son,' Vidur said. 'Today we see the tangled web that has been woven over three, perhaps more, generations. But you must remember that our forebears took decisions as best they could, without the benefit of hindsight.'

'And so you'd have me accept my lot in life, to call it my fate and submit unquestioningly?'

'No, Sanjaya. Your fate is what you make of it.'

'And if I refuse to accept Dharma, or even Syoddhan, as my Emperor? If I question their right to rule?'

'Then you will certainly cause war.'

'It's been caused already.'

'What do you really want, Sanjaya?'

Sanjaya looked up at Vidur in earnest, his eyes tearful and pleading. 'If ever you've loved me as a son, I beg you, tell me the truth… Did you not think of claiming your right? Not even once?'

Vidur smiled at his son and squeezed his shoulder in reassurance, before sitting down next to him. 'Yes,' he replied, 'yes, I did once. Not as long as my brother Pandu lived and ruled, not even when he died. But, for a while, just before Dharma was declared Crown Prince, I did think of claiming my right, as you call it. I toyed with the idea… with many ideas.'

'Why didn't you…?'

'Because I met Govinda Shauri, Prince of Mathura,' Vidur said.

Sanjaya tried to conceal his mixed emotions, but failed. 'Govinda!' he spat out before he could stop himself.

Vidur continued, 'I dare say many people have that reaction to his name. The version that you've probably heard, the story that is most often told, is that of a prince hidden away at childhood, who finally discovered his true identity and saved his people. But the man I met was no prince, despite his crown and his silks and jewellery. He was a common gwala, a man true to the hard earth he'd tilled and tough as stone. And he was proud of it. That's when I decided, Sanjaya. I didn't want to be the kshatta who discovered his identity as something more. I didn't want that for you, either, all these years.'

'What else could anyone want?' Sanjaya was terse.

'A world where there is no shame in being who you are. I don't want to be raised out of my lowly creed, my son. I want to be respected for who I am. Do you understand?'

A silence fell over the two men, and they sat that way for a long time. Eventually, as the sun's blood-red rays faded and darkness crept into the room, Vidur stirred. He went over to the door and opened it. An attendant had left a small wick lamp on the doorstep. Vidur picked it up and walked around, lighting the large earthen lamps that hung around the room.

Sanjaya followed his father's actions with his eyes, realizing for the first time the stark simplicity, the poverty almost, that Vidur lived in. There were many, he knew, who were less close to the king, but had received much greater rewards over the years.

Was this nobility? Or was it merely a stubborn refusal to come to terms with reality?

Dwaipayana had chosen a different kind of power, but he was no less a ruler of men than any king in Aryavarta. But Vidur had chosen to remain the son of a slave, condemning himself and his progeny. Few knew the name of his acknowledged son – a minor clerk in an administrative function, or that of his daughter, a girl married away into comfortable obscurity. Vidur's children, for all practical purposes, barely existed. *No!* Sanjaya noted. *Not all his children.*

He stood up, causing Vidur to turn and look at him.

'I don't believe you,' Sanjaya said. 'I don't believe it was principle alone that stopped you all these years. It was shame. You were ashamed, as your father has been! And that shame is what has led the rest of Aryavarta to trample on us for years. You are as responsible for what happened to us as any Firstborn bastard!'

'And what would I be so ashamed of, Sanjaya? Or my father?'

'That which you pretend to be ignorant of even now, even here. You know as well as I do who your grandmother was, Father. You were young and I was just a child, but I remember the things she said as she lay dying, even if it took me decades to understand. She was proud of who she was. But you, and her son… It doesn't matter. I am proud of being of her blood. I am proud of what she was. And I shall say it without shame: Your grandmother, my great-grandmother, Queen Satya, from whom all of us of the Kaurava clan have descended, was a Firewright.'

15

IF VIDUR WAS STUNNED, HE DID NOT SHOW IT. LIKE THE PATIENT advisor he was, he tried to meet Sanjaya's passionate rhetoric with reason. 'Don't make this personal, Sanjaya. All that matters is the good of the people. You have unleashed an animal you cannot tame. Already, the kings and warriors of the realm have begun to compete with each other, they begin to fear and loathe each other as they struggle for supremacy. If you were to let Syoddhan attack Matsya, then it is the beginning of the end. Not only will you allow war to break out in Aryavarta, but it will be war of unimaginable proportions. Matsya…'

'…is the last bastion of the Firewrights. It is what I need to rule.'

'Sanjaya, please. It doesn't have to be this way. You must think of the people, of the larger good. Dharma's reinstatement as Emperor can make the people believe in themselves, in benevolence and goodness, and that is why I plead with Syoddhan to share his throne. You can't make a man dream of the stars if he refuses to look up. The people must believe that they deserve their prosperity and happiness and shrug off their shackles of fatalistic subservience. Dharma is what Aryavarta needs. And now, with you by his side...'

Sanjaya laughed. 'Dharma? As Emperor? Surely that particular bird fled its roost a long time ago. I cannot believe that you are still hoping...no, dreaming... But then, you always did show exceptional affection for Dharma. Should I start wondering why?' His tone, however, made it clear that he knew too much to truly have to speculate.

Vidur did not appear to be affected by the possibilities of what Sanjaya did or did not think. 'What more will you do just to be rid of Dharma? Sanjaya, I admit it, as does everyone concerned: You are the most powerful man in Aryavarta. You control our destiny. Syoddhan and his allies are at your command. And so it is that I urge you to use your power wisely. You can guide us all to peace, if you will. Please...'

Sanjaya sighed, sounding tired. 'You still don't understand, Father. If I had been born a Suta, I wouldn't have regretted it. It's the fate that the gods would have ordained for me, as I deserved. And my pride, my honour, would lie in loyally serving my masters, not in seeking to be their equal. But that is not how it is. Time and again my right was stolen from me – by Dwaipayana, when he relegated you to nothingness; by you, when you submitted without protest; and by Govinda Shauri, when he destroyed those I consider my true family. It is my duty to reclaim that which is rightfully mine.'

'And in doing so, you'll destroy your own.'

Sanjaya nodded. Vidur did indeed have a flair for the dramatic and much as it could sway Dhritarastra and Bhisma, it had little effect on him. Snidely he replied, 'You and your father have done that already...'

'Sanjaya...'

'Enough. I came here, Father, with the faint hope that you'd understand what I am about to do and why. But you will remain the shame-tainted bastard son of a slave you consider yourself to be, living in your make-believe world and pretending to be wise and noble. I, however, am Arya: a nobleman and a warrior. And I won't rest till I win, or die! Whether you like it or not, I must say this: Tell that old fool Dwaipayana to spend his time in prayer and, if he feels so inclined, contemplation of how his twisted ideas of morality and virtue have led us here. If he tries to interfere, to stop the attack on Matsya, I will bring him down in a way he's never imagined.'

'Stop being a fool, Sanjaya…'

'I'm no fool! No, not at all. You see, Dwaipayana himself taught me that every man has his secrets, dangerous secrets that the wise can use to control and even to destroy. What he forgot, in his pride, was that he too is a man and that his secret is the most terrible of them all. The day all Aryavarta comes to know that Krishna Dwaipayana, the greatest Vyasa of the Firstborn, was born of the womb of a Firewright… Well, that will be the end of him and his precious order. If he wants my silence, he will have it. But in return I want Matsya. As for your precious Dharma… As always, he is a regrettable inconvenience, and I honestly would be relieved if he died and spared me the trouble of going around him all the time. Oh, don't look so shocked! I will leave him alive unless he gets in my way. And the same goes for your dear father, too. Otherwise, I assure you, three generations will pay the price.' With a stiff bow, Sanjaya walked out.

Vidur sat as he was, lost in thought. He stirred only as he felt the weight of another on the seat next to him. 'What now?' he asked the man next to him.

He had never seen Dwaipayana looking so forlorn in all his life. 'He was always the cleverest of the lot. He knows what he's doing. Three generations, he says. You and I are lost for sure, but so are Dharma, Syoddhan and Suka… Hai! Varuna save us! Nothing can stop Sanjaya now.'

Slowly, Vidur began, 'There may be hope…'

'Hope…? Where on earth can we find that?'

'You and I haven't seen eye to eye on many things, Father, and I know what I'm about to propose now may be unpalatable to you. Reach out to Govinda Shauri.'

'And destroy in an instant the only legacy I may have left? He has already eroded our legitimacy and power. If he fails again it will condemn us forever.'

'But he need not fail. Govinda…'

'Stop! Don't even say it! Don't mention that cowherd by name!'

'But there's no other way. You willingly relied on him once…'

'And he betrayed me, just as he betrayed the Firewrights. I can't trust that man, Vidur! We can't. We can't trust Govinda any more than we can trust Sanjaya.'

'Trust yourself then. Trust your upbringing, if not your blood.'

Dwaipayana felt the sense of being old and feeble wash over him once again. It had become his constant state now. He had come to think it was who he really was – an old fool. 'Everything, everything that I have worked so hard for will be taken from me. Was I so selfish, Vidur? You know I've wanted nothing more than a righteous realm, a realm that mirrored the Divine Order on earth. And, yes, I've been human enough to want to leave that righteous realm as an enduring legacy to my son. I wanted him to remain untainted by my past, by the blood and politics that has brought us to our glory. Is that too much to ask for?'

'Perhaps it is, Father,' Vidur said. 'Perhaps, this is the ultimate sacrifice that you must make.'

'You mean…?'

'Yes. Send for Suka. Tell him the truth. Let him decide what must now be done. He is the future Vyasa. Leave Aryavarta in his care. To ally with the Firewrights or not. To defy Sanjaya or not. To trust Govinda or not. They are his decisions to make, and he will do what is right. Suka is a good man. Trust in that.'

Dwaipayana thought for a few moments, each instant an effort of will to persist and not give up completely. At length, he said, 'You're right, Vidur. If only I'd found the courage to do it earlier, Sanjaya would never have had such a hold over me nor would the Firstborn stand in such danger. Now, I don't know of what use it is to tell Suka who I am, who he really is … But I can no longer carry this burden on my own. Let my son bear it for me henceforth. Even so …'

'Yes, Father?'

Dwaipayana's eyes held uncharacteristic agony. 'I fear it may already be too late.'

16

DWARAKA SPARKLED LIKE A PEARL WITHIN AN OYSTER, HELD IN a seamless embrace between the dark sea and the night sky. Viewed this way, from a peak atop the Raivata range, it seemed illusory, an island floating in nothingness, a city of angels and celestials. Philista knew that her fondness for the city was in many ways the result of her fondness for the man she always thought of as the soul of Dwaraka: Govinda Shauri. She wondered what he was doing even as her eyes sought out the tallest cluster of turrets, her gaze misting over as it settled on a familiar tower. But she had to do what she had to, no matter how much it hurt. She sighed, impatient, as she turned away and looked for signs of the man who was to meet her here. But the woods were dark and quiet. Dark, like Govinda's eyes.

Philista sighed yet again. She had proclaimed on more than one occasion that she would never tire of looking into those large eyes, or at the sharp, strong angles of his cheeks and, of course, those perfect lips: neither too full nor too thin. She remembered how, the first time Govinda had visited her native city of Elis, men and women alike had stared at him in admiration, citing his dark skin as a curiosity. Her inquisitiveness had been more philosophical; she had found his ideas and knowledge fascinating.

Indeed, that was why he had come to the Yavana lands, seeking out their philosophers and scholars – her own teacher Pyrrho in particular – to debate, discuss and share, though the first of those debates had been more of a personal argument. Philista had walked in on the two men to find Pyrrho uncharacteristically enraged. 'Leave!' he was shouting at Govinda. 'My family has done enough for you and your kind. I owe Aryavarta nothing. I owe Ghora Angirasa nothing.'

'Acharya, please, listen to me …' Govinda had persisted.

Philista remembered the septuagenarian Pyrrho rising in wrath on hearing the word with which Govinda addressed him – in what she supposed was Aryavarta's native tongue. He had turned to Philista. 'Ask this man to leave, Philista. Or else I don't know what I will do next.'

Govinda had not said another word, but began walking out of the room. Philista had escorted him out. Torn by curiosity, she had asked him who he was. His accent had been strong, but he replied in her tongue, 'My name is Govinda Shauri. I belong to an order of scholars known as Angirasa.' Sensing that she did not completely understand, he explained, 'It means Firewright.' It had not taken her long to see the connection. 'Pyrrho', in her tongue, meant 'of fire'.

When she had gently pressed her teacher for the entire tale, he had told her how he and his family had, many decades ago, escaped from the bloody scourge that had torn apart all of Aryavarta. Over the years, they had become people of Yavana in heart and soul, but memories of their past, of the injustices and horrors they and their kin had faced, remained alive.

'What did that man – this Govinda Shauri – want?' she had asked at the end of the narration.

'He says he has a plan. He wants the world to be united by knowledge, by the light of reason and learning. He aims to do what we have been doing here in Elis – sharing knowledge, spreading it – and asks for my help so that both our realms may prosper.'

'Hah! Another idealist who dreams of changing the world. His plan, can it even work?'

Pyrrho had drawn a deep breath. 'I do not know. This much I will admit – I have never seen a man so rational and immaculate in his thought as he. If anyone can change the world, he can. But whether it will work I do not know. The question he left me with is this: Would I be able to live with not trying?'

'I wouldn't,' Philista had said. 'But that is because I would never be able to look my teacher in the eye if I didn't.'

To that, Pyrrho had laughed and said, 'All right. Send for Govinda Shauri. No, wait. Not immediately. Tomorrow. Do it tomorrow. Let him fester for a day, and then we shall send for him and hear him out completely.'

And so began a long association – part friendship, part collegial affinity and part desire.

Philista wished, with a little regret, that her reasons for seeking him out over the seas after nearly twenty years had not been different. But it was not attraction, whether physical or otherwise, that had brought her to Aryavarta. Her fellow scholars – the Firewrights of Elis, as Govinda had jestingly referred to them – had placed much of their faith in Govinda's proposed plan, in what he had averred would be beneficial to both Yavana and Aryavarta, and perhaps even beyond. Pyrrho, however, had not shirked from pointing out the risks, over and over again.

'If all goes as you say, Govinda, both our lands will prosper. Craft and knowledge shall drive both our civilizations to great heights. If, however, things do not progress as you promise, it will without doubt lead our nations towards war. History teaches us that where power fails to lead to prosperity and peace, it inevitably engenders envy, fear and conflict.'

'Trust in the goodness of men and women, Acharya,' Govinda had said. 'Trust in yourself.'

In spite of herself, it broke Philista to admit that it was this trust, this faith in humanity, that Govinda had now lost. His plan had fallen apart, and there was nothing he could do to set things right. Worse, he was not even willing to try. Already, Aryavarta stood splintered by fear and distrust, and its many nations were competing to build their armies and arsenals. And Govinda no longer cared where it would lead them. He was broken, just as his realm was broken, the remains of a dream gone horribly wrong. It was, Philista knew, the beginning of the end, of the inevitable erosion of a way of life. And nowhere was it more obvious than in Dwaraka.

The city-state that Govinda and Balabadra had built with love and devotion, was now a shadow of its former self. In appearance, Dwaraka lacked nothing of its former glory, but Philista could see the changes, the political conspiracies and skewed views of equality, goodness and justice. The Council was no longer the democratic and representative body it had once averred to be. Kritavarman, Bhurisravas and the other Yadu princes who had given up their sovereignty as vassal princes to join the Confederation of Yadu Nations had taken the opportunity to reassert their dominance, rebuild their personal armies and replenish their personal coffers. Dwaraka was perhaps on the verge of descending into civil war, and that, Philista knew, would be the spark that would light the huge blaze in which Aryavarta would burn as would the Yavana lands, the lands she called home.

There is nothing left to do but act. Thus resolved, Philista turned yet again to glance at the forest behind her. This time she saw the dark outline of a horse and rider. She did not move till the man stepped out from the cover of the trees and into the moonlight.

The sight of Jayadrath, king of Sindhu, filled Philista with revulsion. She had overheard, unseen, Balabadra's careful recounting of the attack on Panchali, and could never forget the sight of Govinda on his knees, broken and utterly devastated. Finding a modicum of satisfaction in the fact that Jayadrath looked a little bruised from his encounter, she stepped forward to greet him.

'Mahamatra, thank you for agreeing to meet with me. I regret that I am not in a position to offer you any refreshment or other hospitality. But such are our circumstances.'

Philista found such politeness from a man of Jayadrath's reputation amusing, but she kept a straight face and came to the point. 'What are the terms? What do you want?' she asked curtly.

'Govinda Shauri.'

'And what do I get in return?'

'The promise of peace with Aryavarta's future Emperor. He sends you a scroll. It is written in your language so you may share it with your ... superiors.'

Philista took the proffered object and ran her eyes over it. 'It is neither in his hand, nor does it bear his seal.'

'Of course not. He's not a fool.'

'But I am, to take him at his word?'

Jayadrath frowned. 'Surely you've been here long enough to know that to an Arya truth is not a negotiable quality.'

'Negotiable, no. But it is adaptable – that much I have learnt.'

'Hence he sends his terms and assurances in writing.'

Philista rolled up the scroll and tapped it against her open palm as she considered the offer. She said, 'Is he that valuable to you? Govinda Shauri? These are generous terms to offer in exchange for the life of one man.'

'We need one other thing. Information ... of a particular kind.'

'And Govinda Shauri has it?'

'Yes.'

'What is it?'

Jayadrath shook his head. 'First, I need your word that you will fulfil this task. Only then can I tell you more. Now tell me, can you do this?'

Philista gave him a doubtful look. 'You know it's not easy. If it were, you wouldn't have sought my help.'

'It is not impossible either. But we would rather that our involvement in this be kept a secret – even from the Yadu leaders we are inclined to think of as our allies.'

'You mean Kritavarman and Bhurisravas. What makes you think I want them for enemies?'

Jayadrath's lips curved in a leering smile. 'It won't make a difference. Do this, and we throw our support behind you. You an your people will have everything to gain.'

Philista said, 'It can't be done in Dwaraka. We need to get him out of there. He is under guard on the Council's orders ...'

'If you invite him to your ship ... I mean, it is well known that you ...'

Jayadrath's tone made Philista's head buzz with anger. She was about to protest against the insinuations, but then decided not to waste her time. 'If I invite him, the Council will certainly not let him leave Dwaraka. They don't trust me and might even suspect that I am planning to help him escape. On the other hand, if you can get one of the traders to ask for Govinda's services – say with a ship's repairs or such ... Make it about money ... the Council doesn't like to lose any. Let me know which ship. I will take care of the rest.'

'Chop his body into pieces and throw it into the sea. That way it won't wash ashore and everyone will think he has escaped. Particularly, if your involvement is not known and you stay at Dwaraka a while to mourn him ...'

The urge to hit Jayadrath hard, to chop *him* into bits and throw *him* off the cliff, coursed through Philista. She fought it back, breathing hard from the effort, and managed a single nod.

Jayadrath raised an eyebrow at her reaction but dismissed it. He continued, 'All right. As for the information we want...'

Philista felt her heart thunder in her chest as Jayadrath told her what it was that he was looking for. She had only to hear the beginning of it before her mind began speeding through many horrible possibilities, including the thought that possessing such a powerful weapon might tempt Jayadrath to turn against his own allies and his liege-lord. Yet she felt grateful for the cold, benumbing fear, for it helped her pretend that her guilt was assuaged. She had no choice but to betray Govinda.

When Jayadrath finally left, she shut her eyes and drew in a deep breath. *One man for my homeland... it is a reasonable trade.* She had been with Govinda long enough to know that if he had been in her place he would have done the same. It helped Philista make her peace with what would happen next.

17

THE DISCOVERY HAD BEEN UNEXPECTED. DHRSTYADYMN HAD ridden east, as Asvattama had directed, and begun scouring the region without much result. Shikandin was a hard man to find if he did not wish to be found. Dhrstyadymn would have counted it his good fortune but knew it was a matter of patience and persistence when he finally heard a piece of gossip in a small drinking-house about arson and rebellion in the Anga kingdom. The fact that no one had ever seen the man, or men, responsible for the acts had been enough to convince Dhrstyadymn that he had found Shikandin.

Dhrstyadymn headed to Anga, but instead of making his way to the capital, he had followed the rumours to a corner of the kingdom that adjoined the nation of Kashi. It gave him an idea. He crossed over into Kashi and sought the help of the captain of a small border garrison, claiming that he was a Panchala soldier in pursuit of a wanted man. As he had expected, the captain was happy to assist, if only to demonstrate how the warriors of Kashi were more efficient than that of Panchala. In the same vein, the captain arranged for all the permissions needed to take their search across the border and into Anga.

Three days later, they came upon the tracks of a single man, hardly muhurttas old. They followed the trail to the scene of a massacre in progress. Dhrstyadymn had no doubt, even from their unobtrusive distance atop a small hill, that it was Shikandin. He watched as his brother methodically disposed of the guards around the simple hut-like structure and he wondered whether he had been right to have come looking for him, after all.

The Kashi captain escorting him intruded on his thoughts. 'You see, this could hardly be the fellow you're looking for. This man is a rebel, a spy the Anga forces have been trying to get their hands on for ages now. Finally, he walks into their trap.'

'Trap? Oh please. There are hardly any men positioned around. What sort of a sorry trap is that?'

'There are soldiers hiding in the woods, on the other side. Not many, because nearly all of Anga's troops have been deployed westwards. In any case, the soldiers are not needed – they intend to kill this rebel, not capture him. You see, this man follows a pattern. He kills the guards and destroys the workshop they protect. This time he is in for a shock… Anyway, make yourself comfortable. The Angas won't want us to interfere, not in this one. The border commandant told me to make sure we stayed out of the way.'

One word in all of the captain's speech caught Dhrstyadymn's attention. 'Workshop?' he asked.

The captain was taken aback. 'Yes. Workshop… forge. Oh, by Hara, you really are a novice aren't you? Else you'd know… unless, you Panchalas are such fools that you're the only nation in Aryavarta that isn't building up its armouries…' Before the garrulous man could finish, Dhrstyadymn drew a dagger from his waist-sash and plunged it directly into the man's heart. He put his hand over the dying captain's mouth, in case he cried out, but it was not necessary. The man was dead in an instant.

Dhrstyadymn began sprinting down the gentle slope. He thought of calling out, but decided against it, since he might alert the other waiting soldiers. He saw that Shikandin was done with the last of the guards around the forge, and was making his way towards the dark doorway.

A blast of heat, like thunder and lightning, exploded out from the bowels of the earth, and Dhrstyadymn felt himself thrown backwards and on to the ground. He pulled himself up, horrified to find that the forge, if it was that, had been reduced to burning rubble. By the light of the fire, he saw Shikandin's still outline on the ground, his limbs splayed at an awkward angle. With a yell that was part rage and part fear, Dhrstyadymn ran to his brother. He was just in time, for more Anga soliders poured out of the woods.

Dhrstyadymn counted nine of them. He skidded to a halt as he reached where Shikandin lay, and took up a position with his bow. He knew he did not have much time, but this was his only chance to reduce the enemy's numbers as much as possible before they got too close. He let his arrows fly in quick succession, moving without hesitation from one target to the next. He managed to down seven men, one of them taking two arrows to fall, before the remaining two were upon him. Letting his bow fall, Dhrstyadymn drew his sword and met them head-on.

Metal rang against metal, and birds stirred near and far, taking to the air with chilling shrieks. Dhrstyadymn added a cry of his own as he felt a burning pain run from his left shoulder all the way down his arm and back. His vision blurred, but as he staggered back he realized that two men had come at him from the side. Only then did he realize what an odd number nine was. Why hadn't it occurred to him earlier? A group of ten, with the eleventh in command, was a basic army unit. His failure to see the obvious sent panic coursing through him. He pushed it out of his mind. *Four against one. I can do this.* But even as he made the assertion, he felt the heavy, cloying emptiness of doubt spread through his body, slow down his limbs. He told himself it was impossible, that no weapon, nothing but his mind could defeat his own will. But his will was fast fading.

This is why. This is why Dron did not think me worthy. It does not matter how many years I train, how hard I try. I lack a warrior's spirit. I was willing to doubt my own brother. I am not worthy.

Blood trailed from his hands, his wrists, down his arms. From the corner of his eye, he could see the drops falling off his elbow and on to the mossy earth, creating dark, wet patches. He thought of Panchali, of the dark stains on her body and robe as she was dragged through the halls of Hastina. He thought he heard a crowd far away, cheering and screaming, but all he felt was silence. Silence, and then the small voice that was always there, telling him to let go, to lose, because he would be defeated anyway. He tried not to listen to it but the voice, *his* voice, grew louder and louder till it was shouting in his ear. It taunted him, broke him and rent his very being till he knew that giving up was all he had to do, and he would know relief, the lightness and freedom he constantly longed for. He would have let go at that very instant, except that one of the four men made the mistake of turning away from Dhrstyadymn to kick the prone Shikandin hard in the ribs out of sheer malice.

Dhrstyadymn's heart quailed as Shikandin neither stirred nor made a sound. With a yell of rage he threw himself at the man who had dared touch his brother. Anger made him near-invincible. He was aware of a whiplike stinging again, this time on the back of his thigh, but he didn't care, snarling in satisfaction as the first soldier went down with a dazed look on his face and Dhrstyadymn's dagger in his throat. Another burst of pain, and Dhrstyadymn realized his mistake. Intent on the first soldier, he had nearly ignored the other three.

Childish mistakes! Dron's harsh reprimands came to mind. He always made childish mistakes such as these, errors that even a boy smaller than a sword knew not to make.

Your anger is your strength. Right now it controls you. You will have to learn to control it.

'Aaaaah!' the cry was a roar, not of physical pain but a sensation far more unbearable. Dhrstyadymn ran his sword clean through the first man, and then lashed out at the second soldier, his back turned completely to the third. If the choice was between anger and dismay, he would gladly choose anger; he would gladly go down ablaze than live without hope. In his fury, he had no clear notion of what he was doing, but a few moments later, the second man lay at his feet, dead. But he too had paid the price. He knew he had been slashed at least

253

six times and stabbed at least once. His head throbbed and spun from exertion. His stomach heaved, threatening to bring up a few inner parts along with the bile in his chest and it was all he could do to stand. His eyes closed as he swayed from side to side. He tried to hold on, but felt his sword slide out of his grasp. It seemed to fall a long, long way, as though the earth had opened up to claim it deep inside her core. Dhrstyadymn knew she awaited him the same way.

The last man rushed at him and slashed downwards, right on target towards his neck. Dhrstyadymn felt his knees buckle but remained upright and caught the sword with both hands. It remained inches away from his head. All his training told him that he ought to hold tight and try to sidestep the man, whirl around him, pull his arm into a twist which could give him the upper hand and then he could try to fight on… He forced himself to keep his fingers curled around the blade, ignoring the unbearable pain as the soldier tried his best to rip his sword out from his grasp.

Give up! It will all be over! You cannot do this anyway! You are nothing!

Dhrstyadymn could feel his strength ebbing away as his blood fell, drop by leisurely drop, each speck heavy and rounded with its own weight, each globe shimmering red with life. The next few moments lasted an eternity. Time, he thought, had decided to wait, while his entire being turned into an ocean of red, a cohesive union of millions. *Like rain. Each drop complete in itself.* He closed his eyes. *I am what I am,* he told himself, neither the slayer nor the slain, nothing more and nothing less. Trusting in the instinct that spoke to him without words, he let go of the blade.

Before the soldier could react, Dhrstyadymn turned and stepped in close, mimicking the soldier's stance like a live shadow. Grabbing the man's wrist with his left hand, he added his own strength to his swing. He heard a scream. It sounded like him, yet it was not completely human. He felt the soft resistance of flesh, the iron tang of blood as it filled his mouth, the warmth of it satisfying in its own way, as it drenched his face and flew generously down his chest. The blade stopped inches from his own neck, even as his right hand came up and across in a precautionary gesture, his palm meeting the sharp edge before it could touch him. He let the headless torso fall to the ground and stood as he was, his chest heaving. Slowly, the world stopped spinning.

'Shikandin!' Dhrstyadymn ran to where his brother lay still. He placed his head on the warrior's heart, but he could neither feel nor hear a beat. 'Shikandin! No!' He shook his brother, thumped his chest and tried his best to revive him, but it was of no use.

Soon, dawn brought the forest around them alive in a melody of sound and activity but still Shikandin did not stir. As the sun forced its way through the canopy, Dhrstyadymn could hold on no longer. He felt himself fall over his brother's torso. The last thing he remembered was the stinging in his eyes as the tears broke through.

18

DHRSTYADYMN OPENED HIS EYES TO FIND HIMSELF IN A BOWER in the forest. Sunlight and shadow fell in dappled patterns of green and gold, and the musical hum of honeybees filled the air. Yet, it was a gentle, familiar, touch that sent life and joy coursing back through him.

'Shikandin!' He sat up at once, the action causing a sharp pain to pierce through his abdomen.

'Easy…' Shikandin cautioned, helping his brother up into a sitting position. He looked tired and worn, but otherwise unhurt.

'How…? Where are we?'

'We are, politically speaking, in the Kashi kingdom, but these forests are… well, they are like our Eastern Forests: a world unto its own. As for the how – I carried you here. I was stunned by the explosion, but have a faint recollection of you dancing on my chest before you fell over me. Still it appears you managed to revive me with that battering, so I shall not complain about it. Especially since you look like you've tried to mate with a crocodile.'

Dhrstyadymn looked down at the profusion of cuts on his body, most of them already cleaned and bound. He knew he should not have survived, but was glad that he had. Slowly, as he began to take stock of himself and his surroundings, he noticed that his wounds had been treated with a green unguent that had an unfamiliar smell. He also noticed two lithe, dark men sitting on their haunches, preparing what he supposed was the same unguent by chewing certain berries in their mouth to a paste-like consistency and then spitting out the paste into a bowl made of woven leaves. Dhrstyadymn let out a sullen curse at which the men looked up, waved their greetings and resumed their chewing.

Shikandin laughed. 'It's a mighty useful healing salve, brother. Saliva activates the healing power of the leaves – even crushing them won't have the same effect. And if you're feeling well enough to notice these things, I'd say the medicine has served its purpose. So I suppose you can return the favour and tell me how it is you came to be at the forge last night.'

'Asvattama sent me.'

'Asvattama? That is a surprise. But…'

Dhrstyadymn continued, 'He said, "Shikandin is one of the strongest men I know, but even the strength of the greatest man can fail if he loses hope. Your brother needs you; he needs you to believe that he is not a traitor to his people." The rest of that conversation was in his usual, insolent style, so I won't bother with it, if you don't mind. But this seemed important. It… it stayed in my head.'

Shikandin smiled, deep wrinkles fanning out from the corners of his eyes as he did so. 'Some things never change. Asvattama always loved to prove that he was the most intelligent man of the three of us.'

'Three of you?'

'He, Govinda and me. Asvattama was forever berating me as impulsive and reckless. Govinda was more like him back then – he was a serious man in many ways, though to see him now…' Shikandin trailed off as the irony of the statement struck him. 'Anyway, if those were Asvattama's words, then he was doing more than telling you where to find me. He was sending me a message: even the strength of the greatest man can fail if he loses hope. And just as I needed you to give me hope, brother, Govinda now needs us to find his own strength.'

'Govinda? But why…?'

'Yes indeed. Why?' Shikandin frowned. 'It can only mean one of two things. Either Aryavarta is in great peril, and Asvattama believes Govinda can help. Or…'

'Or…'

Shikandin took a deep breath and let it out. 'Or Panchali is in trouble.'

Dhrstyadymn's heart skipped a beat. 'Asvattama also said something about you… and your friends… being in danger. You don't suppose he meant..?' He nodded towards the two swarthy men, who politely ignored the brothers' conversation.

Shikandin did not answer the question. Instead, all he said was, 'Come on, it's time to go.' With that, he got up and signalled to the two men to break camp. He set about putting his own things together.

Dhrstyadymn tried to stand up, but felt his head spin.

'Sthuna!' Shikandin called to one of the men for help.

Immediately, Sthuna was at Dhrstyadymn's side, holding him up. With his other hand he pulled out a container, which he opened to reveal a dry powder inside. 'Ashwagandha,' Sthuna explained, in an accent that Dhrstyadymn found new but not incomprehensible. 'It will make you immune to the pain. Your heart will beat faster and you will find some energy. It won't last long and you will feel like a skinned snake later, but for now…'

'Thank you.' Dhrstyadymn took the proffered container and poured the contents down his throat in one go. Sthuna passed him a skin of water right after, which he gratefully consumed. To his surprise, Dhrstyadymn found a fiery heat coursing through his body. He could stand, no, walk even, and his head felt much clearer than it had. The pain from his wounds, too, seemed dimmer.

'No wonder people think these forest-dwellers are magicians. Imagine how useful that little box of magic dust would be after a long night with a concubine,' Shikandin teased, falling in next to his brother as they began making their way through the forest.

Dhrstyadymn said, 'Who are these people?'

'They are the native inhabitants of these forests. People we pretend don't exist anymore. In many ways, they don't. Most of them have given up their old lives to become one more body in the teeming mass of commoners that we call our subjects. Others remain here, living reclusive lives. Our soldiers are often ordered to hunt them down as troublemakers and thieves ... or magicians.'

'Magicians? You mean these people are Firewrights?'

Shikandin laughed. 'What is a Firewright, Dhrstyadymn?' He waited, letting his brother ponder over the question. Eventually, he said, 'It took me a long time to understand. Fire is more than an object, it is an element. The first Firewrights were ordinary people – probably children of the earth like these forest dwellers. Look what has become of them now. Look what has become of us all.'

Dhrstyadymn's head ached with the many questions that he had, but Shikandin was in no mood to continue the discussion. The four trudged on in silence for the rest of the day.

A smile lit up Shikandin's face as a dim outline of huts was seen on the far side of a gurgling stream. It disappeared as Sthuna let out a pained yell.

Before Dhrstyadymn could react, his three companions ran forward, splashing through the stream towards the village. He followed as fast as he could, feeling glad that his strength had returned, but the sight that greeted him made him bend over and retch. Ahead, stood the village, quiet in the smoky haze that hung over it. Right at its entrance, set on stakes a foot high from the ground, were over thirty severed heads.

After what felt like a long time, Shikandin drew his sword. 'Sthuna, go round the village and make sure it's clear. Give the signal.'

Sthuna appeared not to have heard and stood, rigid. His other companion was already on his knees, throwing up and crying at the same time.

Shikandin reached out. 'Sthuna ... Sthuna? Did you hear me?'

Finally, Sthuna stirred. Pulling out a short spear from the array of weapons on his back, he set off around the perimeter of the settlement, his tread cautious, as though he were hunting a wild creature.

Shikandin took a deep breath and began walking towards the gate, and the severed heads. He stopped when he was closer and took a count under his breath. 'None of the children are here,' he noted, with relief. 'But ... we have six women missing.'

'Over here,' Dhrstyadymn said, from between the first cluster of huts. 'The women … are here …'

Shikandin walked to his side with the heavy tread of one who knew what to expect. The women lay dead, their bloodied bodies and naked forms leaving no doubt as to what had happened to them. Shikandin picked up one of their discarded robes from nearby, tore it in two, and covered up two of them. For three of the others, he pulled off and used his upper robe. As he walked over to the last woman, Dhrstyadymn held out his uttariya. Shikandin took it, and dropped to his knees next to the dead woman. He wrapped the robe around her with a tenderness that Dhrstyadymn had never seen in his brother and kissed her dirt-stained forehead.

By the time Sthuna returned, having finished his rounds of the area around the village, Shikandin and Dhrstyadymn had begun digging a large grave.

'The children?' Sthuna asked, a quiver in his voice.

Dhrstyadymn nodded to a still-smouldering hut.

Sthuna took a few steps towards it but as the smell of burnt flesh hit him, he stopped, not daring to go any closer. He turned to Shikandin. 'Did you … ?'

'I did. About seven of the children are missing. Six boys and one girl. I think they must have gone to the forest to play or pick berries, and so have escaped. Kshtradharman and Uttamaujas are, I hope, among them. Their bodies are not here.'

'And Guhyaka? My sister?'

Shikandin merely pointed. Sthuna fell to his knees and began sobbing.

'Sthuna, your daughter too,' Shikandin said. He picked up one of figures he had wrapped in his robe, and carried her over to where Sthuna was sprawled on the ground and laid her in his lap. It was all Dhrstyadymn could do to not scream, as he realized the dead girl could hardly be twelve or thirteen years old.

Unable to take it, he spat out, 'Yabha! How … ? What animals could do this?'

Shikandin replied, 'Human beings do it, Dhrstyadymn. You've seen battle, but you haven't seen massacre. There is something about war that fuels rage and lust and fear and every dark emotion there is. The best of soldiers turn into demons, and even the most noble generals and commanders cannot stop them.'

'This is not war!'

'Isn't it? It is as much war as what is fought on a battlefield. You...you don't know what the Great Scourge was like, brother. What has happened here...it is a re-enactment of those hunts. I guess, Devala has finally had his revenge against me for all those Panchala raids I once led.'

'You? You'd have never let this happen if you had been in command.'

'You didn't know me when I was younger. I've made my share of mistakes.'

'And so? So we forgive that bastard Devala? And Vasusena? It was his men who did this, wasn't it? They must have planned to attack exactly when you were out. I don't understand, Shikandin; nothing makes sense any more. What world is this, where we say: "This is how men are, this is how kings are." Hai, is there no hope?'

'There is always hope,' Shikandin said. He spoke a few words of consolation to Sthuna and finally got him to his feet. 'Get your brother,' he instructed. Sthuna went back to where the other man had collapsed outside the village, but returned alone. He held out a bloody knife to Shikandin.

'He didn't have the courage.'

'Neither do I, Sthuna. But this doesn't take courage. It takes... emptiness.'

Together, the three men buried all the bodies in one grave. It was well past midnight by the time they finished.

'What now?' Dhrstyadymn asked, numb.

In response, Shikandin and Sthuna exchanged glances and began walking into the forest. Dhrstyadymn followed in silence. The men came to stop at what appeared to Dhrstyadymn as a relic of sort – a large stone pillar that bore the marks of the elements and worship both.

Sthuna broke into tears again at the foot of the pillar, while Shikandin stood resting his forehead against the stone.

'What ... who ... what is this?' Dhrstyadymn asked.

'She is Amba. She is the spirit of all those who were burnt alive during the Great Scourge, the eternal spirit of the thousands of innocents whose sacrifice we remember and honour.'

'But ...'

Shikandin shook his head. 'Not now, brother. Now is not the time for stories.' He wrapped his fingers through the white beads around his neck, placing metal and flesh against the stone. He then drew back and began taking off his armour. 'Sthuna. Stay here. The children know to come back here once it's safe. Take them to your mother's tribe. Give my armour to my son, to Uttamaujas. Tell him to train hard, for the next time we meet, we shall avenge his mother's death together. Tell him ... tell him to take care of his little brother.'

With that, he turned away and began walking back towards where they had tethered the horses. Dhrstyadymn refrained from asking any questions.

Shikandin said, swinging into the saddle. 'I'm heading to Dwaraka. You should go home.'

'Shikandin, please. What's the point? Look, I don't care that Govinda is a Firewright – not after everything that I've seen and heard now – but that doesn't change the fact that he's a broken man. In twelve years, we've not heard from him. Rather, we hear of him, of how all he cares about now is drink and women. Is that the Govinda we knew? And if the Govinda we knew still existed, would he have watched and waited all these years?'

'We watched. We waited.'

Dhrstyadymn shouted, 'But he has lost all hope!'

In response, Shikandin urged his horse forward.

Dhrstyadymn threw his hands up in exasperation. 'Wait! Wherever it is you want to go, I'm coming with you,' he said as he swung on to his steed. Muttering to himself, he added, 'Might as well mate with crocodiles together.' Sullenly, he spurred his horse, the forced humour doing nothing to dispel the smell of blood and burning flesh from his mind.

19

'OUR PEOPLE CAN'T FIND ANYTHING WRONG WITH THE SHIP. BUT the sailors insist that there is a problem with the rudder, and that the ship lists and veers at the slightest cross-current. They are demanding that Govinda Shauri himself check the vessel, else they won't pay us the port charges due to us for docking and maintenance.' The attendant tried to put all the authority he commanded, which was not much, into his voice. Failing at the effort, he conceded, 'Or so I was instructed to tell you. And to ensure that Commander... I mean... that is... Govinda... accompany these soldiers here...' He trailed off, partly embarrassed at having used a designation that Govinda no longer carried, and partly at now having to address the man in question with undue familiarity.

Balabadra did not care in the least for the messenger's discomfort, certainly not after he had been woken up in the dead of night. 'Surely,' he argued, 'the loss of a single ship's charge is not worth the time of an emergency council meeting?'

'It's not just one ship. They refuse to pay for the whole fleet and also for the many times they have docked here this year. Commander Kritavarman says it may be best to indulge them. The Council agrees with him.'

'Where is the ship now? In port?'

'On the sea. Beyond the harbour. But one of the smaller sailboats can get us there.'

Balabadra looked questioningly at Govinda, who nodded. It was not enough to convince him. 'Be careful,' he cautioned, in a low whisper. 'I trust these soldiers, and I think the Council has not yet stooped so low as to harm you, but I still don't like this middle-of-the-night affair or the fact that they went on to call a meeting without me. That I could not be found is the silliest excuse I've ever heard. Keep your eyes open, and your sword close.'

If Govinda took note of the warning, he did not show it. Nor did he show the slightest suspicion when, on reaching the trading ship, he found no evidence of any defect or repair. Before he could comment on this, the Yadu soldiers escorting him were asked to return to shore and wait while he was taken below decks, ostensibly to meet the captain of the ship. He smiled the moment he was left alone in a small room. This would be his prison, but he gladly made it home, for he knew what it meant. If Syoddhan was coming after him, Panchali was, at least for the time-being, safe.

With that reasoning warming his heart, Govinda stretched himself out on the small wooden bunk that was the only fitting in the room, save for the shuttered wick lamp of the cautious make that was typical on ships. He had hardly closed his eyes, when the door opened and four men came in. Mercenaries, Govinda noted, wondering what the world had come to that men such as these could be found in plenty. He did not protest or resist when they threw him onto the floor and stripped him, or when the relentless whipping began. Govinda grit his teeth against the pain for as long as he could, but when the lash, wet with his blood, hit raw, broken flesh, he screamed.

Govinda waited for the burning sensation to drive him to unconsciousness or even death, but it did not. The whipping stopped, and he felt afloat in a sea of fire, his body in flames yet whole. He willed himself to let go, as though holding on to the idea of being alive was all that had kept him so, and now it was time, it was finally time, for the release he had been waiting for all these years. Reason told him that it was meant to be so. It was the only thing that gave meaning to everything, to believe what he had once stood for was not flawed, though he himself was; a creature with the same frail, flawed humanity that he so loved.

Blood flowed from a cut on his forehead to pool, hot and searing, in his eyes. Govinda tried to wipe it away but he could not move. Through the blurred haze he saw a familiar figure, her red hair framing her face in a soft glow.

'Philista?' he gasped as the sting of betrayal hit him, forcing him to focus beyond the physical pain.

'I'm sorry, Govinda,' she evenly replied. 'But you have to understand that you ask for the impossible. Your ideas, your dreams – assume that we … people … always act rationally, and that there is nothing more rational than goodness. It is not so. I am not so. You made me believe and hope in the idea of greater good. Now that you have lost hope, though my mind still sees the power of your ideas, my heart fears for my people, my nation. I will not act towards the greater good, Govinda. Nor will anyone else. Fear distorts reason. Chaos is inevitable. I am sorry.'

She paused, waiting for Govinda to speak, but he remained silent. Philista continued, 'I … my people have been promised a favourable alliance with the new Emperor – Syoddhan of the Kauravas. All I have to do in return is to …'

'Kill me?' Govinda grit his teeth against the pain, trying to find the strength to speak clearly. 'I knew it was to happen, sooner or later. But, I'm curious: did they specify how badly torn up I must be?'

'That is … personal. Though not in the way you think. I need to know, Govinda. The last astra-weapon Agniveshya created, when he was in hiding after the Scourge, I need to know where it is.'

'And how much will Syoddhan pay you for that?'

'I said it was personal. By which I meant it is for my country, my people. Each kingdom in Aryavarta is now bent upon outdoing the other. Can you imagine what would happen if they all came together – if this Syoddhan really does hold the empire together? What about the rest of the world, Govinda? We wouldn't want to trade with such an empire; we would fear it, and would defend our land against it. Now tell me where this last weapon is … this Naga-astra …'

'And you think torture will make me talk?'

Philista said, 'I should have known it wouldn't, but my benefactors insisted. I know that the only thing that matters to you is cold reason. And cold reason says you should tell me the secret. You know why? Because it is your fault that the entire world is in danger now. Can you imagine the horror if all the nations of the world went to war with each other? Isn't that terrible prospect what made you and Ghora Angirasa want to break the Firewright order as it was? Well, you should have done a better task of it. You should have done a better task of building your peaceful, glorious new empire, and then none of us would be in this position. This is your fault, Govinda, and this is your last chance to save the world. Tell me. Where is the Naga-astra hidden? What is it?'

'Syoddhan is far from a bad man, Philista. He is capable of bringing peace and glory to Aryavarta, and beyond. If my death is what it will take for him to do so, it is not a bad trade, at all.'

'Aah yes … one for a family, a family for a village, a village for a nation, a nation for an empire … That is how the saying goes, no? I hope you are right, Govinda. That your blood, and that of the Matsya nation, is enough.'

'Matsya?' Govinda's voice shook, just a little.

Philista did not miss it. 'Sentimental? I believe that was home to the Firewrights once, was it not? Now that its protector, General Keechak, is dead, perhaps it can be home to them again. Are you still willing to die, Govinda? Are you still willing to trust Syoddhan?'

Govinda did not answer with words, but Philista could see him transform, shrink into something smaller than the pathetic creature he had already been reduced to. For the first time in all the years that she had known Govinda Shauri, she saw his eyes brim and overflow, his tears mingling with blood to stain the dark skin of his cheeks. She gasped, and it took her every bit of self-restraint to not go to him, to not comfort him now that she saw how utterly broken he was.

Biting her lip to keep herself from breaking down, Philista said, 'It's not too late, Govinda. Help me. Tell me about the Naga-astra, and we of Elis and the other Yavana lands can stop Syoddhan before it's too late.'

'No.'

'You trust him still?'

'Yes.'

Philista looked disappointed. 'Why?'

'Because I make the last sacrifice I have left to make. He better be worth it.'

Philista stared at Govinda, trying to read his lifeless eyes. At length, she turned to the sole mercenary with her – a tall, lanky fellow with the lower half of his face shrouded in the typical style of his profession. 'Kill him,' she ordered the man, adding, 'Do it quickly. He's already been through enough pain.' With one last look at Govinda, Philista left.

Govinda let his head hang heavy. A quiet sob escaped him as he realized this was not over yet, that his body and mind both had much left to pay for. The mercenary's voice, surprisingly gentle, intruded on his misery. 'Quickly? Is that how you really want it?'

Govinda shook his head. 'Make it hurt. Make it last. I deserve it. Please...' He let himself hit the wooden floor with a thud, the world spinning around him. As his will to hold on faded, Govinda began slipping into darkness, an endless darkness that would offer no peace. A voice sounded, dull and in the distance. It took him a while to figure out that it was the mercenary speaking.

'I knew this warrior once...' the man said, 'a tough, no-nonsense fighter he was. He taught me that reason was the ultimate weapon, the most powerful of all forces. He told me that the one who walked the path of reason could never lose. Of course, that warrior is an old man now... maybe he was an idiot. Maybe he was wrong. Maybe that lady – Philista – speaks truly. Fear distorts reason. Fear rules us all. Even you.'

Govinda knew the man was right. Fear did rule him, and it had happened because he had let go of reason. Till that day in Kamyaka, he had let reason guide him, he had made every sacrifice that had been needed of him, including... *Panchali.* By letting her be a symbol for life itself, by letting her mean that much to him, he had turned his ultimate sacrifice into his ultimate mistake. At the admission, the part of Govinda's mind that had been trained into rational methodicity flared in a last, defiant thought. He knew that the mercenary ought not to be speaking to him, certainly not in his own tongue and in such familiar words. Perhaps there was no mercenary other than his own guilt, the final, oppressive sense of failure.

There is no need for guilt, Govinda told himself. *Sacrifice is the meaning of all things. For the sake of all that exists, the Primordial Being sacrificed himself. From him came all existence, this world we perceive through reason. Sacrifice is everything.*

The words sounded in his memory, in a child's voice: *But why, Govinda? What the Primordial Being did is all very well, but why? Now* that *is a question!*

Govinda heard himself speak before he realized what he was doing. 'He was not wrong,' he spat out with vehemence. 'Your warrior … he was not wrong. Fear does distort reason, but we fight fear. And we fight it not with duty or reason, but with compassion. Compassion is what sets humanity apart from the gods – that we are capable of such benevolence as even the Creator could not show. We were created, not by an act of reason but by an act of love. And to know that is to know the reason of it all. And so we fight because we must. Even when there is nothing left to fight for, we fight for what is right.'

At those words, the mercenary pulled off his shroud, revealing fair skin and a chiselled face. His eyes were dark and large, and filled with once-familiar warmth.

'You?' Govinda wondered for an instant if he were hallucinating, for the man before him looked so much like he once had, not just for his features, but for the light in his heart. But the vision smiled and he saw a glimpse of something more. It stoked the last of his strength, and he pulled himself up to his knees.

Abhimanyu Karshni held out his hand to help Govinda stand up. He said, 'Prove that old warrior right, then. Let's get you out of here.'

20

ABHIMANYU KARSHNI WAS NOT A MAN TO HOLD EXTREME DISLIKES. Yet the one thing that irked him no end was when people told him, as they often did, that he bore a strong resemblance to his younger maternal uncle, Govinda Shauri. In his childhood he had seen it as a compliment. Now it was a whispered caution shared by people mostly with his mother or with his uncle Balabadra. His reason to dislike it, however, was the same as what had made it a compliment so many years ago: In his mind, Govinda Shauri was incomparable.

When Dharma and the others had gone into exile, Balabadra had brought Abhimanyu and Subadra back with him to Dwaraka.

Perhaps it was silent anger against Partha that fuelled them all, but Balabadra and Pradymna had trained the young Abhimanyu with a vengeance, determined to make him better than his father in every craft. Better and braver. Yet, paternal affection, the one thing that Abhimanyu truly longed for, was denied him. He had grown up addressing Govinda as 'father' simply because his cousins and companions – Pradymna and Samva – called him that. Since then no one, not even his blood parent, had been quite able to replace him.

Not that Abhimanyu ever had the chance to let Govinda know – the Council was adamant that the young warrior be kept far from his errant uncle's influence and, in any case, Govinda, had no desire to see his nephew. 'I cannot!' he had declared, barely days into his seclusion. 'It would be more than I deserve. He is as much *hers* as he is mine. Tell him never to come here again!'

Abhimanyu, who had been waiting in an adjoining room, had overhead and misconstrued. He had rushed to Subadra. 'Who am I?' he had asked, far too distraught to see how the question insulted and pained her. 'Why am I called Karshni?'

His mother had not flinched. 'You are born of my womb and the seed of Partha Savyasachin the Kaurava. My *husband*. Yet, your soul, Abhimanyu, was forged by the will of the two who stood over me as you came into this world – your uncle, Govinda, and your mother in the eyes of law, Panchali. And so, you are Karshni, for the father who sired you is sometimes called Krishna, the dark one. But in my heart, you are Karshni, because the light in you comes from Krishna, the dark-skinned cowherd, and Krishna, the brave princess of Panchala.' At that, Abhimanyu had thrown himself into her lap and cried his heart out for a while before abruptly standing up and walking away. Subadra had let him go with a knowing smile. Her son was no longer a child.

And so Abhimanyu had waited, watched and learned as much as he could in the many years since. He saw how Aryavarta was changing, and with it his own nation. Politics, trade, negotiation, diplomacy and even war: he observed it all with curious eyes and a keen mind. He also watched as Govinda Shauri sank deeper into the depths of despair and as, one by one, all those who loved him lost faith in him. In the recesses of his mind, Abhimanyu fought his own private war. The more people lost hope in Govinda, the brighter he let his faith for his uncle burn in his own heart. And now he finally knew it had not been in vain.

Govinda was shivering from head to toe, partly on account of his nakedness, and partly from fever. Abhimanyu suspected that his uncle's whiplash wounds were already starting to fester.

'Right…' he began, but before he could say anything more, he realized Govinda was already hobbling over to the corner where his clothes and his sword had been unceremoniously thrown. The soles of Govinda's feet left bloody stains on the floor. He tried to get dressed and hissed in pain as his lower robe touched the torn skin on his thighs. He let the material drop from his hands before falling to the ground again, unable to move.

Abhimanyu reached a decision. 'Wait here…' he said and slipped out of the door, though he did not bolt it from the outside. There was no one in the narrow passageway – after all, the prisoner was hardly a threat in his current condition, and that too with a mercenary on guard. Wrapping his robe over his face once again, Abhimanyu cautiously made his way up a set of stairs to the deck.

The ship was of a different shape and construction than the ones used by the Yadus, but growing up in a bustling port like Dwaraka, Abhimanyu knew his way around all seacraft well enough. Govinda had been kept just one level below deck, so all Abhimanyu had to do was to get him out of the room, down the passageway, up the stairs and on to the deck. Then he had to signal to the small boat waiting just out of sight of the ship's lights, wait for it to draw up alongside and help Govinda down into it – all of it while avoiding detection. Yet, as he had observed even while planning this daring rescue, the situation was not without benefit. Being anchored in Dwaraka's waters, and that too claiming to be unseaworthy, the ship could hardly afford to show undue strength in the form of armed guards or regular patrolling beyond the usual nightly checks. Most of its sailing and trading crew were already on shore, as might be expected, and only a few men remained on board ship. Of course, that still left Philista and her mercenaries, barring the one Abhimanyu had subdued and was now impersonating.

They have no cause for suspicion. Success lies in audacity, he reminded himself, echoing Pradymna's oft-used words.

Drawing in a deep breath, Abhimanyu let out a seagull-like cry and repeated it twice in quick succession. The sound itself was not unusual though the pattern was, but not enough to raise an alarm. The men in the waiting rowboat, however, knew it for the signal it was and would soon draw up alongside the ship.

Feeling a little light-headed at how easy it was, Abhimanyu made his way back down the stairs and into the passageway at a light run. He realized at once that he had rejoiced too soon. One of the other mercenaries stood at the door and was just about to open it, but turned at Abhimanyu's approach and went for his dagger. Abhimanyu was in no doubt that his deception had been found out. He responded by drawing his sword – the mercenary's serrated long-blade that he had appropriated. The weapon was heavy and its unfamiliarity placed him at a disadvantage. He swatted aside the mercenary's dagger with the blade, but lost his balance in the move. By the time he had recovered, the mercenary had drawn his own long-blade and now came at him with a vengeance.

The fight was short and bloody, particularly since Abhimanyu was wary of alerting others on the ship. He dropped down to one knee, swift and unexpected, and slashed at the mercenary's abdomen. The serrated blade cut deep, pulling out flesh and entrails as he whipped it out and around to face the attacker he sensed advancing behind him. The second attacker was closer than he had estimated, leaving him with no choice but to chop through his leg. The man cried out, but Abhimanyu cut his scream short by rising to a squatting position and lopping off his head. The man was dead before all three pieces of his body hit the wooden floor.

Panting hard, Abhimanyu surveyed his handiwork, pleased with the results. It distracted him enough to not see the third man till it was too late. The man brought his twin-faced axe down hard, intending to sever Abhimanyu's sword hand at the wrist. Abhimanyu dodged just in time, and the blow fell on the lower part of the blade. Still, the impact was enough to knock the weapon out of his hand and cause him to lose balance on the blood-slicked floor. He kicked out at the mercenary, first trying to land a direct blow on his kneecap and then, when that failed, to get him off-balance. But he was too far away. His only choice was to try and make a run for it.

The mercenary moved in, resolute, to the point that he merely kicked his companions's severed limb out of the way. Abhimanyu tried to stand, but he was too slow. Just when it seemed there was no avoiding the heavy axe, the mercenary froze, arms raised to strike, mouth open in a silent scream. With a soft tear, the tip of a blade emerged through a blossoming wound in the man's chest. Abhimanyu scrambled away as the man fell face down. In the narrow passageway, tired, mangled, yet with a defiant spark in his eyes, stood Govinda Shauri.

The single blow had taken all of Govinda's strength. He swayed unsteadily as he pulled Nandaka out of the mercenary's flesh, falling back as the blade came out clean. Abhimanyu caught him, and wasted no time in moving towards the stairway.

'You'll never make it to the shore in time. Our ships surround this one. We won't even have to fight. One command from me and they will make it look like an accident...'

Abhimanyu turned to face Philista.

She gasped, visibly taken aback. For once, Abhimanyu's resemblance to his uncle served him well. 'Who are you?' she asked.

Abhimanyu did not answer but just stood there, his chest heaving, his gaze defiant.

Philista looked from him to the insentient Govinda and then back again. This time, it was Abhimanyu who was astounded at the range of raw, honest emotions he saw on her face: jealousy, love, anger... and, finally, hope. He knew she would let them go.

He bent down to hoist the inert Govinda over one shoulder and had one foot on the first step of the stairway that led out to the deck and to safety, when he turned around to face the Yavana woman.

'Come with us. You'll be safe, I promise. If you stay here, they'll surely blame you for his escape… Come with me.'

'I just tried to kill you both… Are you sure you're not Govinda?'

Abhimanyu grinned. 'I'm not sure I can explain it as well as he does, but it has something to do with the fact that we were all created not by an act of reason but by an act of love. And so… well, we should do what's right… and, you know, be compassionate and all that.'

Philista laughed. She shook her head: his words had helped her reach a decision she had been struggling with. 'No. My place is at home, in Elis. There are young women and men like you there. They are the future, and it is to them I must now look. Go. Take good care of him.'

Abhimanyu rushed up the stairs and on to the deck. He glanced over the ship's side, weighing his next decision, when he heard indistinct sounds of activity. Gritting his teeth against the agony he knew Govinda would feel, he threw the wounded man overboard. He waited till he heard the splash, and the immediate sound of paddles that told him a waiting rowboat was headed towards Govinda. Then, tucking Nandaka tightly into his tunic, Abhimanyu jumped into the dark waters below.

Strong arms pulled both men out of the water and into the boat, even as the small vessel turned for shore. On board the Yavana ship, there was no activity. Philista had raised no alarm. Abhimanyu gave a sigh of relief, which turned into a gasp of surprise when he realized who his rescuer was.

'Uncle…? What… what are you doing here?' he addressed the burly outline that could only be Balabadra.

Balabadra did not reply. With a grunt of effort he forced Govinda up into a seated position and poured a goblet's worth of spiced wine down his throat. The drink made Govinda retch at once, and he came to his senses only to throw up over the side of the boat. By the time he was done, he was beginning to look more alert than he had in a long time, the sting of salt water in his wounds adding to the jolt of agony he felt in his arm.

Balabadra set about examining his brother's wounds as he finally answered the pending question.

'How I got here is a simple thing, Abhimanyu. There is more than one rowboat available in Dwaraka, and you are not the only one who knows how to be surreptitious with its use. The point is *why* I am here.'

Abhimanyu nodded. 'I know. Philista told us…him.'

'Yes. It has begun. The militarization of Aryavarta, the race to develop and use terrible weapons. And much else will soon begin too: bloodshed, intrigue, death and destruction.'

Govinda's strained voice added, 'It… It all began long ago, and goes as expected. The question now is how it will end. Syoddhan is set to attack Matsya. I don't have much time.'

Balabadra turned to him. 'You want to go there…to Matsya?'

'Yes.'

'And that which you find there… Do you mean to take it or destroy it?'

Govinda smiled, a shadow of his former self but with at least a spark showing through after years. 'What…what is it you think I will find there?'

'Weapons? Firewright weapons. That is what Syoddhan seeks. That is what everyone would look for in Matsya.'

'No, Agraja.' Govinda willed strength and clarity back into his speech. 'You see, I thought that I had more time, that Syoddhan would not turn towards Matsya as yet. And so that is where I sent Panchali. I have let her suffer the consequences of my decisions enough. Now…how soon can I ride?'

Balabadra's shock was obvious. He blinked, as though coming out of a trance and said, 'Yuyudhana is waiting on shore with our horses.'

'Will you come with me?'

'Yes, Govinda. I have let *you* suffer the consequences of your decisions enough. Besides, I've always wanted to see the great desert of Matsya for myself. Call it a childhood ambition, if you will. And before you say anything about the Council, this once let me worry about it.'

Govinda said nothing, but threw himself flat in the boat and remained there in a half-dazed state for the rest of the journey to land.

'THIS IS MADNESS!'

Bhim ignored Dharma, still in his ministerial attire as would befit his guise as Kanka, and set about tightening the straps around his armour, looking all the while at the desert plain before him, now the site of a soon-to-be battle. Chief Virat's massive forces had been divided into four, one part under his command, and the others under Sankha, Swetha and Bhuminjaya, Virat's three sons. Chief Virat himself had, on Bhim's advice, remained at their temporary command tent. Dharma took the Chief's position as an indication of cowardice, though Bhim knew otherwise. Whatever the chief may have lacked in military acumen, neither he nor his kinsmen were short of courage.

'I don't see why I need to be here either. Especially if I can't fight,' Dharma grumbled.

Bhim sighed, irritated, and said, 'You're here as Virat's envoy and overseer in this war. It is not uncommon for chieftains and emperors to send others out to do their dirty work while they stay in their palaces. You know that from personal experience.'

'I stayed at Indr-prastha because I had to! Someone had to maintain government and hold the empire together as it was being built. I would have traded places with you in an instant if I could, Bhim.'

'But you couldn't. Just as you can't now.'

'Exactly! Virat is just being a coward. This is not even a war; it's just a battle. Look ... look at Susarman's forces – they are one-fifth the size of Matsya's army. And with you as its General ... Oh well, let's finish this and get back to the city. Have you appointed Nakul and Sadev to key positions?'

'I have,' Bhim nodded, 'as best as I could, given they are meant to be groundskeepers. But they know what needs to be done. They'll make sure that each of the divisions they are part of swings out from the main army and flanks the enemy from either side. Still, it all seems too easy. Why would Susarman attack now? He knows Matsya's strength.'

Dharma said, 'Because he thinks the General is dead ... ? I mean, the former General.' He laughed, hollow. 'I still cannot get over that, you know. Keechak, the mighty, mysteriously dead in his own land. How many men do you know who can choke ... no ... crush a man to death like that? If I didn't know better I'd say it was you who did it, Bhim.'

'Are you saying it, Agraja?'

'No, not at all ... I just meant ...'

'Whatever you may have meant, if the General's death is truly the reason why Susarman has attacked, and that too with such a small force, it's all the more reason to suspect a trap.'

'You think too much, Bhim.'

'Someone needs to,' Bhim said. He muttered a prayer under his breath before calling out the orders to advance.

The battle did not last long. Trigarta's army was no match for the larger and better-prepared Matsya forces. No doubt, Matsya's soldiers were well trained and brave, but for the first time Bhim saw the true value of Matsya's forges and the skills of its craftspeople. The endless supply of arrows – lightweight and deadly, and fine enough for a man to hold a stack of a hundred in his fist – was the first indication of the superiority of the Matsya army. Their armours, their carriages – all their equipment was sturdier and more effective.

Panchali had explained to him what she understood as Govinda's plan. As the General had demonstrated to her, isolation had forced the people of Matsya to extend their abilities with metal-crafting into directions beyond the needs of warfare and armament. When news came in of Susarman's impending attack, and Matysa's soldiers began their preparations, Bhim saw pieces of iron and metal being transported for a week to the border and assembled in less than half a day to form catapults and ballast that would have taken even a herd of elephants much longer to transport in their finished form. He saw wounded men healing faster with the metallic splints used by medics, many of the soldiers even returning to battle – so light were the braces on their limbs. Bhim noticed how fine needles were used to close open wounds with precision, leaving little chance of them getting infected. Water, the most essential and scarce resource for soldiers in the harsh desert lands, was pulled out of the deepest aquifers under the sandy earth by using a system of metallic pipes with bellow-like devices of leather attached to them. Wick-lamps lighting the army camp were housed in shuttered containers that ensured the flame would go out if tilted, thus protecting the camp from accidental fires.

Many of these smaller devices had been obvious to Bhim even during the course of his life as a cook in the kitchens of Virat's palace, but to see them come together, particularly with the benefit of knowing how these inventions had taken place, was truly remarkable. Unambiguously absent, however, were weapons made of Wright-metal, or any devices that suggested Firewright astra-weapons. It was then that Bhim fully understood. Govinda had shown the world that it did not take a powerful, secretive order to drive humanity forward to discovery and invention. Bhim only hoped the Dharma would see it too.

Another thing niggled at his mind. Despite the odds, the weakening Trigarta army had fought with a will that had only affirmed Bhim's suspicions. 'You don't suppose this was just a distraction? That Susarman has more forces?' he asked Dharma as the two men walked towards the command tent. Both of them were fresh off the battlefield and eager to give Chief Virat news of their victory.

'And what would they attack?' Dharma countered. He was enjoying the taste of victory in open battle after many years and was not willing to let the thought of further fighting mar the moment.

'The city. If they took Upaplavya...'

'Don't be silly. Chief Virat's scouts would have reported troop movement. The only tract that remains unwatched, and with good reason, is the old riverbed to the south. There isn't a drop of water in those parts. You couldn't get a man through there alive, not to mention an army.'

'I suppose you're right. I suppose we should be grateful that it was so easy...' No sooner were the words out of Bhim's mouth than he regretted them. Ahead, the Chief's tent stood in disarray, a pale

Sankha standing in the middle of it all. 'They've taken him,' he said. 'They've taken the Chief.'

'What!' Dharma looked horrified.

Before Sankha could respond, his youngest brother Bhuminjaya came running into the tattered shelter. 'Susarman sends a message. He's holding our father hostage. He says he is willing to trade.'

'Trade?' Sankha said. 'Trade for what?'

'Matsya. They want our surrender, and they will let Father live.'

'If you weren't my brother, Bhuminjaya, you'd be dead for even bringing those terms to me!'

'Peace!' Bhim intervened.

'Stay out of this, Vallabha! What does a cook know of honour and war? We will die before we surrender. And if the first to fall is my father, so be it.'

'Sankha,' Bhim raised a calming hand. 'The reality of war is that it is not always honourable, and far from absolute. There are other alternatives to surrender or death. Listen to me ...'

'What alternative can you offer me, Vallabha?'

'Let me bring your father back alive. Then we will unleash more death on those cowards in Trigarta.'

'And how are we to do this?' Sankha said.

Dharma sounded even less convinced than Virat's son. 'Yes, how? Don't be foolish, Vallabha!'

Bhim met Dharma's gaze, understanding full well the folly that Dharma spoke of. If he were seen and recognized by Susarman, not as Vallabha of Matsya but as Bhim Vikrodara of Kuru, it would invite great danger upon them all. Especially Panchali. But that did not change what had to be done. That did not change what was right. Turning to Sankha, Bhim said, 'I have a plan. I will need the help of Granthika and Tantripala – two of your groundsmen whom I personally trust. I will also need a scout who knows this region like he does his lover's eyes.'

Sankha nodded at Bhuminjaya, who left to see to the arrangements. 'I hope you know what you're doing,' he said, turning back to Bhim.

Dharma muttered under his breath, 'I hope so too, Prince. I hope so too.'

22

PANCHALI BURST INTO THE ROOM WITH A LITTLE MORE FERVOUR than Malini the handmaiden was wont to show. 'Have you heard?' she began, her eyes on Partha, but fell silent as she noticed the young woman with him. 'I beg your pardon, Princess,' she immediately added, though she shared more than a congenial relationship with Uttara, Chief Virat's only daughter.

The young woman was about nineteen or so, but she stood taller than Panchali. Her fair skin had turned an alluring golden brown under the desert sun and her brown hair had been stained a few shades lighter. Her features were as hard as the stone of the land but in her own way the princess was rather beautiful. Influenced in her growing years in equal measure by her soft-hearted father and her tough maternal uncle, the dead General, Uttara reminded Panchali in many ways of herself when she had been that young. Yet, the girl was different, far bolder and far more responsible than Panchali had ever been at that age, and way more outspoken.

In the past year, the two women had built a relationship that bordered on friendship, though Panchali had been careful never to overstep her bounds as Malini, the handmaiden. She also had this inexplicable feeling that there was an assailable, even mysterious, quality about Uttara, and so kept an eye on her – more out of concern for the younger woman than curiosity – while maintaining a distance. Rumour among the handmaidens was that Uttara went out of her rooms at night to meet with a secret lover. Panchali did not think that was the case, but she would also not put it past Uttara to sneak out, if only to wander her beloved city by night, making sure that all was well.

'It's all right, Malini. Don't go,' Uttara said, waving her in. 'And yes, we've already heard. A great army, led by Syoddhan Kauravya, self-proclaimed ruler of Aryavarta, is set to attack us. They are at the south-west pass and have sent a message asking for our surrender. In the absence of my father and brothers, the decision as to what should be done falls, unexpectedly, to me. What do you think I should do, Malini?'

'Princess, it is hardly my position to offer advice on this. But since you ask, I think we should stall for time. Our forces would have surely overcome Trigarta's army by now.'

'They are three days' ride away, at the least. Victorious or not, they are not here to help us. The herds are a priority.'

'All this for a herd of cows?' Partha-Brihannala blurted out, earning himself a harsh look from Uttara. 'Well, I mean, they're important but…'

'But it's brilliant! Don't you see?' Panchali said. 'Trigarta's attack was a diversion so that Syoddhan and his men could achieve their true purpose, which is…'

Uttara chuckled. 'Which is what, Malini? The annexation of Matsya? Control over our forges, our foundries? Is that why Syoddhan sent you here? To kill my uncle and… oh, don't look so shocked. I was there, that night in the dancing hall. I saw the two of you, and Vallabha too. I heard everything.'

Partha began to offer a flustered explanation, but Panchali remained calm. She said, 'In that case, why didn't you intervene? You could have raised the alarm, even done it in time to save him. Or at least you could have had us arrested.'

'For what? A known enemy is far better than an unknown one. If you were indeed Syoddhan's spies, you would at least work to protect his interests. The moment Keechak was dead Vallabha was more important to Matsya than ever before. I am not a fool to have him arrested and condemned! Besides, ever since I've been old enough to understand the situation, I've known that Keechak was going to be our doom. His ideas of bloody revolution and the rise of Matsya were fascinating to hear, but they wouldn't do a thing for my people. Salvaged pride lasts for only a generation. My people need more. They need a future. Surrendering to Syoddhan might just give us the chance to become a part of Aryavarta once again. That is how it begins, with peace and trade and the sharing of knowledge. And that is why I have decided' – she turned to Partha, a cold haughtiness in her eyes – 'Brihannala! Have a rider take the message to Syoddhan. We will agree, in principle, to surrender provided we are able to negotiate the terms of peace.'

'You cannot!' Panchali sprang forward. 'Uttara, I don't know what political game you think you are playing, but this is not such a simple matter.'

'How dare you talk to me that way, Malini!'

'I dare to speak how I like, Uttara,' Panchali said. Softening her tone, she said, 'I dare speak, not because of who you are, or who I was or am. I dare because I must. The truth is bigger than you or me. This story is bigger than you or me... My name is not Malini. I am Panchali Draupadi, once Empress of Aryavarta. The person you know as Vallabha is Bhim Vikrodara and Brihannala is Partha Savyasachin. Both are brothers to Dharma Yudhisthir of Kuru.'

To Panchali's surprise, as well as Partha's, Uttara shrugged, unconcerned, and remarked, 'Brihannala. I always wondered about that name: *big reed*. Rather egotistic a euphemism for a eunuch, don't you think? But then, all of Aryavarta knows what a Kaurava thinks of women. As for you, Panchali, forgive me if I don't fall on my knees and grovel before you. I have no interest in the legitimacy of your claim to the empire any more than I have in Syoddhan's.'

Partha looked distinctly uncomfortable. He opened his mouth as if to speak, but could find nothing to say. Panchali said, 'It's best you leave us to talk this over, Partha.' He nodded and with a glance at Uttara exited the room, this time without the customary sway of Brihannala's hips. Panchali waited till he was gone and took a seat. She gestured for Uttara to follow suit.

The subtle gestures, the assertion of dominance, were not lost on the younger woman. She sat, but did so with condescension.

Panchali said, 'You'd make the perfect puppet, Uttara. You're so easy to manipulate and predictable in your thinking. I could make you do exactly what I want you to, while you remain convinced that you act of your own free will. I've learnt that from the masters of masters, the best politician Aryavarta has ever seen, and I won't hesitate to do what I have to.'

'So why don't you?' Uttara said. 'Why do you argue with me, instead of manipulating me as you claim you can so easily do?'

'What makes you think I'm not? What makes you think every word I've just said was not meant to achieve my ends?'

Uttara muttered under her breath as she saw the riddle.

'Well, I am not manipulating you,' Panchali said. 'I have no way to convince you of that except to say that Matsya is as much home to me as it is to you, and that I would never wish it harm. Matsya is the future; it is hope. I did not want Keechak dead, Uttara. But I did what I had to … All I asked him for was the chance to explain. It is all I ask you for too.'

'Or else what? You'll kill me too?'

Panchali shook her head and then, rising, went down on her knees before the seated Uttara. 'I was once a princess, an empress, but I learnt the hard way that position, power and status mean nothing in a world where being just a person has no value. Please, trust me. Do not surrender to Syoddhan. If you do, there will be nothing left of Matsya but its forges, and the people will be merely slaves who work in them.'

Uttara stared at Panchali for a while. Then she reached down and helped her up. 'Don't,' Uttara said. 'It doesn't feel right. Not because of who you are, but it just doesn't feel right. Oh, Malini. You act like you're the only woman with a brain and a conscience. I admit, you're different, but whatever gave you the right to presume you are unique? I don't think I'm anything like you, but I do find it offensive that you think you alone can lay claim to being capable of complex thought.'

Panchali said, 'If you are trying to provoke me, Uttara, it's not working. I'm beginning to like you all the more, in fact.'

Uttara laughed out loud. 'You know what they say – most friendships are based on trust and respect. A few are based on mutual insult, and those are the strongest.'

'My brother has a friend, with whom he's like that. But they'd die for each other.'

'He's a lucky man. And his friend is luckier still. Though I would like to know if this affinity for strange friendships runs in your family.'

'Ask him yourself.'

'Your brother?'

'His friend, though before that I need your help to bring him here.' As Uttara frowned in puzzlement, Panchali added, 'His name is Govinda Shauri.'

281

23

GOVINDA SHAURI.

Uttara knew the name well, but the only recollection she had of the man was a fleeting, childhood memory from over a decade ago. He had come to Matsya, she had seen him, and she remembered how the older girls of the palace had whispered things about him that she had not understood then. More than anything else, she remembered the horrible argument that had ensued between her parents and her uncle the night Govinda Shauri had arrived. Keechak had held a dagger to her mother's throat, saying that he would rather kill his sister than let her serve as a whore to those forsaken Firewrights. Uttara had asked her brother Sankha what a whore was and he had told her to leave the room. But she had stayed, and watched as her brothers and her father reassured Keechak that never again would they welcome Govinda Shauri into Matsya.

As she had grown older, Uttara came to understand what that conflict had been all about. Keechak had insisted that Govinda Shauri was a traitor – why else had he not made Matsya a part of Dharma Yudhisthir's empire? He had cursed Satya and her descendants, the clan of Kuru, to eternal damnation and sworn that if ever a Kaurava or that lackey Govinda Shauri set foot in Matsya he would drink their blood.

And now Uttara was helping a Kaurava fight another Kaurava who sought to invade Matsya, and even considering the idea of bringing back Govinda Shauri to her homeland.

I must be crazy, Uttara cautioned herself. Yet, she also knew why she was entertaining Panchali's suggestion: Deep in those childhood memories were other, pleasant recollections. She could not remember why, but the thought of Govinda made her think also of swings and laughter and running playfully over hot sand. It made her remember her father as he had once been – a boisterous, wholesome man who had been quick to humour and slow to anger. A part of her had once thought, and still did, that Govinda Shauri could bring back her father's laughter.

'This way, is it not?' Partha, or the man Uttara had known as Brihannala, whispered in the darkness.

Night had brought a fearful silence over all of Upaplavya and no one ventured out of their homes but for the city guards on duty. Uttara had the authority to order the guards to let them pass, but Partha insisted that secrecy was better. She did not dissent, and now led her companions silently through the darkness. 'No, there is a passageway here between the army barracks that leads directly to the funeral ground,' she told him. He did not look convinced, but Panchali gave him a reassuring nod. The trio walked on in silence.

A short while later, Uttara said, 'There! See, we are almost on the other side of the grounds. I think you must have entered from the other side, when you ...' She stopped, realizing she had no idea what Partha was doing. 'Why did we come here?' she asked.

Partha said, 'We hid our weapons here before we came into Upaplavya.' He turned to Panchali. 'I will need your help.'

Together, the two clambered up a solitary sami tree that was used by the people of Matsya to dispose of the bodies of the worst of criminals. The corpses of the convicted were bound in cloth and tied to the branches of the tree, and left to rot at leisure – ensuring, it was hoped, that the deceased had as difficult a passage into the afterlife as possible. Uttara flinched when Partha examined one of the cloth bundles by sniffing at it. With a look of satisfaction, he nodded to Panchali, who helped him untie the bundle and bring it down.

'Weapons?' Uttara asked. 'But we make the best weapons in all Aryavarta. Why did you have to go to such trouble ... Oh!' She said nothing further as the cloth covering the corpse-shaped bundle fell apart to reveal a bow, the likes of which she had never seen. The metal looked light and supple, every curve and line of the bow crafted with sleek precision, as though fire had been tamed and given form.

'Gandiva,' Partha said, as he reverentially picked up the bow. 'Forged by Agni and wielded by Indra, king of the celestials, it is said.'

'You can gape at it later,' Panchali told an open-mouthed Uttara. 'Now help me tie up the rest of these.'

Panchali had taken out her own sword and bow, as well as the rest of Partha's weapons. That still left an impressive, gleaming collection on the ground. Uttara complied, though not without confusion. 'Who … to whom do the rest of these weapons belong?'

'To my husband, Emperor Dharma Yudhisthir, and his brothers,' Panchali replied, tightening the last knot in the bundle.

More questions spun inside Uttara's head, but Partha said, 'Ready? Let's go.'

'Where?' Uttara asked.

'You and I are going to face my cousins. Panchali is going to get us help.'

'I am?' Panchali did not look pleased at the prospect.

'You have to, Panchali. You need to let Govinda know what has happened here, where we are, and what is going on. Get out of Matsya. Find him, find your brothers. Bring them back here before it is too late.'

Panchali stood where she was, frowning.

'There is a way …' Uttara offered. 'There's a path across the plains from the old riverbed. My uncle ordered it destroyed, but it can still be used … if one is careful. I've used it myself. Head due south-east from the marker beyond the palace. You won't be able to keep a straight line, because it will run through the marketplace and the dwellings beyond, but once you are out of the city you can follow the stars. I can get you to a horse, and you should be able to reach the cliff before dawn.'

'What about the two of you?'

Partha replied, 'We will need a horse and a rig. If we ride out now, and then rest for a while, the two of us should be able to meet Syoddhan's armies by first light. They are holding their position just west of the city. It's a good position – they will stand between the city and the returning armies, if needed.'

'A siege?' Uttara said.

'In time, yes.'

'Two of you can't fight an army by yourselves. What are you thinking of, Partha?'

'I'm thinking of challenging Syoddhan to single combat, Panchali. He and whoever else might be willing to fight. I can't defeat them all at the same time. But one by one ... ' He smiled, though it was not one filled with mirth. 'If we create multiple obstacles – first me, then the city guards – it may hold back Syoddhan's forces for long enough. It will only be a few days before the Chief and his men return. We need to hold out till that time.'

Panchali said, 'No, Partha. This is wrong. Not your plan, but that *she* is a part of it.' She turned to Uttara. 'You go. I'll ride with him.'

Partha was about to protest, but Uttara cut in. 'No, Panchali. I might get out of Matsya, but I wouldn't know what to do next. I've never been too far from our borders, and I certainly have no idea how to find Govinda Shauri ... or your brothers. Besides, I think it is a matter of honour that at least one Matsya soldier stand before Syoddhan. Else, my father will die of shame! Go. *Brihannala* here is enough to entertain me.'

Realizing that protest was futile, Panchali agreed. Less than half a muhurtta later, she set off from the stables on a dark stallion that would be difficult to spot by night.

Partha watched her leave, then looked at Uttara. 'Thank you, Princess. That was kind and brave of you.'

'It was sensible of me, that's all,' Uttara said. 'I don't know why you wanted her out of harm's way, but I supposed that unless you got what you wanted you weren't going to be in best form. And that I cannot risk, considering I want to stay alive.' She laughed softly and added, 'You do know there is no chance whatsoever that she will be back in time with help?'

'Yes,' Partha said. 'But there is a good chance that if we hold the enemy back and make them wait, your father's army will return. That apart, the point of sending Panchali away was to keep her safe, as you rightly guessed.'

Uttara looked amused at the confession. 'Why?' she asked, her eyes twinkling.

Partha caught her insinuations, but did not share her mirth. He replied with a straight face, 'Because I owe her safety to a friend.' Feeling inexplicably happy at the thought, Partha pulled Gandiva off his shoulder, strung the bow and tested the string. A loud, solemn note boomed through the night, travelling as echoes off the cliffs and resounding ahead till it faded in the distance. 'Now,' he said, 'are you any good with chariot rigs? Think you can handle two horses?'

'Hah!' Uttara said as she began measuring out reins for four.

24

BALABADRA WOKE UP WITH A START. BREATHING HARD, HE SAT in his makeshift bed and looked around. Their campfire, small and hidden from view by a pile of stones, was smouldering but had not yet gone out. The night was quiet, the air, cool, and little appeared amiss other than the fact that the makeshift bed next to his was empty. As his eyes got used to the darkness he could make out the dark shape of a man sitting on a rock at the cliff's edge. With a weary groan, Balabadra got out of his warm bed and made his way over.

'Can't sleep, Govinda?'

Govinda turned to look at his brother and shook his head. 'I thought I heard ....'

'Hmm?'

'Gandiva. I thought I heard Gandiva.'

Balabadra sighed. 'Wishful thinking?'

A voice called out from behind them, 'Wishful indeed. You can hear an absent Gandiva, but neither you nor your watch could see this ambush coming, could you?' At the sound of the voice, the rest of the men sleeping around the campfire rose to their feet, swords drawn.

Shikandin laughed at the sight, though not unkindly, as he and Dhrstyadymn stepped out of the nearby thicket and on to the rocky ground of the campsite. 'Oh please! A little too late for that, don't you think? Whatever happened to the Yadu hunters' instinct? Or has your inner gwala taken over?'

'Considering the inner gwala of this Yadu hunter has an arrow aimed at your head, you ought to be a little more polite in your greeting.'

Both Shikandin and Govinda turned to look at the new speaker, who swung down lithely from a tree, and then at each other. Shikandin said, mock disappointment lacing his voice, 'By Hara, we weren't like this, were we?'

'We had better lines,' Govinda said. 'This boy thinks he's in a play at a village fair.'

At that the company burst out laughing. Yuyudhana, still bleary-eyed from having been woken up, but delighted to see Shikandin and Dhrstyadymn stepped forward to greet the brothers with vigorous embraces. 'You're a sight for sore eyes, my friends.'

'You can say that again,' Shikandin replied.

'How did you get here?'

In response, Shikandin pointed to the dim outline of a lone eagle perched on a rock nearby.

'I didn't send you a message,' Govinda protested.

'No, but Subadra did. We were heading for Dwaraka, but our feathered friend found us on the way. Anyway,' Shikandin gestured to Govinda's whiplash wounds, 'what happened to you? You look like you mated with a spiked sea-creature.'

Dhrstyadymn screwed up his face in disgust. 'Why the sudden references to mating with different animals, brother?'

It was Govinda who replied, 'It means Shikandin has been spending a lot of time with old friends.' As Dhrstyadymn started, he explained, 'These are turns of phrases unique to their tribes. How is she, Shikandin? And that brother of hers – Sthuna? Does he still sing as well as he used to?'

'She's dead, Govinda. And there hasn't been much cause for Sthuna to sing of late.'

'I…' Govinda struggled for words. Giving up, he squeezed Shikandin's shoulder. With a deep breath, he declared, 'I'm tired, Shikandin. I'm tired of losing those we love. I'm tired of hiding the pain and pretending to surrender to a greater cause. I'm tired of fighting battles for others. One last fight, one last plan, and I'm done.'

Shikandin said, 'Let's get Panchali out of there and go home. But first, there is someone I'm eager to meet.'

'Abhimanyu,' Govinda called out. The young man standing by the tree came forward.

Shikandin let out a low whistle, even as Dhrstyadymn gasped.

'Now, my friends,' Govinda cautioned. 'You don't want to say anything about his resemblance to me. He hates it!'

'Who in Rudra's name said he looks anything like you, Govinda?' Shikandin said. 'This man has Subadra written all over him. He has her eyes.'

Abhimanyu looked at Shikandin with newfound curiosity. It served to remind him of his manners, and he bowed to the two brothers and greeted them respectfully. Then he straightened up and said, 'Well, what now? Reunions are all very well, but I prefer either sleep or strategizing to sentimentality.'

'And there the resemblance to Subadra ends and Pradymna's influence begins,' Govinda affectionately complained. 'But he has a point. Since it is less than a muhurrta to dawn, I suggest we decide on the next plan of action.'

Dhrstyadymn said, 'The plan of action is simple. We go into Matsya. We get Panchali. We come back out.'

'Except for one problem,' Balabadra pointed out.

'Which is?'

'That,' he pointed over the cliffside into the gorge that lay far below. 'The pass?'

'No, what's in it. More soldiers than it can hold, Dhrstyadymn. Syoddhan is here with his entire army, as well as Vasusena and Asvattama's men. How do you suggest we get past that?'

Shikandin threw himself down and stretched out on the ground. He said, 'By waiting till the inevitable happens.'

'And that is?'

'After an expected and rather jaded dramatic pause, Commander Govinda Shauri will tell us there is another way.'

They turned in unison to look at Govinda. He shrugged.

'Well?' Balabadra urged, with learned impatience.

'What can I say?' Govinda replied. 'There *is* another way ...'

25

'AGRAJA ...'

The voice that called out to him was a familiar one, yet Dharma Yudhisthir knew he had not heard it in years.

A dream, he noted, and himself an observer suspended between the waking world and the one inside his mind. A memory flashed within the dream – his grandfather teaching him how to let the conscious self retreat into sleep so that one's inner voice would speak, revealing truths that remained hidden in daylight. Except, Dharma did not know what it was that he had sought out his inner voice for.

'Agraja!'

This time, the voice was urgent. In his vision, Dharma turned with a tired sigh to face the speaker. 'What is it, Syoddhan?'

'Agraja, you must come at once. Bhim and Dussasan...'

'They are fighting again? By Hara, these boys... What is it now?'

'Something about nothing, as usual. Bhim called my father a blind snake and Dussasan called yours a spineless coward...'

'That's all? And they're fighting over this?'

'Well...' Syoddhan looked a little uncomfortable. 'Their choice of words wasn't as mild as mine. But please, Agraja, come with me. Bhim won't listen to anyone but you.'

'Bhim is your younger brother too, Syoddhan. He ought to respect you.'

'Hah! I can't get Dussasan to respect me or listen to me. Bhim is a far cry from that lout. One day my brothers will be the death of me. Yours will be your strength. I'd give you my crown, my throne, any day if I could have brothers like yours.'

Dharma laughed, restrained and adult-like, even in youth. 'That is destiny, Syoddhan. Yours is the throne, and mine is the means to rule.'

'Then, perhaps, the throne too should be yours. All I can do with it is what my father already does – sit on it just so that it does not fall into the wrong hands. I often wonder what I am, a warrior or a sentry.'

'Dear brother, you have no idea what a noble function that is. There are only two things worth guarding in the world – uncorrupted good and undiluted evil. Good is a great power, and it must be preserved and passed on. As for evil...'

Syoddhan's unlined boyhood face lit up in a way few ever saw. 'Dharma Yudhisthir, wise beyond wisdom and mysterious as an elephant's backside. You've got my attention, Agraja, so I shall ask: Why would anyone guard evil?'

Dharma threw his arm around Syoddhan's shoulder, pulling him into a fraternal embrace as they began walking. 'Because, my dear crown-prince-who-knows-the-answer-but-is-too-lazy-to-explain-it, evil must be guarded if only to keep it out of the wrong hands.'

'In that case, we'd better hurry. Dussasan may or may not be undiluted evil, but right now Bhim's hands are certainly the wrong ones!'

The dream continued, a garbled version of true memory. Dharma the observer found himself getting impatient: *Why am I here? What's in this dream?* His mind protested, watching himself observe a young but still powerful Bhim beating his cousin Dussasana to near-death.

'Patience!' The voice that now counselled Dharma came not from memory but from imagination. It was a voice he had always longed to hear.

Grandfather, the observer called out, as Dwaipayana took form in his dream .

'You promised me, Dharma. You said you wouldn't let me down. I told you after your coronation that it did not matter how you had become Emperor. What mattered was why you were on the throne. Your rule was the beginning of a new era. I chose you over Syoddhan for that reason alone. But you... look what you've done.'

I did my best, Acharya, Dharma protested. *Everything I said and did as Emperor was to keep the realm free of Firewrights, of their craft...* He stopped, as in his dream, a young Syoddhan walked out to stand next to Dwaipayana. The old scholar's eyes filled with pride, an expression that Dharma had always seen used for himself and never for his cousin.

Dwaipayana turned to Syoddhan and asked him. 'What will you do when you are Emperor of Aryavarta, my son?'

Syoddhan dutifully answered, 'I will protect all that is good, Acharya. I will protect Divine Order and our way of life.'

But that is what I did!

'And? Is that all, Syoddhan?'

Syoddhan said, 'No, Acharya. I will guard evil from itself.' He turned to face Dharma and said, 'You taught me that, Agraja. You taught me that.'

'Agraja...'

Dharma opened his eyes.

'Agraja… wake up.'

'Bhim?' Dharma sat up and looked out of his small camp-tent at the dark skies outside. 'What happened? Is everything all right?'

'All is well, Agraja. Listen, I'm leaving with the others. One way or another, I will bring Chief Virat back.'

Your brothers are your strength. Protect the good. Guard evil from itself.

Dharma got out of his bed with renewed will. 'I'm coming with you.'

'Agraja? But…'

'I am coming with you, *Vallabha*. It is my duty. And in Varuna's name, stop calling me "agraja". Here, I am Kanka.'

Dharma found the same mix of surprise and delight that he had seen on Bhim's face on Nakul and Sadev's too, as they watched him walk up to them in the full armour of a Matsya soldier. Sankha, too, looked pleased.

'Well, Kanka. Looks like you're good for more than just playing dice.'

If Dharma or his brothers saw any irony in the statement they did not let it show.

Sankha continued, 'Right. Are we all here? All right, Vallabha, what is this plan of yours?'

Bhim stepped forward and took command of the situation. 'It's very straightforward,' he said, crouching down to draw on the sand with his finger as he spoke. 'The Trigarta forces came at us from due west. We met them in battle along a rather wide line – over here. In fact, Sankha, you chose this spot because it gave us a strategic advantage.'

'Yes,' the prince confirmed. 'The cliffs run at an angle north and south of the point to form a small ravine. It forced the enemy into a confined space but allowed us to spread out wide. Of course, the plan worked only because we outnumbered the enemy at least five to one. I suppose that is redundant now,' he finished.

'Not completely,' Bhim said. 'The Chief was taken from our camp while the battle was on. Which means the men who took him had to be behind us. Also, once they captured the Chief they could not take him directly westwards because we were in the way.'

Dharma said, 'What if they went along or around the ravines...'

'Which they could, given time. But it would be a huge risk to take a hostage in the open over such a distance. Also, they overpowered the Chief's personal guards at the camp. No matter how stealthy their approach, that would have taken at least ten men, maybe more. It's too big a group to keep moving in the open, especially when we have such a vast army at our disposal to look for them and give chase. They would have gone into hiding as soon as possible.'

'But where?' Sankha asked. 'There is no place to hide between the camp and the battlefront, and if they did not climb up the cliffs or go around into the ravines on the other side, where could they have gone?'

Bhim said, 'Eastwards. Behind us. Into Matsya.'

'But,' Bhuminjaya said, 'even if they did try something so audacious there's no place to hide there. It's just desert land with the occasional nomads' settlement.'

'Which is why,' Bhim explained, 'I requested you to send for Granthika and Tantripala. Along with the scout, these two men have been to every settlement within a day's ride of here. Of course, they pretended they were heralds taking messages back to the capital, but both Granthika and Tantripala found us the one sign that could help us identify the settlement the enemy was using to hide in – livestock.'

Nakul continued, 'Human beings can lie, or be scared into silence and submission. Horses and cattle are another story. It didn't take us long to find a settlement where new horses had been added to a group of the old even though they all looked dirty and worn. Horses behave differently when in groups... When we also found that in the same settlement the cattle had been fed in their bowers and not been let out to graze on the nearby scrub it left no doubt.'

Swetha, who had been silent all the while, let out an angry yell. 'Yabha! The entire village of traitors should burn for this!'

'Don't be hasty, Swetha,' Sankha cautioned. 'They may not have had a choice. What would you do if the enemy brought the Chief to your doorstep and told you to follow their orders or they would kill him… And for all we know they may have taken the villagers hostage too.'

Sadev said, 'We had the same suspicion, and that is why we kept an eye on the settlement from afar. Even Matsya's sun wouldn't stop children from coming out to play. When we saw none running around, we realized that they too were probably being held hostage.'

'Maraka! A plague on all Trigarta!' Swetha swore. 'Don't they have any regard for morality? Using children and innocents to hide…'

Bhim said, 'I know a very wise man, who would often say that morality is a subtle thing. It has taken me years to understand his words. But now that I do, I see how morality becomes the most powerful value of them all. Which brings me to the plan. It has to be a surprise attack, or else we will place the Chief and the villagers in danger. I propose this: We ride, just a few of us, to this village. We say we are raising muster for the Matsya army and all able-bodied men must join us right away. The enemy is most likely to let all the men of the village go, with the caution that if they reveal anything, their women and children won't live. Perhaps an enemy soldier or two will join them. Once that happens, the advantage is ours. Any and every able-bodied man, barring the Chief, who remains in the village, is clearly one of the enemy. We can kill without hesitation. Unfortunately, the plan puts the women and children at greater risk, not to mention the old men left in the village. That is my only concern.'

Dharma said, 'But it is a risk we must take. A village for a nation is good trade, and what is a nation without its chief?'

'Father would never approve!' Bhuminjaya blurted out.

Sankha waved him silent. 'I won't let even a single innocent die, brother. But I won't lose Father, either.' He looked around at the small company. 'Let's go. We should reach there at dawn and catch the enemy unprepared. Come, Vallabha, Kanka. Let's ride out and bring back the Chief!'

Exchanging calls of resolution and determination, the men mounted their horses and began riding east.

26

THERE WAS LITTLE, IF ANYTHING, TO SUGGEST THE PRESENCE OF enemy soldiers in the village as the party of six – Bhim, his three brothers and the three sons of Chief Virat – came up to the village. The number was, Bhim had argued, a strange one, but none of the others had agreed to being left behind. They had changed into the simpler armour of common soldiers, which Nakul and Sadev already wore, and tried their best to adopt a tired, war-worn look that would go with it.

Sankha called out to the woman who was filling water from the small oasis-well by the mingled light of the setting full moon and not-yet-risen sun as a man looked diligently on. 'You there! Summon your head or village elder.'

The frightened woman did not answer and looked instead to her escort. The man stepped forward. 'Who are you and what do you want?' he questioned Sankha.

'Can't you see, you blind fool? We are soldiers. Soldiers of the Matsya army, in case you wandering idiots don't know the difference between friend and foe. We have orders to gather all the men in this region, to come fight for the Chief. Quick now, get all the men out. We haven't got all day.'

Sankha set his face in an expression of weary impatience. The others began guiding the horses through the village, repeating the instructions as and when men and women emerged from their hutments. In truth, each of the seven was making his way to an assigned position, as per plan. Except for Bhim. His task was to find Chief Virat and protect him at all costs.

The opportunity came when he saw an ashen-faced woman being pulled back into the shadows of her doorway. She re-emerged to ask, in a trembling voice, 'But…. But if you take all our men away, who will protect us?' It was, Bhim noted, a tactical mistake on the enemy's part. Matsya's women were anything but dependent on their menfolk, and he could hardly imagine the burly matron asking him that question of her own will.

'And is your man teaching you to give such excuses? Bring him out! Bring him out before I come in there and drag him all the way to the battlefront.'

The threat worked. Rather than letting Bhim in, a sullen-looking, bearded man stepped out of the hut. 'Go in,' he roughly commanded the woman. He looked around him, exchanging discreet glances with three other men, before all of them joined the group of villagers – pretended and otherwise. Assuming all four were Trigarta's soldiers in disguise, that would leave at least six or more to deal with, Bhim reasoned. They could easily harm any of the hostages, or even the Chief, unless the rescuers acted carefully.

'Right,' Bhim turned in his saddle to address Bhuminjaya. 'Get that lot of men outside the village and lined up in marching order.'

The group of about twenty-five men were herded outside the makeshift perimeter of the settlement, where both Bhuminjaya and Swetha stood guard over them. Bhim realized it was now or never. He slid off his horse, declaring casually to Sankha, 'I'm just going to take a look around, make sure there are no more cowards hiding in their homes.' Knowing he had to move fast, he ran towards the hut in which he suspected the Chief was being kept, ignoring the rising sounds of activity around him. Men and women were screaming, shouting, threats filled the air, as did the sound of weapons being drawn. Bhim left his companions to deal with it all and rushed into the dark doorway of the hut as the burly matron got out of the way.

'Drop your sword or the Chief dies,' a hoarse voice commanded. Bhim complied, letting his weapon fall to the ground, biding his time while his eyes got used to the dark.

'Now, on your knees.'

As Bhim slowly got down on his knees, he could see the outline of two soldiers in full armour. The third figure was that of Chief Virat. The Chief's mouth was tied with a piece of cloth, and his arms and legs were bound with rope. His eyes, however, were open and bright, and he looked at Bhim with recognition.

'Down!' one of the men barked. Bhim placed his palms on the straw-strewn floor and went down on all fours. An instant followed in which he could hear the bustle outside, but he could not make sense of the situation. Apparently, neither could the Trigarta soldiers.

The second of the two was about to step outside, when the first one ordered him back. 'Tie this one up first. Or, better still, kill him.'

To dissuade Bhim against any attempt at resistance, the man drew a knife from his belt and held it to Chief Virat's throat. The second man grabbed a length of rope and began moving, with caution, towards Bhim. He bent down to grab at Bhim's hands and made the fatal mistake of taking his eye off the man.

In that instant, Bhim acted. He bounded lightly to his feet, catching the head of the bending Trigarta soldier in the crook of his left arm. At the same time, he pulled a thin, sliver-like dagger out from where it was strapped around his ankle and hurled it with all his might at the first soldier. Using both his hands he snapped the second soldier's neck in a move that he realized had now become characteristic of him. The man fell dead to the ground. Bhim turned to Virat. The captive Chief was safe, not even shaken from the experience. The soldier who had held a knife to his throat lay sprawled next to him, Bhim's thin dagger driven into the middle of his forehead like a nail.

Bhim sprang forward to cut the Chief's bonds. Virat gave him a nod of gratitude and warmth, but wasted no further time. Bhim drew his sword and handed it to the Chief, who took it. He then bent down to retrieve the dead men's weapons.

'Wait here,' he told the Chief, who merely growled his refusal and strode out the doorway, eager for battle. Bhim shook his head and followed.

The scene that greeted them outside was, given the circumstances, an agreeable one. Three of the captors lay dead, Swetha and Nakul's arrows pierced through them. Dharma stood over another fallen Trigarta soldier. The villagers had beaten the four other pretended enlisters to death.

'The children?' Bhim asked. Sankha gestured towards a large hut, which Sadev had begun hacking down with his sword. Bhim saw the children were already outside and safe though still looking afraid, being seen to by their mothers and fathers. The last two Trigarta soldiers were lying face down on the ground, the matron, who he surmised was the leader of the settlement, standing proudly over them with a blood-smeared iron pestle in her hand.

Bhim bowed in respect, and she returned the gesture.

At the villagers' insistence, Virat, Bhim and the others waited till the settlement was returned to order and refreshments were served. With many thanks and an emotional farewell, Chief Virat prepared to lead the men back to camp.

By the time the company returned to the front, the victory over Trigrata's troops was complete. Scouts reported that what remained of the enemy troops were drawing back into their kingdom. To the resounding cheers of his men, Chief Virat raised his sword in a sign of triumph. The soldiers responded with unrestrained adulation, beating their shields, and calling out praises till, with one voice, they began chanting 'Jayeti! Jayeti! Victory to the Chief! Victory to Matsya!'

Dharma, delighted and amused by the scene, whispered, 'Have you ever seen anything like this?'

Bhim frowned as the remark stirred an old memory. 'Yes, Agraja,' he said. 'I've heard and seen people adore Jarasandha this way. What does that say about what we believe?'

Dharma did not reply in words, but placed a reassuring hand on Bhim's shoulder. For the first time in many years, Bhim felt younger, less burdened. He had found Dharma Yudhisthir, the brother he had once sworn to obey and follow till death, once again.

27

PANCHALI DREW DEEP, EVEN BREATHS AS SHE WAITED FOR THE sun to breach the horizon. Timing and patience were imperative to her task. She had not wanted Partha to worry about her and had left him and Uttara without much argument. But she had not ridden far, staying well within the city limits so as to not draw attention from the city guards on her return.

Even as Partha, Uttara and she had made their plans, Panchali had recognized how redundant her task was. She reasoned that if there was an old Firewright path in and out of Matsya, Govinda already knew of it. What she feared was that he was not the only one. There had been no question – she would have to stay back at Upaplavya.

By the time Panchali returned to the palace, Partha and Uttara had slipped quietly out of the city and were long gone. Panchali set about making sure that their absence would not be discovered for as long as possible – a precaution that the two of them had not discussed at all, intent as they had been on moving towards their dramatic encounter with Syoddhan's armies. She went through the usual actions of settling a pretended Uttara into bed, leaving strict instructions with the other attendants that the princess was not to be disturbed, for she had a tough day ahead, considering the nation's plight. After that, Panchali visited Sudeshna, Virat's queen and Uttara's mother, reassuring her that her daughter was indeed in control of the situation, and that the best she could do was to show faith in her daughter's leadership. These matters settled, Panchali went back to her rooms and sat in silent contemplation. At first light, she had made her way out of the palace and across the grounds towards the forge.

For a nation at war, life had changed little in its capital city. It was quieter in parts of the city, with entire garrisons being called away to battle, but in most other respects daily life continued uninterrupted. Panchali wondered whether this ambivalence came from the generations-long seclusion the people had faced from the rest of Aryavarta, or from a quiet confidence that their armies would prevail. Indeed, security around the city had not been intensified – though she had no doubt more scouts had been sent out into the countryside. As she had expected, there were no guards around the forge, dawn being one of the few instances when a change of guard left the structure unattended. Panchali quickly slipped inside.

Inside the forge, it was silent: the craftsmen were yet to come in for the day. Panchali waited till her eyes adjusted to the darkness, and began her descent into the forge. She made her way across the work floor and towards the small room she had earlier been brought to.

The night Keechak had died, Panchali had considered taking his keys. But she had rightly guessed that Chief Virat would change the locks the moment the General's disappearance came to light. She had concluded, too, that the only way to put in new locks would be to change the door. And the Chief had done exactly that, replacing the old iron door with one made of the new alloy from Matsya's forges.

A simple mistake, Panchali noted. There was a reason why the Firewrights of old had put in an untempered iron door to seal off a forge where Wright-metal was in constant use: It took different means to melt down the two metals. Now, entering the inner room would not take much. She found what she needed next to the smelting area. Carefully picking up a small wooden bowl filled with a thick, black liquid and the wooden ladle lying next to it, she carried it over to the new door. Using the ladle, she began applying the liquid to the edges as though she were tempering the door with oil. Unsure of how much to use, Panchali waited, stepping away a fair distance to be safe. It took time, but she saw the effects – subtle at first but rapidly becoming more pronounced. The door was softening around the edges, curling away from its surrounding jamb as its inner layers peeled off.

Panchali applied more of the corroding liquid – this time only to at the hinges. A short wait later, she pushed at the door, nearly laughing out loud with delight when the door swung open with a soft yawn. Panchali stepped inside. A pang of regret hit her as her eyes ran over the array of bottles and containers on the shelves of the room. But time was running out and, resolute, she set herself to the task at hand.

Panchali stared at her own handiwork, wondering how it was that she had not killed herself with some potion or the other. It crossed her mind that the power of the old Firewrights may just have been nothing more than a symbol, a dead force.

The sound of a person descending the stairs made her turn. She felt sick to her stomach at the sight of the man who came into view. Fists clenched tight, she turned and stepped out of the small room, revealing its empty shelves to the new arrival. Asita Devala took one look at the debris, the broken shards that were all that was left of the Firewrights' greatest creations, and his delight turned to despair. 'No! What have you done? How could you do such a thing?'

Panchali sneered. 'How could *you* do what you have been doing? Don't you see? This is why the Firewrights had to be destroyed!'

'You think it's just the Firewrights? You're a fool then, just like your dear Govinda Shauri. You two think the world runs on reason, but there is no greater reason, no greater justification in the world than power. Power makes its own morality, Panchali. You should know that by now. And the one who has power gets to make the rules, dictate morals, and call himself whatever he likes. Firstborn, Firewright, rebel – these names are but illusions. Power is the only reality. It is the only thing that distinguishes man from man. There are those who have power. And there are those who fear. I think you know what that feels like.'

'Yes, I do. I think you will too, soon, if you don't already. You have failed. I know you came for the Naga-astra. You may now leave, empty-handed.'

Devala advanced on her, as though to hit her. Panchali stood her ground, defiant, but the Firewright did not raise his hand. Instead he put his face close to hers and laughed, cold and mocking, and said, 'You think that by destroying the Naga-astra, you will balance power in Aryavarta, don't you? You believe in all that prattle about trade and equality and new ways of life that Govinda has filled into your head. When will you come out of your make-believe dreams to see that the world is much larger than Aryavarta? There are many more lands to conquer beyond these tiny borders, Panchali. When the world goes to war, what is it that you wish for Aryavarta – that it will conquer, or be conquered?'

Panchali felt tears brimming in her eyes, for it drained her to stand, tiny and weak, against the undeniable truth of Devala's assertions. But she did not flinch. She said, 'There will be war, Devala, within Aryavarta and beyond these lands. You are right. There will be war, and the lust for power and fear will rule us all. But there will be war because in every age there will be those who fight for what is right, those who stand defiant against men like you. Now, we can discuss the eternal battle of good and evil for as long as you like. It doesn't change the fact that you cannot have what you came here for. The Naga-astra is gone.'

Devala stared at her, still disbelieving, and then turned once again to the multi-hued liquids that mingled on the stone floor of the inner room, slowly coming to terms with the enormity of his loss. He turned to Panchali, his eyes blazing. 'Do you truly remember nothing? Who you once were? What you once did? And what Govinda Shauri did to you? If you cannot remember the distant past, surely you remember your life as Panchali? Have you not endured enough? How much more will you bear for him? After all that he has done to you, how can you trust him?'

'Really, Devala. That is such a silly question,' Panchali smiled, completely at ease. 'As for this,' she gestured to the destroyed bottles. 'I didn't do it for him. I did it because it is the right thing to do. You are right. Power is the only reality men like you understand, and it is unfortunate that the world is filled with men like you. But I think you know the old story... At the end of the day, neither the Indras nor the demons of the world get to own Sri. She cannot be owned or kept, but will remain a companion to the one who sees her for what she is.'

'Hah! Stories... Who believes them? And who do you imagine *your* Vasudeva Narayana to be? Foolish girl!'

Panchali raised her chin, feeling within her a wholesomeness and pride that were new to her, but at the same time so natural as if it were a childhood quality pushed forward from her subconscious mind. 'I don't remember who I was, Devala. But I remember some of what I was taught. And if there is one thing I know, it is that behind every myth lies a meaning, a meaning that is housed equally in reason and benevolence. Vasudeva Narayana is each one of us, he is a symbol of the goodness that is inherent in humanity... Humanity, Devala, not these inconsequential, egotistic illusions you call you or me, or other men and women. Sri is the essence of that humanity, the manifested form of the potential within us that we can either embrace or destroy.'

Devala snarled. His eyes showed betrayal and disappointment. He brought up his right hand, curled his fist and opened it to reveal a tongue of flame that appeared to be dancing on his hand. He said, 'In that case, it is settled. I owe you nothing. I owe your family nothing.'

Panchali started at the statement, but Devala had made up his mind. He raised his hand and swung it to throw the ball of flame at her. The flame missed Panchali as she moved back, but hit a stone receptacle which burst into flames, billowing smoke. The sudden occurence knocked her to the ground. By the time she was back on her feet, her eyes watering from the smoke, Devala was gone. She took a few deep breaths to compose herself, and then made her way up the stairs and towards the entrance.

She had not given much thought to how she would leave the forge because, she silently admitted to herself, she had not thought she would leave. As she stepped forward cautiously, wondering what to do next, she came upon the inert body of a guard – the man posted within the forge, who had perhaps taken up his position by the time Devala had entered the building. Devala had no doubt taken the man unawares, and there was no sign that the dead soldier had raised an alarm.

With a word of prayer, Panchali stripped the dead guard of his uniform and put it on, hiding her own robes and the precious item she had secreted away inside them within its folds. She tucked her long hair under the soldier's metal helmet, covering it as best as she could. She waited as she reached the top of the stairs, listening intently to the footsteps of the guards on their rounds outside, counting their paces, till she was sure of her timing. Then she opened the door to the forge, stepped out into the sunlight and began walking towards the palace with all the confidence she could muster.

Panchali reached the attendants' room without incident. Cleaning herself up and changing into fresh robes, she made her way towards Uttara's rooms, as was her morning duty. Just as she had instructed, no one had intruded on the princess. Settling herself into the appropriate state of mind, Panchali entered Uttara's chamber all set to discover that the princess was missing. With careful tending, the matter would grow to obscure the inevitable discovery of the dead guard and the destroyed potions, not to mention a small item that had disappeared from the forge, once the craftsmen arrived for their daily labours. It would, she estimated, give her till evening at the least before things got too complicated, and by then ... Panchali felt sad but content at the thought. By then anything could happen. By then Matsya could fall and she herself could be killed, or in Syoddhan's captivity, or worse, in Dussasan's custody. No doubt he had every intention of finishing what he had started on the day of the dice game. But the possibility no longer inspired fear, at least, not in the helpless, hopeless way it once had. Panchali closed her eyes and smiled. *I am Existence itself.*

28

'WHAT ARE THEY WAITING FOR?' UTTARA SAID, SHADING HER eyes with her hand as she looked at the army. She knew what she saw was just a meagre portion, a hundredth possibly, of the entire force, but the leaders were all there, right at the frontline. Yet, they had neither attacked nor sent a response to the shouted challenge to single combat that she had issued at the break of dawn.

Partha checked his bow for the third time in the last half-muhurrta before putting it down and looking up from where he sat on the floor of the chariot rig. The small and light rig was space enough for two to sit on without too much discomfort, but Uttara remained standing, one hand lightly holding on to the reins of the horses. He said, 'They suspect a trap. To be precise, they suspect a Firewright trap... like the earth opening up under their feet or the mountains falling upon them.'

'Heathens and magicians. That is what we have always been to you all, haven't we?' Uttara said with ill-concealed contempt.

Partha replied, 'Just as we have always been blood-sucking oppressors to you.' He added, 'I don't want to fight about this, Uttara. I've learnt the hard way that the past is important, but not at the cost of the present or future. For what it is worth, I now believe that your people are among the bravest I have ever met, not to mention the cleverest. This is a fine location for an imperial capital.'

Uttara opened her mouth to retort, but Partha went on, 'I mean it, without condescension. Imagine, in times past, when the river flowed through these regions: Your imperial capital would have been nestled in a verdant plain, surrounded by these mountain ranges for protection. True, the mountains are not tall, but they are steep and difficult to scale. The only way in or out would be through these mountain passes.'

'Unless,' Uttara pointed out, 'the enemy came from the north or the west. Of course, one could argue that there is enough of a distance between the borders and the capital city to hold attackers back, but still…'

Partha shrugged. 'Exceptions are inevitable.'

'So you think there is a chance Susarman's forces may overcome our armies? I mean, in the west?'

'The chance always exists. But the last message we had from the western front was that our forces outnumbered the Trigarta troops many times over. Of course, now we know that the attack by Trigarta was merely a distraction. Perhaps your father should not have led the entire army there.'

'Hmm… I remember Bhuminjaya saying as much. And I did too. But when it comes to the cattle… Our herds are tough and hardy and manage to graze well enough on desert scrub and still yield milk and plough what little farmland we have. In fact, the nomads of the west depend on their herds completely for their sustenance. It is tough not to react to a threat to the herds. Your *cousin* probably expected that.'

Partha frowned. 'Considering my brothers are fighting Susarman in the west, and I am standing here with you and not with my cousin, as you call him, a little more charm from you would not be amiss.'

Uttara was undaunted. 'If it weren't for you lot, we – Matsya – would not be in this situation in the first place. But, as you said, this is neither the time nor the place for a fight… I'm sorry.' After a while she said, 'I'm just on edge, not knowing what we are waiting for or why.'

Partha said, 'I'm sorry, too. It's been a while since I was as young as you. I've forgotten what it is like to be impatient, though now I wonder if that is a good thing, after all. If it makes you feel any better, we can surmise what the enemy is up to. The moment you issued your proclamation, Syoddhan would have gathered his advisors to debate on it. His dearest friend Vasusena would have insisted that they ride us down. Grandsire Bhisma would have cautioned against it, pointing out that such an action is contrary to the rules of battle just as single combat is permissible within the rules of engagement. Kings may choose to let a duel decide the outcome of an entire war in order to prevent bloodshed. Or, should a nation lack an army, it may issue a similar challenge. Acharya Dron would have emphasized that a challenge has indeed been issued and that to ignore it would reek of cowardice. He would suggest that he ride out to face you, that is, us, in single combat. At that point, Syoddhan would ask if it were not better to check the rearguard of their armies to negate the possibility of another attack. Asvattama, Acharya Dron's son, would inform him that messengers were already on the way to check this.'

'He can do that? Without Syoddhan's permission?'

'Asvattama is not a man to wait for anyone's permission. He has a mind of his own. His father trained the two of us together, and I ended up being Dron's favourite simply by keeping my mouth shut. Asvattama would get himself into trouble, sooner or later, every time.'

Uttara was impressed. 'Is that how you know so much about each one of them?'

'Yes. I grew up with them. Some of them brought me up, some of them taught me ... They were not all my friends, but none of them were really my enemies, till ...' He trailed off.

Uttara did not press him.

At length, Partha said, '*He* is like that ... Syoddhan. He does very little without asking for counsel. It is both his strength and his weakness.'

'How can that be a weakness?'

'Because thought and debate are all very well when plans are being made, but not when plans are falling apart. My cousin is not a bad man, Uttara. But in my opinion he lost the right to be Emperor, even the king of Kuru, the day he could not stand up to his own brothers, the day he could not stop those under his command from transgressing their bounds.'

Uttara laughed. 'It's strange,' she said, 'how neither Kaurava who has stepped up to lead Aryavarta has the fundamental quality that defines an emperor. It makes one wonder who is fit to lead us ...'

'Maybe, Uttara, no one person is meant to lead. Maybe people, we, all of us together make the best leaders.'

Before Uttara could reply, a horn sounded along Syoddhan's frontline.

'What in the name of ... Are they retreating?'

'No... Yes!' Partha said, with a puzzled frown. 'They are retreating, but not all of them. But yes, they are falling into marching ranks. But... I wonder?'

'Don't speak too soon. The soldiers have stopped moving. This makes no sense...'

As Partha and Uttara watched, two riders left the frontlines and headed towards them, one of them holding aloft a white flag of truce. When they came to stop just outside arrow range, Partha recognized them as Syoddhan and Asvattama. It was Syoddhan who spoke first.

'Princess!' he called out. 'Can you hear me? I must ask you to identify yourself once again.'

Uttara stood tall. 'I am Uttara, daughter of Virat, Chief of Matsya. And I remind you that my challenge remains unanswered.'

'It is the matter of the challenge that I need to discuss, Princess. But before that I need to ask you, who is the other person with you?'

Partha hissed a curse, but Uttara remained unruffled. 'This is my charioteer and fellow warrior. I know her as Brihannala.'

The response drew a chuckle from Asvattama. He said, not bothering to hide his amusement, 'You're a clever girl, Princess. And I have no doubt your companion is, too. Which is why I would like to hear... her... identify herself. You there, upon your honour, who are you?'

Partha felt his heart skip a beat. He had no qualms about revealing his identity, but was afraid that it would place Uttara in grave danger. If Syoddhan found out the truth, he would not hesitate to cut them down where they stood, flag of truce or not. He chose his words carefully and spoke in the lilting tones that he was now used to. 'Did you not hear the princess Uttara? She said my name was Brihannala. I have served in her palace as an attendant excelling in various fine arts.'

'Battle included, no doubt,' Asvattama replied. 'I ask you again. What is your name?'

Partha remained quiet.

'What is your name, *eunuch*?' Asvattama said, rolling the last word off his tongue with all the derision he could put into to it.

It was more than Partha could take. He drew his shoulders back, firm and strong, as he proclaimed. 'I am Partha Savyasachin, by birth a Kaurava and by right a king amongst kings. Fight me, if you dare.'

Asvattama urged his horse closer. He said, 'Oh, I dare, Partha Savyasachin. I dare. But I will not. What happened that day at the dice game ought not to have happened. That I was not there to stop it lies as a debt on my head.' Before either Syoddhan or Partha could speak, he raised his hand and said, 'I am not here to debate whose fault those events were, for enough fault lies on all sides. All I know is my own omission. And so, today, I will not fight you. I suspected it was you, when we set up camp last night. Few bows sound the way yours does. But Syoddhan here had his doubts ... Well, that is settled, Syoddhan. I owe you my loyalty, and I shall fight as the least of your soldiers in any war of your choosing. Bring me Virat, bring me the entire Matsya army, and I shall stand and fight till my last breath. But *him* ... I cannot fight. Not today.' With that Asvattama spurred his horse back towards the frontline.

Syoddhan stayed as he was for a while, glaring at Partha. Then he too turned and headed back to join his troops.

'What just happened?' Uttara asked amazed as, slowly, the enemy forces came into formation and, at the signal from many horns, began to retreat.

'I think,' Partha said, equally astounded, 'we just won.'

The counsellors and commanders of Syoddhan's forces had gathered in a circle. Three men stood at the centre of it all, fighting their own silent battle of wills. Around them, the sound of troops, marching as they fell back, filled the air.

It was Vasusena who spoke first, giving form to the tension in the air. 'How could you, Syoddhan? Just because he said so ...' he pointed to Asvattama.

'He had a point. We came here to conquer Matsya, not fight private battles.'

'And you will turn away from Matsya with your tail between your legs because one man stood in your way? I don't understand. What perverted sense of honour is this? Just because *he* told you he wouldn't fight.'

Asvattama cut in, '*He* is standing right here, and can speak for himself.'

'Then,' Vasusena turned to face Asvattama, 'I suggest *he* explain how an advice to retreat in these circumstances constitutes loyalty. You said you had an obligation not to fight. That sounds like you owe them more than you owe your liege-lord here.'

'A man is not defined by one allegiance alone, Vasusena. If he were, then reason would have no value, nor would loyalty have meaning. I am capable of remaining true to a greater principle and yet serving Syoddhan as a faithful vassal. If it is my loyalty you question...'

'If I may interrupt...' Sanjaya's voice gently intruded from those gathered around the trio.

Asvattama turned on him, visibly irate. 'Welcome, Suta. Amazing how you are never to be found when we ride to battle, but as soon as we stop to talk there you are! An enviable talent, if cowardice were a thing to envy!'

'Stop it! All of you!' Syoddhan called out. His raised a hand, firmly forbidding Dron or Bhisma from adding to the argument. 'My decision is final. And my reasons are my own. We fall back.'

'And if,' Vasusena persisted, despite the caution, 'Susarman should have won in the west?'

'Vathu, Vasusena!' Bhisma did not pass up the opportunity to put down the other man. 'Use your head, if you have one. We used Susarman to draw out the Matsya army, knowing full well that it would be difficult for him to win that battle. It was to be a distraction while we took Upaplavya. That which was difficult in any circumstances is surely impossible if Partha's brothers ride with the Matsya army, which they most likely do. Susarman could not have won in the west.'

Dron added, 'That being the case, if Matsya's army is riding back towards Upaplavya before we take the city, we will have lost our only advantage. Our strategy was to take the capital in a surprise stroke. That may not be possible anymore. We lack the strength to meet Matsya's forces in war. From what my spies tell me, they are about four to five divisions strong.'

Sanjaya edged his way into the triangle of confidence. Asvattama refused to move, forcing Sanjaya to stay a foot behind and to the left of Syoddhan. Sanjaya ignored the slight, and directed his words at Vasusena, 'If Susarman has indeed lost in the west, then it is all the more to our *advantage* that we withdraw. You heard what Partha said. Clearly, he and the others have been living here in hiding. Now that he has revealed his identity, and that too in the presence of Matsya's princess, Matsya's Chief will take care of them for us. Won't they, Grandsire?'

Bhisma was taken aback at being suddenly addressed. Recovering quickly, he gave a firm nod.

Vasusena said, 'I'm not convinced.'

Sanjaya sighed. 'What we need from Matsya we will get. Let us go.'

'What do you mean, Sanjaya?' As the implications of the statement dawned on him, Vasusena spat out, 'Where is Devala?'

Sanjaya merely smiled.

Syoddhan frowned. 'You should not have acted of your own accord, Sanjaya. Devala ...'

'Is expendable. If he fails, he will be seen as a traitor who wanted to take advantage of the situation. If he succeeds ...'

As though the statement settled all concerns, the group slowly began to disperse. Each of the men went to oversee the retreat of their respective divisions, and to impress upon their men that it was a tactical move. Dron could be heard muttering an old adage about commanders who retreated not remaining in command for long. Syoddhan ignored it, and turned his attention again to Vasusena, who had not moved. 'What is it now?' he asked.

'Let me go after him, Syoddhan. Alone, or with just a few men. Just as your outstanding debt makes you retreat, mine compels me to go after him. I cannot forgive or forget my humiliation at Panchali's wedding contest. I want Partha's blood.'

'What ... After all these years?' Syoddhan looked at his dear friend with incomprehension, for he had thought that nothing meant more to the Anga king than loyalty and friendship. Vasusena, however, brimmed with vengeance, an old vengeance that had been all but forgotten. Seeing his friend this way left Syoddhan at a loss for words.

Vasusena said quietly, 'I have always been your friend, Syoddhan. Please be mine. If I fail, you can disavow all knowledge of it. The blame for anything that comes of this shall lie on me alone.'

Syoddhan started at the words, then he said, 'Is that all you want from me, Vasusena? All right. Go. I will lead your divisions back for now.'

Vasusena pulled Syoddhan into an impulsive embrace and then went straight for his horse. He let out a low whistle as he mounted his steed. Ten of his best men fell in behind him. Syoddhan watched as they rode out before anyone could notice. Except Asvattama. 'I didn't know, Syoddhan, that to you friendship means letting your friends do things that are foolish, even wrong,' he remarked.

'Friendship means respecting the other person's priorities even if they are not your own,' Syoddhan said, adding, 'I learnt that from you, my friend.'

Asvattama did not answer. He watched the lone eagle circling the sky above, as he placed his hands behind his head and brought his elbows together, stretching his upper back till muscle and bone settled into place with a creak. 'I grow old. We all do. What now? I suppose it's too much to expect that it is over?'

Syoddhan was about to answer, but stopped short as he felt a strange chill descend on him. The hair on the back of his neck stood on end and his spine tingled. He turned to see if anyone were watching him. He saw no one in the vicinity except for Sanjaya.

Turning back, he said, 'No, Asvattama. Something tells me that it is far from over. And I cannot help but feel a little … afraid … of what might come next. I do not know or understand what it is we do anymore. What has happened to us, to this realm? Or is this what all who live to see such times, who stand as emperors and kings, feel? Is this our destiny? Or can we make our own? No, Acharya,' Syoddhan respectfully stopped Asvattama, who was about to speak, 'no philosophy, no advice, no observations. Not now. If you must speak, just say that you will stand by me no matter what comes next.'

Asvattama squeezed Syoddhan's shoulder. 'I will. You've always helped me meet the demands of my conscience. The least I can do is help you meet yours. You have my word. No matter what comes next, I will stand by you.'

Syoddhan smiled. 'On that note, let us go home.'

29

'WE ARE OUT OF WATER,' UTTARA SAID. 'WE NEED TO STOP AT THE next oasis and let the horses drink.'

Partha said, 'You make it sound like we need to stop at the next wayside inn! I don't suppose you have any of those between here and the city?'

Uttara laughed. 'One year in Matsya and you still haven't learnt anything about the desert, have you?'

'It's not my fault,' Partha grumbled. 'All Brihannala ever had to do was string garlands and play music and dance and ... I'll have you know, I've learnt to plait a woman's hair in thirty-seven different ways! How is that for a survival skill?'

'It might be, depending on who you marry!'

Partha thought of the simple, bold Subadra. 'I'm not sure she'd care about it ... my wife, that is.'

'You are married?'

'Yes, to Govinda Shauri's sister. We ... Wait, what are you doing?' he said as Uttara brought the horses to a halt in the low valley between a cluster of sand dunes.

'Water,' Uttara replied, pulling out what looked like a cylindrical metal vessel from where it had been secured to the side of their chariot rig. The vessel was open at both ends and had a perforated partition in the middle. 'Could you unharness the horses, please?' she instructed.

Partha complied, but asked, sounding puzzled, 'This is an oasis? There is nothing here!'

Uttara did not reply as she got down on her knees. She ran her hands across the sand till she found what she was looking for. Slowly, but with what appeared to be the ease of experience, she forced the cylinder into the sand at that precise point, pressing down on it with all her strength. She stepped back and waited as, slowly, clean water gathered in the upper half of the receptacle. Uttara filled both their waterskins before letting the horses drink their fill from the ground. She passed one to Partha, and raised the other to her lips, drinking in a slow, measured way. Then she lifted the skin high to pour some water on to her face. Both of them heard the dull thud before the waterskin burst from the impact of an arrow.

'Down!' Partha cried, but Uttara was already on the ground. She crawled towards the rig, whistling to the horses, which had wandered beyond the dunes and into the attackers' line of sight.

'No!' she shouted as a flurry of precise arrows took three of the horses down. She was about to run to them, when Partha grabbed her hand and pulled her under the cover of the chariot rig. She realized the futility of her actions, but still shrugged off Partha's grip and jumped up, grabbing the reins of the fourth horse. She coaxed the animal down on to all fours, trying her best to get him behind the rig. As one of the other horses let out a dying whinny, Uttara settled into a cold rage.

'Stay down,' Partha instructed. 'They can't see us as long as we stay behind the dune.'

'Yes, but we can't see them either! Wait here.' Before he could protest, Uttara wrapped her upper robe around her face, and dived into the sand, as though it were water. Crawling low, she made her way up to the edge of a dune and peered over without letting herself be seen.

Partha could see her hand as she signalled to him. She counted eleven men, all mounted. She moved her hand in an arc, indicating the direction of their approach. It was enough. Partha closed his eyes, trying to focus his hearing to locate his quarry, but the sand dulled all noises. He made a swift calculation from the speed and number of soldiers advancing on them, and estimated the distance between them. All Partha had to do now was find one by sound, and he could shoot them all down. He looked up to find Uttara staring at him, waiting for him to act. He tried to signal his predicament and urged her to fall back to safety. She nodded, and then did something that Partha had not expected. She stood up, letting herself be seen. As she had hoped, one of the attackers shouted out to his companions even as he raised his bow to shoot at her.

It was all Partha needed. He let fly a quick succession of arrows.

Uttara threw herself back on to the ground. The impact drew a gasp of pain from her, the sound of which immediately attracted more arrows. Scrambling to her feet, she ran down to join Partha. 'What sort of training do they give you Kaurava archers?' she said. 'Not only do you shoot by sound, so does whoever it is out there.'

'In that case, it can only be Vasusena. And just so that you know…he is not a Kaurava!'

'I don't care what he is, what do we do now?'

'You said there were eleven. I'm sure I got five of them in the last round, maybe six.' He let loose another round of arrows, aiming in the general direction of Vasusena and his men. He heard a faint cry, possibly from a man wounded by one of his shafts and he followed with another volley of arrows. This time, the loud screams told him that two more men were down. 'That leaves just three,' he counted.

'Which might include your not-a-Kaurava-but-can-shoot-by-sound Vasusena,' Uttara pointed out. 'What is he doing chasing us, anyway? This is treachery! Syoddhan said…'

'Never mind what Syoddhan said!' Partha snapped as another rain of arrows descended on them. Partha pushed himself and Uttara under the rig just in time. Many of the arrows hit the floor of the chariot rig, but none of the shafts could pierce through the metal-overlaid wood.

The horse gave a chilling shriek as a dart pierced one of its haunches. Uttara grit her teeth. She said, 'Let's charge at them.'

'What?'

'Let's charge at them. We are not going to get out of this anyway. We might as well die honourably.'

Partha was not amused. 'Stupid girl! Take it from a veteran: Stay a little afraid, and you will stay alive. Dead men…and women…are of no use to anyone, and…'

'Out! Now!'

'What?'

'Can't you smell it? That's a flame-tailed arrow.'

'We'd feel the fire if it were a flame-tipped arrow. Calm down, you are panicking!'

Uttara gave him a disgusted look. 'I said flame-*tailed*, not flame-tipped! Once the shaft burns all the way down to the arrowhead, it ignites the ... Oh never mind, we aren't arguing about this now. Just move!'

Partha weighed the dangers of coming out from under cover of the rig against staying there. He had heard of flame-tipped arrows but flame-tailed ones, he knew, were still an imperfect, no, an impossible, weapon. Frowning, he said, 'But ...'

'Out! Go!' Uttara shouted. Her voice drew a fresh rain of arrows, another one of them hitting their equine companion. 'Mih!' Uttara crawled closer to the animal. Even as she tried to she scramble out from under the rig, she slapped the horse on its rump, trying to get it to move. Finally, the horse staggered to its feet. 'Come on!' she called out again to Partha. This time, he did not protest, for the smell of burning wood filled the air.

He half-emerged from under the chariot to see that the arrow had already burned down to a thumb-length from the explosive tip. 'Uttara, hurry!' he called out and reached under the chariot to help her out. He grabbed her hand and pulled at her.

'Aaah!' Uttara cried out, and slid out of his grasp with a jerk as the horse got to its feet and moved a few feet away from the rig, dragging her along the ground.

'Yabha!' Partha said. 'The reins ... they are tangled. Uttara, your foot, cut it loose. Cut the reins.' More arrows fell. Partha had no choice but to take refuge under the chariot once again.

'Run for it,' Uttara told him. 'Just go! They will be aiming at the rig, they won't expect it. Run!'

Partha smiled, as though they had all the time in the world. 'I have a son a little older than you, Uttara. No father would run for it.' Uttara stopped struggling to free herself and closed her eyes, reaching out at the same time for Partha's hand. He said, 'You'll make your father proud, just as you have made me proud.'

Silence. And then they heard the hiss of a single arrow, the crack

314

of breaking wood and, all at once, many voices, shouts and the sounds of a fight.

Uttara opened her eyes to find Partha listening intently.

A man's voice said, 'Give me a hand here!' and she felt the rig move. She cried out despite herself as the tangled reins pulled at her foot.

'A woman! There's a woman!' A second man's voice said.

'By Rudra, you're a genius!'

To Uttara's utter confusion, Partha began laughing. Aloud, he said, 'If it's no bother, I'm here, too, Shikandin. And stop pulling at the rig, Princess Uttara's foot is tangled in the reins.'

At that, a wild-looking man, his many tight braids of grey and black hair pulled back and tied together at his neck, peered under the rig. His eyes gleamed with amusement as he saw Partha, who still bore the traces of having been Brihannala. 'And who might you be, my beautiful one? An apsara from above?'

Uttara recognized him as the first man whose voice she had heard earlier. She prickled at the statement and prepared to rudely counter it, but realized that Shikandin had not referred to her but to the long-haired Partha. She turned away as the second man crouched by her feet and began cutting the reins with his dagger. He was, she noticed, young and handsome. He smiled at her, and Uttara recognized it as the self-assured grin of a man used to having women swoon over him. She decided she did not like him and indicated as much by rejecting his offer of help to slide out from under the rig. Her next thought was for the hurt horse. Already, another man was tending to the animal despite the fact that he only had use of one arm – the other was in a sling that hung around his neck. He turned and rose to his feet as she rushed forward, sensing a familiar sense of comfort coursing through her.

'Govinda Shauri?' she gasped.

Govinda said, 'Surely, this is not little Uttara with the two tight plaits and the many dolls she kept wanting new clothes for? And you, Partha! Why, I'd wager that you are the most beautiful woman in all Matsya. Aah, those dark tresses would drive even the best of poets mad with wordlessness.'

'You gwala, you!' Partha retorted. He then asked, 'How? And Vasusena ... ?'

'Oh, we sent him running as if a hive of bees were attacking his backside,' a man replied, riding up.

'Yuyudhana!' Partha greeted him.

Uttara saw that Yuyudhana's bow was in his hand. Two more men were with him: a large, fair-skinned man, who still looked grim, and another man with impeccably chiselled features and an arrogant bearing.

Yuyudhana continued, detailing how their group had come down the cliffs and seen the attack in progress. '... but it wasn't fair sport, really. Vasusena and his second turned back as soon as they saw us, so there wasn't much for us to do. The other man didn't take much killing. I must protest, Partha. You always end up taking the pick of lot, whether it is soldiers to kill or courtes ...' he stopped mid-word as he realized that a young woman was present in their midst. 'Mahamatra ...' he respectfully acknowledged her, and Uttara in turn responded with a bow.

Partha said, 'If you come late to the banquet, all you will get are leftovers. Besides, that was remarkable archery, my friend – shooting off the burning shaft before it could explode. I salute you!' he declared, indicating where the small broken-off piece lay charred and harmless, on the sand.

'That was not me. That was a boy who has archery in his blood. You might know him ...' The young man who had freed Uttara's feet from the tangle of reins stepped forward. Despite her dislike of him, Uttara thought it only polite to thank him for his help. But before she could say a word, Partha had run forward and thrown his arms around the young man, embracing him tightly and with unrestrained affection. Not sure how to respond to the emotional exchange and backslapping between the two men, Uttara stepped back.

At length, Partha turned to her. 'Uttara, this is Abhimanyu, my son. Abhimanyu, this is Princess Uttara, daughter of Chief Virat of Matsya. She is one of the bravest people I've met in all my life.'

Uttara acknowledged him with a polite bow. She turned to Govinda, the one she felt most comfortable addressing, and said, 'You should get that arm looked at, and soon. Come, Upaplavya is not too far a ride away. We can be there by early evening.'

'Is that an invitation?' Abhimanyu called out. 'If it is, it's not much…'

Uttara twisted around to look at him. 'Would you like to wait here in the desert while I send someone along with a group of dancing girls?'

Govinda cut in. 'We'd be delighted to follow you, Princess. Please lead the way.'

Uttara nodded, and went about fixing the harness and reins on the surviving horse. She thought she could feel Abhimanyu's eyes on her for a long time.

30

DHARMA YUDHISTHIR WAS, BY HIS OWN BRUTALLY HONEST reckoning, a man of considerable intellect. As such, it was not unusual for him to condense events around him into singular questions of philosophical or moral importance, which then allowed him to make his decisions. He was, therefore, not in the least discomfited by the news of all that was transpiring around them, nor the fact that it was his cousin, Syoddhan, who was behind the events.

He received the news that Syoddhan rode under the elephant banner of Emperor Hastin with a knowing smile. What he had not expected, however, was the enemy ranks also flying flags with symbols of a golden altar and a white umbrella, for those belonged to Kripa and Bhisma, respectively. Alongside theirs was another flag with the symbol of a flame – a sign that Dron, acharya to the Kuru clan, no longer felt the need to hide his origins. That his teachers and Grandsire Bhisma had taken up Syoddhan's cause was the final sign Dharma needed to understand fully the many things Vidur had told him a year ago. The insight made him feel lighter than he had in a long time. He thought yet again of the man he loved and respected as a father and sent him silent thanks. Vidur had been insistent that Matsya was the answer to all the questions of morality Dharma had struggled with. By the time he, Chief Virat and a few of the others had ridden ahead to the capital, Dharma had made up his mind.

When rulers forgo what is right,
Know that evil shall delight…

My fault was not that I played dice, but that I lost at it. My duty was not only to protect, but also to guard. I failed at it then, but not anymore. He had his brothers; they were all he needed. It was time to act.

With this conviction, Dharma turned his attention to the missive that awaited them at Upaplavya: Uttara and Brihannala had challenged the Kaurava leaders to single combat. Syoddhan's army had retreated. Virat had insisted on riding out again to meet his daughter and her companion at once, but Sudeshna, urged gently on by Panchali, had prevailed on her husband to wait and to ensure that the armies were refitted before being deployed again in case the enemy should decide to return. Still, nothing could dull the anticipation with which Virat took his seat in the assembly, and went about giving the appropriate orders.

Dharma saw the situation as destiny providing him with an opportunity, one that he would be a coward to ignore. Virat was beholden to him and his brothers in more ways than one. This was a gamble he could not lose. And then, with the military might of Matsya at his disposal… He found his chain of thought broken as Virat began speaking. 'Kanka, Vallabha… and you too, Granthika, Tantripala and… Brihannala, is it not – the one who is not here yet? Never mind. Tell me, what can I give you to show you my gratitude? Ask, and it shall be yours.'

Dharma thought, once more, of Vidur. He said, 'Give us that which is ours by right, Chief. Give us Matsya.'

Virat laughed. 'What do you mean, Kanka? I'm not a man without honour to disavow those who have served me well, and it is true that I might owe Vallabha my life. But Matsya belongs to the people, to these brave soldiers who fought for it, and the thousands who have stood behind them.'

'What is *your* right to lead them, Virat? For mine is the same right.'

'Silence!' Virat thundered. A moment of silence ensued, followed by the sharp scrape of metal against metal as Bhim, Nakul and Sadev drew their swords. In response, Sankha, Bhuminjaya and Swetha too reached for theirs. Alert to the danger to their chief, Virat's personal guards quickly surrounded their charge.

'Father!' Uttara's voice rang out from the doorway, Partha and Panchali by her side. Sankha ran to pull her away, even as Nakul shifted his position, anticipating an attack. In the middle of it all stood Dharma, unperturbed and unshaken. In fact, he looked all the more majestic for not drawing his weapon.

'Chief Virat,' he began. 'Do you know who I am? I am your kinsman.'

'Kinsman? Hah! I don't care who you are, Kanka,' Virat replied, pushing past his guards to come face to face with Dharma.

'Oh, but you must! I am Dharma Yudhisthir Kauravya, the true Emperor of Aryavarta. The one who stood by your brave daughter, the one whose presence caused Syoddhan to retreat from battle – he is my brother Partha Savyasachin. My other brothers, Bhim Vikrodara, and Nakul and Sadev Madriputra, you already know as men in your employ, and the handmaiden Malini is Panchali, daughter of Dhrupad. Most importantly, I am descended from Satya, Queen of the Kurus, whom many believe to be a woman of Matsya. But both you and I know that she was more than that. She was Crown Princess of Matsya, was she not, Virat? It is only when she left these lands to live in hiding as a fisherman's daughter that her brother – your great-grandfather – became Chief to hold the throne in trust for its true heirs. By all law and all morality, your throne is mine.'

Virat stared at him, incredulous. Then, slowly, he raised his hand and laid a single, resounding slap on Dharma's cheek. A silence hung over them all.

It was Sankha who stirred first. He turned to Swetha and said, 'Arrest them. The woman too.'

'No!' Uttara protested.

'This is outrageous!' Bhim growled.

Bhuminjaya and Swetha both came forward, exchanging confused looks. 'Arrest them all right now,' Sankha insisted.

Sadev said, 'But why? What is our crime?'

Sankha glared through bloodshot eyes. 'Your brother's crime, firstly, is that he is a fool! Have you never wondered why even Bhisma of the Kurus never dared step into these lands – though he is the only one of that line who might have survived, for he is not of Satya's blood. If you truly consider yourself my kin, on account of Satya, then wouldn't your cousin Syoddhan be my kin, too? And he just went running from our borders, did he not? Yes, Satya was from Matsya. That is well known. But do you know why she left these lands? Because she was a traitor, she betrayed those whom you and your family have spent years hunting down. You see, Dharma Yudhisthir, *your* ancestress Satya was trained as a Firewright by the man who loved her, and whom she eventually betrayed. Generations later, Matsya still pays the price, we stand alone and forsaken. Finally, we shall have our vengeance and the barren earth of our motherland, the parched course of the river, shall slake its thirst with your blood.'

'But…' Dharma had no words, merely the vague thought that he wished Sankha would kill him right there, right then. He did not know whether to feel shame at the tainted, Firewright blood that ran in him, or to rejoice that his ancestress had dared bring those heathens down. Yet, at the same time, questions stirred in him, all the more for his recent experiences. *Had Vidur not known? Had Dwaipayana not known?* But the answers came to him even as the questions formed in his mind. *No… of course, they knew. That is why Dwaipayana had chosen him and not Syoddhan to become Emperor. Protect the good, guard the evil.*

Bhuminjaya's touch on his arm drew him out of his introspection. The prince still remained hesitant and respectful. 'Come, Kanka.'

'Sankha, please…' Uttara interjected.

'Vathu, Uttara!'

'My lord, Chief Virat…' Dharma felt a searing pain as he heard the voice, far worse than what his body or honour had endured when Virat had struck him or Sankha had ordered him arrested. The speaker's next words, however, stirred a whirlwind of emotions: shock, confusion, joy and sadness, and others sensations that he could not identify. 'You owe that man your greatest allegiance, Sankha.

Because truly this throne is Dharma Yudhisthir's. In him survives the true legacy of Matsya, and the secret of the Firewrights.'

31

GOVINDA FELT BLOOD RUSH TO HIS HEAD, RISING WITH THE HEAT of fury, self-loathing and rage. Guilt and recrimination followed as he realized he had betrayed the one secret that had allowed him to weave his web of intrigue over Aryavarta, the one secret that Ghora Angirasa, once Secret Keeper, had left in his possession. The secret had bought him his legitimacy, his influence with the Firstborn despite the burden of his own origin and allegiance; it was the one thing that had kept him even remotely useful to Dwaipayana and, so, alive. It had been the one thing he had left to trade. But it had taken just one glance to dismiss all reason and do what he had to do.

As Bhuminjaya and Swetha had advanced, following Sankha's command, Panchali had remained where she was, summoning courage to stand firm. But, for just an instant, she had turned to glance back, not quite seeing him. Her eyes had held, again, the look of a trapped, desperate animal, one that longed to live even as it was being led to slaughter. He had seen it in the eyes of a young girl, whom he had promised to protect, only to fail time and again.

In that moment Govinda knew he would do whatever it took to to shelter Panchali from any further suffering. He did not care any more for half-truths and conspiracies, for politics or honour. And, he admitted, a deep, angry part of him longed for Dharma to know the truth, the complete truth, and to see if that could finally pierce through his insufferable self-righteousness.

Govinda turned to Virat and said, 'Dharma Yudhisthir, great-grandson of Queen Satya of the Kurus and once Crown Princess of Matsya … Nothing happens in isolation. Satya's story is part of a larger, inevitable change. Even as the Firewrights grew unfettered in power and arrogance, within their own order there rose rebels – men and women who believed that fire is the light of knowledge and that it ought not to be tamed by a few. Ghora was one of those. He was the one who trained Satya, though she was an outsider – just as he later trained me, and many others.

'Satya saw, as Ghora did, that the order had to be destroyed for the sake of all Aryavarta. And so, when the Firewrights failed to harness the waters of the Saraswati and turned all of Matsya into a desert, she set into motion a plan. I cannot say whether she intended vengeance on the order or not … But she did intend their downfall. She agreed to let her father send her away to live with Chief Dasha, but by that time she and Ghora had already begun to spur on the only power capable of bringing down the Firewrights: the Firstborn. You all know how the story goes after that. Satya kept the birth of her son, Dwaipayana, a secret till such time as Dwaipayana became surrogate father to her grandchildren, the Kuru princes. That was not without reason, for by her actions she had inextricably bound the fate of the Firstborn and the Firewrights – not the old, entrenched ones she wanted to destroy, but the rebels who would gladly disappear into obscurity if they could leave their craft and knowledge as a legacy for all Aryavarta.'

Govinda paused, aware that his audience hung on to his every word. After all, he was for the first time telling a tale that many had heard in bits and pieces, never in its entirety. He was also aware that with each word he spoke he was revealing Aryavarta's greatest secret, tearing apart the immaculate plan that Ghora had set into motion with his own death.

All this for a woman? The memory of a voice reared its head in his mind.

All this, because it is right, Govinda answered.

Out loud he continued, 'But we failed. I failed. Where there should have been no order of Firewrights in this empire, we now have two. The Secret Keeper …' He looked up as gasps filled the air. 'Yes, there is a Secret Keeper – Ghora Angirasa's successor. I serve him … Virat, I once asked you to trust me, because there was something that I knew and you did not. This is that secret. Ghora Angirasa left it in my keeping as he died, and my knowledge of it was the reason Dwaipayana and the Firstborn have wanted me dead, but never exposed me as a Firewright. But now, I have put my faith in you. You must choose, Chief. Are we traitors? Or are we rebels, a few who stand for what is right against the might of many? Isn't that what your nation is? An island of equality and hope within the moral desert that is Aryavarta? Do you not understand?'

'Enough!' Sankha stepped forward, drawing his sword. 'Your lies and trickery won't work on us, rebel! What happened to this land was punishment for Satya's treachery. But since you feel so strongly for her cause, you can be the first to die for it.'

But before he could raise his weapon, Chief Virat was on his feet. 'No, Sankha, wait! If it is him…if he has come back, then…then there is hope. Govinda? Govinda Shauri, is it really you? I thought you had forsaken us…'

Govinda opened his arms in a gesture of peace. 'I had, Chief. I nearly had. But don't lose faith in your fellow men and women just yet.'

As though punctuating Govinda's words, the rest of his companions entered, the group dominating even the large hall. Balabadra and Yuyudhana were faces Virat and his sons recognized, though Shikandin and Dhrstyadymn were new to them. Abhimanyu, looking less youthful now and more sombre, stood behind them. Govinda looked around at them, their presence bringing a smile to his face. He said, his characteristic mischief returning to his voice, 'I hope we are not unwelcome, Chief?'

Chief Virat laughed, the sound a boom that matched his bulk. The sound of her father laughing filled Uttara's heart with joy, and she ran forward to embrace him. She whispered in his ears – apparently words of counsel from the thoughtful frown on Virat's face. When she was done, he placed an affectionate hand on his daughter's head as he turned back to the man before him. 'Unwelcome? Govinda, you are a sight for sore eyes and a thirsty heart. Every day I have prayed that you would return, that the future that was promised us was not just a dream. Seeing you here today…' Realizing the implications of the situation, Virat gestured to his sons to lower their weapons. 'Dharma Yudhisthir…?'

Govinda said, 'Dharma Yudhisthir. Dwaipayana promised Satya that he would see her line on the Kuru throne. He kept his word to her, but at the same time he was determined to fulfil his duty as a Firstborn. And so he did all he could to hide the truth of his origins even as he brought the Firewrights down. But in doing so, he subsumed much of the Wright's craft and knowledge into his own fold. In a few generations we would not have remembered the Firewrights, but their skills would remain.'

Sankha said, 'In a few generations…? That can't happen anymore, can it? Not after what you've said and done right here. Unless you want to make us all part of your conspiracy? Wouldn't that be sheer incompetence on your part?'

'Absolutely, Prince. But I have no need for this particular secret anymore. You can send out heralds with proclamations for all I care.'

'And why is that?'

'Now *that* is a secret that I might have use for yet. Not a secret, really, but just a story for another time. What do you say, Chief?'

Virat looked at Govinda and then again at Dharma, seeing him through new eyes. 'Dharma Yudhisthir! I understand now why Govinda urged us to wait. He said that your empire would be Matsya's chance to rise to its rightful place of respect among its neighbours. He insisted that our patience and sacrifice would light Aryavarta's future. But we didn't believe him. We thought him a traitor too….'

Dharma frowned, but said nothing. The Chief did not notice. Instead he rested his hands on Govinda's shoulders, and looked him up and down with unrestrained joy. 'What now, Govinda?'

'Now the true Emperor rules. We of Ghora Angirasa's legacy stand by him and his empire. I see no better place for the Emperor to return to claim what is rightfully his than here, where it all began. Unless, Dharma, you have any objections…?'

Dharma finally brought himself to look at Govinda. Both men knew that the one objection he had raised, years ago at Kamyaka, was no longer relevant. Dharma had thought himself tainted by Govinda's association, but now he knew, everyone knew, that Syoddhan was as tainted as he was, as were those to whom they all turned for counsel and justice: the Firstborn, and Krishna Dwaipayana, the Veda Vyasa, not the least. He nodded.

Govinda smiled. Silence was, Govinda knew, the closest to warmth Dharma could show in the circumstances, and it was enough. He stepped back and let Virat guide Dharma to the Chief's seat of honour.

To muted but respectful greetings, Dharma Yudhisthir sat on the throne of Matsya, the seat, heralds announced, of ancient emperors. His eyes remained on the man who had brought him this, his third crown. Govinda's gaze, however, remained on Virat's silent but disgruntled sons.

'What was that?' Shikandin pulled Panchali aside, making no effort to hide his amusement.

'That, my dearest brother, is called politics. It so happens that I've had a lot of time on my hands these past years and I have spent much of it contemplating this rather consummate art.'

'You're good at it. I can't imagine who else Dharma might have learnt from.'

'You see it too?'

'Yes. Dharma wants Matsya. He tolerates Govinda for he reasons that the ends justify the means, though he begrudges the fact that even now it has taken Govinda's word to settle his affairs. No wonder Govinda wanted you to marry him. No matter what he does for Dharma he will always be the lesser man, because there is one thing that our esteemed Emperor has that Govinda can never have ... You. Hai! The intrigue never ends. And so much so for Dharma's moral stand.'

'Ah, but morality is a subtle thing, as Dharma would say. Duty is constant. And Dharma Yudhisthir believes he is doing his duty.' Panchali's smiled faded as she thought of all that lay ahead, but she forced it back on to her face as Govinda approached them. She tried to give a name to the confused sensations that coursed through her.

Govinda said, 'Panchali, I need you to speak to Uttara.' And then he was gone, weaving through the crowd to fall in step with Virat and Dharma as the assembly concluded and they left the room. He struck up a conversation with the two monarchs as though the occasion were nothing but a pleasant visit.

Dhrstyadymn walked up to Panchali and Shikandin, looking at Govinda with displeasure, and said, 'What just happened?'

Panchali sighed. 'Ah yes, you wouldn't see it. You never did. It's rather simple, brother. This realm isn't quite Dharma's yet. Sankha and his brothers are not fully convinced. No doubt their father will explain things to them in private, but we need a bond stronger than Virat's word and his sense of ancient honour. We need another kind of alliance to hold this together.'

'I don't get it. I simply don't understand. Why, after all that has happened… Why would Govinda let Dharma Yudhisthir reclaim a throne, any throne?'

As if of one mind, Panchali and Shikandin looked at each other and burst out laughing.

'What?' An uncomprehending Dhrstyadymn stared at his siblings.

'My dear brother,' Panchali began.

Shikandin continued, 'If after all this while there is just…'

'…one thing you should know…'

'…about Govinda Shauri, it must be this…'

Panchali concluded, 'Govinda Shauri always has a plan.'

32

PANCHALI SUSPECTED THAT A CLEVER WOMAN LIKE UTTARA KNEW well what was to come, but facing her now, she found no satisfaction in knowing that her assessment had been accurate. No sooner did she enter the room than Uttara came striding forward to face her, confusion writ large on her face. 'Are you here to help me or to counsel me, Panchali?'

'What if they are one and the same, Uttara?'

'The last time you and I were alone in a room, I made a few choices. Choices I did not regret till a short while ago, but now…'

Panchali sighed. 'I take it, then, that your father has already told you of his plans to wed you to Abhimanyu.'

In response, Uttara grunted, disdainful.

Panchali went on, 'I also take it you don't want to marry Abhimanyu?'

'What makes you think I'd want to marry him? Or do you think me obligated to do so? Yabha! I'm not some puppet for you to treat me this way, nor am I a child who plays with them that you can cajole consent out of me.'

'Your father initially offered you to Partha, Uttara. But Partha can't think of you that way, not after he's cared for you and protected you as a daughter. That's why I suggested you marry his son ... '

'I don't want to marry his son! I'd rather die than ... What is this, Panchali? Conquest without bloodshed? I have seen my father bow to the General and bend under the weight of ancient promises and lies that meant nothing. How do you expect me to have any regard whatsoever for a man who comes to my home, lives under my father's protection and in return takes away my father's throne and honour with it. And what of my brother? The throne is rightfully Sankha's! Just because my family has been the custodian of a right that Dharma now claims, I don't have to like it. And even if Matsya is Dharma's by law, it certainly doesn't come with me as tribute!'

'Your father should have thought of that before ... '

'Before what, Panchali? Before he kept his oath as Chief to give up his throne to Satya's heir? Or before he put me up as a prize? Isn't that what happened to you? Where were your ideals then? Where were your brothers? And where was your precious Govinda Shauri?'

'Uttara, please ... '

'What now, *Malini*? Will you cry and plead? Will you counsel me that this is the fate of our kind? And what kind is that? Women? Princesses? Or just those of us unfortunate enough to be of political use? And don't give me all that piss about putting my nation's interests before mine. We both know what this wedding really means. As it stands, every monarch in Aryavarta would give an arm and a leg to call himself kinsman to Matsya!'

'And does that make you feel less like an object of use, a political puppet?' Panchali snapped back. 'At the end of it all, you're obsessed with your own self-worth, aren't you, Princess? All that ... what did you call it ... "piss about my nation's interests" ... I've been through that and more. I've seen the one I trusted the most throw me away, trade me in the interests of all Aryavarta, and I've felt more anger and rage than you can begin to imagine. But there is a difference between use and sacrifice. Do you even know what that word means? Sacrifice? It

327

is when you surrender ... not because you think you mean nothing. One cannot give up that which means nothing. I was not a puppet, Uttara, I was a sacrifice. Just as *your* ancestress Satya was. There are many who have given up everything because they believed in the ideal of Aryavarta, of a united realm beyond the politics of Firstborn and Firewright. I will leave you to choose what you believe in and what you wish to be.'

Panchali turned to go and was almost out of the room when Uttara called out, 'Wait.' Panchali stopped, but did not turn. Uttara continued, 'If Abhimanyu touches me, he dies. Him, not me, be clear. I'm not one to suffer anything and everything. I will agree to this wedding, because I know it is what Govinda Shauri wants. But it is an arrangment – that is all it is. You can tell that brat to stay away from me.'

'All right.' Panchali left without looking at Uttara. She also did not bother with tears, not then, nor later as she lay sleepless throughout the night.

A week later, on what turned out to be a fine, cloudless morning, Abhimanyu and his kinspeople, including his mother Subadra, were led through the city of Upaplavya amidst a jubilant convoy of dancers and musicians. The moment they entered the palace, Govinda slipped away from the ceremonial procession. He moved around the chief's court, joyously greeting old friends and allies, jesting and striking up conversations. He was constantly flanked by Shikandin and the recently arrived Dhaumya, who had been sent for to perform the wedding ceremonies. The sight of the three old friends took Balabadra and Yuyudhana back many years.

'Keep him out of trouble, will you?' Balabadra jovially ordered Dhaumya.

'He *is* trouble!' the scholar pointed out in return.

When Dharma stood up from the Chief's throne to formally welcome all the guests to the wedding, the three of them made their way back to the front of the assembly. As everyone took his or her place for the wedding ceremony, the groom was led away for a ritual bath and to change into wedding finery, while Dharma and

Virat exchanged gifts and made pledges of friendship and alliance. Govinda looked around, but could not see Panchali anywhere. They had exchanged no words, not even socially, since the day he had told her to speak to Uttara, and he wondered if she were avoiding him. He had caught a glimpse of her now and then from a distance, but before he could approach her, she had always disappeared. And now, too, she remained elusive.

Subadra noticed his preoccupation and whispered, 'She is with Uttara... Look!' she exclaimed softly, as Abhimanyu was led back into the hall.

'Pradymna's spoilt him!' Subadra lovingly complained.

'What can I say? He's such a gem.'

Abhimanyu approached Dharma and Virat where they sat, and greeted them both. Virat stood up and offered his son-in-law his place, as was custom. Abhimanyu was visibly hesitant, but he went forward to stand in front of the carved seat. His discreet refusal to sit on it did not go unnoticed, and the burly Chief drew the younger man into an impulsive embrace. Sankha, Swetha and Bhuminjaya, too, were discernibly warmer towards Abhimanyu after that.

Princess Uttara was led out by a group of women. A light, golden veil covered her face, and her eyes remained on the ground before her. Govinda knew better than to mistake it for modesty, and he felt a new emotion tug painfully at his heart. He tried yet again to find Panchali. She was not there.

'Come on, we can't stand here like some distant cousins!' Subadra hissed and led Govinda to the foot of the ceremonial dais. There she let go of her brother's hand and went up to join her husband.

Shortly, Dhaumya called for everyone to bless the wedded couple. Abhimanyu grabbed Uttara's hand with an air of familiarity, and the two sought blessings from the assembled guests. 'Flirt!' Govinda muttered to himself, beaming with delight at the scene.

'He's *your* son, remember?' a very familiar and welcome voice sounded in his ear. Govinda turned, a rare expression of absolute surprise on his face. 'For once, I managed to sneak up on *you*, Govinda. You have no idea how hard it was! But I must admit that the look on your face just now was worth the effort...'

'How, Panchali...?' he asked her, referring to the couple before them.

'I trust your upbringing, Govinda. Abhimanyu won't touch her unless she lets him. As for her... I made her see reason. Just as you once made me see reason. One woman for an empire is a very fair trade, is it not? But, I must admit, I was afraid for a while that Uttara was already in love with someone else, maybe even an incorrigible, flirtatious cowherd... But no. It wasn't as bad as all that.'

'Was it not? Is reason truly everything, Panchali?'

'You know it isn't. You know there's more inside you. And that is what keeps me going.'

Govinda stared at a Panchali he had not known before. Ruthless and calculating, yet hopeful and spirited. After all that had happened in all this time, she seemed... *Reforged. Tempered by fire.* 'Panchali...' he began, but fell silent, unable to find the words to tell her how much he admired her. How much he had missed her. How much he cared for her. Finally, with a smile of contentment, Govinda took her hands and held them tight.

33

'YOU CAN'T BLAME ME FOR NOT LIKING MATSYA, PANCHALI. I'M a cowherd – I need greenery, pastures, rolling fields. Not sand... and then more sand!'

Panchali clucked her tongue in mock sympathy as she led Govinda across a dry stretch of ground from the forge towards the quarters that Chief Virat had surrendered for Dharma's use. Despite her playful tone, her words were serious. 'Are you angry with me?'

'For destroying those potions? Or for letting Devala escape alive?' 'Both.'

'Neither, Panchali. In fact, I am not angry at all. You did what you had to do, and I...' Govinda stopped in his tracks and stood looking at the building ahead. It was alive with the bustle and flurry of a wedding just concluded but a strained sobriety lay under all the activity. 'How is he?' he said, 'Our lord and master, the Emperor?'

'Surprisingly content and settled. The advantage of being a man of principle is that once your values are indulged, it is easy to find peace.'

'He's not unlike his grandfather, Dwaipayana. Or perhaps it is a Firstborn trait.'

Panchali laughed. 'Is that why you find it so easy to manipulate him?'

'Manipulate? You make me sound evil, Panchali. Am I evil?'

'Never! You're just highly useful, Govinda, as evil sometimes is. You were useful to Dwaipayana by keeping a secret. Now, you've made yourself useful to Dharma by sharing the same secret. Where is the evil in that? But, I wonder, did you get what you wanted out of it?'

Govinda turned to face her. 'What do you think I wanted, Panchali?'

'What you've always wanted.'

'Are you going to accuse me of ambition and hunger for power yet again? I did not at all enjoy our last conversation along those lines. Besides, I'm overdressed for it.'

Panchali could not help but smile. She said, 'You sent us here, didn't you? Vidur was acting on your instructions. Why? Why here?'

'So that all I needed kept safe, would be so. I did not want anyone to find you, Panchali. I did not want anyone to hurt you. But the mistake I made, one of many, is that I thought Matsya had more time.'

'What do you mean?'

'Matsya's isolation was meant to foster change. You've already seen the evolution of their craft – Uttara found nothing strange about a flame-tailed arrow, even though Partha could not even think of it, as he told us. But more important was the change in their way of life. Matsya's is a far more equal society than the rest of Aryavarta. I admit, it is far from perfect, but it is a step. You see, the rest of Aryavarta concentrated power – not just moral or martial power, but power over effort, over resources and the produce of the earth – in the hands of a few, and did so in the name of Divine Order and a righteous way of life. And the few who have the power tend to struggle with each other over it – just as the Firstborn and Firewrights. But today, when faced with the unique creature that is Matsya, a place where equality is intrinsic to justice, and power lies in the hands of the people and not a chosen few, a man like Dharma Yudhisthir does not know whether he owes his loyalty to the Firstborn or to the Firewrights. And so, his decisions will come not from blind allegiance, but from reason and greater good. As will Syoddhan's, for that matter.'

Panchali frowned, trying to understand. 'So you needed to isolate Matsya long enough for this change to happen? But how could you force something like that to happen?'

'I … we … didn't force it, Panchali. The isolation began as a result of many events, most of which were socially inevitable and all of which were beyond our control. The failure of the Firewrights to divert the river, Satya's own actions, the resultant escalation of the Great Scourge and the rise of the Firstborn – all these are part of the greater cycle of Time. All we could do was to try and ensure that the isolation lasted long enough for it to allow these changes to happen within Matsya.'

Panchali was unconvinced. 'You make it sound so easy, Govinda. But how could you … or Ghora, or your fellow Wrights, know what to do, or for that matter what path Matsya would, in fact, take?'

'Because, my dear, the Creator doesn't play dice. The universe is a very efficient place, and we are its rational products. Matsya was a result of social evolution – as was Dwaraka. But the mistakes we made with the younger, newer idea of Dwaraka taught us better how to deal with Matsya. We Yadus were a society based on our livestock, not unlike Matsya, and that made it easier to give each person some degree of power over their lives. Although, we could never completely change the structures of power – even at its height, Dwaraka's Council members were mostly all former Yadu vassal princes despite our pretence at equality by calling them leading citizens and such. And so, at the first opportunity, Dwaraka begins to regress to what it once was – a bunch of infighting tribes, led by a few men acting in their own interests. Dwaraka lacked isolation. It lacked balance.'

Panchali said, 'So, the imperial campaign … You wanted to build an empire, not just because you wanted to unify Aryavarta but also because you wanted to isolate Matsya …'

'Absolutely! The empire never really did cover Matsya. And to ensure that the isolation would last adequately long, I fostered internal dissent – or balance, if you will – within Matsya. The tensions between Virat and Keechak, for example. This ensured that at any point Matsya would not only resist conquest, but also that the ruler of Matsya couldn't upset the plan and rise as a tyrant to conquer the unified Aryavarta.'

Panchali felt a pang of guilt. 'I … we … Keechak …'

'I know. Bhim told me. It's all right, Panchali. These actions don't change the larger tide of events all that much; not at this stage, anyway. The point is, Aryavarta would move towards this moment, towards Matsya, irrespective of who sat on the throne. What Dharma would have done, had he remained Emperor, is not very different from what Syoddhan did.'

'Then … then why did you stop Syoddhan? Why did you come here? What is Matsya to you, Govinda? Your secret stash of weaponry? A private army at your command?'

'I think you already know, Panchali, and you're just teasing me. Matsya was an opposite. An antidote. The other that makes the whole, just as you and I make each other whole.'

Even as Panchali struggled to place her emotions, Govinda said, 'I didn't come here for Matsya. I came here for you. Telling Virat the truth about Satya, placing Dharma back on a throne, Uttara's marriage … all of that has no other purpose than to protect you. Dharma, Syoddhan – it makes no difference to me who rules Aryavarta or what becomes of the Firstborn and Firewrights. All I know is that I can't let you be hurt again, not by Syoddhan, nor Dharma, nor Virat or anyone else. My arrogance and my ambition have brought you great hardships. Can you ever forgive me?'

Panchali wanted nothing more than to laugh; no, all she wanted was to cry. But the sensation passed, and she settled into quiet contentment. 'Do you regret your actions?' she asked lightly.

Govinda answered in all seriousness, 'Not in the least.'

'There is nothing to forgive, Govinda. You have done with me as you would with yourself. But if that was your way of telling me this conversation is over then I must ask your forgiveness, for it most certainly is not.'

Govinda laughed, quiet but wholeheartedly, as he hadn't in a long time. His eyes looked just a little less shallow, a little less tired, as though something within him had stopped tearing itself apart. 'It is over for me, Panchali. Not just this conversation, but this whole journey. Now that you are safe, it is enough.' He paused and chose his words carefully. 'When we met at Kamyaka, you refused to come with me. I understand why. The secrets I have kept bound me to Aryavarta, to its fate. Now,' he took a deep breath, 'I am a free man. I am free of Dharma, of the Secret Keeper, of Dwaipayana … I owe them nothing. I hide nothing. It is over, Panchali. Let us leave Aryavarta.'

'You want me to come with you?'

'I want you to come with your brother. We shall take Shikandin with us. He's been through unspeakable pain. I find myself unable to look into his eyes, there is so much … so much sorrow and …' Govinda shook his head, and said, 'Oh Rudra, Panchali. Leave for yourself, of your own will. I will not be judged by another, and neither should you. Let us do as we will.'

'That sounds selfish, Govinda. It is not a quality I'd readily associate with you – dispassionate creature of reason that you are.'

'Some things are more important than reason, Panchali. And for that you can call me selfish, or an idiot, or anything else you like.'

'Selfish idiot?'

'That too. I look forward to hearing many more such compliments from you. It promises to be a worthy application of whatever time may be left to us. But as far as Aryavarta is concerned … our days here are finished. It would be foolishness to not admit it and let go. It is over. There is nothing left here to fight for, anymore.'

Panchali heard herself say the words, 'Nothing left to fight for, Govinda, is nothing left to lose.'

For all his unflappable equanimity Govinda Shauri the cowherd looked as though he had failed to tell a cow from a bull.

34

IT WOULD, GOVINDA KNEW, BE A DRAMATIC EXAGGERATION TO pretend that Panchali had not aged. True, age sat better on her than it did on many others, and he found nothing but beauty in the fine lines by her eyes and the creases that her smile left behind. Her hair, once as black as the darkest night sky, held traces of grey elegantly distributed in streaks as though to be otherwise scattered would be a disservice to her grace.

He imagined her older, further wrinkled, a little shrivelled, bent over with the burden of her years, hair white as the snow-packed reaches of the Great Mountains. But her eyes would remain the way they were now, and he would long to look into them as he died. There was a fire in their depths that nothing, no travail, could extinguish, and it served as his last solace to know that there was at least this one thing left, this one goodness that he could not destroy, no matter what mistakes he made. Govinda let the thought pass. Some things, he knew, could not happen, not any more, but to feel intensely the bitter pain of that loss was better than living in the empty happiness of oblivion. He was content to watch her in the moment, admiring the proud line of her shoulders, the defiant upward thrust of her chin. As he watched, she seemed to grow, not in size but in courage, walking through flames to emerge unscathed.

'Do you know,' Panchali began, 'not a day has passed since Dharma, and... even I... have wondered if I did not bring this misfortune on myself, on us... Wait, let me explain,' she interjected, as Govinda began to protest. She went on, 'After the game and after you met us at Kamyaka, on many occasions Dharma argued with me and cautioned me that my arrogance was my undoing. There have been times, during the darkest of nights when I have lain awake wondering if what I did was wrong. Perhaps I should not have been defiant. Perhaps I should have begged for Syoddhan's mercy, for the kindness of the elders present. I should have said, yes, I am your slave, but have pity on me... I should have implored Dussasan to let me go, called him "brother" and begged him to look on me as his sister. I should have cried instead of arguing, I should have asked for mercy, instead of justice. I should have submitted and kept what honour was left me by my masters and by my destiny. But I did not, and I don't regret it. Do you see why?'

Govinda shook his head. He did not dare meet Panchali's eyes and his gaze remained on her fingers. His nostrils flared as he tried hard to remain calm.

Panchali extracted her hand from his grasp and placed it on his cheek, tilting his head up so that he would look at her. 'You did that to me, Govinda. Just as you did to thousands of gwalas who had believed that their birth and destiny condemned them to the life they led, that power was an end in itself and that to be weak meant to give up, to surrender. I could not beg, I could not give up, because you showed me that to be human is to have the right to be free, to be my own person and be worthy of basic respect, my birth and gender and stature notwithstanding. You taught me that my body, my soul, were my own, and not meant to be taken from me by force. You taught me that the true role of a ruler is to protect the rights I was born with just by the virtue of being born. That society, law and justice were all human creations – systems made to preserve what we can call righteousness or dharma or whatever we like. To surrender would be to give up that which cannot, ought not to be ceded.

'Dignity is not someone else's to give me, Govinda. It is mine, to keep. You showed me that. You've shown your fellow citizens at Dwaraka that. We shall not forget. Twelve years ago, it was just me. Today, I know for sure that Nakul, Sadev, Partha and Bhim would stand with me, as would my brothers.'

'Panchali …'

'Listen, Govinda! You wish to blame yourself? Yes, you are to blame, but only for making us what we are. Revolution is here! It is time. What Satya began is not over yet. Destroying the Firewrights as they were is not enough. Removing the distinction between those who fight to hold power is not enough. We need to remove the distinction between those who have power and those who don't.'

'You don't know what you're saying, my dear. I understand you want to find meaning for your suffering but …'

'You did not fail. The system failed. The kings who promised to protect me, righteousness, morality, law – the institutions I called on to defend my right as an individual … they failed! Not you, Govinda. Not yet. But if you were to give up now, you would fail, just as everyone else has failed me. The choice is yours.'

'It's a choice I cannot make. I cannot bear to put you at risk. I've had enough of believing in my own rhetoric, in the nobility of sacrifice and the greater good of Aryavarta. Who am I trying to convince, Panchali? You and I both know that I am a selfish man who does what he does because it makes him feel good to do it. I am no different from Dharma or Syoddhan or any of the others. All I've ever wanted is for you to understand me. And you do. That is enough!'

Panchali held back a sob as Govinda averted his eyes. She had never seen him this way: angry yet vulnerable, honest yet fighting the truth, both selfish and selfless at the same time. She wanted to say so much, explain that she not only understood, but that she also admired and cherished him just as he was. But she could not. She nodded, conceding the point, and walked a few steps ahead.

Govinda stood where he was, in silence, expecting that she would stop and she did. But she did not turn around. She continued to look into the distance as she said, 'You've never really told me about your mother, you know. I've asked before, but you've never quite answered me.'

'What do you want to know?' Govinda said, frowning at the unexpected mention of the woman he thought of often but never spoke of.

'What is your oldest memory of her? No, tell me, what is your most cherished memory of her?'

Govinda crossed the distance between them slowly, deep in thought. 'I remember her singing to me as she went about her chores. Most women in the vraja would sing to themselves as they worked, but she ... she sang to me. She would speak to me even when I was an infant, and not the meaningless sweet cooing that everyone does with babies. She would tell me things as if I were an adult, like how the harvests were coming along, or how the village was worried that there was no rain. She'd talk about taxes and tax collectors, vassal lords and river and mountain spirits and ... and so many things. And she'd always end with a song, a song to me ... Don't ask me how I know what she said, Panchali, but I did ... or I feel I did.'

'You loved her?'

'Of course!'

'And yet, when you left your village in the countryside behind to become the Prince of Surasena, you never saw her again. At least, that is what I've heard...'

Govinda said, emotionless, 'It's true.'

Panchali said the words as kindly as she could, 'Do you even know if she is alive, Govinda?'

The reaction was muted, but Panchali knew Govinda well enough to imagine his clenched jaws, the slight throb at his throat and, finally, as he pulled himself together, the near-imperceptible swallow. 'No, Panchali,' he stated. 'I don't know if she is alive.'

'Why?'

'Why what, Panchali?'

'Why didn't you go back to her... or for her? Why did you turn your back on the woman who raised you, protected you and loved you, and made you the man you are – a man who has been a prince and a commander and so much more...'

'What are you implying...?' Govinda began, defensive. He fell quiet as he understood. 'Oh Rudra!' he swore under his breath.

Panchali said, 'Everyone thinks *you* made this sacrifice, like every other one that you've made. But it wasn't your sacrifice to make, was it? It was hers. She let you go. And her loss made you see what you had to do for your people, for Aryavarta. We cannot sacrifice that which isn't ours, Govinda. And that which is truly ours, we never sacrifice in vain. You dared defy a tyrant because your mother thought that the life of a simple, poor gwala was fighting for. Great things happen when the weakest rise. You knew this in your heart when you swore to make me queen over all kings, for when you said that there was none weaker, none more desperate in all of Aryavarta, than I. You know this now, when you say compassion is greater than reason, than duty, because compassion is what makes you rise, to do right.'

Govinda asked, 'What do you want me to do?'

'That is not for me to decide. Mine is the honour of sacrifice. I did not always understand, you know. So many times I've blamed you for what happened to me... from the very beginning of it all. In moments

338

of weakness, I rail against you still. But never so much that I forget that you would not give up what you don't honestly think is yours.'

Govinda stood stunned for an instant, and then he threw his head back and laughed. Panchali felt herself smiling at the mere sight of his mirth, for it had been far too long since she had seen him laugh this way – open, fearless and with unfettered joy. When he finally settled down his eyes once again held the spark that she knew so well and loved. 'I asked you a simple question, *Princess*. I might have thought twice about it if I'd known that your host of enviable talents does not include brevity.'

Panchali was all set to retort in a similar vein, but the smile faded quickly from her face. She was painfully direct now. 'The answer to your question is this: I want you to take us to war, Govinda.'

Govinda frowned. 'War is not mine to declare, Panchali. Rightfully, it is for your husband, the Emperor, to deal in such terms.'

'And he will fight because it is his duty. As will Syoddhan, because it is his. As will the Grandsire, and the acharyas Dron and Kripa – and Dwaipayana and Vyasa Markand will bless them all for it. But who will fight for what is right, Govinda?'

'It's not that easy. Dharma may not even agree.'

'Many won't agree. But when has that stopped you?'

'I don't want war, Panchali. All I've ever wanted is peace.'

'No, Govinda. The price for peace will be too much to pay. The different kingdoms compete to grow their armies and arsenals, to lay claim to more and more power, and that can never lead to peace. This is no longer about Firstborn and Firewright, heretics and rebels. This is about why we do what we do, the very meaning of being Arya, of being noble. It is time for revolution. It is time for Vasudeva Narayana, he who sleeps on the Eternal Ocean, to rise.'

35

IT WAS NOT UNCOMMON FOR THE MEN, WOMEN AND CHILDREN of Upaplavya to empty out on to the streets to cheer Govinda and the others as they went about their business. When that happened,

Govinda would gratefully mingle with the crowd, relishing for the first time the sense of acceptance, even respect, that the identity of Firewright brought him. He spoke plainly and politely to all, often thanking them in earnest for their good wishes, and nodded and smiled at those who were too far away to hear him. It was on one such occasion, when he was walking back from the stables with Shikandin and a still-sullen Dhrstyadymn by his side that he noticed the silent group of travelling seers that stood in the crowd. They were less boisterous than their neighbours as could be expected, but they raised their hands in blessing as he passed them. Govinda bowed his head in respect, but his eyes remained on the bright-eyed man in the middle of the group, a man reclusive enough that he remained unrecognized by any of the others. He turned away as a few boys ran up to him.

In all the boldness of childhood, one of the boys said, 'Aren't you Govinda, the great Firewright warrior?'

He laughed and said, 'I'm Govinda, yes.'

'Is it true that you can kill ten men with one stroke? Are you really as strong as an elephant? Can you do magic? My brother told me you can fly!'

'And who might your brother be?'

In reply, another wide-eyed boy was pushed to the front. Govinda went down on one knee in front of the two children. A throng of adults gathered around, curious to see what he would do.

'I can't fly,' he said, in a sombre tone. 'But,' he pulled out a distinctly deformed brass coin bearing the Panchala emblem from his waist band, 'I *can* do magic.'

Laying the coin out on his right palm, he waved his left hand over it in a grand gesture. The coin disappeared, to the amazed gasps from the children. The adults laughed at what they thought was a sleight of hand. Govinda stood up, glanced around him, and bent down to address the children. 'Where's it gone?' he asked.

The children gestured their puzzlement, while the adults murmured that it must be concealed on his own person. Govinda dramatically shook his head. He nodded at Shikandin, who, with an expression of great surprise, searched around to find the coin tucked into the leather bindings on the hilt of his sword. It was unmistakeably the very same piece, bent out of shape in the very same way. The adults gasped and the children broke into spontaneous applause. Grinning widely, the warriors walked on.

Govinda waited till they were away from the crowd. 'I hoped you still had it with you, old friend. Otherwise, it might've been rather embarrassing.'

Shikandin said, 'The keepsake of our very first battle ... err ... together? Of course I still have it, I always do.' Turning to Dhrstyadymn, he added as an explanation, 'When Govinda and I first met, we placed bets on who was the braver man. These coins were the stakes.'

'And who won?' Dhrstyadymn asked.

Govinda and Shikandin burst out laughing. 'We need to have yet another wager on that!' Shikandin said.

Dhrstyadymn shrugged. 'Well, now that I think of it, it was a rather simple trick. I mean, what you just did in front of those boys there – I too was taken aback.'

'It's the way he does it,' Shikandin said, 'the confidence and persuasive charm ...'

'Well, it was supposed to be Firewright magic ...' Govinda irreverently teased. 'Or do you prefer Firstborn miracles? Repeat a fantastic tale often enough and it becomes the truth, that sort of magic?' He chuckled dismissively.

'You know, you're not only insolent but you're really apathetic too.'

'No, Shikandin. Not apathetic. Merely ... overwhelmed. But I've been self-indulgent for too long now. It's time to change that.'

Dhrstyadymn regarded him keenly and was about to speak, but reconsidered. After that, his behaviour towards Govinda was almost normal, as though the unstated issue between them had settled itself for the time being. He did not think Govinda noticed either way.

It was nearly evening by the time Govinda was able to make his way through the palace kitchens to the courtyard behind them. As always, people waited in the hope of alms or even leftovers from the royal

341

scullery. Many of the travelling mendicants he had seen that morning were there too. Govinda made sure the one he was interested in saw him distinctly before he continued to walk, heading into the agrarian sections of the city. He turned back just once, casually, to make sure that he was indeed being followed. After that, he did not look back again.

After a while of wandering along the city's roads, Govinda made his way into a barn that stood at the edge of the city, abutting the dry, hard grounds that passed for a farmer's fields. He waited in the shadowed doorway, watching as the man who had followed him approached. The seer drew near and looked around, unsure of where to go. Govinda waited to make sure that no one else was in the vicinity before letting out a low whistle. Immediately, the seer turned to look at the doorway and made his way inside.

The man wrinkled his nose a little as he entered the barn. He took a look at the animals around him and said, 'I'm sure my predecessors in this position have many mighty deeds to their name, most of which I cannot even aspire to match. As it stands, I am likely to go down in historical accounts as the Secret Keeper who held most of his meetings in particularly pungent places – cowsheds and stinky inns not the least of them.'

'Well, you could blame it on me. I am a gwala.'

'Oh please! You chose this place for a reason and you chose well. Not only is it secluded, but you're relying on the cows' behaviour to let you know if anyone approaches.'

'Yes, it does offer that simple advantage too.'

'A valuable one. It wouldn't do for me to be recognized, particularly not at this point in time. But leave that be for now, Govinda. I'm pleased and relieved to see you again, and that too in one piece.'

Govinda acknowledged the sentiment with a nod. 'And you? How have you been, Acharya?'

'Do you really want an answer to that question, Govinda?' With a sigh, he reached out for Govinda's arm. 'How did this happen?'

'Apparently when Abhimanyu threw me off the side of a ship. It didn't help that I ignored it till Dhaumya got here and gave me a tongue-lashing about taking better care of myself now that I'm an old man.'

The Secret Keeper examined the bandage. He said, 'This is a new method, and an interesting one. Using splints to set a bone is well-established, but this...this method offers far more mobility to the limb. Dhaumya has excelled himself.'

'This was his student. A boy named Charaka. I have great expectations of him. He has immense talent and Dhaumya is a great teacher.'

'Remind me to meet him. It would make me wistful, I suppose, but it would also give me great pleasure.'

'And hope?'

'And hope, yes.'

'You deserve it. This has always been a hard fight, but your lot has been a particularly lonely one.'

'Has it? I suppose, yes. It is difficult to hide things so deep from your own self that no one could ever see who your really are. To look at one's own reflection and wonder who you are at any given instant, and if anything you are is real or true. Frankly, I admire Sanjaya for the way he has been able to do that. He fooled me, and I must take responsibility for what has since come to pass. You told me long ago that the person behind Devala's rise had to be one who held authority to act in the Vyasa's name. I suppose I have been as blind as the Vyasa, to not have admitted it all this while. That has been my fatal flaw.'

'Every man and every woman has a fatal flaw, Acharya. It is these foibles that are the very foundations of humanity.'

'Flaws are the foundations of humanity? That's a new philosophy, Govinda. Whatever happened to emulating divinity?'

'Its overprized. Humanity is wonderful, just as it is. Have you ever heard of gods striving to be more? But that's how we human beings are – we seek courage to overcome fear, in suffering we find compassion, and without anger we would never know the meaning of forgiveness. Most of all, without passion we would never know the true depths of Oneness, for passion is our flawed title for what is a sense of unfettered potential, of infinity and of love. That is a lesson that took me a while to learn.'

The Secret Keeper clucked his tongue. The light moment hardly lasted, though, and he was sombre again. 'So, once again, Govinda Shauri comes to Aryavarta with a plan. But after what has happened here, I don't know if I can trust you.'

'Do you doubt me?' Govinda asked, the hint of a smile in his eyes.

The Secret Keeper found it difficult to meet the gaze and looked away as he said, 'I'm not sure you act in the best interests of Aryavarta anymore. We had a plan. Things were going well. Matsya had been the isolated womb of new skills and new methods and if Syoddhan had brought it under his sway, as he intended to, then the entire realm would have benefitted. I admit, it happened sooner than was expected, but it was not contrary to our plans. Once Dharma lost his empire, Syoddhan became the next and most obvious choice. All would have turned out exactly as we had once wanted it to. But instead of staying away and letting it happen, as you were supposed to, you intervened. Do you realize what you've done? Keeping the secret of Satya's true allegiance was not only in the interests of the Firstborn, it was in our interests too. We've lost our influence over the Firstborn, and we've created a new struggle for power. Now every petty ruler in Aryavarta will claim allegiance to us, if not link us to their ancestry. You've destroyed everything that we worked for, Govinda. Where the Firewrights ought to have disappeared into ignominy and legend, you have resurrected them, made them real. In short, you've set us back three generations.

'Are you blaming me, Acharya?'

'I'm *asking* you, Govinda. I'm asking you how it is that the most rational, selfless man I know could suddenly take a personal decision, a decision that served the interests of a few over that of many.'

'You're right, it was personal.'

'That's not an answer. I want to know why. You have thrown this very same woman away time and again; treated her as nothing more than an instrument, a puppet; let her suffer things that no person should have to endure. Why this newfound concern for her safety and well-being?'

Govinda reached out instinctively to pet a calf as he considered his next words. Then he turned back to the Secret Keeper. 'For years now, both Firewright and Firstborn have fought over what has been best for Aryavarta. They have both considered themselves justified in all that they do, all that they achieve no matter what the means, because they have thought themselves as righteous and good.'

'This is an age-old dilemma. The fact is, both have been right and both have been wrong.'

'Yes. And in that conflict lies progress. Everything has a counter, an opposite. The Firstborn and the Firewrights have not only been opposites, they have been complementary, even essential to each other. It is in the constant debate between philosophy and science, between faith and reason, and imposed morality and uninculcated virtue that we of Aryavarta have grown to glory. You remember men like Ghora Angirasa … even Parashara Varuni or his ancestor Shakti, and the many tales we have heard of their famed dialogues, the endless dialectic and fearless enquiry that has led to what we today revere as sacred knowledge? They were rivals, enemies even … but Aryavarta prospered under their rivalry.'

'Then how did it come to this, Govinda? All you or I have ever known is blood and politics. Who brought it to this? The Firewrights? The Firstborn? The kings of Aryavarta?'

'Human failing.'

'But whose?'

'The failing of every man and woman who refused to stand up against what was wrong. The failing of every one of us who did not stand by what was right. What happened with Panchali …' He trailed off.

'Is that what this is about, Govinda? Revenge?'

'It's about that which you long for, too, Acharya. It's about hope.'

'I don't understand.'

Govinda considered the honest admission, all the more humble for the unquestionable wisdom of the man who had made it. He said, 'When we first met, a long time ago, you told me that for a cowherd to rise to be a prince was nothing less than the work of either divinity or destiny … do you remember?'

'I do. I also remember what you said. You told me that your rise was the work of neither divinity nor destiny, but of humanity.'

345

'And that, I think, has been the only other occasion, Acharya, when you've said you didn't understand me.'

'Surely an explanation is now overdue?'

'Indeed. You asked me who is responsible for the state of things around us – Firewright, Firstborn, the kings of the realm. The answer is simple. The only person who is responsible for any situation is the one who has chosen to do nothing about it. The only people responsible for the rise of a tyrant are those who choose to submit and suffer. The only people responsible for evil are those who choose not to fight it. That the gwala you once knew rose to be prince was nothing but an instrument, a means to an end. It was the people of Surasena who raised him to that position, because they decided that enough was enough. And I don't know about you, but I think Aryavarta has reached that point. Enough.'

'Because a man sworn as Emperor to protect these lands wagered them away? Because a good woman was humilated and hurt in the most terrifying of ways?'

'Because after all that happened, someone stood up and said: Enough. But it wasn't me.'

The Secret Keeper was taken aback. 'Panchali. But ...'

'This isn't about vengeance, Acharya. When we watch, silent, while a wrong is done, we make it all right for wrong-doing to become the new right, the new established way of life. Syoddhan allowed a wrong to happen, even though he had the power to stop it. Today, he rules us all. Dussasan, Jayadrath, Vasusena ... noblemen, monarchs, mighty leaders. And Bhisma. But why blame them when I have been equally guilty – not because I could not protect Panchali, but because I did not protest when everything I want Aryavarta to stand for failed. I let despair take over ...'

'It's only human, Govinda. We do not fight battles we cannot win. It is survival.'

'No, Acharya, it is surrender. To not fight is to surrender. It is not for us to judge the worth of a battle by its outcome. We must do what we must. And so it is that human failing is its own redemption. Humanity will rise. It's who we are.'

'And so?'

'Acharya, my friend ... we were willing to go against our own, we rebelled against the order we swore loyalty to. Why? Because we knew that the order had failed. Now it is not just the old Firewright order that has failed, but the entire system around us that has shattered. Panchali simply asked for justice. The Firstborn, the Firewrights, the empire and its kings – none of them could give it to her. They all failed. I care for none of them anymore. All we can do is to be true to our convictions, be the instruments of change, till together we become change itself. Kali, the age of darkness is upon us, and I swear by Time that I shall not stand and watch in silence while humanity is lost. I swear to you, I will change Aryavarta as you know it, and the world will remember Panchali, the one who dared to stand up for what was right when no one else did.'

As the full implications of Govinda's words sunk in, the Secret Keeper let his concern show. 'This ... this is ...'

'Treachery? I've been accused of it more than once. It is time I earned the distinction.'

The Secret Keeper cleared his throat, but said nothing. Govinda's calm certitude was terrifying. Eventually, he spoke, but all he could say was, 'You put me in a difficult position. My mandate as Secret Keeper is beyond doubt. I am sworn to preserve the spirit of the Firewrights, their knowledge and, above all, to act in the best interests of the whole realm. What you propose will reduce us to nothing. At best we will become slaves to those kings who will patronize and protect us. At worst we will be hunted down once again. Where will that leave Aryavarta, Govinda? No,' he shook his head, 'the only way forward is to salvage the situation, to work out a peace arrangement, an arrangement that will let me fulfil my ultimate task, the last element of our plan. I will personally ...'

'Peace? We can want peace all we like, Acharya, but the time for peace is past. You underestimate the power-lust, the ambition, that is seeded into our society. Duty is a good thing, yes, but not at the cost of reason. And even reason cannot be upheld at the cost of compassion. It is compassion that we have lost, Acharya, and your illusions of peace cannot bring it back.'

'Vathu! Consider this a command, Govinda: Stop this madness

at once. Throw your might, your support, *our* support behind Syoddhan. We can still make this work.'

'No.'

'You disappoint me. I did not expect you to act this way!'

Govinda shrugged. 'Do you expect me to apologize?'

'I am not a man you want for an enemy.'

'I am not your enemy.'

'You are, Govinda, if you stand in the way of what I am sworn to do. And I will do whatever it takes to meet this great responsibility, to fulfil this one last, crucial task that was left to me.'

A feral glimmer shone in the Secret Keeper's eyes. For all his kindness and benevolence, the scholar was a man of cold reason. 'Think about it before you answer, Govinda,' he urged. 'Before we reach a point we cannot turn back from, think hard and tell me: Are you sure this is how you want things to be?'

Govinda took a deep breath, reaching into the fount of Oneness that had never truly faded away, not since the day he had seen Panchali standing there in the forests of Kamyaka. He surrendered to the sensation, fading into insignificance, inexistence, till he was nothing at all. And in that nothingness, stripped of all ego and identity, he truly came into being.

When he spoke, it was Vasudeva Narayana himself who formed the words, 'I am sure. It is time for revolution.'

36

HASTINA WAS ASTIR. EVERYWHERE SANJAYA WENT, BE IT THE great assembly hall, Syoddhan's private chambers or even the usually quiet temples, a buzz followed him, and the words that seemed to reach his ears the most were: 'Satya the Firewright'. No, they were, 'Satya the *loyal* Firewright'.

Conversation, argument, debate, he did not care what it was. To listen would be to invite madness, for he knew there were many, many interests he had goaded and spurred on to weave his tapestry of deceit. And now each of those voices, those interests, pulled at the warp and weft of his plans in their own self-interest. It was not an insurmountable problem. In fact, Sanjaya knew that once things settled a little, the ground would be more fertile than before for him to plant the seeds of destruction. It would be the ideal climate for him to see his plan through to its end.

He saw Syoddhan and Grandsire Bhisma together in the armoury bonding over weapons that had previously been stored with utmost discretion to look as if they were of no importance. Vidur, uncomfortable but dedicated, described the inimitable gleam of the Wright-metal to an accompanying Dhritarastra, whose blind eyes lit up with delight. Elsewhere, he saw Dron and Asvattama in deep discussion, each man radiant with the glow of having found that which they had always been denied – acceptance by those who had earlier dismissed them. Vasusena and Dussasan alternated between sullen, excited and inebriated, even as Dussasan's spies brought him timely updates on all that transpired in the palace as well as the on-going search for Devala throughout the realm.

Of course, the fact remained that the recent developments had cost Sanjaya his personal hold over Dwaipayana. But a public revelation of the old scholar's shameful secret, and that too by one such as Govinda Shauri, had only served to diminish Dwaipayana's stature. It was only a matter of days now before the Firstborn would stand destroyed beyond recognition He nearly laughed out loud at the thought of how simple it now was: Govinda had destroyed the Firstborn and legitimized the Firewrights. Now all he had to do was destroy Govinda and the rebel Firewrights, an easy enough task. Those fools would soon be crushed under the might of Syoddhan's empire.

Though the situation was cause for joy, Sanjaya's heart held a strange foreboding, a sense of impending doom, made worse by the fact that he was not usually inclined to place any worth in such irrational premonitions. He could not ignore that his calculations had been incorrect, and that Govinda's unexpected revelations had swung the balance of power in the latter's favour again. The thought brought to mind Dwaipayana's old lessons on the true nature of strategy, of seeing the field of conflict as a fluid, everchanging, living creature. Another thought followed, this one self-recriminating –

that despite the many years that had passed, Sanjaya still thought of Dwaipayana as his teacher and found himself applying Firstborn aphorisms to his life and actions.

It had been a long and very lonely journey and he was tired of constantly sifting through the clutter of human minds, trying to manipulate people into doing what he wanted of them while they were convinced they were doing so of their own will and volition. A few muhurttas of silence and solitude was what he needed.

Sanjaya headed to his small but lavish rooms in search of exactly that, but a curse escaped him as he saw his attendant waiting at the door.

'Mih!' he swore again as the identity of his visitor became apparent. Determined not to entertain the unwelcome guest with even a smattering of warmth, he burst into the room with quick, angry strides.

He stopped.

He was familiar with the silent nod with which his guest greeted him. But the visitor's cold gaze, the way he reeked of arrogance and power, made him a stranger. Sanjaya could not remember the last time he had felt this unsettled, afraid from the pit of his stomach – not mortal fear, for the man before him was no warrior, and despite his considerable stature was not likely to pose any personal danger. The fear he felt was more subtle. He could smell it in his own sweat, the tang of rust and salt that overcame the perfume he was fond of wearing. For the first time in his life Sanjaya was afraid he would fail.

'Come on in, Sanjaya.' Suka was positively cheerful, startling Sanjaya. 'Come, come, sit down. We have much to talk about and unfortunately very little time.'

Sanjaya could only stare and wonder what had happened to the timid, reticent man he had known all these years. The Suka who stood before him looked no less self-assured than a king, an emperor even. Enraged, he lashed out, 'Whatever you're here for, Suka, you're wasting your time. I've told your father and your half-brother this already: I will bring the Firstborn down, if it is the last thing I do. There is nothing you can say to change my mind.'

Suka sat back, adjusting the cushion behind him for comfort. 'Why not?'

'What?'

'I said, why not? Why can't I get you to change your mind?'

'Because, unlike your father, I am not ashamed of who I am… I am not ashamed of my heritage and blood, whereas your father… Yabha! Your father finds it such a shame that he has never told you, even once in all these years, who he really is, has he? And what that makes you! Now that the whole world knows you have come to me begging for my help.'

'Really, this is confusing – your father, my father, their blood, our blood. It's all one, you know. But that's not the point. I have no intentions of insisting on formality, so there's no need to stand in my presence. Do sit down and let's talk about this in a civilized manner.'

'Civilized? You talk to me of being civilized when your father…'

'Enough about my father. Personally, its my grandmother I'm more interested in – as, I think, are you.'

Sanjaya clenched his teeth in a bid to show no response. He sat down.

'That's better,' Suka said, leaning forward. 'So, my grandmother. Queen Satya of Kuru. Of course, my grandfather… Parashara Varuni, met her before she became a queen. She was a lost princess, fleeing her tormented land… We both know the story, so there's no point restating it. After she gave birth to my father, Dwaipayana, she met Shantanu, which makes her your ancestress by custom as well – through King Vichitravirya. You are, after all, a bastard child of the Kuru clan, are you not? For all legal purposes you are Kaurava… as much as Syoddhan and Dharma are, at least.'

Sanjaya sprang to his feet, growling.

'Sit down,' Suka instructed, as though Sanjaya were merely a troublesome student.

'How do you know all this?'

'What difference does it make? You thought my father would go to any lengths to keep the truth about Satya from me. And now that its public knowledge you think this revelation will destroy the Firstborn completely. Yes, you're right, my father is ashamed. But you have to understand, Sanjaya, he's human too. I think you can imagine what it is to be… shall we say… residual, like the leftovers of a sacrifice that no one wants but that still cannot be fed to pigs because it was sacred once. For what it's worth, my father, *your grandfather*, Dwaipayana, still feels the same way. He does not know why he was concieved, and for whose vengeance. I think he just wanted to spare me the self-loathing that he, and in your own way you have gone through.'

'And you ... now that you know, you are not ashamed?'

'Ashamed? Frankly, I couldn't care less either way,' Suka stood up and paced around slowly, weighing his next words. 'You don't really know me. I don't know what you've thought of me so far, but whatever it is I assure you that's not what I am. I am a practical man. But also a patient one, unlike you. Your problem, Sanjaya, is that you don't deal well with priorities. You're dedicated and focussed, and you have the resilience of a tiger, but you're not good at delaying gratification.'

'Hah!' Sanjaya did not agree with Suka's assessment of what he considered his greatest strength. 'Considering the Firstborn are nothing more than an impotent group of hymn-chanters sired by the blood of Firewrights, a decrepit order led by a feeble, bumbling Vyasa like Markand. I'd thought of letting your lot fade away quietly but I swear by Agni that your arrogance won't go unanswered, Suka. I will have the Firstborn hunted down, ravaged and tortured and verily plucked off the face of Aryavarta, the way your family had us hunted down during the Great Scourge.'

Suka smiled and Sanjaya could not help but notice how handsome, how impressive he was when he did so. 'You mean *our* family, Sanjaya. Our family has been both the hunter and the hunted, depending on how you look at it. As for everything else ... Oh well, I suppose I might as well tell you. I *wanted* Markand to be Vyasa before me. I wanted that docile, god-fearing hymn-reciter to become the Vyasa because I knew the Firewrights would rise again – one way or another. And, finally, when Aryavarta stood fragmented and leaderless with its kings and their mighty armies ready to fly at each other, in threat of war, of foreign invasion and internal dissent, when its kings trembled in fear because each one had outdone the other in a race to weaponize their forces, I would step forward. Yes, I, Sukadeva Vashishta Varuni would become the Vyasa of the Firstborn. Now, do you see?'

'I ... I don't understand,' Sanjaya refused to accept it. 'Why bother to weaken the Firstborn and then rebuild their influence ... assuming you could, that is.'

'Oh but I can, and I will. You see, Sanjaya, despite what everyone says, I don't take too much after my father or my grandfather. It is my grandmother's blood that runs true in me ... as it does in you.'

Sanjaya tried not to show it, but his eyes held curiosity and uncertainty both. Suka stood up and stepped forward to squeeze his shoulder, the gesture affirming every impossible speculation that Sanjaya entertained.

'I'm not a man to destroy that which can serve me well, Sanjaya. And that is what you will now do ... you and your fellow Firewrights, such as you call them. No ... don't bother to protest,' Suka held up a hand, shutting the other man off. He said, 'You and I have our differences. Very simply, we are both men who want the same outcome. Power and peace are mutually compatible ends, Sanjaya. One cannot exist without the other. And so, there is no reason why we both can't have what we want. Now, who would you rather trust for this trade? A Vyasa you know to be your friend, or a puppet rebel Secret Keeper you don't even know exists?'

Sanjaya's eyes shone with frantic curiosity. 'You know! You know who the Secret Keeper is!'

'But of course,' Suka said. 'Surely you see it too ... ? Oh, don't disappoint me, Sanjaya – I had great hopes of you!'

'Who? Who is he?'

'Let me finish,' Suka imperiously cut in. 'All that I have said so far has been out of courtesy. The fact is, you rolled the dice on this one. You held the secret of your grandfather – my father's – birth over him and you thought you could hold it over me. But that is no longer a secret, thanks to your dear fellow Wright, Govinda Shauri. Nor can you hold whatever I've told you now against me. I assure you, no one would believe you if you told them that I, Suka, am not what I seem. Not my father, not Syoddhan and certainly not Dharma Yudhisthir. You have failed. Unless you have any other tokens to move, I'd say this game is over. It is up to you whether we play the next game as allies or foes.'

Sanjaya sank into a seat and let his head rest in his hands. He was not a man to concede defeat, leave alone doing so in haste, but to see Suka here, this way, speaking as he did … It made him wonder if treachery was less brutal than the sheer shock of having been fooled, of being shown up as a blind imbecile. 'If …' he began, but could not put his thought into words. 'If I … we … ?'

Suka said, 'For now we'd continue exactly as you had planned, Sanjaya. Though my methods might be a little more direct than yours. Building forges, getting into these little skirmishes … the time for that is past. If you truly want these kings, these overlords, to fall at your feet, you need to show them the true reach of your craft. It's not just one vassal lord here and there who needs to be touched by the Wrights, my friend. It is every man, woman and child in Aryavarta. You see, at the end of the day, these names, these orders – they are just ideals. What matters is power. You have the means, I have the motivation. The Firewrights hold scientific and economic power in their hands, but we, the Firstborn, control the political and the spiritual. It is time we began working together.'

'And why would I do this when I stand so close to victory? I have brought Dharma Yudhisthir down by my own effort, Suka. I don't need you to make the Firewrights win.'

Suka laughed. 'What Firewrights do you speak of, Sanjaya? The ones in Matsya? The Nagas? Or the mercenaries under Devala's control? There is only so much use he can be to you. With such power at their command, neither Dharma nor Syoddhan can resist the temptation to conquer, and we know where that will lead us all. Yes, either way, the Firewrights will win. But the question is, will *you*? You need me, Sanjaya. Just as I need you, to keep the legitimacy and influence of the Firstborn alive.'

Sanjaya's eyes held a calculating gleam. 'What can you give me?'

'The one thing you want for yourself, the one thing that was denied you, and given, with what you believe to be no due cause, to your brother … Ah yes. I know. Rather complicated, these secrets of birth and ancestry. Be that as it may, give up this antiquated notion of being *the* Firewright. It means nothing. Become, instead, the Emperor of Aryavarta. You promised my father, did you not, just as he promised his mother, that a Kaurava would sit on the imperial throne? Are you telling me that you've never wanted that? Are you telling me that knowing in your heart that you'd make a better ruler than either of your brothers, you've never wondered what it might be like? An incompetent Dharma, an unambitious Syoddhan, both men have the power of the Wrights on their side now. Only I can give you more. And so, that will be our trade, Sanjaya. Help me legitimize the authority of the Firstborn over all Aryavarta. In return, I will legitimize your rule and the power of Wright-craft. Once that is done, nothing, no one, can stand in your way. In return, you will give me the peace I want for Aryavarta. You will do what either of your *brothers* have failed to do.'

It took Sanjaya a few moments to form any coherent words. When finally he found his voice, he heard himself saying, 'How can I trust you?' It was, he knew from experience of having been on the other side of many conversations such as this, the last, defiant question to ask before the final concession was made.

'Maybe you shouldn't,' Suka noted with malicious amusement. He added, 'But that is not the point, that is not the point at all. We have work to do.'

'And the plan, Acharya?'

'History teaches us that there is one thing, above all, that changes the world as we know it. It turns every hearth in every home into the fire of a forge, spurs new inventions, new discoveries and new political arrangements. Few things are ever as revitalizing, and when it is over it brings peace, undisturbed and lasting peace.'

For a while, he fell into a strange silence, as though rolling his next words on his tongue without speaking them aloud because they were strange and new, having never been used before. Finally, he made his peace with them, with nothing less than a childlike amazement of discovery, or perhaps the lighthearted joy of ultimate enlightenment. Sanjaya did not care. All he knew was that he was on his knees. He would have bowed at the scholar's feet but for the fact that he could not bring himself to take his eyes off Suka's face as it glowed with all-pervading joy, the bliss of fulfilling the purpose of one's existence.

As Sanjaya Gavalgani let his heart brim with adoration – though for an instant he wondered if it were fear – he heard Sukadeva Vashishta Varuni say, matter-of-fact and resolute, 'Let it come, Sanjaya. Let there be war.'

Standing on the Shoulders of Giants
A NOTE ON SOURCES AND METHODS

The Aryavarta Chronicles is the product of research and analysis, with the latter drawing on the former. A slew of work is out there – critical, unconventional, even controversial – that revolves around the world of the Mahabharata. Many are in regional and vernacular tongues, existing as folklore and tales that have never made it into print as a cohesive tome. The Chronicles rely on a mix of these scholarly and popular sources, on histories that tend towards established fact, as well as those based on socially constructed beliefs of what constitutes fact.

THE EVOLUTION OF AN EPIC

The Bhandarkar Oriental Research Institute (BORI) version (also known as the Poona Critical Edition) of the Mahabharata, which remains the dominant source for most retellings and reinterpretations today, is estimated to have been prevalent around the fifth century CE, that is, the Gupta Age. That leaves a fair 3,000 odd years or so during which the story was told over and over, endlessly, forming a final 'layered' narrative filled with explanations and interpolations. The bard–narrator of the mainstream edition, Ugrashravas Sauti, states that he recites what he heard from the scholar Vaishampayana, who in turn is one of the five students who learns the epic from its original author, the Vyasa. Add to this the fact that the epic itself recorded its growth from 8,800 verses composed by Dwaipayana Vyasa to 24,000 verses, and then to the 100,000-verse version we have today. Somewhere along the line, the Harivamsa is added on, as an appendix. And there begins a journey – for history is not stagnant, nor is its narration.

UNRAVELLING THE EPIC

Bibliographically speaking, my study began with C. Rajagopalachari's *Mahabharata* (Mumbai: Bharatiya Vidya Bhavan, 2005). My main source, which forms the broad canvas of 'canon' Mahabharata, is the translated version by K.M. Ganguli (*The Mahabharata of Krishna-Dwaipayana Vyasa, Volumes 1–12*, Calcutta: P.C. Roy/ Oriental Publishing Co., 1884–96; Republished, Delhi: Munshiram Manoharlal, 1970) available online through www.sacred-texts.com. I read this in conjunction with J.A.B. Van Buiten's three-volume translation which goes up to the Udyoga Parvan (*Mahabharata, Volumes 1 to 3*, Chicago: University of Chicago Press, 1975–78); P. Lal's lyrical transcreation of the epic (*Mahabharata of Vyasa*, New Delhi: Vikas Publishing House, 1986); and Ramesh Menon's more contemporary retelling (*The Mahabharata: A Modern Rendering, Volumes 1 and 2*, Lincoln: iUniverse, 2006).

I have relied also on Pandit Ramachandrashastri Kinjawadekar's version of the *Harivamsa* (Poona: Chitrashala Press, 1936), as translated by Desiraju Hanumanta Rao, A. Purushothaman and A. Harindranath (http://mahabharata-resources.org/harivamsa), and on M.N. Dutt's version of the text (*The Harivamsa*, Calcutta: Elysium Press, 1897). H.H. Wilson's *Vishnu Purana* (Calcutta: Punthi Pustak, 1961; original copyright 1840) was invaluable especially when it came to cross-checking genealogies and timelines, as was the Bhaktivedanta Book Trust International's version of the Srimad Bhagavatam, available through the Bhaktivedanta Vedabase Network website (www.vedabase.net).

The subsequent analysis, such as it is, was not without method. D.D. Kosambi notes: 'Against the hypothesis of "pure invention", one must ask why the invention took these particular forms …' ('The Autochthonous Element in the Mahabharata', 1964, *Journal of the American Oriental Society*, 84-1, pp. 31-44). This has been the dominant principle I have chosen to hold on to, focussing on the *why*.

Two stalwarts have influenced my approach to this issue. First, I have borrowed liberally from Bankimchandra Chattopadhyay's deductive principles in his *Krishnacharitra* (trans. Alo Shome, New Delhi: Hindology Books, 2008). Chattopadhyay's analysis is based on a categorical rejection of supernatural events, interpolations and 'events that can be proved to be untrue in any other way' (p. 27). A similar perspective is evident in K.M. Munshi's series *Krishnavatara* (Volumes 1-7, Mumbai: Bharatiya Vidya Bhavan, 1990). While Munshi admits to using his creativity freely in filling what may be gaps in the facts, he remains true to the notion that Krishna-Govinda was a man who eventually became a legend. In his view Govinda was not god, but a (near-perfect) man. I have gratefully followed his lead in beginning with the premise that this is the story of human beings, exemplary ones who are well-deserving of their consequent elevation to divine status. But it is not a story of gods.

Alf Hiltebeitel, a leading Mahabharata scholar, is one of those who speaks of a symbolism-rich Mahabharata; that is, the idea that many expressions in the Mahabharata cannot be literally interpreted ('The Mahabharata and Hindu Eschatology', 1972, *History of Religions*, 12-2, pp. 95-135). Hiltebeitel's *Rethinking the Mahabharata: A Reader's Guide to the Education of the Dharma Kings* (Chicago: Chicago University Press, 2001) also deserves mention for fuelling many ideas; as does James L. Fitzgerald's broad piece covering many topics on the Mahabharata, including the historical evolution of the text itself ('The Great Epic of India as Religious Rhetoric: A Fresh Look at the Mahabharata', 1983, *Journal of the American Academy of Religion*, 51-4, pp. 611-630). Mary Carroll Smith's analysis of the variation in meter, narrative structure, and the subtle moves from Vedic to Classical Sanskrit in the text as we have it today, to identify possible additions and interpolations ('The Mahabharata's Core', 1975, *Journal of the American Oriental Society*, 95-3, pp. 479-482) was central to my reconstruction of the story.

Such a reconstruction also requires political, social and even psychological explanations. For this, I have drawn on ideas from many analytical and creative works, first among them being Irawati Karve's *Yuganta: End of an Epoch* (Hyderabad: Disha Books/Orient Longman, 1991). Karwe is particularly notable for her critical approach to the question of Dharma Yudhisthir's father. Buddhadeva Bose in his *Mahabharater Katha/The Book of Yudhisthir* (trans. Sujit Mukherjee, London: Sangam Books/Hyderabad: Orient Longman, 1986) attributes to Dharma Yudhisthir's character the many frustrations and exasperations that I find likely, and though I am less inclined to glorify Dharma as the protagonist of the epic I cannot deny that I benefitted from reading Bose's book.

Alf Hiltebeitel's work on Panchali (*The Cult of Draupadi: Volumes 1 and 2*, Chicago: Chicago University Press, 1988, 1991) and Pradip Bhattacharya's essay on the *Panchkanyas* of lore ('She Who Must Be Obeyed – Draupadi: The Ill-Fated One', 2004, *Manushi*, 144–Sep/Oct, pp. 19–30) provides deeper insights into her compelling character and even the intricacies of her relationships. Panchali is symbolically and overtly equated to Sri – the consort of Vishnu in terms of the pantheon and the symbol of nature at a deeper level. This clearly places her as the heroine of a story which has Govinda as its hero; an idealized symmetry that is alluded to in Prathibha Ray's *Yajnaseni* (trans. Pradip Bhattacharya, New Delhi: Rupa, 1995.)

The tale, however, unfolds in a different way. The consequent asymmetry, anomaly even, is explained away in canon Mahabharata and its derivative tales (many of which speak of Panchali's preference for Partha) using the concepts of rebirth and divine manifestation. But, if we do away with such interpolated justifications, what might it mean?

I do not have the answer to this riddle, but only a question. Behind the implied and admitted romances, is there a story of affection so obvious that it is easily overlooked? Is it a kind of Freudian transference, whether in the original itself, or perhaps created post-hoc in the interests of sanitizing and legitimizing the epic but nevertheless hinted at by the triangle of three dark-skinned Krishnas – Panchali, Partha and Govinda? Or is the asymmetry itself the story – the tale of a world where many such things are not right? To borrow Govinda Shauri's words: 'The world as we know it would not make sense unless Ahalya were turned to stone.'

ALTERNATE MAHABHARATAS

At this point, I shall admit that I was occasionally surprised, perhaps even shocked, at the alternate theories that seemed to suggest themselves, particularly since I had been brought up on strong doses of canon Mahabharata. The ideas, however, were not as 'alternative' as I had first thought – I discovered the existence of alternate versions of the Mahabharata, many of which were equally canonical in their own right. These included the Bhil Mahabharata and the Indonesian Kakawain versions, both of which I highlight for a reason – The Bhil Mahabharata was (in my view) the nearest I could get to a subaltern version of the epic, and took a very different view of the socio-political status quo (for variations and tales from the Bhil Mahabharata see Satya Chaitanya's blog, based on his research of this folklore: http://innertraditions. blogspot.com).

The Indonesian Kakawain version (http://www.joglosemar. co.id/bharatayuda.html) was equally exciting, since it was possibly shipped out of Aryavarta and to Indonesian islands in a form that was closer to the 'core' or original Mahabharata – that is, an epic with fewer interpolations. A list of resources and essays on the Mahabharata variations across Bengali, Bhil, Oriya, Tamil, Malayalam and Rajasthani cultures (to name a few) is available at A. Harindranath's stunning website: (http://mahabharata-resources.org). Essays on the Oriya *Sarala Mahabharata* are available on B.N. Patnaik's site: http://saralamahabharat.blogspot.com.

BUILDING THE WORLD OF THE EPIC

W.G. Archer (*The Loves of Krishna in Indian Painting and Poetry*, New York: MacMillan, 1957) points to the small but immeasurably important link in the Upanishads that has opened the door to a larger story-world that revolves around the group of scholar–sages known as the Angirasas. With that in mind, the Vedic–Upanishad symbolism in the epic pointed out by Alf Hiltebeitel ('The Two Kṛṣṇas on One Chariot: Upaniṣadic Imagery and Epic Mythology', 1984, *History of Religions*, 24–1, pp. 1–26) begins to make sense. Many reinterpretations and interpolations fall into place and can be logically identified, keeping in mind the basic symbolic themes, as well as the body of philosophical knowledge that the epic seeks to encompass. Most importantly, the Mahabharata starts becoming a story of technological evolution and the associated social change.

I turned to the broader Vedic and Upanishadic literature in an attempt to decipher what the astra-incantations might have meant in a secular and scientific sense, and to understand the technology that hid behind metaphors. For this, I have relied strongly on Karen Thomson and Jonathan Slocum's work on ancient Sanskrit, available from the Linguistics Research Centre at the University of Texas at Austin; particularly their translations of Barend A. van Nooten and Gary B. Holland's version of the Rig Veda (*Rig Veda: A Metrically Restored Text*, Boston: Harvard University Press, 1994). Also deserving reference are Subhash C. Kak's 'Science in Ancient India' (In *Ananya: A Portrait of India*, S.R. Sridhar and N.K. Mattoo (eds.), 1997, AIA: New York, pp. 399–420); Aurobindo's *The Secret of the Veda* (Pondicherry: Sri Aurobindo Ashram, 1993) and Shatavadhani R. Ganesh's audio commentary on the PurushaSuktam and the NarayanaSuktam (K.V. Raman, *Vedic Chanting*, Bangalore: Sagar Music, 1999.)

The Vedic texts have also been of relevance to understanding the socio-political-economic context of the epic itself. For example, M.B. Emeneau and B.A. van Nooten approach the notions of *Niyoga* and polyandry in the Mahabharata from the broader Vedic context ('The Young Wife and Her Husband's Brother: Rgveda 10.40.2 and 10.85.44.', 1991, *Journal of the American Oriental Society*, 111–3, pp. 481–494). Also deserving mention here is Janet Chawla's feminist reading of the Rig Veda ('Mythic Origins of

Menstrual Taboo in Rig Veda', 1994, *Economic and Political Weekly*, 29–43, pp. 2817–2827).

LIFE AND WAR IN EPIC TIMES

In terms of setting the descriptive stage for the story, my first stop was Romila Thapar's *The Penguin History of Early India: From the Origins to 1300 AD* (New Delhi: Penguin Books/Allen Lane, 2002). City descriptions are based mainly on details in the epic narrative, but I also referred to marine archaeologist S.R. Rao's *The Lost City of Dvaraka* (Goa: National Institute of Oceanography, 1999); David Frawley's *Gods, Sages and Kings: Vedic Secrets of Ancient Civilization* (Salt Lake City: Passage Press/Morson Publishing, 1991) and A.S. Gaur, Sundaresh and Sila Tripati's 'An Ancient Harbour at Dwarka: Study Based on the Recent Underwater Explorations' (2004, *Current Science*, 86–9, pp. 1256–60) for ideas on the layout of Dwaraka city, particularly its fortifications and defences. Gaur, Sundaresh and Tripati's 'Evidence for Indo–Roman trade from Bet Dwarka Waters, West Coast of India' (2005, *International Journal of Nautical Archaeology*, 35, pp. 117–127) inspired the notion of Dwaraka as a maritime power.

The military history of India, from the AllEmpires.com historical information website, Sushama Londhe's page on war in Ancient India (http://www.hinduwisdom.info/War_in_Ancient_India.htm), S.A. Paramahans's 'A Glance at Military Techniques in Ramayana and Mahabharata' (1989, *Indian Journal of History of Science*, 24–3, 156–160) and The Sarasvati Web (http://www.hindunet.org/hindu_history/sarasvati) also deserve reference.

GENEALOGIES

In constructing genealogies, I have relied on the texts of the Mahabharata and Harivamsa mentioned above, as well as the Srimad Bhagavatham. My tables were supplemented and cross-checked against two sources: Desiraju Hanumanta Rao's genealogical tables of the Yadu and related dynasties (www.mahabharata-resources.org)

and the tables in Irawati Karve's *Yuganta*. Vettam Mani's classic *Puranic Encyclopaedia* (Delhi: Motilal Banarasidas, 1975) has filled many gaps and provided essential details.

THE CONSTRUCTION OF TIME

My approach to Time has been a mix of the literal and the symbolic. Myth suggests that lifespans were much longer in the previous yugas, lasting perhaps up to three or four hundred years in the Dwapara-yuga – the era of the Mahabharata. However, these figures take on a different meaning if we apply the notion of ashrama or stages of life. K.N.S. Patnaik (*The Mahabharata Chronology*, Pune: Annual Research J. of the Institute for Rewriting Indian History, 1990) compares how childhood (*baalyam*) lasted forty years in the times of the Mahabharata, whereas it lasts approximately 15 years in the current age of Kali. Similarly, youth or *youvanam* lasted till the age of 120 years in the past, as compared to about 45 years in today's age. We are, in essence, dealing with a different basis of measurement of time and age.

Time, in the *Chronicles*, is therefore scaled down to contextualize the main actors as the middle-aged individuals they were, relative to the period of the epic. As a result, the age of the characters is given in contemporary terms.

Interestingly, ancient units of measurements ran by seasonal and sidereal time, along with the common solar. The possibility, therefore, of a year as we know constituting a shorter period of time, cannot be discounted. Subash Kak ('On the Chronological Framework for Indian Culture', *Indian Council of Philosophical Research*, 2000, pp. 1–24) mentions how one of the bases for variation in the dating of the events of the Mahabharata may be the calendar system used (more precisely, the number of stellar constellations in a given cycle).

LANGUAGE

My work would have been near-impossible but for these amazing dictionaries and glossaries, accessed primarily through the Cologne

Digital Sanskrit Dictionaries website (http://www.sanskrit-lexicon.uni-koeln.de). Included in this database are the well-known Monier-Williams, Apte and MacDonnell dictionaries, as well as Kale's work on Sanskrit grammar. I also used the simpler but wonderful Spoken Sanskrit Dictionary (http://spokensanskrit.de) and relied on the Sanskrit Heritage Site (http://sanskrit.inria.fr/sanskrit.html) for grammar reference.

Acknowledgements

'Imagine that you have nine men struggling to lift a large rock. Strong as they are, they fail. Then you have someone like, say, Bhim here, who decides to give them a hand. And the rock moves. Would you say that Bhim is the reason it does?'

'But of course! Without him, the nine men could not have lifted the rock.'

'Without the nine men, without even one of those nine, *Bhim* could not have lifted the rock. Doesn't that make each one of them as important as him?'

'What do you mean, Govinda?'

'No one person is the cause for or consequence of all that happens. I am just the tenth man, the threshold, the turn in the tide. I stand here on the shoulders of humanity, a mere instrument of time.'

– *The Aryavarta Chronicles Book 3: Kurukshetra*

To all those who helped lift my rock and made this book possible, though you may know it not: Thank you.

Poulomi Chatterjee
Jaishankar Krishnamurthy
Shobana Udayasankar
Boozo Iyer and Zana Iyer

Saiswaroopa Iyer
Sukanya Venkatraghavan
Sachin Dev
Pradip Bhattacharya

Jaya and K.S. Krishnamurthy

Alvin Pang

Aapriya Vasudevan

...ind N.V.

Murali Neelakantan

Zafar Anjum

Vinod George Joseph

Helen Mangham and the entire team at Jacaranda.

Thomas Abraham, Sohini Bhattacharya and the team at Hachette India.

Kunal Kundu and Gunjan Ahlawat for yet another fantastic cover.

The entire 'gang' at #TSBC (special call-out to Sudha, Rahul and Raghav).

All the regulars on *The Aryavarta Chronicles* FB page.

Many known and anonymous reviewers – I've tried my best to learn from the feedback.

The reader – who brought Aryavarta to life.

And finally, always, A.R. Udayasankar.